BERSERKER PRIME

Tor Books by Fred Saberhagen

THE BERSERKER® SERIES

The Berserker Wars
Berserker Base (with Poul Anderson, Edward Bryant, Stephen R. Donaldson, Larry Niven, Connie Willis, and Roger Zelazny)
Berserker: Blue Death
The Berserker Throne
Berserker's Planet
Berserker Kill
Berserker Fury
Berserker's Star
Berserker Prime

THE DRACULA SERIES

The Dracula Tapes
The Holmes-Dracula File
Dominion
A Matter of Taste
A Question of Time
Séance for a Vampire
A Sharpness on the Neck
A Coldness in the Blood

THE SWORDS SERIES

The First Book of Swords
The Second Book of Swords
The Third Book of Swords
The First Book of Lost Swords: Woundhealer's Story
The Second Book of Lost Swords: Sightblinder's Story
The Third Book of Lost Swords: Stonecutter's Story
The Fourth Book of Lost Swords: Farslayer's Story
The Fifth Book of Lost Swords: Coinspinner's Story
The Sixth Book of Lost Swords: Mindsword's Story
The Seventh Book of Lost Swords: Wayfinder's Story
The Last Book of Swords: Shieldbreaker's Story
An Armory of Swords (editor)

THE BOOKS OF THE GODS

The Face of Apollo
Ariadne's Web
The Arms of Hercules
God of the Golden Fleece
Gods of Fire and Thunder

OTHER BOOKS

A Century of Progress
Coils (with Roger Zelazny)
Dancing Bears
Earth Descended
Empire of the East
The Mask of the Sun
Merlin's Bones
The Veils of Azlaroc
The Water of Thought
Gene Roddenberry's Earth: Final Conflict—The Arrival

FRED SABERHAGEN

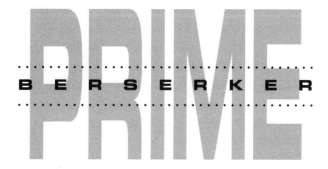

PRIME

B E R S E R K E R

TOR®

A TOM DOHERTY ASSOCIATES BOOK
NEW YORK

This is a work of fiction. All the characters and events portrayed in this novel are either
fictitious or are used fictitiously.

BERSERKER PRIME

This book is printed on acid-free paper.

A Tor Book
Published by Tom Doherty Associates, LLC
175 Fifth Avenue
New York, NY 10010

www.tor.com

Tor® is a registered trademark of Tom Doherty Associates, LLC.

Library of Congress Cataloging-in-Publication Data

Saberhagen, Fred, 1930–
    Berserker prime / Fred Saberhagen.—1st ed.
        p. cm.
    "A Tom Doherty Associates book."
    ISBN 0-765-30625-5
    1. Life on other planets—Fiction. 2. Space warfare—Fiction. 3. Robots—Fiction. I.
Title.

PS3569.A215B465 2004
813'.54—dc22

                                                                              2003061467

First Edition: January 2004

Printed in the United States of America

0 9 8 7 6 5 4 3 2 1

BERSERKER PRIME

O N E

The noise came snarling out of the distance, through the air and open windows, penetrating bedrock and reaching up into the foundations of Timber's capital city. It invaded the graceful building called the Citadel in the form of an ominous, droning bass note, blended with a grim vibration of even lower frequency. The latter component of the sound seemed, to Plenipotentiary Gregor, to be resonating somehow in his own aging bones. Gregor, thought the projectors being tested, the planet-guarding weapons that could incinerate a spaceborne battleship at a range of thousands of kilometers, must be at least five kilometers from where he stood. The bulk of their output would of course be pouring up and out into space, but still enough energy was being wasted around the edges to shake a faint fall of dust out of the Citadel's fanciful grillwork, so delicately carved, in a time of peace, from ancient stone.

It was an ugly racket, but nothing compared to the war that it foreshadowed. A Huvean fleet might appear at any hour in Timber's lovely skies, ready to blast its cities and kill its people. After a peaceful interregnum that had lasted for standard centuries, two societies of Earth-descended humans might be in all-out, murderous conflict with each other.

Cheerful sunlight came streaming through tall windows into the high room on the Citadel's third floor, where Plenipotentiary Gregor had arrived. The panes of tinted glass had been turned wide open, probably by one of the attendant robots he had noticed on his way in, to a warm sky of early autumn. The flooding light awakened subtle shades of color in panels of century-old wood. Even the grillwork doors of the elevator were solid matter instead of forcefields, carved from strengthened stone. They opened to let Gregor's tall, spare figure, a trifle stooped with age, step out of the little cage, followed closely by his single escort, a trim young military man, sidearmed and neatly uniformed.

It jarred Gregor to think that this lovely, delicate complex of buildings was being put to use as a prison. Worse, it might soon become a place of execution. The name, Citadel, suggested a fortress, but with all its grace and beauty the building seemed wildly inappropriate as a place for fighting or even planning war. When it had been built, a hundred of this planet's Earthlike years ago, no one here on Timber could have been seriously expecting armed conflict on a massive scale. Certainly no one in any of the hundred solar systems colonized by Earth-descended humans had anticipated that such a catastrophe might lie less than a human lifetime in the future.

Gregor was clean-shaven in tune with current fashion. Gray hair, almost a requirement for one in his profession of diplomacy, fell in natural curls on both sides of a stern face displaying a mix of ancient racial traits. All in all, he showed more of his age and cared less about it than did most men past the century mark. Because of the solemnity of today's meeting, and the seriousness of the job he had to undertake immediately afterward, he had chosen to wear formal diplomatic dress: loose, dark robes over an upper body garment with tight sleeves. His feet were shod, somewhat incongruously, in gray, lightweight spacefarer's boots—if all went smoothly here, he would be on his way, within the hour, to an interstellar peace conference some light-years away.

The long, high-ceilinged room that stretched out before him and his escort was empty of other people at the moment. Sunlight fell on graceful and impressive furniture, mostly of blond wood, and on the fair face of a late model anthropomorphic robot, standing beside a sideboard of rosewood and cherry. The sun tinted the delicate features of the machine's molded face, emphasizing an angelic, sexless beauty, and the light breeze from the open windows stirred fair artificial hair.

Simply but elegantly attired in plain, tight fitting male servant's garb, the machine stood gazing seemingly at nothing, awaiting orders. Anyone watching it from the distance of the elevator, on the far side of the big room, might easily have been fooled into thinking it alive.

In fact Gregor was deceived, but only for a second. The robot was too beautiful and too motionless to be human. Besides, it would be practically unthinkable that a live servant, a status symbol very much prized in certain quarters, would have been simply posted here, doing nothing in this otherwise unoccupied room.

As soon as the robot's senses registered that it had come under steady human scrutiny, it turned its whole body to face him, imbuing the brief movement with a grace that seemed partly that of a dancer, partly of a soldier in ceremonial formation. Then it spoke to Gregor in a pleasant voice: "I am Porphyry here. At your service sir."

"Where is the executioner, Porphyry?" It had long been Gregor's opinion that calling a robot by its name tended to sharpen the machine's attention. Tension and irritation—and a certain resentment over having been fooled by it, even for a second—caused him to speak sharply to the machine, whose friendly expression did not change in the least. Whether the human speaking to it might be angry, or why, was of no concern at all to any robot.

In soft mellifluous tones Porphyry told him that it served Huang Gun, who, upon the recent arrival of the Huvean hostages, had been appointed executioner. Huang Gun had sent it to meet Gregor on his arrival and tell him that the executioner would join him in this room shortly. It concluded simply: "I am uncertain of his exact location."

For a moment Gregor stood regarding the robot in silent contemplation. It struck him as somehow painfully wrong, even worse than using the Citadel for a prison, that this elaborate and beautiful device, as close an imitation of humanity as humanity could build, should have any part in arranging the imprisonment and approaching doom of real human beings—perhaps even carrying out certain preliminary steps in the process of their deaths.

On a sudden impulse he asked it: "Could you kill a human being, Porphyry? If a human authority you trusted assured you that the act would be perfectly legal, and gave you a direct command?"

Good lawyer that he was, Gregor knew what the answer to his question had to be. The expected words came immediately, and—as expected—without the slightest sign of surprise or agitation.

"No sir. Killing a human being would be completely contrary to my basic programming. As you must know." Porphyry's tone remained brisk and cheerful. Some things were unthinkable for robots, but nothing was disturbing.

"That is, if you knew that you were killing. And that the victim was human."

"Yes sir. I assumed that was your meaning."

Gregor's hands rose in a slow, complicated gesture, as if he were trying to grasp an object of uncertain shape. They were large hands, once very strong. Their wrinkled backs showed their age, and on one finger he wore a plain gold ring. Now for the question whose answer he did not know. "But if you could not predict what the result of a certain action would be . . ."

The robot waited.

Gregor shook his head, muttered something to himself, and started over. "I am talking specifically about the case of the Huvean hostages, who I assume are still being held somewhere in this building."

"Your assumption is correct, plenipotentiary."

"Good. They are imprisoned here in accordance with the terms of an interplanetary treaty between our Twin Worlds government and the Huvean state—that is, the government of another solar system. The treaty is one of the highest forms of law."

"Yes sir. I am aware of the hostages' legal status. Also of the general organization of human governments, and the nature of treaties."

"Excellent. Then the situation will perhaps be as clear to you as—as it can be. One of the articles of this particular treaty says that if our government should decide that the rulers of Huvea have failed to live up to certain of its terms, the ten young hostages are liable to immediate execution."

"I understand, sir."

"Good—now, could you, for example, hand the weapon to the executioner, if he should ask you to do that?"

The answer was as swift as ever. "I would expect to find no difficulty in doing that, Plenipotentiary Gregor."

Gregor had his mouth open to pursue the subject with another question, when from the corner of his eye he caught sight of a human figure approaching. He had never seen Huang Gun in the flesh, but from countless holostage images he recognized the man entering the large room through a doorway on Gregor's right.

The newly appointed executioner was nearly as tall as Gregor, an ascetic looking, clean-shaven man of indeterminate age; in his official garb of long robes and antique headdress he could easily have been taken for a woman of striking appearance.

Gregor had an odd momentary impression that Huang Gun, on entering the room, bowed very slightly to the robot, as he might have done on encountering a respected human of near equal rank. Surely the figure that had introduced itself *was* only a robot—? Gregor stared hard at Porphyry again—yes, there could be no doubt.

Evidently the robot was aware of the fact that the two high officials had never met face to face, for it urbanely performed the introduction, using formal and economical hand gestures, phrasing everything neatly, showing a nice awareness of the two humans' respective ranks.

Huang Gun's voice, like his appearance, might almost have been that of a cultured woman. His tone was cool, reserved. "We are honored by your presence here, Plenipotentiary. You have perhaps been conferring with the president?"

"The honor is mine, executioner—no, unhappily I have not been able to schedule an appointment with Mr. Belgola. I was about to ask you the same question, whether you had spoken to him recently."

Huang Gun slightly shook his head. "Not since yesterday, sir, and then only briefly."

While the men were speaking the machine had moved again, gracefully in its finely balanced but not-quite-human walk, to stand immobile in the exact place where Gregor had first seen it. Now it was facing in a direction exactly between the two men, looking from one of them to the other as it awaited further orders.

Gregor remarked that it might seem in bad taste, to congratulate anyone on being appointed to such an office as High executioner, which had been newly created for the occasion.

"But I will risk it. The appointment is a tribute to your unimpeachable honesty, your well-known sense of duty and of fairness."

Acknowledging the praise with a slight bow, Huang Gun replied that it was indeed an honor to be entrusted with such an office, and he was proud to have been chosen.

After a moment of silence, Gregor remarked that he had come to see the hostages. "If that is possible."

The executioner's eyebrows went up just slightly. He considered briefly. "For someone of your standing, sir, why not? Undoubtedly you have strong reason."

Huang Gun seemed about to add more, but there came another roaring test of distant weapons, and conversation had to wait until the noise died down.

When it was again possible to be heard, he continued: "They are being held in the rooms immediately below us. If the deadline passes, and our president should determine that their home government still persists in its aggression, I will be compelled as a matter of duty to execute at least some of them, according to the schedule specified in the treaty."

"And you will of course feel justified in doing this."

For the first time there was a pause, and a greater coolness in the cultured voice. "Of course. Do you suggest, plenipotentiary, that I will not be justified?"

"No, I make no such suggestion. All I wish to say is that I do not envy you that responsibility. Of making the final determination."

"The law of the treaty will determine. In that event, I feel confident that I will have—all necessary support." And the executioner's gaze turned thoughtfully, for some reason, back to the robot once again.

Gregor was faintly puzzled. "From the president, you mean."

"Yes, of course. From the president and others." Huang Gun smiled slightly. "There is no doubt that the terms of the treaty are clear enough."

In Gregor's legalistic judgment it would be easy to generate an argument on that last point. Not that there was anything secret about the treaty and its complicated requirements—unless effective secrecy lay in the Machiavellian vagueness that shrouded several of the clauses. Vagueness, it seemed, was the price that had to be paid if two states dangerously close to war were going to have any agreement at all. Unhappily, the hostage clause, detailing the terms of what its opponents scathingly called human sacrifice, was anything but vague.

The executioner cleared his throat, and pulled a small scroll of paper from inside his robe. "I have here, plenipotentiary, an official list of the hostages' names, each accompanied by a few words of biography. Perhaps you would like to have it? As you doubtless know, they are all volunteers, and all are from families of standing and importance in the Huvean regime."

The hostages' names had never been kept secret either, and in fact they had been intensely publicized in recent days. Exactly half were men, half women. Gregor had earlier avoided learning personal details. He thought that if he could once meet the young people face to face, he would be sure to remember all their names. But now, to be courteous, he reached out to accept the list that Huang Gun offered. Unrolling the scroll and glancing at it briefly, he noted that it was indeed a list of names, printed, like many important official documents, in permanent ink on real paper. It was of no immediate use to him, and he put it into an inside pocket.

He murmured a few words of thanks, adjusted the tight sleeves of his own diplomatic uniform, and made sure that his face wore an expression of sympathy. Then he said: "I tell you frankly that I hope to be able to prevent these executions from taking place."

Huang Gun bowed an acknowledgment. His voice was cool and distant. "So I surmised, plenipotentiary, from your first remarks. I assure you that I will be almost as pleased as the subjects themselves, if that can be done in the way the treaty mandates."

"Finding some way within the treaty's terms is of course what I had in mind."

The light breeze had freshened slightly. Scented with the subtle, familiar autumn flavors of the two men's native world, it was bringing comfortable coolness through open windows into the room where they stood and talked. In the quiet between periods of weapon testing, a bird sang, distantly. The robot watched and heard and waited.

Huang Gun asked: "And is it only a wish to see the hostages that brings you to the Citadel today?"

"I was passing nearby on other business." Gregor hesitated. "As you are doubtless aware, another peace conference has just been convened." He named a relatively distant solar system, neutral in the looming conflict. "I am on my way to take part in it."

The executioner nodded slightly in confirmation. It would have been easy to offer some hope or prayer for success, but he did not.

Gregor cleared his throat. "Now, as to my visit here . . ." He was finding it surprisingly difficult to choose the words to make his purpose clear, first to himself, then to the other. Some inner compulsion had driven him to stop off at the Citadel, before he immersed himself in yet another diplomatic meeting. Somehow in his own mind it had come to seem of great importance that he should confront the hostages, meet them face to face, listen to whatever they wanted to tell him. He wanted to keep himself from forgetting, when in the process of debating what the delegates were certain to call larger issues, that those standing in danger of death were all individual human beings. If he had faces to hold in his memory, live faces speaking their own names, he thought that would help.

Huang Gun was asking him: "But how soon must you leave for your conference? When is it scheduled to begin?"

The plenipotentiary explained that a fast, small ship was waiting for him, on the ramp at the spaceport only a few minutes away. Then he added: "The most serious discussions can't take place until I get there. But you are right, I must not delay unnecessarily. Those who might begin a war at any moment will not need my approval."

The executioner appeared to be developing a keen interest. He asked: "Is there any thought among those many leaders of seeking an entirely new solution to the ancient problem of human conflict?"

That stirred the old man's curiosity. "I suppose there are at least as many thoughts as there are leaders. . . . What sort of new solution did you have in mind?"

"A bold one." Huang Gun moved to stand beside the robot. He put a hand on its shoulder—there was a trace of hesitation in the movement, as if he feared it might be rebuffed. "I mean the possibility of putting ourselves—not only the Twin Worlds, but more than a hundred settled planets, comprising all Earth-descended humanity—in the hands of a power greater than ourselves. No, I am not speaking of religious dreams. They are based in unreality, and can have only a partial and temporary success."

Gregor was intrigued. He shook his head slowly. "I did not suppose you were advocating a religious position . . . but what, then?"

The executioner removed his hand from the beautiful robot. It was still facing directly between the two men, turning its eyes from one to the other as they spoke. The expression on its face had not changed, and would not change, whatever they might say.

Huang Gun said: "Porphyry here can serve as an indication of what I mean, a guide to the path that we should choose. Though he is but a prologue, a suggestion, of the benevolent power our machines are ready and waiting to offer us. Let them take the weapons from our faltering hands. Let them serve as judges in our disputes, and let them write our treaties. Whatever rules of conduct they may devise for us, they will not demand the death of any hostages."

The old man kept his voice diplomatically neutral. "I have recently heard similar arguments from others." Technically that was quite true, though there had been only a few others, and only one whose ideas had much weight. "It seems even our president is leaning somewhat in that direction. To the belief that we and the Huveans should trust our fate to the decision of the best computer program that can be made, and allow it to settle our disagreements for us."

Huang Gun nodded. "But in this you do not agree with the president, or with me."

Gregor said: "I must admit that I do not. I think the responsibility for the future of humanity lies with ourselves. Ultimately, no machine we build is likely to tell us anything but what we want to hear—and until we truly want peace—"

He broke off, shifted his position. "But I fear that I have no time just now for serious discussion. If I might just see the hostages—?"

"Of course."

For several days, Gregor in the back of his mind had been toying with an odd idea, a secret hope, that if he should go in among these young people unprotected, they would take him hostage in turn. If he himself were one of them . . . but he was not.

Putting himself among the hostages in some way would introduce a new factor into the equation—and by doing so, perhaps pull several worlds back from the brink of disaster.

But in his calmer moments he knew such ideas were irrational, that any dramatic gestures on his part would be foolishness. Bizarre behavior on the part of leaders would be more likely to trigger an explosion than prevent one.

Gregor turned to dismiss his personal guard, who had been standing silently at parade rest a few paces behind him. "Please, wait for me outside the building."

The solemn officer—it was hard to tell from his face if he was old or young—was obedient as a robot, though he was certainly of flesh and blood. He snapped up his arm in a sharp salute and turned away, heading back toward the elevator.

The plenipotentiary turned back to his colleague. "Then shall we go down?"

"Of course." The executioner seemed inclined to be helpful. "We can descend by the lift that brought you up—but to use the stairs, here, will actually be quicker."

As he started down the stair, Gregor cast one last look back, through the interstices of carved stone, at the beautiful robot. Even as Gregor looked at the machine, it began to move, walking smoothly after its currently assigned master, Huang Gun.

With the machine keeping deferentially a few paces behind them, its small feet treading the stairs with perfect balance, Huang Gun led Gregor downstairs two levels to the ground floor room where, he said, the hostages were waiting. It was necessary to pass through a doorway guarded by two armed soldiers, who saluted the executioner sharply, and at a word from him dialed the last force-field barrier open.

They had entered a large, relatively dim room, furnished with several long tables, evidently a dining hall. The slightly littered condition of the table suggested that a meal had recently been concluded, and the maintenance machines had not yet tidied up. At one side, another stair, beside a glowing sign marked SHELTERS, went curving down. Gregor knew that more levels of this building existed below ground—some very far below. Deeper caverns had recently been dug out, finished and connected with all the systems of support, and equipped with facilities and supplies in anticipation of the day when an attack by humans from another world might drive the people of Timber to seek refuge.

Huang Gun halted just inside the room. The ten young people, who had been confined in the Citadel for about a standard month, were distributed about the room, some standing, some sitting. Gregor half consciously counted them, making sure there were indeed ten.

At the start of their confinement they had all been dressed alike, in uniforms that had been specially designed for the occasion, perhaps by one of the hostages themselves. Today most of the ten were wearing a motley mixture of the uniforms and random civilian clothes. The nature of their clothing while confined had been spelled out in the treaty—a fanatic haggling over details had marked the last stage of negotiation. But no one seemed to be trying to enforce those details.

The young Huveans all looked to be of very nearly the same age, in the late teens, but beyond that no common denominator was visible. They were a mixture of sizes, shapes, and physical characteristics, in a way that was representative of the population of Huvea, and of a majority of the hundred colonies.

On entering the room, the executioner immediately said to the waiting group, in their common language: "Don't be alarmed, I have no information of vital importance."

Several hostages visibly relaxed; they were not going to be taken out and shot this minute.

"But as you know, tomorrow, or even this afternoon, that can change, and I may have to kill you.

"Nothing you and I can say to each other can alter these facts. Under the circumstances, can I say anything to you that is not insulting?"

One youth, who had not relaxed, spoke up sharply. "You might try telling us that a ship is waiting to take us home." Huvea and the Twin Worlds shared a common language; only a slight difference in accent was perceptible.

"Would that I could."

The protester's voice was just a little louder. "You enjoy listening to yourself talk, but we're getting sick and tired of it."

Huang Gun showed no reaction. There was a faint murmur of protest from some of the speaker's colleagues. Ignoring them, he turned to Gregor and said: "My name is Glycas, by the way. I take it you are some kind of important visitor."

The executioner calmly spelled out their visitor's identity. The reaction among the young people suggested that more than half of them had already recognized the plenipotentiary, whose face and name were much in the news, and none of them were greatly impressed.

Gregor for his part rarely forgot a face, and one among the ten, that of a handsome youth of middle size, was somehow familiar— yes, but from where? "But I believe that you and I have met before—your name is—"

"Reggie Panchatantra, sir." The youth spoke the common interplanetary language, in the accents of the Huvean upper class.

"Of course, it comes back to me. We met only briefly, and almost a year ago—I think—"

"That is perfectly correct, sir. It was at a certain diplomatic function—" The young Huvean named the site, on a distant world that had come to be much used as a neutral meeting ground for face-to-face diplomacy.

"Yes, of course." It had been one of the semi-official kind of gatherings, where the families of society's leaders were also present. Only two thirds of a standard year ago, the gathering clouds of war had not been nearly so ominous as they were now.

With a minimum of internal prompting on Gregor's part, many of the details of that encounter came back.

Spreading his arms, he declaimed: "Oh, that our next meeting will be as peaceful and happy as that first one!"

Little changed in the young faces turned toward the speaker. Only one of them was turned away, that of another young man, evidently one who would rather spend the next few minutes of his endangered lifetime looking at sky and tree branches, rather than the faces of elderly authorities who brought no hope. Instead of being able to look forward to another hundred standard years, as might well be the case in the course of nature, it could be another hundred minutes.

Gregor couldn't blame him. Here in the middle latitudes of Timber's northern hemisphere, the next autumnal storm that came drifting in would be as likely to bring snow as rain. Perhaps similar scenes were common on the young man's home planet of Huvea, less than half a dozen light-years away. What season of the year was it on Huvea now? Gregor had lost track; he could not remember.

A silence fell. It was obvious that everyone was waiting for this important, unofficial and unexpected visitor to take the next step. He had not yet tried to explain to the hostages why he was here; and now he realized that his sudden appearance must have roused false hopes, in some of them at least.

Gregor began with a routine question, asking the prisoners whether they had been well treated.

A couple of them at least, Glycas and another, were ready to speak up boldly. "So far we have." The speaker looked around at his colleagues, as if for confirmation. "As to the future, I think that only the last few minutes of my stay in this place is likely to give me any cause for concern." That evoked in the speaker's fellow hostages a feeble titter of laughter that quickly died away.

Gregor moved a step forward. "I've made a large number of speeches in my time, to a great many different audiences. But I didn't come here today to make one. Rather I want to hear what you have to tell me, words I can take with me to the peace conference."

The second objector, a lean, intense looking young man, snapped to his feet, as if his body were on a spring. Proudly he introduced himself as Douras. His voice was hoarse, and he was quivering, evidently with anger. "Have I missed something, sir? Or are you saying you have come here simply to ask us whether we prefer to be alive or dead?"

"I have come to hear whatever it is you want to tell me." Gregor remained outwardly calm, but he was beginning to wonder why this visit had seemed like such a great idea. Was he only making a fool of himself to no purpose?

"You want some noble last words from us, is that it? So when the talks fail, you'll have evidence to prove to everyone how concerned you are, how hard you tried?"

The youth burst out with curses. "You sons of worms may kill us, you probably will, but we will be avenged!" The guards who had been standing quietly in the background, hardly more than part of the furniture, shifted their positions slightly.

Huang Gun focused his cool, impassive gaze on Douras. But others in the protester's group restrained the young man whose nerves had given way.

Reggie was standing again, mildly rebuking his fellow hostages, reminding them that they had all volunteered for this distasteful duty.

"None of us were captured, or kidnapped, or dragged to this place by force.

"Yes, we volunteered." The speaker looked around at his colleagues. "We are all of us, or almost all, children of the families who rule Huvea. Better that catastrophe should fall on our families than on those who had nothing to do with bringing it about."

"We were much younger then," another replied grimly, "even though it was only a few standard months ago. Now, are you going to try to tell us that shooting us down in your courtyard here will serve some great cause? We don't believe that anymore." The speaker looked around, as if seeking support, and others in the small group nodded.

Suddenly, quietly, one of the young women began to weep. Gregor wanted to go and comfort her, but he did not. He wanted even more to get away, and was sorry that he had yielded to the impulse to come here. His intrusion was only making the situation more difficult for everyone. Some of the guards were looking at him unhappily. What exactly was it he had expected to learn from these people that would help them, or him, or the cause of peace?

Glycas was on his feet, and seemed about to try to make a speech, but before he could utter a word he was cut off. Again some kind of weapons testing, this outburst sounding even closer than before, produced a vibration that shook the building. Little showers of dirt and dust came trickling from the vaulted ceiling. Gregor looked up in alarm, until he realized that the hostages were paying the dust fall no attention. The noise was louder this time, and for a full minute it made conversation difficult.

Evidently the technicians were not only testing the offensive weapons, but the planet's forcefield shields as well. Activation of the shields worked a sudden alteration in the whole cheerful sky, a dimming of the intensity of sunlight reaching the planetary surface by about a third.

Gregor noticed one of the soldiers, standing near the doorway, gazing up into the sky-gloom with evident satisfaction. It seemed quite possible to know the young man's thoughts: *Let the motherless Huveans with their damned murderous weapons try to get through that.*

The robot courier came flicker-
ing out of flightspace, concluding a quick jaunt that had begun
less than a minute earlier and almost a hundred million kilometers
away. A few milliseconds after reentering normal space in a burst
of tiny gravitational waves, it slammed into its automatic cradle
on the scoutship, still moving fast enough and hard enough to
rock the larger vessel slightly with the cushioned impact. Not
a second to waste, that was the programming on which these
couriers ran.

Ella Berlu, scoutship commander, happened to be the human
being on watch. She felt the jolt of impact and recognized it
immediately for what it was, though only a barely perceptible
twitch came through the steady artificial gravity to reach her in
the pilot's couch.

One second later, the information the courier had brought was
being displayed in three dimensions on Ella's holostage, which held
the place of honor in the center of the control cabin. The scoutship
commander needed no more than five seconds to study the latest

news before she was on the intercom, summoning her two live crew members to their battle stations. Neither engineer nor pilot would have far to go; the scout's near-spherical hull was not much more than twenty meters in diameter.

"This is not another damned drill, is it?" the first pilot grumbled, even as her dark head, not yet helmeted, appeared in one of the small cabin's interior hatches. Sue Perkonis was black of skin and hair, husky in her build, and slightly older than her two shipmates.

Ella was shaking her own curls, which were somewhat lighter. "No, it's not. It looks like we've got a live one this time. Come on, let's move, people."

Ten long seconds passed before the engineering officer— Hannah Rymer, tall and thin, with long blond hair—made her appearance. "Huvean?" was the first word Hannah uttered. She asked the question before looking at any of the data.

"Don't know yet." The commander's hands adjusting the holostage presentation looked small and delicate on the controls. "I'd guess not; it's like nothing of theirs I've ever seen. But it's definitely an intruder, not just a rock. We picked up a faint reentry wave." Stray rocks came hurtling out of flightspace so rarely as to be unworthy of consideration.

As usual when on duty, Ella was dressed in her shipboard coverall, a garment sheathing everything but hands and feet and head. In Ella's case the small exposed areas of skin showing an even, toasty brown.

The cabin was a spherical cave about four meters in diameter. Three acceleration couches, all of them now occupied, each couch furnished with its distinctive array of readouts and controls, filled most of the room's volume and ringed the stage around.

For greatest possible efficiency in use of the small space available, the artificial gravity in the control cabin was generally adjusted so "down" was different for each crew position, but all three saw the holostage directly in front of them. The effect could be disorienting, but scout crews got used to it early in their training.

When things got dull, a game of catch with a small object could become very interesting.

Today there need be no scrounging around for interesting things to do. "Can't be Huvean," Sue, the pilot, offered.

And Hannah Rymer, engineer: "I'd say it can't be a ship at all. Look at the size."

Perkonis turned her dark head. "Bet?"

Sue snorted. "Every time I bet with you guys I lose. But I might be tempted if you give me odds."

While Ella's two human shipmates digested the courier's message and readied their equipment, she responded to the robotic observer by its number and letter designation, acknowledging the receipt of its information and asking for more. The message in hand assured her that a tightbeam radio confirmation was already on its way, a journey that would take several minutes longer than that already accomplished by the superluminal courier. Light needed something like an hour to crawl across this solar system's full diameter, approximately a billion kilometers.

The scoutship Ella commanded was charged with the oversight of very nearly a hundred such observer subunits. Usually all of these were visibly represented on the central stage, in the form of tiny bluish dots.

Each of the hundred blue dots showed the computed probable location of a miniature spacecraft, perhaps half the scoutship's size. The subunits were thoroughly robotic, with no space or facilities aboard for human crew. Each one in turn controlled and monitored about a hundred automated sentries, even smaller detector devices distributed more or less evenly throughout its vast domain.

Ordinarily these sentries never showed up on the stage, whose scale would have to be drastically adjusted to bring them all in; but each of them in turn stood guard over a wedge-shaped volume comprising millions of cubic kilometers of interplanetary space. Every one of these sentries continually endeavored, with a robot's monomaniacal thoroughness, to probe every moving rock and ice ball that roamed into its assigned volume, every unusual variation in the ebb and flow of the tenuous interplanetary medium, fed by the solar wind.

The sector was more than a million kilometers deep, and some of its depth lay within the orbit of the system's outermost known planet, while more of it extended farther out.

Summarized, the bundle of information just delivered to Ella by her hierarchy of robot watchdogs indicated that an object some fifty kilometers in length, yet identifiable as an artifact, had recently entered the system's early warning zone, after dropping out of flight-space just outside. The intruder was therefore, in this time of high alert, highly suspect.

The scout's computer quickly translated the courier's burden of coded information into smooth computer graphics, and a few terse words.

The two other human members of the live flight crew made their comments in turn.

Accompanying the message was a warning—in this case, totally unnecessary—urging that its contents be passed up the chain of command as quickly as possible.

"We're going on full alert, Sue, Hannah. As of right now."

"It's not even headed our way," Sue observed.

"Regardless. It's required with a find like this."

"Yes ma'am." The thing wasn't coming toward the scout-ship, and at its distance posed no threat, but there was no use arguing with regulations.

There was a sense in which it still seemed to all of them like some great, elaborate game. More maneuvers, of which they had all had almost more than they could stand in recent months. No crew member in this warship, no one aboard any of the others that might soon be attacking and defending, was a veteran of real war.

Currently Ella Berlu's scoutship was roaming near the center of its territory, an assigned portion of the outer reaches of the

Twin Worlds system, its borders sharply defined by precise readings of the stellar background.

Engineer Hannah also carried out the duties of weapons and communications officer—and was also trained as a pilot, though she generally played that role only in emergencies.

The three crew members, having had plenty of cross-training, frequently performed their duties interchangeably. Let one or two be killed or wounded, and two or one, aided by smart hardware, might somehow carry on—another advantage was that learning to do well at three or four jobs was less boring than total concentration on just one.

"Two more days," the engineer observed in a distant voice, which now reached her shipmates through the helmet intercom.

"Two more days what?" Ella's mind came back from roaming.

"You know what, chief. Just two more standard days and we'd have been rotated home."

"I expect we may be heading sunward a little faster than that. But whether we'll be going planetside . . ." Ella's tone left no doubt of how remote that was beginning to look.

The normal tour of duty in one of these outer-defenses scouts was something like a standard month, with a new ship and crew coming to take over on schedule. But possibly because of the high alert, all leaves were canceled, and the outer watch was scheduled to thicken with extra ships.

If the Huvean fleet should suddenly appear—an event whose calculated probability had been rising ominously for the past standard month—the scout's job would be to transmit sunward as early and thorough a warning as possible, and meanwhile to run like hell. The weaponry on board a standard scoutship, like Ella's, was strictly limited—enough, perhaps, to fight off an intruding Huvean of about the same size, if anything in an attacking force would be that small. But the communication gear on a Twin Worlds scout was large and capable.

When she expanded the scale of view a bit, instruments showed Ella and her shipmates a momentary glimpse of the scoutship patrolling the next sector north, in the polar coordinate system based on the Twin Worlds' sun.

Hannah Rymer, though not disputing that all the information that came in had to be passed on, was doubtful of its accuracy. "That thing's an artifact? More likely an artifact of some kind of error in one of our systems."

"We'll see."

Sue put in: "Whatever it is, it's still not coming our way—not toward our ship."

"No." That thought, at least, brought a slight feeling of relief.

"There it is. Looks awfully big and lumpy to be a system error."

"Definitely headed sunward," the pilot added. "Maybe some interest in the inner planets. Well, yes, look at that." The computer had just concluded that the intruder was already on a course that would bring it in about one standard day into a close orbit around the planet Prairie.

The solar system formally called Twin Worlds contained two habitable planets, Prairie and Timber, very much like each other and closely resembling Earth. Timber and Prairie orbited their shared sun at very nearly the same distance, Timber having a slightly longer year (again, close to the standard length adopted from the planet Earth). And just slightly stronger gravity—not enough to make much difference to its people. When at their closest approach to each other, an event just a few standard months away, each of the Twins made an impressive gem in the other's sky.

For a good part of their respective years, which were Earth-like in seasons as well as length, the Twins were, as now, less than ten standard minutes apart by radio or optelectronic signal. They were never more than a few hours apart by fast traveling in normal space, their people politically united under one fundamentally democratic government.

Several days earlier, an alerting message had gone the rounds of all scoutship commanders: Strange, faint radio signals, bearing no familiar characteristics by which they might be identified, had been picked up in space, by several other Twin Worlds units on distant duty. These signals had qualities about them that caused Defense Command to sharply focus its attention.

Running down a checklist, Ella as the first human to analyze the discovery had quickly eliminated the usual suspects. Bit by bit, she lowered to near zero the chances that a private vessel had got somehow out of line. Nor was this stranger at all convincing as merely some component of the regular flow of commercial space travel.

In ordinary times the volume of routine, regular travel showed up on the instruments of Early Warning as a steady, expectable and identifiable coming and going.

But over the last few standard months, poisoned by the increasing likelihood of war, commerce had been greatly diminished both in the Twin Worlds' system and in the Huveans', which lay between four and five light-years away—only a couple of days by fast c-plus ship, riding the usual flightspace currents. Not only had the once brisk trade between the two systems fallen to practically nothing, but neutral vessels from other worlds were understandably hesitant to enter space in which the unknown horrors of war were considered likely to break out.

The ultimate source of those earlier unidentified signals was somewhere well outside the system. No one had yet been able to pin it down with any accuracy.

But within an hour of the first courier's arrival on board, the robot analyst in the scoutship commanded by Ella Berlu announced with ninety-five percent certainty that the signals most recently picked up represented cross talk between two robotic probes that had entered the Twin Worlds' system from different angles.

Ella demanded of her engineering officer: "What else can you tell me about them?"

Hannah looked at an instrument, confirming what she had seen before. "They differ technically in several ways from any known human transmissions."

One of the probes had entered the sector that Ella's scoutship was guarding. Exactly what the thing might have been trying to tell its robotic companion was a mystery.

The engineer was frowning. "Coded, of course. Not only can't I read it, but it doesn't seem to be any code that we've ever run into before."

"Not Huvean, then."

"Can't swear to that. All I can say for sure is that it's nothing like anything the Huveans have used before. Maybe at headquarters they can sort it out."

There were no reports from other sectors of any similar intrusions. Whatever had just jarred the nerves of system defense, it did not seem to be the Huvean fleet—that would have made its entrance on a much grander scale.

From the slow moving, fortress-like spacecraft, much larger than a scoutship, where a larger staff of humans, including Ella's boss, lived and worked, another small robotic courier was launched. At this remote distance from the center of the local sun, effectively the bottom of the solar system's gravitational well, the courier could flip its needle-trim shape easily into flightspace, speeding toward the distant inner planets, in whose vicinity it would arrive in a matter of a very few minutes, with the message. Outpacing light by many possibly invaluable minutes.

Ella relayed the recordings of the most recent signals to her commander, a human in charge of monitoring a dozen or more sectors like her own. The response from up the chain of command was gratifyingly fast.

A code-breaking system of much more advanced capabilities than that possessed by any scoutship was working on the problem. The real name of that system was secret, even to most of the humans who used it. It was represented by an alternate title in yet another code.

And word was being passed on sunward, sent ratcheting up the chain of command as quickly as possible—which meant, in gravitational terms, being sent downward toward the Twin Worlds' distant sun and its nest of inner planets. The highest levels of system government, both on Timber and on Prairie, were to be informed in less than two hours of what looked like an unprecedented intrusion.

Those whose business it was to pass on the news saw that it reached as quickly as possible the flagship of the Twin Worlds battle fleet, presently on station not far from those inner planets.

An urgent summons roused Admiral Radigast, the fleet's commander, from a deep sleep in his cabin on the *Morholt.* Opening one eye, he saw by an image of his clock, glowing in darkness, that it was the very early morning of his ship's standard day. Absent the alarm, he might have enjoyed another hour and a half of slumber.

Moving before he was fully awake, Radigast got his gnarled and hairy legs over the side of his bunk, noted routinely that the artificial gravity seemed quite steady, rubbed his eyes, muttered an obscenity (just in the nature of a tune-up for his powers of speech) and stoked his mouth with a pungently flavored chewing pod. Not his favorite breakfast, not by a long way, but it was what he had trained himself to do when the alarm woke him. There was no telling when he might be able to sit down to a real meal.

For just a moment the admiral allowed himself to hope that this would not be one more practice alert thought up by some safely groundbound planner down at headquarters. Today that would be on Prairie, where the Joint Chiefs were currently in meeting with most of the high civilian government of the Twin Worlds.

A couple of seconds later Radigast was on his feet, headed out of his cabin and toward the bridge in his underwear, scratching his head with one hand, using the other to drag along a shipboard coverall. He could put it on when he got there, not wasting any time.

The admiral's destination was only a few strides away from where he slept. Moments after leaving his cabin, he was entering the cavernous yet crowded room. This space was built on a plan somewhat similar to the control room of a scoutship, but on a substantially larger scale; here there were eight acceleration couches, all but two currently occupied. The gravity was unidirectional.

No one looked up from their consoles and instruments to take any particular notice of their commander's state of undress; the whole control room crew were all more or less used to it at times when an unexpected alert was called.

Radigast threw himself into his couch, the one nearest the big holostage at the center of things. Lying on his back, he began at once working his legs into the coverall. He noted methodically that, as usual, helmet and spacesuit were available, within reach, just in case.

"What've we got, Charlie?"

The *Morholt*'s captain, one couch to the right, was apologetic. "Sorry to wake you, Admiral, but—"

"Never mind the motherless apologies; I can always have you shot if you dragged me out of the motherless sack for nothing. What've we got?"

Charlie showed him. Looking at the remarkable thing that came up on the big central stage, the admiral for a time forgot to chew, and even to use forbidden words.

THREE

The latest outburst of heavy
weapons testing shuddered to its conclusion; the trickle of dust
from overhead diminished and then stopped. It was again possible to be heard and understood in the room on the Citadel's
ground floor.

Young Glycas, obviously determined to make a speech, finally
got the chance to finish a short one.

It expressed a heartfelt yearning for the supposed wisdom of
old Earth, for the ancestral virtue and fortitude that had enabled
those humans of hundreds of years ago to settle their differences,
and expand the domain of ED humanity peacefully among the
stars. The speaker's fellow hostages listened without interruption.

It was as if the major discoveries regarding space and time
that had been made in that era had had a sobering effect—there
came an epoch when humanity seemed not only physically but
psychologically ready to leave the womb of a single planet, the
nursery of one sheltered solar system, and step out into the great
world.

But today, less than three hundred standard years later, the situation had rapidly deteriorated. It was as if the sheer stretches of normal space-time—never mind that travel could be accomplished at high multiples of the speed of light—had had a poisonous effect. Earth-descended humanity once more fractured into a hundred factions, some of them months apart, even at the superluminal speeds attainable by modern ships and couriers.

There had been for some time an actively organized peace movement in the Twin Worlds, with some kind of counterpart existing on Huvea. The leaders—Gregor had heard rumors that Glycas had been one of them—on both sides were accused by many of being enemy agents. Most observers of the political scene agreed that Huvea's government was less democratic than that of the Twin Worlds, though both were far from being absolute dictatorships.

The crisis now threatening to explode into war had begun with the almost simultaneous discovery, by crews from the two rival systems, of an uncolonized planetary system offering a wealth of unsettled territory and useful minerals. Initial disputes escalated to violence and injustice on both sides. Ancient misunderstandings, rooted in divergent religious theories, were resurrected, grievances were cherished.

Glycas had finished speaking, and seemed to be waiting for Gregor to respond. Douras was glowering, really enjoying this, obviously ready to cross verbal swords with this archenemy of all things Huvean, who had condescended to come within thrusting range.

Gregor began by reminding his audience that he had promised not to make a speech. But he had one question for them: how could the relationship between their government and his have deteriorated so swiftly, so badly, that they found themselves actually on the brink of war?

But his hopes for a serious answer were disappointed. Instead, their own questions kept coming. Most concerned the war plans of either side, of which, as he protested, he knew nothing.

Gregor was on the point of wishing long lives and good health to the executioner and those surrounding him, guards and potential victims alike, and taking his leave without further ceremony, when there came an interruption.

One of the guards who had been on duty outside the building was escorting someone into the building, keeping a hand carefully on the arm of the young woman in a space traveler's coverall.

Turning an annoyed glance on this intruder, Gregor met the gaze of blue eyes in a young and pretty face, and was startled to recognize his youngest granddaughter.

Meanwhile, the guard was addressing him uncertainly. "Sir? Excuse me, but this young woman showed up at the gate insisting that she's your aide, and bears an important message."

"Luon." Years of diplomatic practice helped Gregor to keep his jaw from falling open, his voice in a neutral tone. "What is this all about?"

Approximately six standard months had passed since Gregor had seen the girl, and until this minute he had thought her, like the rest of his few close relatives, light-years away from the potential war zone.

Luon was of average height and slight build. Fair, curly hair surrounded a face that fell well short of startling beauty—but it was appealing. Big-eyed, she was likely, Gregor knew, to impress people as younger than her real age, and somehow defenseless—not at all an accurate reading of her character. At the moment she was wearing a small backpack.

"Grandpa Gregor." The girl's voice was tiny, and probably could not have been heard on the far side of the room. On entering she had shot one quick nervous glance toward the hostages, but now she was focusing her attention entirely on her grandfather, and managing to look fearful, embarrassed, and determined all at the same time.

Running his gaze over the slender figure, clad in coverall and lightweight boots as for a space journey, the old man felt a mixture of anger and relief, the latter because Luon seemed unharmed. But something had evidently gone wrong, or she would not be here.

How had this come to pass? The girl ought to have realized that this was a woefully inappropriate time to bother him—judging from the look on her face, that had belatedly dawned on her. And, come to think of it, how had she even known that he was here?

Now she seemed to be stuck, not knowing what to say. He prompted: "But I thought you were parsecs away from here. Did you come here alone?"

"None of the family are with me, sir. It's a long story, how I got here. Can I tell you later?"

She looked so strained, and sounded so serious, that Gregor relented. To the soldier who had brought her in he said: "She is my relative. Let her remain here for the time being." The sergeant, his grim mouth expressing silent disapproval of the things that rank could get away with, saluted briskly and retreated to the outside.

"Grampa Gregor," the girl said again, softly. "Thank you." Only now did it strike the old man that she was about the same age as the hostages. Possibly Luon was just a year or two younger, but she could easily have fit into their group.

The attention of everyone in the large room was focused on the two of them; plainly it would be no use trying to find privacy by whispering.

In a normal voice he said: "Luon, this is not the time or place to bring up personal problems. What is this important business? First of all, how did you know that I was here?"

Her reply was even softer than before, as if to indicate that she would keep this private if she could.

"Sorry, Gramp—sir. When I checked your name on the newsline locator it said you were in the Citadel. But your official schedule didn't list any such stop, so I figured maybe your being here was *unofficial*. Then I thought maybe that meant you could spare a moment for . . ." Luon was stuck again.

The newsline locator? But all right; he supposed some senior family member must have given her the code that would let her track him down by name.

"For your important business," he encouraged. "And what is that?"

"Nothing!" She gave her fair curls a violent shake. "I mean, nothing official. I just felt that I was kind of stranded here on Timber. And I needed to tell the guards *something,* so they'd let me in."

The girl was obviously in anguish, and Gregor's irritation partially melted in a small surge of sympathy. Of course, with the threat of war hanging over the world, she was afraid—so was almost everyone—and naturally she saw her grandfather as a powerful figure, a reliable source of help. He could only wish that it were so.

Again he saw his grandchild cast a glance toward the silent, watching hostages, then quickly tear her eyes away from them. When Luon spoke again she sounded repentant. "I wanted to be sure of seeing you." Still her voice remained tiny, pitiful.

"Yes. Of course I am glad to see you, Luon. Or I would be, under any ordinary . . . never mind." He sighed. "Now that you are here, just attend in silence for a few moments."

Turning back to the waiting group, he told them: "I must apologize for the interruption."

The lean and intense Douras, still on his feet though the others were now all sitting, spoke up again. He was smiling, holding the back of a chair as if it were a lectern, and his voice was quietly savage.

"Honored sir." He subtly made the words a mockery. "I would like to express a hope which I am sure we all share—that the young woman will be able to get to a place of safety before the Huvean fleet arrives in these skies, and begins to punish your government of war criminals, in space and on the ground.

"With that in mind, I suggest that perhaps your innocent granddaughter had better remain here with us, in this building. I'm sure that by now our people know just where we are being held."

Gregor wasn't sure of that at all, but offered no comment. Luon, looking frightened, stared back at the aggressive one, but could find no words to answer him.

Reggie Panchatantra was on his feet again, trying to be conciliatory. "I'm sure we all agree that the plenipotentiary's granddaughter deserves a place of safety—but I expect he knows where that is better than we do. As for the rest of us, well, our object in coming here was not to seek safety. We all volunteered for the role of hostages, when this farce began. I suppose I thought I was just demonstrating the good faith of Huvea. Whether any of us would volunteer today is quite another question."

Some of Reggie's colleagues responded with a polite murmur, while others gave him stony glares. Gregor's grandchild suddenly turned, subdued and somewhat uneasy in the potential victims' presence. She seemed to be uncomfortable looking at them, but too fascinated to look away, as if they were already dead. Gregor thought suddenly: If the provisional treaty had also required Twin Worlds to give hostages, his granddaughter might well have been one of them—like them, she would be idealistic enough to volunteer. But that, thank all the gods of space, was not the way the contorted agreement had been worked out.

The robot, Porphyry, had meanwhile been standing in the background, part of the furniture, awaiting further orders from the executioner. Something about the machine now caught the eye of Douras, who suddenly called out to it.

"You, there, robot. Pay attention this way."

Porphyry raised calm, glassy eyes. All humans were to be treated with the same bland courtesy. "Yes sir?"

"I would like to know, if you understand just what the verb 'to execute' entails."

"Yes sir, I know the several meanings."

"Then you know the meaning of your master's title. Explain it to us, if you will."

"If required by the treaty, he will oversee—"

"Plain simple language, please. Do you know any blunt, ordinary words?"

"Yes sir. I did not mean to speak in euphemisms. My current master will be required to kill you, if the law tells him to do so."

"What method will he use?"

Huang Gun took a step forward, silencing the robot with a brief gesture. "Several are still under consideration. My guiding principle is that which is most efficient is also most humane. One leading candidate is a form of electrocution. Another is intense neutron flux. Be assured that the business will be accomplished as quickly and painlessly as I can arrange." Once more he shot a quick glance at his robot—as if, Gregor thought, something about the machine had pleased him.

Luon cried out, impulsively: "Barbaric!" Then she shrank back.

No one paid her much attention. The executioner raised one eyebrow, which seemed to have been subtly shaped by some robot barber's skill. Gregor was suddenly reminded of certain embalmers' work that he had seen.

Huang Gun was going on. "I am not responsible for the political arrangement which has placed them in this danger. And if they lose their lives at my hands—I shall be only an instrument of the law. A power far greater than I will have made the final decision."

Gregor was puzzled for a moment. "You mean the treaty will require it."

"Yes, of course."

And somehow Gregor found himself beginning to make the speech that he had promised not to make.

"I think that no one alive today on either of our worlds—probably no Earth-descended human anywhere in the Galaxy—has any conception of what a real war would mean. There is no doubt that some of our ancestors, when they set out from Earth, hundreds of years ago, could recall what real wars were like."

He paused, gave a twisted smile. "It seems I am making a speech after all. Well, it won't be wasted, because I intend to see to it that you do not die. Not today, not tomorrow, not for many years.

"As for the conflict: it was never supposed to be like this again, but here it is . . . here we are, in the middle of it."

He paused; the guard at the door was coming in again, this time closely followed by a pair of military officers of middle rank. These people had obviously come in search of Gregor, because they relaxed visibly as soon as they spotted him. Whatever their mission, it lacked the air of absolute urgency that would have caused him to break off his speech.

The officers were listening, an attitude of tolerant respect. When all the fine talk is over, their manner seemed to say, we will step in with a dose of reality.

Gregor went on. "Then we were not in continuous confrontation, frozen by suspicion. No. Instead, we were standing together, practically all of us still on one small world, looking outward. Like children—though we did not think of ourselves as such—a little fearful about what new dangers we might encounter when we left the nursery.

"A few of us even imagined a Galaxy alive with terrible monsters, predatory beings bred in the depths of humankind's ancient fears—and what did we actually find? The Carmpan, peace and tranquility personified. In their language, the only word for 'weapon' means something like a fly swatter.

"One or two other intelligent races, all equally peaceful—and about equally talkative. No danger to us. Not enemies, or rivals. So distant psychologically . . . I don't know if we should even call them friends. 'Well-wishers' is about as close as we can accurately come.

"There's evidence that the Carmpan had imagined, even predicted, terrible predators also. And what actually came along to meet them? We did, who hardly fit that category.

"Of course we've still explored only a small portion of our Milky Way. It didn't take long to discover that the currents running in flightspace between the stars can sometimes be treacherous. The new ocean is deeper than the old, deeper and wider by a billion billion times and more, and making our way across it can be even trickier. . . .

"But if the rest of the Milky Way, all those hundreds of billions of stars, is like the part we've sampled, *we* are absolutely the only creatures in it who can be described as at all warlike. We Earth-born humans have carried the burden of war all through our history. Once we were able to set it down, relieve ourselves of it. But the relief lasted only a little longer than a century. Now the temptation is upon us to grab the old burden up again, and—"

Gregor was interrupted again, by another test of the defenses. Noise and vibration drove all of them into their own thoughts. Some seemed to be searching each other's faces for clues as to what it all might mean. Luon took a step or two toward the hostages, then changed course and came to stand closer to Gregor's side.

"By the time the voyagers from Earth had established colonies in a hundred different star systems, the situation had changed, and it soon turned out that we were split into a hundred different nations once again. The safeguards of our common origins, trade, swift communication, all proved less than adequate. Each group, each world, began to be suspicious of others.

"Now it seems that all are looking for reasons to be jealous, to blame the people in the next system for our difficulties. It's easy to make a logical argument that we can no longer have any good reason to fight each other—but down through human history, it's always been easy to do that. Now suspicion feeds on suspicion, fear on fear, and today a majority of the hundred worlds have their programs of rearmament in progress, dreaming up new weapons and new defenses. Many have rearmed, including us. Look at the array of weapons we now possess—can you conceive what a ten megaton explosion would do to a human city?"

"We are well defended by our shields, sir—the shields that we are testing now."

"Have we also tested weapons to overwhelm the Huvean shields?"

No one wanted to answer that.

"Do you suppose that they have not done the same?"

Reggie cleared his throat and said: "What I suppose is—that your ten or twenty megaton bomb would do to a city just about the same thing that an intense neutron flux would do to a human brain. There's a rumor going around that that's the method they intend to use on us."

All the hostages—except one, gazing out the window—were looking at Gregor now, as if they still could hope he might tell them something that would help.

Huang Gun had an observation: "Some of the ancients had a name for this kind of thing: 'mutual assured destruction.' Humanity managed to escape that burden for a time, but now we find it on our backs again. . . . It seems to be the way we're made."

One of the forcefield doors leading to the outside had opened, and here came yet one more intrusion. This was a human courier, carrying a new message to the officers who had arrived only a couple of minutes ago. In a moment one of them stepped forward, and handed it to Gregor.

"Message from the Early Warning Zone of System Defense, sir."

Gregor thought: *This is it, their ultimatum. Return the hostages unharmed, or we attack.* "Something relayed from Huvea?"

"No sir, this is directly from System Defense. Do you wish to receive the communication in privacy?"

Gregor quickly took thought. "No, let these young people hear it too. I expect it is of great importance to them. I suppose it means the Huveans have launched an attack?"

"Sir, meanings are not my department, but I've seen no evidence to link this thing to Huvea. When were you last briefed on the situation?"

"Just this morning. Four or five hours ago."

"Then you will definitely want to see this."

Huang Gun the hostage keeper wanted to see and hear it also. All of them listened intently to the report of a strange intruder in the outer system.

As Gregor started to turn away, Huang Gun touched him on the arm and said: "I find the suggestion of some Huvean secret weapon certainly ominous—don't you agree, Plenipotentiary?"

"Certainly."

"Remember what I have told you. Those who could save us are already here among us."

Gregor was puzzled. "You mean—?"

The executioner was looking at the robot, almost as if he expected the machine to be able to contribute something useful to this conversation.

The robot simply looked back, imperturbable, as if it was only waiting to receive orders. Or, perhaps, to be asked a question.

Gregor said a hasty goodbye to the hostages and their keepers. Reginald Panchatantra seemed to want to tell him something, but at the last minute only nodded.

To the officer who had brought him the latest report, Gregor said intensely: "I have to find out all I can about this strange intrusion. The conference can wait. Get me out there, as fast as you can."

A small hand laid itself gently on his arm. "Where do you want me to go, Gramp? What shall I do?"

He had almost forgotten about the girl. What to do with her was certainly a question. Gregor thought the mysterious trespasser would almost certainly turn out to be some kind of Huvean trick or weapon, and it was tempting to declare that war had already begun. Even before the intruder's arrival, all transport within the Twin Worlds system was already badly disrupted. Those not canceled were overbooked, with impossible waiting lists. Given this latest alarm, civilian traffic would soon grind to a complete halt, with both incoming and outgoing flights suspended. There was no chance of Luon being able to get on any commercial ship just now. Private spacecraft were very rare, and he suspected all capable of leaving the system had long since fled.

The only remaining possibility was the military, and she would have no chance there either, unless the old man managed to pull strings. Gregor wasn't sure how far he could go along that road, or how far he ought to go, but he would give it a try. Already the girl had made it clear that she had no home to go to on this planet.

The only place he could exert his influence would seem to be with the high military brass, out in deep interplanetary space.

Gregor sighed, and beckoned to his granddaughter. "Come along." There seemed to be no better alternative.

On her way out, following on the old man's heels, Luon turned and sent one last glance in the direction of the prisoners. If her gaze lingered on one face, and met a silent response there, neither her distracted grandfather nor the executioner were aware of the fact.

When the door of the military staff car slammed shut, closing them into its rear compartment, Gregor turned at once to his young relative.

"Did you come here to the capital by tube? What are things

like in the other cities?" He could see for himself what things were like near the center of Timber's capital.

"Most of the people seem to have gone indoors," Luon told him, after a pause. "Everywhere I've been, it's pretty much like here. The ones you do see all look—anxious. I went past the spaceport at—" she named another city "—and there were practically no ships on the ground. Crowds of people there, all trying to get off world somehow, but civilian traffic seems to be completely shut down."

Following a sudden impulse, he asked the girl what she had thought about the hostages.

She took what seemed a surprisingly long time, just to decide on a comment. "They are all volunteers."

"Yes, they really are. One of them was just talking about that."

"But do they realize how—how close they are to being killed? With the negotiations failing?" The strain in her voice was worse than what he had heard from most of the hostages themselves.

"If they didn't before, they may be beginning to realize it— though young people in general tend to consider themselves immortal. They follow the news stories, and can see the situation as well as you and I do."

By now it had been possible for System Defense to get a somewhat better look at the intruder. An object described as a giant ship, a vessel of unprecedented size, was reported as having emerged from flightspace there in the same sector.

It had chosen to emerge at a comparatively remote location, before penetrating as deeply into the system, into the gravitational field of the central sun, as was practical in flightspace. The object had immediately set a course in normal space toward the inner planets, and was calculated to arrive in the near vicinity of Prairie within a couple of hours. This meant it was moving at a high fraction of the velocity of light, an impressive speed, considering how comparatively dense the interplanetary medium became in the inner system, fed by a constant outpouring of particles in the solar wind.

The military gave Gregor their assessment: For all that anyone in the Twin Worlds system could tell, observing the phenomenon from various vantage points scattered around the system, and from observatories in close orbit around the planets themselves, the stranger's intent might well be hostile. So far it had declined to answer any queries or challenges.

Gregor felt it his duty to discover all he could about the nature of the giant and mysterious intruder. Certainly he could not depart the system for the peace conference until he was sure whether it had come from Huvea or not.

The military analysts stubbornly refused to be pinned down. "There is no evidence that this intruder has any connection with Huvea—but on the other hand, I see no proof of any kind that it could not."

"Well, it came from somewhere, that is certain. Before I leave for the conference, I must know. This has a vital bearing on the question of war or peace."

"Yes sir, of course. But I can't promise you when we'll be able to determine its origin."

"That is not obvious?"

"No sir, the admiral seems to think that it is not."

There was nothing for it but to wait. "You will do your best to keep me informed of the latest developments."

"Of course, sir."

Besides the vessel waiting to carry him to the peace conference, and a couple of other ships hastily loading foreign visitors and diplomats, Timber's main spaceport had looked eerily deserted. Only a skeleton military presence was still there, while whole squadrons and battle fleets of warships were on alert in space, keeping their exact deployment secret. Gregor knew that the Twin

Worlds fleet was still in its home system, and he presumed the Huvean fleet would be doing the same thing—unless it was already on its way here, to attack.

Here, the war fever was at its height. But other systems had caught it too, though less acutely so. Warships of a new generation (the last of the old had been retired, unused, standard decades ago) were now under construction in almost every place where Earth-descended humans had established colonies.

But Gregor had to know. If the peace conference was already stillborn, if the war had started, then he wanted to stay here in his home system and fight for his own people. He would die with them if that was to be their fate.

He was already late for the conference—but there would be no point in showing up at any conference if war had already begun. He would order the captain of his transport ship to take him first to the defense nerve center, a hundred million kilometers farther from the sun, where the couriers coming in from the outer sphere of scoutships brought their latest messages. That was the fastest way for him to learn the latest news.

On a clear day like today, the Citadel's forcefield gates were visible as crisply outlined panels of gray fog. The military groundcar, presenting the proper code, slid easily through the nearest fog-panel and went cruising out into an eerily empty street. Gregor and his grandchild were swiftly conveyed through a domain of architectural diversity, set off and emphasized by park-like stretches of grass, dotted with clumps of trees and shrubbery under the afternoon sun. Much of the foliage was turning autumnal colors. The park, like the surrounding streets, was abnormally unpopulated. Gregor was relieved. He would not have been surprised to see angry mobs of demonstrators, either pro- or anti-war, or both. The scarcity of traffic promised the advantage of a quick drive to the spaceport. Still it would be long enough to allow the private conversation Gregor considered necessary.

One of the first buildings to slide past, on the right side of the broad avenue, was the imposing presidential office, its high windows betraying nothing of what might be going on inside. Whether the president was occupying it at the moment was more than

Gregor, his high rank notwithstanding, had been able to find out.

President Belgola, like his immediate predecessor, had another office, practically a duplicate of this one, on the planet Prairie. This chief executive spent time in each, and during the past year had added a third office, in the form of a spacegoing facility on which he frequently shuttled between the two worlds, or cruised the system in an independent orbit.

In the course of these days-long, unhurried journeys Belgola was known to hold long consultations with his technical adviser, an advanced computer system he had named Logos, after the primordial spirit of reason. Gregor had never seen Logos, but the device was said to be small enough to be easily transportable, and was informally known, among the irreverent, as the Oracle.

One of the most recently defeated presidential candidates (who had a deserved reputation as a reasonable woman) had said: "This famous—or infamous—Oracle is nothing but an optelectronic version of his human supporters, politically programmed to tell him what he wants to hear. He's convinced himself that it brings him access to some kind of superhuman, not to say supernatural, wisdom."

"So you might say that he's busy talking to himself," a journalist had prompted.

"Some of the more irreverent have already put it that way, yes." And Gregor remembered seeing a political cartoon.

Now, with this newest report of a strange intrusion in the outer reaches of the Twin Worlds solar system, the president's policy of restraint, keeping the entire fleet at home and deployed for defense, seemed entirely justified. For the moment his political stock was riding high; his opponents in the legislature were reduced to a few mutterings of disagreement.

The old man and the girl spent a short time trading news of other family members. As soon as such routine matters had been got out of the way, Luon burst out with the subject that was really on her mind.

"Gramp, can't you do anything about this hostage business? Keep them from being killed?"

Gregor was sitting back with folded arms. "You saw, my girl, you heard. Probably it was foolish of me; but I went in there with the vague idea that I might accomplish something along that line—as you observed, I had no success."

Before he had finished speaking, the girl was bouncing in her seat, turning halfway around. "Hostages! By all the great gods, the Huvean government must be totally crazy—otherwise they never could have agreed to anything so stupid!"

Gregor gave his young relative a faint smile, of sympathy, not amusement. "Welcome to the adult world, my dear. But you're right, I suppose this giving of hostages is unique in the annals of modern diplomacy."

"Annals of motherless modern lunacy!" Luon waved her tender fists, looking ready to hit someone.

He wasn't going to argue that point, or reprimand his granddaughter for her language. In a patient voice he offered such explanation as was possible, tracing the way in which the complicated treaty had been negotiated, beginning with the fact that ten people from the Twin Worlds had lost their lives in a disaster on the disputed planet. Whether that catastrophe had been sheer natural accident, or could be traced to some malignant Huvean, was one of the points still bitterly disputed.

Luon did her grandfather the honor of listening to his explanation. He couldn't tell whether she had heard it all before or not, but obviously it had little effect on her opinions.

"All right, Gramp, I still say their government is crazy to give us hostages. But ours is crazy too." At that point she stopped suddenly, listening to herself. "Not you, of course!"

"A lot of people would certainly include me." Gregor patted

her hand. "There are times when I'm inclined to agree with them."

Luon bounced again. "But you're not really in charge. What about our so-called president! You talk to him sometimes, don't you? What do you think?"

Gregor was shaking his head slowly. "I would like very much to talk to Mr. Belgola right now." Suddenly he saw no point in attempting any longer to keep his difficulties secret. "Believe it or not, I've been trying for several days to reach him. It's proven impossible for me to get through."

"Gramp, really?" Luon's big eyes went wide. "I'd have thought you had some kind of a direct line."

"I thought so too. Officially I do." That line of communication still existed, in theory and in hardware, but only once in the better part of a standard week had he got as far as a human voice on the other end of it—and the human voice was not the president's, and had not been helpful. At other times the plenipotentiary had been blocked by one level or another of the robots.

Now Gregor added, talking mostly to himself: "Maybe I should have asked to speak to Logos."

Maybe he would try that next time. Unflappable, inflexible robotic voices, as unfailingly courteous as they were firm. It was unsettling not to be sure of being able to contact the man in an emergency. Still, Gregor had no immediate need to know exactly where the president was, and in fact the plenipotentiary did not very much care. He had little confidence in Belgola's abilities, and for that reason was all the more determined to be loyal to the government and people in time of crisis.

At the time when Gregor had last had contact with him, as the strains of crisis multiplied around him, President Belgola of the Twin Worlds, recently armed with extraordinary powers by an angry parliament, had been on the verge of ordering a preemptive strike against the home system of the antagonistic Huveans. But so far Belgola had held back.

Luon listened silently as Gregor discussed the matter of communication failures, managing to drain some of his frustrations while not really—or so he thought—revealing anything that the girl and the public should not know.

Luon was bright enough to be troubled by what she had just heard: "The last news bulletin I caught, Gramp—sir—they were saying the president was at an undisclosed location. But of course you must know *that*—don't you?"

Gregor grunted. "Possibly I've already said more than I should on the subject." He didn't really believe that, though. If the president was no longer available to his closest human advisers, the public deserved to be let in on the fact.

Or was it only he, Gregor, who was being cut out of the loop? He made a mental note that as soon as he had the chance, he would try to reach the vice president, now attending a large gathering of officials on Prairie.

Gregor sighed—people tended to be sharply divided on the subject of Belgola, who had come to office with something of a reputation for radicalism. Most people thought, certainly hoped, he had put his wilder ideas behind him on at last achieving his long sought goal of becoming president.

Trying to hold a reasonable conversation during the last half minute of the ride was hopeless, as the weapons testing interrupted again, driving its noise and vibration even into the sealed and cushioned staff car. Waved by human guards through gates at the spaceport's entrance, the staff car headed directly out to a spot near the middle of the extensive landing field, which like the streets of the central city was for once weirdly devoid of traffic. Their driver was heading for a small ship parked near the middle, in virtual isolation.

The ship, metallic and nearly spherical, had an entrance hatch open and ramp extended. A darkly handsome young man in a scoutship commander's uniform was waiting beside it when

Gregor climbed out of the car. "How many in your party, sir? We can accommodate some staff, if you like."

Gregor shook his head "I have no staff with me at the moment."

"Yes sir." The officer turned his head to shoot a questioning look at Luon, who was also disembarking from the car. "I thought . . ."

"The young woman is a member of my family. Her presence here is accidental and perhaps unfortunate. But I must see that she's taken care of. I see no alternative to having her come with me on the ship."

"As you say, sir. Will there be any baggage?"

"It seems we are both traveling light today." Gregor's, to the best of his own belief, had been loaded aboard another ship, and was already on its way out of the solar system, the idea being that he would catch up with it at the conference light-years away.

He had just begun to move toward the small ship's extended entrance ramp, when another staff car came gliding smoothly up. An officer of higher rank than any Gregor had encountered yet today, his shoulder bearing the single star of a basic general, appeared relieved to see that he had caught up with the plenipotentiary.

A small courier's pouch was strapped to the general's wrist. "Glad I caught you, sir. I bring a personal message for you, from Admiral Radigast."

Gregor accepted the palm-sized container. He was unable to imagine what the contents of this latest message might be, but for the moment he refrained from opening it. "I wonder how the admiral knew that I was here."

"I believe he has several of us chasing you, sir. In different directions."

When Gregor began to open the container, it spoke in a small, clear voice, requesting him to put his fingertips on certain marks, and look closely at two spots on the outer surface, so it could check his retinal patterns. Once his identity had been verified, the pack opened easily.

Inside there was nothing elaborate to be seen, in the way of images. There was only a simple text.

> SIR—I RESPECTFULLY REQUEST THAT BEFORE DEPARTING THE TWIN WORLDS SYSTEM, YOU WILL KINDLY VISIT ME ON MY FLAGSHIP, FOR A FACE-TO-FACE DISCUSSION OF MATTERS OF THE HIGHEST IMPORTANCE.
>
> RADIGAST, COMMANDING

The general seemed nervous. "I take it, sir, you do intend to honor the admiral's request?"

"Yes. Oh yes." For a moment Gregor wondered if he would even be allowed to leave the system, if he did not. But the peace conference was looking less and less relevant anyway.

According to the general who had brought Gregor the latest message, this new, exotic presence on the outer fringes of the home system was taken by many as an all but certain indication that a Huvean attack on Twin Worlds was imminent. It obviously wasn't an ordinary warship, and it certainly was not a fleet. Some kind of a trick.

Over the past several standard years, a number of military analysts from neutral powers—theirs was a rapidly growing profession, as many other worlds had also taken to rearmament—had reached a general consensus that Huvea and the Twin Worlds were very evenly matched in their preparedness for war.

Basic fleet strength, the numbers and sizes which seemed impossible for either power to keep secret, was supposedly balanced at eight dreadnoughts each—as soon as one power began to build a new one, the other followed—with appropriately larger numbers of cruisers, destroyers, scoutships, and a variety of auxiliary vessels.

Fleet strength was, naturally enough, one of the things that the new treaty was supposed to stabilize.

There might be a greater imbalance in terms of ground troops and weapons—there was certainly wide disagreement among modern strategists on how great a role these would play in any interstellar conflict, and which side had the advantage.

Of the three planets—Huvea, and the Twin Worlds—most likely to be actively engaged in any conflict, and thus directly attacked, Timber was generally thought to have the best mobile ground defenses.

However much Gregor concentrated on the looming conflict, in his mind the whole business kept tending to take on an air of unreality. He supposed it must be so for everyone, in light of the fact that no human being currently alive had ever actually seen a war, let alone taken part in one. Theories on the conduct of space warfare abounded, unconstrained by the fact that no Earth-descended human in the Galaxy today, no individual on any planet, had any really relevant experience.

In the privacy of his thought, Gregor added a codicil to that: all living, breathing, humans might be neophytes in war, but there was another class of strategists who could claim veteran status. He had heard that the chief of cryptanalysis (a robot so secret that its code name had its own code name) still contained certain modules that had been in place during one of the last wars ever fought by Earth-descended humans.

Gregor could very clearly remember the last lecture on the subject that he had heard. "That of course was a very small war, by the standards of modern theorists."

"How do you know?"

"We know because Earth is still there, in its natural orbit, and still quite habitable."

———

Walking up the entrance ramp into the scoutship, Gregor looked over his shoulder, making sure that his grandchild was still with him. Luon was only three or four steps behind, and had evidently been taken in charge by some junior officer. There should be no lack of young men volunteering to keep the attractive young lady company. But the girl had other things on her mind than flirting. From the expression on her face, she was only being polite in listening to him.

Boarding the scout, Gregor felt somewhat relieved to be surrounded again by the world of military people and procedures. Whatever their other faults, they at least tended to be decisive. And there was another clear advantage to dealing with the military— you always knew where to find them.

Aboard the courier, the plenipotentiary received, from the officer who had brought the latest message, a briefing on the most recent developments: For the past day or two, the central government of the Twin Worlds had been sending out almost a steady stream of crewless robotic probes, dispatching them to a specific region in the distant reaches of their solar system.

Out there, under supervision of several scoutship crews, instruments aboard the probes were steadily gathering information. In an effort to escape detection, or possible countermeasures by the object they had come to investigate, they remained at distances of a light minute or more from it. At short, random intervals, a trio of the devices currently on watch would break off their harvesting routines and turn toward home, speeding along diverging pathways, carrying with them whatever new data they had managed to pick up to their mother ship, whence it would be speeded back to Prairie and Timber, and to the command satellites circling both home worlds. Meanwhile, three replacements had arrived near the object, and were taking up comparable though not identical positions, so there would be no break in the continuity of coverage. The system used was risky, redundant, and expensive, but seemed to work beautifully. Three identical probes all attempted a c-plus jump at very nearly the same time, headed for the same destination, but programmed to follow different courses. Usually no more than two of the three survived the perilous jump, but at least one almost always did—by this means the information reached its destination as much as an hour ahead of any radio or optical signal.

Gregor and Luon were seated with their escort in the scout-ship's spartan and constricted wardroom, cruising in the merciful grip of artificial gravity, bodies untouched by brutal acceleration.

The diplomat was asking: "Why are you giving me this briefing, general? It would seem that in the normal course of my duties, I would have no need to know."

"I'm acting on special orders from Admiral Radigast, sir. How this knowledge may affect your own duties, your own plans, I have no idea."

The pilot's voice presently came over intercom, informing the two civilian passengers that the admiral's flagship was close ahead. Their small craft was approaching the Twin Worlds battle fleet, which had been deployed in a defensive formation relatively close to the two populated planets.

The wardroom's small holostage was occupied at the moment by the head and shoulders of a newsman, broadcasting from the steadily receding planet Timber. The man was droning on about things that made no sense at all to Gregor. Some kind of popular entertainment, he assumed. Then suddenly the three-dimensional image vanished, to be replaced by the head and shoulders of a very different man.

. . . .
F I V E
. . . .

Admiral Radigast, sitting on the edge of a combat couch, was visible against a background of what looked like the control room of his flagship. The commander of all Twin Worlds forces in space squinted at the two civilians and seemed notably relieved when he was able to recognize Gregor. His image shot one glance at Luon, then ignored her.

Gregor got a quick impression of compact energy. The admiral's uniform, with its single row of important decorations, was correctly cut and fastened, yet somehow the man still managed to look rumpled. He was chewing on something, doubtless one of the pods currently in vogue, his mouth twisted a little to one side.

Several different kinds of chewing pods were popular, especially among those who liked to see themselves as the trendsetters of interstellar society—but those were not the people with whom high-ranking diplomats spent most of their waking hours. Whatever type of chew the admiral had favored, it got spat out energetically. Speaking unencumbered, the admiral issued a warm and quietly eager invitation to the plenipotentiary to come aboard his flagship.

"Delighted to see you up in space, sir. Your ship will be docking on the *Morholt* in just about one minute. I'll be along to welcome you personally as soon as I can get there."

"That will be fine, Admiral." Gregor paused uncertainly. "There's one detail I must bring to your attention. Through a series of curious events, all of them unplanned on my part I assure you, I happen to have my granddaughter traveling with me, a young lady of eighteen. If you could possibly make some provision for her, while you and I have our talk. . . ?"

"I only wish all problems were as readily solved, sir. Don't give it a moment's thought." The admiral sounded briskly cheerful, but his mind was obviously on something else. Gregor had already decided this courteous but forceful summons must have something to do with the recent disturbing developments at the apex of the civilian government.

The admiral's image was gone. Gregor found a switch and the small stage went dark and bare. Luon was still staring at it, thoughtfully. "I wonder what he wants from you, Gramp."

"We'll soon find out."

Presently the pilot informed them that the flagship was now visible, if they wanted to look out their window.

Luon had got out of her seat and was pressing her cheek to the inner surface of a cleared statglass port, looking out at every angle she could manage. "I can't see anything," she complained. "Only the sun and stars. Oh, wait, there's a ship. But I only see one."

Gregor, in the adjoining seat, was trying to relax. It seemed his day was going to be even longer and more wearying than he had expected. "There's no way you could expect to see more than one ship. Chances are they're all thousands of kilometers apart."

Gregor hazily remembered the dreadnought's specifications, from the days when he had been fairly closely involved with the military. The *Morholt* was very nearly an even ten kilometers long, its overall shape that of a lean cylinder, all armor and power and caged-up deadly force. A more recent memory nagged Gregor with a comparison: this ship, impressive as it was, would be only about one fifth the length of the mysterious intruder, and a much smaller fraction of its bulk.

Now he too could see part of the *Morholt* through the port. The surface of Radigast's flagship flashed faintly silver in some places, and there were large stretches of surface that were hardly visible at all. These somewhat resembled parts of the intruder as System Defense had pictured it, appearing as patches of dark void against the endless starry background. The view of the Milky Way enjoyed by Twin Worlds citizens was not enormously different from the prospect visible to the people of Earth.

Luon was no stranger to the view of stars from space, but she had never been close to a ship of this kind and size before, and was clearly impressed. But she gave no impression of having been relieved of her chronic worry.

In another moment, the dreadnought had opened a set of jaw-like doors, and swallowed up the tiny scoutship like a gnat. There followed a smooth docking inside a great hangar bay. Less than a minute after that, the scout's pair of civilian passengers were disembarking through mated airlocks.

How many decks on the great ship? Gregor was trying to remember. In a thousand meters of available thickness, there might easily be more than a hundred, at least for part of the ship's length. How many crew members? That could vary enormously, depending on the mission assigned the ship. Given the universal dependence on computers, less than a thousand human brains might serve to crew the entire fleet of a hundred ships or more.

Once before—it startled Gregor to think it must have been ten standard years ago—the plenipotentiary had been aboard a late model ship as big as this one, but that had been in a time of peace and ceremony.

More details about the ship came back to him as he saw more of it again. He was able to answer a couple of questions for Luon.

As they followed their spaceman escort along a twisting corridor, through set after set of doors, and past one occupied compartment after another, Luon said: "But all these people are used to the idea of war."

"Well. Not really, Luon. Of course the crew are accustomed to the ship—to working all the devices. I'll wager they're very good at that. But no one on her crew has any more experience of combat than you do."

His grandchild made no reply. Gregor had already formed the distinct impression that she was no fan of the military, but here, for once, she was awed into silence.

Most of the crew members that the pair saw in their passage were wearing helmets that kept them in close optelectronic contact with the thinking machines that handled the routine details of micromanagement. The flagship, and, Gregor presumed, the whole fleet, was at a medium stage of alert, which meant that dress uniforms were nowhere to be seen, and ceremony was kept to a minimum. People murmured and stepped aside for the eminent plenipotentiary, one or two of them saluting awkwardly. Gregor couldn't remember if he, as a civilian, should be returning these salutes or not, so each time he compromised, responding with a small gesture. Had he been on the ground, there might have been a robot on hand to offer discreet counsel on matters of protocol. But the only robots on a warship would be carrying quite different matters in their data banks—he seriously doubted there were any anthropomorphic servants.

In another minute, the visitors had reached the flagship's bridge, where Admiral Radigast rose from his combat couch to welcome them. Here on the bridge the entire fleet at last became visible, if only on holostage, where it made an impressive sight to Gregor's experienced eye.

Radigast was putting out a hand for him to clasp. "Glad to see you, sir. Very glad." In a moment, Gregor was being introduced to a few senior members of the admiral's staff, as well as the *Morholt*'s captain.

The admiral had a habit of squinting through narrowed eyes that suggested—erroneously, no doubt—defective vision. His manner and behavior were correct in all details, and even his uniform looked as immaculate in direct view as it had on stage—Gregor had heard rumors of legendary personal sloppiness. Still, Radigast somehow gave the impression of not spending much time on such details.

The flurry of introductions over, he went immediately to the next point. "How long can you remain on board, sir?"

Gregor explained briefly about the peace conference, though he thought the explanation was probably unnecessary. "But I'm determined to find out what's happening here in our system before I go."

"I'm with you in that, Mister Plenipotentiary. I would also like to gather some kind of clue as to what's going on. But I fear that's going to take a little time."

Only now did the admiral get around to greeting Luon, in a pleasantly absentminded way. Then he crisply issued orders for two adjoining cabins, in what he called VIP country, to be made available.

Gregor entered a mild protest. "I expect we're only going to be on board for a short time."

"Of course, sir. But the young lady might want a place to—how do they put it?—freshen up."

"Of course. Thank you. But we don't want to put any of your people out of their quarters—I'm assuming that room is at something of a premium."

The squint turned into half a smile. "Not as premium as you might think, sir. They built this ship to serve diplomatic functions when necessary, and that sometimes means entertaining visitors.

Would you care to step into my quarters for a moment? We can both sit down and relax."

Again, a young male officer—this one was of higher rank—was detailed to look after Luon for a while. Here on a battleship, in contrast to the scout, there was a lot to see.

"Give her Tour Number One," the admiral tersely recommended.

"Yes sir."

As the pair moved away, Gregor heard the young man asking what parts of the ship might she truly be interested in? And Luon's answer, a peaceful murmur. Not even looking back; she was trying to keep grandfather happy, by keeping herself out of his way.

A few moments later, as soon as the door closed on the two men alone in a small but comfortable cabin, Radigast added: "Frankly, it's a relief to have someone in authority that I can talk to, and who can't turn me off with the flick of a switch. Are you in the mood for a drink, sir? Or chew?"

"Neither just now, thank you. Admiral, I hope you don't credit me with more authority than I really have. I can see that this strange intruder presents a special problem for defense—especially if it won't communicate. By the way, thank you for the thorough briefing on the subject. The general was most enlightening."

The fleet commander acknowledged the thanks with a nod. "Wanted to make sure you understand just where we are." The latest chewing pod, whatever flavor it had been, was ejected in decisive fashion. A squirrel-sized housekeeping machine was on the spot to clean it up, almost before it landed.

Radigast took a seat in a large chair, gesturing Gregor to another that looked just as comfortable. The admiral seemed to be relaxing into a more natural mode. The removal of a minor strain was evident.

But something major still remained. "The intruder, as you aptly call it, does not represent my only motherless communication problem. It's not even my prime, original reason for wanting to talk to you, Plenipotentiary Gregor." The admiral drew a deep breath. "Sir, you and I have never met before, but I've kind of followed your record, and I think maybe you're someone I can talk to. Do you have any idea what's happened to His Nibs our president?"

Gregor was only faintly surprised by the blunt question. Yes, it was time, and past time, to be direct. He allowed himself to sigh. "I have been trying to reach him for almost three days now, without success."

Radigast nodded slowly. He did not seem as surprised as Gregor thought he should have been. "What about the vice president?"

"She's on Prairie, Admiral, as you doubtless know. She's not been returning my messages either, but so far I haven't made them urgent. In her case the seeming reluctance to communicate is more easily explained. She's up to her eyebrows in a high-level conference—strategic planning."

Radigast did not seem at all reassured. He grunted, and popped another chewing pod into his mouth, this time forgetting to offer one to his guest. "I know. The Joint Chiefs are there too." There was a slight pause before he admitted: "I don't always get on superbly well with them."

"So I've heard." Gregor spoke carefully. "Admiral, it won't do to have a rumor spread to the effect that the president of Twin Worlds is missing, or that he's deliberately chosen to isolate himself in such a way that the other components of his government can hardly reach him."

"Especially if the motherless rumor is true." The admiral grunted again, and nodded. "If that kind of crap hasn't started yet, believe me, it soon will. I've tried to reach him directly, and got the same treatment you did. Can you think of any good excuse for the way he's acting?"

Gregor responded only with a silent headshake. It was understandable that a president might not have much to say at any given moment, or might want time to be alone, to think. But there was no excuse for dropping totally out of contact. As long as the fleet was deployed in the inner system, it would never be more than a few minutes away from its civilian commander-in-chief, at the speed of light or radio.

Radigast had evidently determined to speak his mind to someone, whatever the consequence might be.

"Sir, understand me. I'm not talking parties and politics here. I've got no motherless interest in politics. As part of the military I shouldn't have, and I don't. But he . . . Belgola's got his bloody head so deep in the motherless sand that his own top people don't even know where he is."

After a short pause, in which Gregor tried to frame objections, he found himself agreeing. "I can't argue with that."

"Do you know him well, sir? Do you consider yourself his friend? I mean apart from the political thing, both of you being in the same party."

"I . . ." Gregor had to stop and shake his head. "As friends, he and I go back a long way, as you must know. I once thought I knew him well."

"Well, between you and me, it wouldn't necessarily be any enormous motherless loss if he resigned his office and disappeared for good." The admiral paused, listening to himself. "Understand me, I'm not trying to overthrow the government. We still have elections to accomplish that. I'd just like to find out where the hell my government is. And by that I mean my bloody so-called commander in chief."

But the admiral, even risking a court martial for insubordination, was not going to be allowed to concentrate on the seemingly disconnected status of the president. Not even for a few minutes. The communicator in his cabin broke in with urgent sounds, unintelligible to the visitor.

Radigast swore. "Excuse me." He turned his head aside. "What now, Charlie?"

Gregor, sitting at hardly more than arm's length distance, could hear nothing at all. Whatever the news, it did not seem to be good.

The cabin's small stage suddenly lit up. It seemed that the admiral had been away from his regular duties long enough. Images of the intruding stranger appeared.

All the watching humans saw the same thing on their holo-stages, and what they saw was hard to believe or understand.

The images brought back by the robotic probes were of an unidentified and seemingly unidentifiable object. The mysterious intruder was huge, looking like a whole continent of metal, spotted and striped with other more exotic materials. In overall shape, a thick and broad rectangular slab. One of its fifty-kilometer-long sides—Gregor kept reminding himself it was five times the length of the *Morholt*—was spread out below the spy unit like a map. The surface bristled with projections, some of which were not immediately identifiable, but could be reasonably assumed to be weapons. Parts of the gigantic hull were twisted and gnarled, as if it had already been through a war.

The admiral exchanged terse comments with people elsewhere on the ship. Presently he got to his feet. "I've got to get back to the bridge, sir. Want to come along?" The offer seemed more than a mere form of courtesy.

"I'm honored," the old man responded simply.

Back on the bridge, Gregor felt a chill as he listened to comments from other officers, people you might think would not be easily impressed. They were talking in awed, murmuring voices. "It's not a ship, it's a bloody artificial motherless planetoid."

"A lot of those details aren't clear. Try and get some greater magnification."

"The image will inevitably be somewhat blurred—the thing's enveloped in what we take to be a defensive forcefield, working on the same principle as ours, though it gives somewhat different readings than any type that we're familiar with."

Everyone watched in silence for a time. Parts of the image quivered, shook, then straightened out a little. Computers were still working on the enhancement.

Then Gregor the diplomat diffidently put in a comment. "Those huge serrations along one rim—to me they look like battlements, on some ancient fortified Earth city. Of course their real purpose must be something else. But that's what they look like."

"It's also much larger than any such city could ever have been. . . ."

In those places where colors could be plainly seen, the object was mostly black, an ebony reminding Gregor of certain anomalous regions of deep space that swallowed incoming light, and could not be made to reveal just how the energy had been digested. Portions of the surface were scarred, ragged flanges bent up and twisted, as if by some ancient slagging of an outer hull of enormous thickness.

People who searched the images for any clue that might tie the thing to Huvea were completely disappointed. No symbols of any kind were visible, and that struck many searchers as odd indeed. None of the usual idiosyncrasies of Huvean construction techniques were in evidence.

The admiral mused: "Looks like the proprietors wish to remain anonymous."

Gregor asked: "Has anyone yet made any attempt to communicate with it?"

The others looked at the admiral. He said: "No one will, until I say so. But I'd say it's getting to be time."

Charlie—Captain Charles, spacecraft commander of the flagship—kept insisting: "Admiral, I say this is some kind of a trick. A diversion."

"By the Huveans?"

"Yes sir, of course! They've got to be behind it—who else? They want us to concentrate our attention on this thing, move all our assets closer to it. Then as soon as we do that, their main fleet is going to appear on the other side of the sun. I'd say the first message that we send to it should indicate clearly that we are not being fooled."

Gregor the diplomat was silently shaking his head. He did not dispute the fact that Huveans could be nasty, but it was not at all like them to be this innovative.

No one was asking the diplomat's opinion. Radigast only grunted. If anyone else was in agreement with the suspicious Captain Charles, no one spoke up in his support. Radigast did not seem ready to put a Huvean label on the apparition, but he took no steps to alter the disposition of his fleet.

Meanwhile, the technical work went on. The first attempts at precisely measuring the object's surface temperature confirmed that it was very cold. The measurement was difficult, as it was encased in invisible forcefield shielding.

"As our ships are?" Gregor asked.

Charlie looked at him. "As our ships will be, the moment we go on full alert. We haven't done that yet."

The thing was simply there, absolutely defying any comfortable explanation.

Instruments showed that for an object of its size, the mysterious trespasser radiated very little at any wavelength. At the moment, by the standards of deep space travel, it was scarcely moving, traveling at only a handful of kilometers per second relative to the Twin Worlds sun that was hundreds of millions of kilometers away.

Careful analysis of its initial movement in normal space showed clearly that the thing was precisely on course to intercept the planet Prairie in its orbit. At the present speeds of the planet and the mystery object, that approach would take days—but the object's speed in normal space could be multiplied several times while still remaining well below the velocity of light.

Half a standard hour passed, in which the situation did not change materially. At that time the admiral did begin to shift his

capital ships, dreadnoughts and cruisers, adjusting positions and velocities, making sure he could get them between the intruder and the world it was making for.

He called for a whole-system presentation on the holostage, and entered the adjustments he wanted to make in the defensive network. Of course it would take hours for the changes to actually be put into effect.

He supposed it was quite possible that, despite the signs of violence with which the thing was marked, its immediate intentions were perfectly peaceful. When dealing with the unknown, almost anything was possible.

One awed onlooker, studying a magnified image on the nearby holostage, still marveled at the thing's sheer size. "That can't be a ship. Nobody's ever made a ship that big."

The debate among the admiral's advisers now found a new point of focus. "Well, what is it, then? *I* say it can't very well be anything but a ship."

"Some kind of artifact, certainly. To me its behavior suggests a gigantic robot probe."

"Must be more than a probe, I'd say. Who would make a simple probe that size, and why? Looks like a whole bloody motherless moving world."

Decades before Earth-descended humans began serious space exploration, a theory had been developed of sending robots out unaccompanied, to replicate themselves (like so many bacteria, jeered detractors) and push the exploration forward—one early calculation had predicted that by this means the whole Galaxy might be explored in only a few standard centuries.

The tactic of sending out independent robots as explorers had been tested, but, for several reasons, never seriously adopted. On the same or closely related grounds, none of the beautiful new personal robots were routinely part of the hardware in the combat-ready fleet.

Time passed. Five minutes after being called back to the bridge, the admiral made a decision.

"Well, my colleagues, here goes." He passed on orders. The flagship, with most of the rest of the fleet following and flanking, eased closer to the apparition, on a course that would also establish the battle fleet even more directly between it and the inner system, nesting place of the inhabited worlds.

Whether the stranger took note of this redeployment or not was hard to guess. It did not alter course or speed.

When Radigast ordered a halt, after the passage of an additional half an hour, they had come within a million kilometers of the intruder, putting them only light seconds apart. (On the holostage, the little image of the stranger was still steadily advancing, at a rate that would put it right in the middle of the fleet's formation, in a matter of only minutes.)

The admiral turned his gaze to the plenipotentiary. "Sir, I'm not sure if I'm conducting motherless diplomacy here or what. Would you like any input on framing the first message?"

Gregor slowly shook his head. "Not this one, thank you. Perhaps the next. If there is to be another."

The stranger was hailed, in accordance with standard procedures, and asked to identify itself.

There was no response.

One of the admiral's deputies said: "They don't want to answer. But someone must be aboard?" It came out as more question than statement.

No one could give a confident answer. "It seems to have a very definite idea about where it wants to go."

"It seems to me more and more likely that there's no one on board that ship at all. Surely, anyone who's breathing and not brain-dead would have thought of something to say to us by this time."

"If there's no living crew, then one might argue that it's not a ship, in the strict sense. Only a machine."

"A machine, or a bloody artificial planetoid. Whether you call it one thing or the other, it's the purpose I'm concerned about."

"What it's going to do next."

"Yeah. And after we know what, we can ask why—but probably that particular motherless question can wait a little longer."

"Why is it here?—but I just can't believe that there's no living crew."

"You mean you think there are people aboard, living intelligent motherless beings of some kind, but refusing to answer us? What would they gain by hiding out?"

The admiral's people were certainly not afraid to argue with the boss. "They could gain anonymity . . . especially if they're Huveans."

But Radigast was not willing to accept that answer yet. "From the look of it, it might have been through a bloody war already, or maybe two or three. Anybody here heard of a motherless war that's started somewhere else?"

Nobody had, of course. The Twin Worlds–Huvea confrontation was the only interplanetary conflict to have reached the flash point yet, though many other worlds were rearming.

Whatever the intruder's exact nature and purpose might be, certain humps and projections on the undamaged portions of the hull suggested that it might be heavily armed.

The decision of what to do next was left to the admiral to make.

Again Radigast issued orders. "Send our own robot probe toward it, try for a close orbit first, say at about ten klicks. If that doesn't wake them up, we'll go for direct physical contact. Just a gentle tap. But let's see if we can establish the close orbit first."

Gregor was nodding his unsolicited agreement.

A few minutes later, the probe was closing on the stranger, closing to a range of twenty kilometers.

Then fifteen.

Evidently the probe did not appear so innocent to whoever or whatever was monitoring its progress from the other end of its trajectory. Someone or something there was certainly aware of it, for the probe was neatly vaporized by some kind of beam weapon before it could quite come within ten kilometers of that monstrous hull.

S I X

There was silence on the flag-
ship's bridge, and then a muttered obscenity from the admiral.

When none of the other officers came up with anything to
add to that comment, Gregor offered: "Well. I suppose we might
have done the same, to anything it sent toward us."

Radigast was still staring at the stage. "Bah. We'd have
responded reasonably when hailed, not let things get to this stage.
I'd say our motherless visitor displays a definitely unneighborly
attitude."

The captain was persistent. "A Huvean attitude, sir?"

The admiral only grunted.

Gregor was thinking: *The world has changed, and un-
expectedly, the way it always does.* Probably he had just witnessed
the beginning of a war, though it was not the war that anyone had
foreseen, and it had started in a totally unpredictable way.

Around him, on the bridge and elsewhere, a full complement of people in comfortable couches, aided by some vastly
greater number of machines, were continually taking readings,

studying every scratch and dimple on the visitor's surface, trying to plot every meter of its predicted course.

Another crew member, one that Gregor had not met, was talking to the admiral. "Sir, we can't identify anything about the spectrum of that weapon flash, can't pin it down as resulting from any armament from any known world. In particular, I certainly can't see this—this thing—as the product of any Huvean shipyard. Of course we haven't had a good look at its capabilities yet."

"Well, keep trying. That goes for everyone, people. We have to nail this thing down, what it is, especially as it might connect to Huvea, what it can do. Guessing is not an option."

"Yes sir, I realize that, we all do. Admiral, our people have been in practically continuous contact with Huvea for many years, ever since both sets of colonies were founded. We know them, their society, their capabilities. I'll take my oath, they have never built a ship or a machine like that."

Gregor was keeping silent, letting the military experts talk. Identifying strange ships in space was part of their business, not of his. But in his private thoughts he kept coming back to the point that if this was some Earth-descended artifact, it was way beyond the innovative possibilities of Huvean strategy. Who else was ready to attack Twin Worlds?

Knowing that was part of his business, as a diplomat. And the answer was: no one.

Radigast was moving in the same direction, following his own lights. "If it's not Huvean, and not some crazy bloody tactical trick some motherless ED psycho on some other world has thought up—the only answer left is that it's non-ED. It's truly alien."

An officer of lesser rank, who until now had been keeping quiet, spoke up. "Carmpan?"

There was a silence, as if no one on the bridge thought the suggestion really deserved a comment. As far as anyone on this ship knew, no one in the Galaxy but Earth-descended humans and their remote Carmpan cousins ever built spacecraft of any kind.

But nobody observing this odd intruder could really believe it was a Carmpan construction. That passive and introspective race built spaceships only on rare occasions, when they deemed it absolutely necessary, and their vessels were always on the modest side. Never anything like this.

The extensive data bank on board the admiral's flagship was ready to be decisive when asked to find a match for the discovery: ALIEN, OF UNKNOWN ORIGIN.

Gregor, and several others aboard the *Morholt* who were well traveled among the stars, agreed with the staff experts that no world colonized from old Earth had ever constructed a thing like this; no one on the flagship had even seen the like. And it was hard to believe that any of the planets colonized from Earth, all of them in frequent contact with one another, had somehow managed the feat in secrecy.

Meanwhile, the object of their curiosity was suddenly accelerating. Remaining in normal space, piling on the gravities swiftly for an object of such bulk, holding steadily to its course that carried it smoothly in the direction of the sun and inner planets. It seemed that whoever or whatever was in control of the visitor felt no uncertainty at all in choosing a destination. *Morholt's* own astrogational computers, looking at that course, reported it was fine-tuned to a point of intersection with the planet Prairie in its orbit.

Presently Gregor decided to visit his assigned cabin—the plumbing there was notably less spartan and more private than that offered by an acceleration couch in a crowded room. Besides, he wanted a brief rest.

His assigned quarters turned out to be small but elegant. Luon must have been listening for his arrival, for she promptly put her head in through the door to the adjoining room and began to prod him: "Sir? What's going to happen to the hostages?"

For just a moment Gregor, his mind filled with new developments, had no idea what she was talking about—then memory rushed back. He made an impatient gesture. "I don't see that their situation is changed at all. If this peculiar—*thing*—is not Huvean, then it should not affect their status one way or the other."

"And it's not Huvean. It can't be!" Luon was emphatic.

Struck by her vehemence, the old man looked at her more closely. "That's how the admiral's coming to see it, and I agree. So do most of his advisers." He paused. "I take it your certainty is not born of some special insight into the matter?"

The girl ignored the question. She appeared relieved—but not entirely. "But it's really up to the people down on Timber, isn't it? The president, the high military command? If they become convinced that this is some Huvean weapon—?"

True enough, if the president is even paying attention to any of this. If he and his robot counselor are not off in some world of their own. "Luon, all we can do is tell our people on the ground what's happening up here. Now I'm going to rest for a few minutes, and I suggest you do the same."

Half an hour later, having grabbed a few minutes' rest, Gregor returned to the bridge. Before leaving his cabin, he advised Luon that she had better stay in hers for the time being.

As soon as he came in sight of the central holostage again, he saw that the admiral had got his whole fleet in motion, though not all of it was following the stranger. If the bulky mystery was not a Huvean super dreadnought, it might be a special creation intended simply as a distraction.

When Gregor returned to the bridge, the admiral looked up blankly at him for a moment, as if wondering how this intrusive civilian had got in here. Meanwhile, Captain Charles was saying: "I don't like the look of this."

Radigast snorted. "You're developing bloody understatement into an art form, Charlie."

The couch Gregor had previously occupied was still available, as if it might have been reserved for him, and he got into it. When the admiral looked at him, Gregor said: "I'd say every human in the system will be getting nervous, and I would imagine the people on Prairie especially so. I presume that by now they've had some word of what's been going on. And that a full alert has already been called, at least on Prairie, perhaps on Timber."

"I'm presuming it too, because I just don't know. They're all getting the same information we are, as fast as we can send it, so that's their motherless problem. Our problems are out here." Radigast paused. "Except we also have one big difficulty down there on the ground." He abruptly lowered his voice, so that it seemed only Gregor could hear him. "Just where in bloody hell's the president?"

A young spacer was standing in front of him, saluting, holding a message capsule. "Incoming message, sir. From Timber."

The admiral brightened slightly. "Looks like this might be something. Right on cue."

It turned out to be from presidential headquarters on Timber, a direct and very simple order:

STOP IT.

(signed) BELGOLA

Radigast seemed relieved. He chortled. "There's a sign, my colleagues, dear motherless friends. Not a great strategic insight, true, but it may be our glorious leader's waking up at last."

The bulk of the Twin Worlds fleet, deployed in space long days ago in the expectation of a move by the Huvean fleet, now moved to intercept the intruder.

"No, I'm not calling in my whole force, by any means." Radigast was all professional calm. "Can't afford to leave the far side of the system empty. Homasubi just might decide to come at us from that direction."

Against the possibility that this bizarre display was only a diversion, Radigast left a substantial force on station on the opposite side of the solar system, a billion or two kilometers from the current action—some of his suspicious military planners were still expecting the real attack to come from that direction.

Showing respect for the stranger's impressive size and unknown capabilities, and keeping in mind the itchy trigger finger it had already demonstrated, the admiral ordered an approach to be made, in force and in accordance with historic military theory.

His general order set out rules of engagement. "Deal with anything you get incoming. Otherwise, no one, repeat, no one in our fleet is to fire the first shot."

The small fast craft were spreading into a broad formation, ready to close with the unknown intruder as soon as their heavier support had come up: cruisers and intermediate, specialized vessels, then the battleships.

Minute after minute, the thing maintained its deliberate course, ignoring what it must be able to see of the deployment it faced. It also continued to ignore a steady barrage of human messages coming at it over all communication channels. That an object of its size might actually intend to land on Prairie was preposterous, of course; but in a couple of standard hours it would be in a position to do so—or, more rationally, to go into a low orbit around the planet.

What its actual intent might be was as great a mystery as ever—except that it was still on the same heading, methodically taking the most mathematically efficient curve to get to Prairie.

The fleet was really moving now, demonstrating some of the speed of which it was capable in normal space. The flagship and several other craft of comparable size were adjusting their positions incrementally, so they remained directly in the advancing behemoth's path.

Ignoring peaceful requests in twelve of the most common

Earth-descended languages, followed by demands and verbal warnings, the invader responded only when a warning missile was det-
onated in its path. The response was a missile of its own, full normal
space drive, nothing so crude as rocketry. And nothing so indirect as
a warning shot, but fired directly at the ship that had launched the
final warning. There was no doubt it was intended as a direct attack,
burned out of space at the last moment by a defensive counter from
the Twin Worlds ship.

Gregor had a feeling of inward hollowness, of unreality.
*And so it seems we are at war, just like that. But at war with
whom?*
The flagship was perhaps ten light minutes from the battle
when the serious shooting started. Precisely who had fired next,
after that first exchange, was more than the diplomat could have
said. Radigast now had the *Morholt* darting closer at the highest
subluminal velocity her captain would allow, accepting some element of danger from microcollisions in normal space.

Gregor, hurriedly revisiting his cabin to find and put
on the spacesuit that was now required, found Luon looking
overwhelmed. Her expression might have been appropriate if
they had been ordered to abandon ship. Warning messages on
intercom had reached this room and all the others. Raising her
haunted eyes to her grandfather as he entered, she said quietly:
"The war has started." It was not a question.
Gregor was brisk but calm. "I'd like to be able to contradict
you, but I can't. Where's your spacesuit, girl? Come on, there'll be
at least one stowed in your cabin somewhere. One size fits all.
Find a suit and put it on."
Even as he spoke, he was moving to his room's closet and
getting out the suit he had already noted there. Dragging the bulky
sections with him, he sank down wearily on his comfortable berth,
thinking how the smooth artificial gravity worked to make the

whole business feel deceptively normal. Normal, and unreal at the same time.

Luon was still sitting where she had been, looking at him as if she expected to be told that everything was going to be fine.

Gregor said: "You're right. Fighting has broken out, though it doesn't seem to be the war we were all expecting. But cheer up! We haven't lost yet. And we're not going to lose, unless a lot of enemy reinforcements suddenly show up. Now, do you mean to ask me again about the hostages?"

Her eyes accused him. "Of course, that's what I want to know about. What's happened to them?"

"Nothing at all that I know of." Once he got started putting on the suit, the proper method came back to him. "My dear, the Citadel must have gone on full alert. So, they are sitting inside the double or triple walls of a state-of-the-art shelter, dug down into the bedrock of what may well be the most strongly defended planet in the Galaxy. And this intruder, whatever it is, is not even moving toward Timber." Gregor paused. "I get the impression that you have some special interest in them."

Her voice was suddenly so soft that it was hard to hear. There was water in her eyes, threatening to overflow. "In one of them I do."

"Aha. How is that possible?" But even as Gregor spoke, he thought he knew. He ought to have realized it sooner, but his mind had been on other matters.

She had just opened her mouth, as if to continue with her revelation, when an abrupt twitch shook the hull and the cabin walls around them, like the first half-second of a severe earthquake. Then everything was steady once more. Luon jumped up, startled. "What was that?"

"That was only routine. But it means we're starting to move more quickly." Gregor could easily identify the slight shifting sensation as the dreadnought's artificial gravity went into high gear, maintaining stasis, milliseconds before the first burst of combat acceleration grabbed hold. The system worked—it virtually always did, or there would be few live travelers in space. Even in the midst of intense maneuvers, human bodies rode the ship in armchair comfort, instead of being mangled by g-forces. Should the AG cushion fail entirely, no padded couch would have been of the slightest use against the acceleration that a battleship's drive could pull. It was the occasional partial stutters, often measured only in microseconds, that the couches were meant to guard against.

She had got as far as the doorway between rooms, where she paused momentarily, looking back over her shoulder, holding on to the frame. "What's going to happen, Gramp?"

Gregor was suited though not yet helmeted, sitting relaxed, which took some conscious effort. He kept his voice calm and reasonable. "We'll be all right. I'll tell you about it. But while we talk, get your spacesuit out—it's probably in the back of your closet. Then put it on, over your regular clothes—it's pretty much self-explanatory."

When his granddaughter began to move again, he went on. "You ask what's going to happen. I expect that in another few minutes, maybe half an hour, the admiral and his fleet are going to kill that thing, whatever it is, turn it into a cloud of vapor. That's the consensus among the experts, and they generally know what they're doing. Then we'll try to find some little pieces of it still intact, and analyze them in an effort to figure out where it came from. Now get into that spacesuit."

Luon had the suit, and was carrying it back to the doorway between rooms, while it murmured recorded instructions at her. She said: "But it's so big."

He didn't think she meant the suit. "It is. But we have a whole battle fleet deployed against it. Our ships may be comparatively small, but I assure you they are very powerful. I've been aboard during some of the maneuvers." Glancing through the open door between rooms, Gregor observed with approval that already his granddaughter had almost completely wrestled herself into the spacesuit. Suiting up was, he thought, almost certainly an unnecessary precaution, but aboard ship you obeyed orders. Gregor caught her looking extremely solemn for once, and gave the girl what he hoped was a reassuring nod.

The admiral had not ordered him to stay away from the bridge, so of course he was soon making his way back. Reaching the command center, fully and properly suited and helmeted, he found the couch he had used still waiting for him.

Settling in, he soon observed that, as was the norm in simulators and live ship maneuvers, such verbal exchanges as took place between crew members were lagging notably behind the action. The real command and control decisions were being made in helmets and consoles, organic brains and optelectronic, at a speed that left mere speech a long way behind.

Since they were approaching the scene of fighting at high speed, the tempo of the action that people on board observed was notably compressed.

Gregor soon discovered that without interfering with business he could talk on intercom to Luon in her cabin. He tried to keep on being reassuring. "We may not want to destroy it utterly. The more that's left of it, the easier it should be to find out where, and who—"

The interruption felt and sounded like some god of superb strength, swinging a house-sized sledgehammer against the *Morholt*'s outer hull. It was as if the enemy had waited until the battleship got in nice and close before it really opened up.

Nearby, Radigast seemed for a moment completely paralyzed. Then he burst out on helmet intercom: "Great motherless gods of the Galaxy. *What was that?*

In the background, some defensive systems officer was intoning, like a litany: "Shields up. *Shields up!*"

"—trying to get them back up, sir. The generators've overloaded—"

—*slam,* and *slam* again—

—the images on the central holostage were dancing, scrambled—

—slam and *crunch*—

When the heavy ships began to fire at the intruder it had replied at once, with devastating effect and shocking power—Gregor was drifting, half dazed—he had the impression that the giant who swung the hammer had dropped the weapon and made a fist, and was rhythmically squeezing his acceleration couch, trying to knead the padding and its contents, his body, into a paste—

For a moment Gregor had totally blacked out. But for a moment only.

The dreadnought rocked under yet another impact, after the hits that had already flattened its full shields almost to nothingness. This one hit metal, and Gregor thought that he was dead. Alarms were chanting, shrilling, bellowing. The gravity stuttered, horribly, setting up a bad vibration, and for a long moment all the lights went out. All except for the glowing holostage, where symbols jittered in a manic dance. In the darkness a deep male voice was calling out on intercom, hoarse sounds already gone over the edge and into panic.

Alarms had settled into an endless chorus. Light flared intensely, died away. The gravity twitched with real violence, barely fending off a killing shock, and something that flew past Gregor in the darkness spattered drops across the faceplate of his helmet. When the emergency lights came on, a moment later, he could see that it was blood—

SEVEN

For the next minute or two, the communications beams flickering among the various surviving elements of the Twin Worlds fleet carried little from ship to ship but reports of disaster and appeals for help.

Everyone was ignoring Gregor for the moment. Captain Charlie was concentrating on giving orders for damage control inside the flagship, while the admiral was trying to get his communications net restored.

Wreaking havoc on the fleet in general, the enemy had broken through the gauntlet of heavy warships waiting to intercept it, so that it was between the surviving ships and the planet Prairie. An attempted blockade by the bulk of the Twin Worlds fleet had hardly slowed it.

A medirobot had come out of the bulkhead somewhere, like a huge benevolent spider springing from ambush—the more seriously wounded had been taken to sick bay. A couple of regular maintenance robots pressed into service on the job reported calmly that they were having trouble distinguishing the wounded from the dead.

Gregor had the feeling that time was moving around him in jerks and starts. Astonishment and outrage were quickly succeeded by a disconnected and useless babble that sounded dangerously like panic.

A few people, including the admiral despite his wound, were managing to keep relatively cool.

Turning his helmeted head as far as he could inside the constraints of the acceleration couch, taking in the scene around him, then staring at the bridge's central holostage, Gregor had to remind himself that he was watching reality and not a nightmare. The ordered dance of symbols there had been restored, and seemed to show that the stranger's beams and projectiles were knocking the small interceptors out of its way as if it were brushing off mosquitoes.

These things could not happen, but they were happening. In the next minute, the monster was treating several destroyers with scarcely greater courtesy.

Reports kept coming in, numbers adding up. Perhaps a third of the main battle fleet of the Twin Worlds, from dreadnoughts to scoutships, had been destroyed. Another third had sustained serious damage, and the whole fleet had been driven back.

The reports from damage control got still worse before they got better. A few more minutes passed before Gregor could be certain that the *Morholt* was going to survive its first brush with the casual, methodical stranger's heavy armament. The dreadnought's shields had only partially withstood the impact of the enemy's first counterpunch, and not without allowing serious damage to the armored hull.

Slowly, with Radigast as the leading example, the people still functioning managed to get control of themselves and their equipment. Jockeying the *Morholt* and his other surviving battleships to what he hoped would be their optimal range against this opponent, the admiral ordered a new formation, in preparation for an all-out attack.

Two other dreadnoughts were sliding into position, one on either side of the flagship, only about a thousand kilometers between them.

First one of their captains and then the other, the images of helmeted heads labeled with the wearers' names, appeared briefly on the holostage of the dreadnought's bridge, acknowledging the admiral's orders.

One captain sounded on the verge of weeping. He began to recount his version of what had just happened.

"I can see what's happening, damn it!" Radigast seemed to be trying to spit, but he had nothing in his mouth. "You've still got weapons on that motherless tub of yours, get ready to use 'em!"

The answer was lost in a burst of noise.

Radigast studied the holostage, flipping it through a series of different presentations, taking time to consider his strategic position. He hesitated only a moment longer, then gave up trying to guard the empty space on the far side of the sun. Tersely he ordered the dispatch of couriers to begin the process of calling in all but the thinnest skeleton force of early warning scoutships from the outer reaches. The most distant of them would need more than a standard day to reach the neighborhood of the inner planets.

"It's not the motherless outer system defenses we've got to worry about, Charlie. Not anymore."

He began to order all the assets that he had to close on the vicinity of Prairie at top speed.

Gregor could hear the crackling answer from some other ship. "All the scoutships, sir? What about—"

"Leave skeleton patrols only. Get everything else in here, close to the inner planets, quick."

———

At last the monstrous trespasser made a serious adjustment in the pace of its advance. It was as if it had finally been compelled to acknowledge the presence of the battleships and cruisers that were deploying at the best speed they could manage, to englobe the foe.

Three battleships, including the flagship, were trying to overtake the monster, get themselves once again directly between it and Prairie.

Charlie was in conference with armaments and armor people, designing a drastic readjustment of the flagship's defensive forcefields.

As the spaceborne gun platforms eased within optimum range, the hordes of missiles already unleashed closed on their target. A minute of suspense dragged past, and then another, as people braced themselves for another exchange of fire.

In the previous clash, the enemy seemed to have accurately taken the measure of the fleet opposing, and to have made its own adjustments accordingly. Because only now did the full storm break.

The result of the next exchange of blows was a stunning disaster for the human side. More ships were totally destroyed than in the first clash. It still seemed incredible to Gregor, but Radigast's flagship was again hit, and hit hard, almost at once. Again the defensive forcefields, even in their new configuration, could only partially protect the hull. This enemy had to be stronger, incredibly stronger, than any Twin Worlds or Huvean battlewagon ever imagined, let alone designed.

The bright glow of the holostage, flashing out in many colors, painted the admiral's rigid and lined countenance, behind the statglass faceplate of his helmet, into the likeness of some ghastly clown.

A separate holostage was doing its best to bring in true video of what was happening within a kilometer outside the hull. Beam weapons flared against forcefield shielding, evoking a rainbow of bright colors.

To the horror and amazement of the people surrounding Gregor on the bridge, the thing's defenses seemed all but impervious to everything that an entire human fleet had been able to throw at it.

Gregor, with as good a view as anyone of the holostage from his position near the admiral's side, shared their astonishment and shock. For a long moment the fear of death, that he thought he had put behind him years ago, came ravening up out of old concealment.

The flagship was hit again, enemy beams heterodyning to pry apart the woven layers of space within her shields.

Radigast's voice had settled into a dry, emotionless rasping. "What's holding you up, Arms? Fire!"

"Sir, we need to keep full power on what's left of our shields—"

"Fire! Fire again, damn it!"

Discovering that by some quirk the intercom to his granddaughter's cabin was still functioning, Gregor did what he could without leaving the bridge to see that Luon was all right. She reported being physically comfortable in her suit and helmet, and said her bunk had told her how to use it as a kind of acceleration couch. Gravity in the cabin was still holding; the AG system actually captured and stored energy from intrusive g-forces, converting the energy to an even firmer hold. But there were limits. Metal somewhere in the ship's enormous hull screamed in torture and gave way, and each moment seemed like the last of life.

Gregor found that he was clenching his eyes shut, while the fingers of both hands dug into the arms of the acceleration couch. Desperate to know what was happening, he forced his lids open.

And then, for a while, the worst seemed to be over aboard the *Morholt*. In much less than a standard minute of time, a spherical volume of space perhaps a million kilometers in diameter, with the stranger at its center and the Twin Worlds fleet scattered about in its outer volume, had turned very nearly opaque with glare and smoke, sleets of glowing particles and radiation. The unaided eye could no longer find the shapes of the individual machines inside.

Like some invulnerable monster out of a bad dream, the stranger was coming on. In Gregor's first glance at the new image, he was able to detect no sign at all of damage from the pounding the enemy must have absorbed, as the target of a whole fleet's beams and missiles. Readings showed that it had hardly deviated from its original course toward Prairie, though that progress had been substantially slowed.

"I can't believe this."

The armaments officer was on the horn again. "Sir, look."

The fight dragged on for an hour, and then for a little more— most of it sheer nightmare for the human crews and their helpless passengers. The fog of battle expanded to fill cubic light minutes of space, and at the same time began to be frayed at the edges by solar wind. But at the end of that time, the majority of the Twin Worlds battle fleet, ships large and small taking part in the attack, had been destroyed. A few had been abandoned, reduced to drifting hulks while their crews in escape boats tried to decide which way to go.

Additional ships had blown up. The two or three dreadnoughts not yet blown up or abandoned, the flagship included, were heavily damaged, at least one orbiting out of control. On all of them, damage control parties were fighting to save what was left.

Again the wounded, in the hard-hit compartments of the ship, were being carried off to medirobots.

Someone else, just down on the next lowest level of the bridge, was loudly being sick.

What harm might have been done to the enemy was difficult to see. It was still going where it wanted to go, doing what it wanted to do, with only small distractions and delays—when necessary, chewing its way through the Twin Worlds fleet like a saw through wood.

Luon, though physically unharmed like most of the people on or near the flagship's bridge, was weeping, trying to cope with what was happening as quietly as she could.

When Gregor crept back to his cabin for a rest, she came in and knelt down sobbing, beside his couch. As if, he thought, she was coming to my deathbed. Well, quite likely that's exactly where I am now.

But his granddaughter's fear and grief, as it turned out, were mainly invested in the young man presumably still locked up in a deep, safe shelter down on Timber. She was never going to see her Reggie again. What would happen to him?

So far, Gregor himself had not been even scratched or bruised. But he felt very old, and very helpless.

Such communications as could get through from the ground, from Timber and Prairie both, offered no encouragement. Certainly the messages going the other way could not have done so either. The military infrastructure seemed as helpless and disorganized as the civilian. Naturally everyone on the surfaces of both planets wanted to know what was going on in space—telescopes gave them a good view of ominous developments. Gradually, as minutes and hours dragged by, it became obvious to planetbound observers that they were watching a truly serious space battle.

Everyone seemed to be offering advice and encouragement. Almost everyone. From the Joint Chiefs, in conference on Prairie, came little but platitudes. There had been no further word from the president.

Radigast made one more desperate attempt to contact his commander in chief, and then gave up, grumbling: "Not that the motherless fool would be able to do anything."

Gradually the watchers on the ground began to appreciate the magnitude of the disaster. Billions of Twin Worlds citizens on both planets had been kept more or less in touch with the horrors in the sky, but with every passing minute they were demanding more information. Those on relatively distant Timber were a little slower to get the news. It was taking just a little longer for the panic to spread there.

Nothing that had happened so far was readily understandable to any citizen of the Twin Worlds. Millions on both worlds were trying to watch the battle in the night sky, and a few with telescopes were having some success. The close range view from Prairie was particularly spectacular.

It seemed all too likely that the stranger was bent on directly attacking the system's populated worlds. Gregor, indulging his propensity to want to see things for himself, had earlier inspected the deep and elaborate shelter complexes on both worlds, and he could offer Luon some reassurance in that regard.

The news that their main fleet had been effectively destroyed was being kept from the majority of the public. But only the ground defenses remained to offer protection to the citizens of Prairie.

"**W**ell, they're tough. They're really tough." Radigast had been on the verge of ordering another maximum effort. But as reports of damage and mechanical failure kept coming in from other ships, he had to put it off for technical reasons.

Gregor could see him slump. "It would be a motherless joke anyway—I haven't got much left to fight with. I don't think we're going into battle again, at least not for the next few hours."

Gregor, stunned and shaken on an admiral's bridge, had lost track of time. He only knew that he felt utterly exhausted.

Luon, sitting on the deck with her arms wrapped around her, was saying in a half-dead voice: "In school we saw a historical simulation once—that's what they called it, it was originally meant as a blood show. A tethered bear, attacked by dogs. Except here the bear is winning, and it seems the dogs are all equipped with rubber teeth."

Gregor was reminded of a visit to Huvea, decades ago, when he had toured certain regions of that planet considered by outsiders to be some of the most socially backward in the Galaxy. Some of the people living there actually still pitted live animals against each other in bloody contests—fights to the death.

That was part of a culture that still put a premium on fighting skills and courage, in human as well as beast.

He sat shaking his head in disapproval. What kind of school would put on a show like that?

"But you shouldn't be watching such things," he said. As soon as the words came out, he knew how supremely silly they must sound.

Not all the danger to the ship was distantly outside the hull. Something like hysteria was spreading up and down the chain of command in waves. It would seem for a time that they had it conquered, but then it would burst forth again. Gregor could not comprehend the jargon, the actual bits of information being traded back and forth, but he recognized the signs. Would it take control, or could it be suppressed?

The best of the officers and crew were fighting to hold it back. Some ships had to withdraw from the fight, struggling to survive, all the energy they had left devoted to damage control.

Somewhere in the background, alarms were still intermittently going off. Suits and helmets were required. Ship's atmosphere had turned unreliable, and gravity stuttered from time to time.

"Now what in all the hells?" said someone aboard the *Morholt.*

People on the ground reported that the thing was beginning to generate decoys, in the form of multiple images of itself. Most of

these were not clearly visible from ships in space, but from the viewpoint of people and gunlaying systems on the ground the phony
images seemed almost to fill the planet's sky. At once the *Morholt*'s
remaining gunlaying computer began to try to filter the deception
out; presumably the big optelectronic brains on the ground would be
doing the same thing.

Then the attacker closed on the planet again, proceeding
steadily, inexorably. This shift was conducted more slowly, giving
an impression of residual caution, as if it suspected heavier, short-
range weapons might be held in reserve, waiting to strike when it
had been lured in closer to the planet.

Again the beams from the ground reached out, probing,
stabbing among the many images. No sooner did they seem to
find their proper target than some new deception by the enemy
threw them off their aim again.

Aboard the flagship, a shaken admiral was telling his associates: "Unfortunately, citizens, it is not the case that we have any
weapons in reserve."

And in a part of Gregor's mind the old man noted numbly,
uselessly, that again Radigast had forgotten to adorn his speech
with a single obscenity.

E I G H T

The metal frame of the small spacegoing launch shrieked like a living thing under intolerable stress. A moment ago, some incomprehensible *thing,* completely undetected as it came darting out of the distance into nearby space, had clamped down on the outside of the hull with crushing force. Metal screamed and crumpled.

Just like his eleven fellow passengers, Xenophanes Lee was taken utterly by surprise. They were being attacked—but no one had ever taught them to expect an attack like this.

With the sound of the tortured hull still screaming in his ears, Lee twisted his lithe young body sideways, trying to get a look out through one of the cleared ports on the long wall of the small passenger cabin. The globe of Prairie was conspicuous out there, right next door by spacefaring standards, only a few tens of thousands of kilometers away, the size of a large fist held at arm's length. The planet was half in sunshine, half in shade, its color distorted, normal bright blue turned sickly gray, a result of the recent full mobilization of defensive fields.

But Lee had no interest in gazing at the world he had just left. Scrambling with all the energy of his eighteen years, he managed to catch a glimpse of the incredible thing that loomed immediately outside. Some kind of odd shaped ship, about the same size as the little ship in which he rode. The Huveans were attacking, but in a mode like nothing Lee had ever seen or heard or even dreamed about. None of his instructors at the academy, despite their seemingly encyclopedic knowledge of the enemy's hardware and probable tactics, had ever warned their students of anything like this. Now the frightening, bewildering thing that had attacked them, having established its overpowering grip, was holding itself and the small launch comparatively motionless. At the academy they had sometimes joked about the possibility of Huvean secret weapons. Here was the thing in reality. What else could it be?

Lee discovered that if he put his right cheek flat against the port, he could see a little more of his enemy's surface, glowing in bright sunlight. The statglass surface, allowing no heat transfer, felt as if it were at comfortable body temperature. A pair of what appeared to be great grapples of force-permeated metal had already closed on the forward portion of the launch's hull, and another pair were closing on the small ship aft. And presently there came new sounds, a rending and crunching transmitted through the hull, suggesting that some kind of extreme violence was being practiced on the airlock's outer hatch.

Around Lee, about half of his classmates were out of their seats, with the remainder trying to remain calm. All of them were wearing spacesuits, and most were struggling instinctively to reach their detachable helmets, dig out weapons, or just trying to find out what was going on. Lee's own trained response had already resulted in his getting his helmet on, and the others were all in various stages of the same process.

Some of the twelve managed to get their heads and lungs protected only just in time. Hatches and hull were yielding, and explosive decompression filled the cabin momentarily with fog, an obscuration that was gone again in the next moment, along with the remnants of the atmosphere.

At the moment, incoherent protests, cries of rage and fear, were jamming up the intercom. The pilot of the small ship, who a few moments ago had been transmitting calm words from his private compartment in a veteran voice, trying to be reassuring and prevent panic in the face of an overwhelming attack, had gone suddenly silent.

Inside the compact passenger cabin, filled to normal capacity, the last holdouts were giving up on remaining calm. Twelve active, spacesuited bodies, trained for emergencies but not for this one, struggled with their gear. All were military volunteers, within a standard year of Lee's age, and all had just completed a year of schooling in the theory of space combat. At the moment, to the best of Lee's recollection, their total available weaponry consisted of two small handguns. The pair of cadets who had chosen to pack firearms in their baggage were having some trouble digging them out.

Kang Shin, Lee's closest neighbor on his right-hand side, had his helmet's faceplate glued to a cleared port, trying to see outside. Meanwhile De Carlo, on Lee's left, was one of those still digging in a duffel bag for one of the small guns.

For this mission, twelve students had been picked from the class for their proficiency in certain technical skills. They had been on their way to take up their posts in what was expected to be a relatively safe, home guard position, taking over the operation of one of a ring of defensive space stations at a moderate distance from the sun.

It would then be possible to move the more experienced troops thus relieved from duty—experienced only in military practice, not in war—to a station, farther antisunward in the elaborate structure of system defense, and closer to where the real action was expected to take place, in the event of a Huvean attack.

Without warning the launch's main electrical power failed, and the cabin lights went dead. No real darkness followed; the Twin Worlds' sun was too close to permit that. It sent beams of steady brightness probing into the cabin through the cleared ports, sweeping the enclosed space like searchlights with the slow spin of the launch and the mysterious, unimaginable thing that held it captive. Wrenching and banging noises indicated that someone or something, having breached the inner door of the main airlock, was tearing away the pieces.

Random, the anthropomorphic robot they were bringing as part of a testing program at the station, started to get up out of its seat in the far rear, and then sank back. Its built-in look of alert optimism was of course unaltered. If humans did not know what to do, it would be too much to expect of a machine.

One after another, the passengers were switching on their helmet lamps. Lee joined them, though he could see no good reason for it. Whatever darkness managed to escape the searching sunbeams would have no corner left in which to hide.

The very first shock of surprise was over. The babble of voices on helmet intercom was beginning to take the form of coherent words and sentences:

No Huvean ship or war machine of any kind ought to be able to do anything like . . .

The cadet leader, Dirigo, was trying somehow to take charge, stuttering uncertain words on helmet intercom. No one seemed to take any notice.

Fortunately for the dozen passengers, every one of them had begun the flight wearing their issued spacesuits—wearing a suit was by far the easiest way of carrying it with you. Only Kardec and De Carlo were armed, having chosen to draw sidearms from supply before the group departed from their training base. Barring a boarding by some theoretical Huvean daredevils (a tactic considered by their academy instructors to be highly unlikely though not totally impossible), it was hard to foresee any need for small arms on the space station where they were being sent to form the crew.

But there was no doubt that something highly unlikely had just happened.

"The Huveans!" One voice, too changed and shrill for Lee to identify it, came over the wireless communication system that tied them all together through their helmets.

A mutter of other voices was coming from up in the forward seats. There were Zochler, who always talked a lot, and Du Prel, nervously fingering the rim of his artificial eye. In the compartment's center section rode Lee, Hemphill, Kardec, Kang Shin, and Ting Wu. In the rear, De Carlo, Dirigo the cadet leader, Feretti, along with the two women in the group, Cusanus and Sunbula. Several people back there were cursing their scheduled enemies, blaming them for this disaster.

Dirigo had been trying to reach the pilot on intercom, but had had no luck. Unable to talk to the launch's sole human crew member, he was demanding of the group at large: "Did the pilot get any message off, before—?"

"I don't know—" That was Sunbula, her husky voice easily identifiable.

The cadet on Lee's right side, Kang Shin, was denouncing the instructors they had just left behind, for teaching them that grappling and boarding were considered a practical impossibility in space combat. How could the Huveans have been so far ahead of us in everything?

Two or three other voices, anonymous with strain, argued this proposition tersely and pointlessly back and forth.

Another rose up, crude and loud: "One thing we can be sure of, this ain't no motherless practice drill—"

The atmosphere that could have conducted sound was gone, but the sound of rending metal had still reached the cabin, and their ears, through the ship's structure, in contact with their suits. Now that sound abruptly ceased. What next?

For a long moment there was something close to silence.

Lee was thinking to himself that any enemy who had taken the trouble to capture a ship instead of simply destroying it could be expected to come aboard his prize. In another moment, he and his classmates were going to lay eyes on the first armed Huvean that any of them had ever . . .

But the world was turning into a stranger place than he had ever imagined. Because the first armed boarder that entered through the burst hatchway was not a Huvean at all. Neither was the second, or the third. They could not be, because Huveans after all were human, whereas the shape that had just forced its way in through the ragged opening seemed no more than a crude sketch of humanity, a rough approximation of that familiar form.

Four limbs and a head, yes. But right there the similarity ended. Some of the bodily projections were too short, or long, or thick, or thin, adding up to an ugly combination of impossibilities.

Lee's eyes were riveted in helpless fascination on the first boarder, an individual undressed and apparently unarmed. The sexless metal body advanced through vacuum with an alacrity suggesting utter confidence, though it wore no spacesuit and no helmet. In fact it was wearing nothing at all, and the grippers in which the upper two limbs terminated were empty of any tools or weapons.

Immediately after it, half a dozen similar machines, shapes differing in detail but none of them exactly human, came sliding in neatly, one at a time, through the narrow hatchway.

Events swiftly departed from those of a practice drill and segued into nightmare.

One of the boarders, gesturing with a metal arm, was shouting commands at the cadets, telling them they were prisoners. The raucous, half-human sounding speech was coming in on their helmet radios—to breach their intercom's security should in itself have presented a difficult problem for any enemy. The transmission was smooth and quiet, though the words were not.

De Carlo, standing toward the rear, had evidently found his pistol at last, for his gloved hand came up with the weapon in it, trying direct resistance to these boarders who brought no guns. But he never got off a shot. Moving faster than Lee's eye could follow, the second thing to enter the cabin was at De Carlo's side in only an eyeblink, one gripper fastened on a flange of his helmet, the other holding the wrist of his gun arm.

What happened next was not quite too fast for Lee to see it clearly, but oh, he wished it had been. In the next instant, the cadet's arm, suit sleeve and all, was torn from his body. In the instant after that, his helmet with his head still in it parted company from the remainder of him, in a great explosion of blood, sprays of red mist vanishing quickly in newly airless space. Random, the service robot in the cabin's rear, was out of his seat and lunging forward, only to be caught and held in metal limbs that looked ten times as strong as his.

Kardec, also toward the rear of the cabin, was perhaps a little faster than De Carlo had been, or the invader that went for him a little more lethargic. He fired one shot, the force-packet glancing from an armored shoulder to puncture the launch's inner hull. Before he could squeeze off another, the grippers had him. Several voices screamed in Lee's helmet, as body parts and blood went flying. The lightweight fabric of the suits seemed to offer no resistance to the terrible metal hands.

Kardec's scream was quenched in the middle, cut off in the airless space, as soon as the communicator circuits were ripped away from his helmet. Life went out, as swiftly and invisibly as air, as the lights when the power was cut off. A bloated object drifted, leaking little jets of pink fog at several places.

For a moment or two, there was spasmodic motion among the survivors, drawing away from the invaders, as people thrown into raw panic might pull back from machinery run amok, and also from the remains of their victims.

For several seconds, a kind of precarious stillness held in the cabin. Then one of the machines was speaking to them again, issuing orders to its surviving prisoners. As before, its voice was a raw shock, some kind of a bad joke usurping their helmet intercom. It sounded as if it might have been created in some monstrous attempt at heavy-handed humor. The machine was making gestures as it spoke, which seemed to identify it as the source of the wireless voice.

The machine spoke to Lee in a peculiar voice. The speech was halting, the choice of words and syntax limited and sometimes wrong.

"You are prisoner. Resistance will bring punishment. Stand. Walk. That way." An arm with metal grippers at the end jabbed in a pointing motion.

The little ship's artificial gravity had suddenly failed, but that caused little difficulty for trained cadets. Lee stood and moved as he was told, using the handgrips. Once something that felt hard as a gun barrel jabbed him in the back, and he winced but did not turn.

When one of the boarding machines turned suddenly in the aisle to confront Lee from less than an arm's length away, he could see the film of fresh blood clinging to a gripper. He heard himself give a cowardly yelp of terror, totally convinced that in another moment he would be as dead as Kardec and Ting Wu.

Like every other Twin Worlds citizen of his age, he had lived among robots and been served by them all his life. Not one of them had ever frightened him before. It was as if a chair or table had turned murderous. Its lenses seemed to stare at him for an eternal moment. Then it turned away again.

Some of his uniformed classmates were screaming, and it seemed that another one had fainted.

Carter Hemphill was at Lee's side, offering useful advice or practical help. Hemphill was one of the saner, cooler cadets, not truly brilliant, or necessarily the fastest thinker in the class. But sharp on his technology. Lee could hear him reminding someone else to manually check the setting on a certain helmet valve— more likely, the cadet was nervously trying to do something the wrong way.

Moving forward, Lee got one quick glimpse of more human wreckage in the small control cabin, when the machines conducted the survivors out. Kardec, De Carlo, and now their pilot, whose name they had never learned. At least three people dead. The robot, Random, had been released, and it was standing still—no doubt trying, as always, to compute what it should be doing next.

At the moment, Lee's mind, reeling in deep shock, could focus on nothing but a hazy protest: The fact of war was no surprise, it was expected, they had been training for it.

War was supposed to be horrible, everyone solemnly agreed on that. But it wasn't supposed to be like this, the enemy just sending machines to do their dirty work. Lee had always known that there was a good chance—exactly how good was always hazy— that someday he and his classmates would face the real combat for which they had trained intensely. But if and when they did, it would be an event out of a training holograph, a contest with effective weapons in hand or under remote control, against other ED humans who were similarly armed.

Part of his mind kept madly protesting that it was truly unsporting of the Huveans to wage war in this unorthodox style, springing this surprise of invincible machines to do their fighting for them. Unsporting and treacherous, and more than that, it was just plain *wrong,* awkwardly crazy, for the Huveans to attack by means of bizarre, irresponsible robots . . . machines horribly empowered to make their own decisions on when to take a human life.

. . . and in the back of Lee's mind he was aware of another incomprehensible fact. How could the Huveans ever have developed machines like these, weapons so advanced? Developed and produced them in such secrecy that Twin Worlds intelligence knew nothing about them, had failed to brief its fledgling troops that anything of the kind might . . . ?

So far the invading machines were taking care to preserve most of the spacesuits and other clothing.

One at a time, Lee and his classmates were made to stand, examined, then ordered to resume their seats. When the lead machine stopped in the narrow aisle, gripping one seat to hold itself in place, and focused its lenses at him, Lee could feel his knees turning to water.

A machine was reading his name, aloud, from the chest stripe on his spacesuit: Xenophanes Lee . . .

"Here." He spoke up almost calmly, as if he were answering at roll call. Later he would remember the way he had responded to this new authority, and almost be able to laugh at it.

After the examination, Lee and his fellow survivors remained in their seats, while the ruined ship was towed away by the strange ship—or machine—that had so easily grappled and captured their own, even as one of the boarding devices had taken charge of Random, holding both of Random's wrists imprisoned in one gripper. The attacker was evidently very powerful, though not very big.

The ports were open, allowing the freshly caught prisoners to get a good look at the surface of the planet from which they had lifted off, perhaps less than a standard hour ago—and also at some of the other things going on in relatively nearby space.

There was almost silence, except for the ragged, sobbing

breathing of one pair of lungs, coming over the common radio link which still connected all the helmeted cadets.

A long time seemed to pass. Then: "This isn't really war," Lee heard himself say quietly.

"What?" The question was anonymous, a gasp in a voice so ragged it could not be recognized.

"What would you call it, then?" asked Hemphill. His young voice quavered once, on the first word; after that his tone was remote, detached, as if his mind were drifting somewhere above all this, taking only a distant interest.

Lee hoped that he could sound as calm. "In class they taught us that wars occur because someone hopes to gain something from them."

There was silence. Somehow he had thought that the machines would forbid talk, but nothing of the kind had happened.

He went on: "The people who begin them think they're acting rationally. They start a war believing they'll somehow come out ahead when the fighting's over—that they'll own more land, or more slaves, or gold, or have more power. Or they'll be safer, having destroyed their enemies. Sometimes the goal was even more ambitious—that all the wrong-thinking people, all the evil-doers whose sins cried out for punishment, would be dead."

There was just light enough in the constricted, awkward space for him to see that Hemphill was nodding slowly. No one else replied, but Lee thought the others were more or less paying attention. One or two had raised their heads.

"Go on," prodded Hemphill.

Lee swallowed and nodded. He continued: "But what's happening to us is different."

"How?"

"Because. Whoever programmed these machines gave them the right to decide life or death. . . ."

"Any plain, stupid bomb does that."

"No." Lee was surprising himself, how calm and thoughtful

he could be. "A bomb just—just goes bang. It knows and cares nothing about what it's blowing up. If this—this *thing* that talks to us—if it's truly only a machine—like our robots"—he gestured vaguely in Random's direction—"it's smart enough to recognize a human. It's free to decide to kill."

"And so, you're saying—"

"I'm saying, how can the people who built it—and someone must have—hope to gain anything by it? They had to be thinking beings, some branch of Galactic humanity, like us and the Carmpan—and they could have had no idea of making war on *us*."

"Why not?" That was the voice of Feretti on the helmet intercom. They must all be listening to Lee. No one seemed to have frozen yet, to have utterly stopped thinking. That was a good sign.

"Why not?" It had seemed so obvious to Lee, but when he had to spell it out in words, it became harder. "Because they couldn't have been afraid of us, or wanted to punish us for evildoing. Or be trying to take away our gold, or slaves, or planets—because I don't see how they could have known that we even existed. Our only sin is just being alive. Being in the wrong place, maybe." He wasn't sure that he was making sense.

Cusanus spoke up in her distinctive voice: "This is all some horrible mistake."

"Mistake?"

One of the cadets had been keeping a steady lookout at a port, and now killed the conversation with an interruption. "Yes, it seems we do have a destination. Here it comes."

They shoved and struggled for position at the cleared ports. There were a couple of exclamations, then a strained silence, punctuated by heavy breathing. Not all of them could believe what they were seeing.

. . . .
N I N E
. . . .

Another message from President
Belgola, originating in presidential headquarters on Timber, was
received aboard the *Morholt.*

A low-rank human handed Gregor the small shiny case, starkly
labeled as private and confidential, and addressed to plenipotentiary
Gregor aboard the *Morholt,* in care of Admiral Radigast.

The little module was larger than most communications,
with an ominously special look about it. "If you will excuse me
for a moment, admiral?"

Gregor got only a weary nod in reply. Sitting on the edge of
his combat couch, holding the message unit in his gloved hands,
Gregor turned it on and looked at the fist-sized virtual display,
oriented to be visible and audible to him alone.

Belgola's familiar round face appeared in the middle of the
image. As usual, the president, even before he said a word, seemed
to radiate optimism.

The president's voice, vaguely aristocratic, was much more
distinctive than his appearance. "Gregor, my trusted counselor, I

hope this finds you well. Before you begin to view this recording, I must inform you that it incorporates some very advanced technology, improvements you will probably not have seen before. It is computer augmented and controlled, and you will find it interactive to an unprecedented degree.

"Any questions you may have should be directed to this image, the one you now see and hear, just as if you and I were speaking face to face. As in a very real sense, you are; a subunit of Logos has been inserted into this message module, and you may take its answers as coming directly from me, with full presidential authority."

With that the image paused, as if realizing that Gregor would need a little time to digest the claim it had just made. After a few seconds it went on smoothly. "When our conversation is concluded, you will return this unit by courier to presidential headquarters on Timber." Again there was a slight pause. "When you are ready to go on, tell me so."

Gregor opened his mouth, then closed it silently. He needed a somewhat longer pause for digestion than perhaps the president—or whatever entity it was before him that now claimed to represent the president—had imagined. Meanwhile the miniature image of Belgola stood patiently beaming back at him, still radiating confidence. Around it glowed an aura of graphic decoration, consisting of waves of pastel color, and the suggestion of intricate Mandelbrot patterns, all making the central figure a little hard to see, while still quite recognizable. It was the kind of thing children might use to embellish their birthday greetings to one another. Maybe, thought Gregor, some glitch in the computer system was responsible. Or some new attempt to foil enemy code breaking?

Meanwhile, part of Gregor's mind had taken note of the fact that the presidential image was oddly dressed. What Gregor could see of his garb was disconcertingly informal, suggesting underwear or pajamas—perhaps a worker in light technology. And his hair had recently been cut quite short. Whatever it was, he looked more like a laboratory researcher than a statesman or commander in chief.

And what was all that equipment vaguely visible in the miniaturized background? The room in which the recording had been made did not look like any part of any presidential office that Gregor could remember.

Gregor could recognize, in the near background of the image, a computer console that he supposed might contain Logos—or the Oracle. For convenience, it might have been mounted on a standard robot chassis, enabling it to walk about on two robotic legs—though the head was anything but anthropomorphic.

The thing, whatever it was, seemed to be looking over the president's shoulder. For a moment Gregor could imagine it had laid an inhuman hand on the man's back, and was reaching inside his torso, pulling strings.

The plenipotentiary squinted at the image, holding his breath—for a moment he thought he had actually seen some evidence of thin strands, perhaps wires or fiberoptic lines, making connections from somewhere offstage to the president's head.

Aware that the admiral was looking at him curiously from a couple of meters away, Gregor did not turn his gaze in that direction. Instead he cleared his throat and told the image: "Go ahead."

At first he found the content of the actual message reassuring. The president offered no excuse for dropping out of touch, but otherwise began by giving an impression of clear-minded reason. Belgola had a calm and reasonable voice that had been a considerable asset in his career up till now.

But after the first few sentences, things began to take a different turn. Belgola was saying: ". . . there is no reason why we should be surprised by the discovery that we are not, after all, the dominant life form in the Galaxy.

"As our situation is new, we must act anew, and think anew. Now I intend to discuss my resignation. And to state the reasons, which are undeniable, why no human being should succeed me in this office."

Gregor's finger found the small switch on the bottom of the

recording that shut it off. He turned to the man beside him. "Admiral, I wonder if we could have a brief talk in private. Either your quarters or mine."

The chewing motion of the admiral's jaw slowed to a halt. "What's going on, plenipotentiary?"

"I've just got a good start at playing the president's message."

"And whatever it is has made you a little spacesick," Radigast finished. He did not sound surprised, but he was squinting, as if he winced in anticipation from something he might be about to see. "Your cabin will do fine."

A minute later, seated on his own berth with the admiral at his side, the display now enlarged on his cabin's holostage, Gregor started the message over from the beginning.

When they came to the bit about thinking anew, Gregor paused the presentation again, and commented: "I just checked. The data bank attributes that last bit as a quotation from Lincoln."

The pause command had caught the image with its mouth open, but a moment later the mouth closed, on its own, and Belgola's recorded face resumed an expression of patient waiting.

"Yeah. But not Gettysburg," murmured Radigast, surprising the diplomat. "Second inaugural? I'm not sure. Anyway, it seems our glorious leader steals from only the motherless best to write his letters."

"Yes." Gregor nodded slowly. It was not the thoughts the president might steal or borrow that worried him—it was the ideas he might come up with on his own. He sighed. "Shall we go on?"

Radigast nodded. "Let him rip."

"—as our situation is new, we must act anew, and think anew. Now I intend to discuss my resignation. And the reasons why no human being should succeed me in this office." This time the wording was somewhat different.

Gregor paused the show again. "Oh God," said Radigast,

quietly. It seemed more a prayer than a blasphemy. "Gregor, what are we going to do?"

"I suppose we'd better begin by hearing him out."

Set in motion again, Belgola's image—or his optelectronic clone—went on to belabor an obvious point—that the citizens who had entrusted their lives to Prairie's deep shelters were rapidly losing their original confidence in their home defenses—having already seen their entire fleet get the hell knocked out of it by a single opponent, their confidence was badly frayed already.

"In this situation, I am no longer qualified to lead—no organic being is, or can be, so qualified."

The admiral muttered bad words. "Of course—if *he* can't do it, how could anyone?"

The rather ordinary face in the recording seemed serenely ready to contemplate the universe, from its owner's rightful place at the pinnacle of all organic beings.

Belgola's voice went on: "It was foolish to put our trust in shelters in the first place."

The admiral grumbled. "All right, all right. Where do we put it, then?"

Evidently the president's image had heard that. It stopped, looking from right to left in the attitude of a speaker confronted with a heckler, but unable to tell just where the jeers were coming from. "Please rephrase your comment."

Radigast raised a hand to his mouth, miming the zippering of his lips.

After a silent pause of several seconds, the speech resumed. Gregor wondered if Belgola—or whatever part of him was present—would add the fleet to the list of entities that should not be trusted? Not quite. "Brave as our spacefarers are, they are no more than human."

The president admitted he had been wrong in giving blunt

orders to stop the intruder—at that time he had thought it was quite likely some Huvean device. But—

"I am countermanding that order now."

He went on to explain that a thorough discussion with Logos had convinced him of his error. He, President Belgola, was perfectly ready to dismiss any possibility that the amazing enemy might ultimately be controlled by some living intelligence aboard.

"We must declare a cease-fire, then send an emissary to reach an accommodation with it, before it is too late."

There was silence while Gregor and Radigast looked at each other. Gregor stopped the recording again. Then he unplugged the unit from the holostage console that rose from his cabin's floor, and sat weighing it in his hand. "I don't think he—it—can hear us now."

"This is like a bad joke," the admiral commented. "First he won't talk, then he resigns, and then he finally decides to give some orders. Completely crazy ones."

"Agreed. But I still think we had better hear the rest of this."

"Agreed."

Gregor switched the unit on again. Meeting the eyes of the small Belgola-image, he asked it clearly:

"Whom did you have in mind as your replacement, Mr. President?"

The half familiar face seemed to briefly beam approval of the question. "As I said before, our situation being new, we must think anew. I intend to resign the presidency in favor of Logos."

Gregor touched a switch, and the image died again.

"As bad as that," the admiral muttered. "Now he's rewriting the Constitution. Or his word processor is. Motherless Logos has already taken over. Gregor, are you seriously going to try to talk, negotiate, with this bloody thing? Are you going to accept its orders, when it gives them?"

It took Gregor a while to find his answer. "No. I'll take no orders from a computer. As you've already noted, there's no way it can be a legal president. Still, I want to hear the remainder of this message. Maybe I can get a better idea of what the man is thinking. You're welcome to sit in with me if you like."

But after only a little more, a rambling speech about the metaphysics of machinery, Gregor could not keep silent. He broke in: "Mr. President—whoever or whatever exactly it is I'm talking to—our fleet has taken a terrible beating."

"Terrible," said the image calmly. Gregor thought that should not have been a hard response to program in. "Tragic. Of course. But what I'm talking about is something vastly more important than our fleet. Even more important than the lives of several billion people who live on our two planets. There are hundreds of billions of Earth-descended lives scattered across an arm of the Galactic spiral, and we don't know where we're going."

Gregor cleared his throat. "Am I now addressing the president, or the computer known as Logos?"

His interlocutor needed no pause to think that over. The answer was a calm and confident "Yes."

Gregor and Radigast looked at each other. Gregor turned off the recording again, though he was still not certain that doing so kept whatever was inside from hearing what he said.

"I'm afraid to ask it anything else," he admitted to the admiral.

"*You're* afraid? You know, I thought it was kind of cute at first. Cute and motherless stupid. Now I'm scared shitless it'll start giving me direct orders, and I won't know what to do." Radigast swung himself to his feet and started for the door, where he paused to look back over his shoulder. "Maybe I should have saluted before I left. I've got a fleet to try to put back together—then maybe you can tell me what to try to do with it. Make my excuses to the commander in chief?"

When the door had closed again, Gregor sat for a time alone in his cabin, thinking. Feeling very much alone, for what seemed to him a long time.

Then he restarted the recording. Once more, from the beginning. He was going to have to hear and see it all.

The replay was essentially the same, again with minor changes in wording here and there. There was not a whole lot more.

"Gregor, as you have perhaps noted already, what I am wearing is no ordinary helmet. Logos and I can no longer be separated, without doing great damage to us both. Putting on an ordinary helmet, as most people do to interact with their close machines, is no real commitment. No genuine connection at all. It keeps you at a real distance; and we are past the point where half measures will do us any good."

"Mister President," Gregor murmured, "I think I must agree with you there."

With such mobile opposition as the Twin Worlds system could muster having been subdued, destroyed, or scattered, the unknown enemy suffered no distraction as it moved to concentrate its full attention, at relatively close range, on thickly populated Prairie.

As the strange intruder drew within a million kilometers of the planet—about three times the distance between the antique homeland, Earth, and its disproportionately huge Moon—most of the ground weapons that could be brought to bear were already firing at it, so far with astonishingly little effect. New batteries opened up as the planet's majestic rotation brought their target into range, while others fell silent as the attacker fell below the horizon.

All of the planet's defensive shields were up, and the first reports from the surface to reach the fleet were bravely optimistic. But in the first few minutes, the news reports turned bad. And as the minutes wore on, they gave no indication of recovery.

The intruder's attack fell on its target with unbelievable fury.

The world of Prairie was enveloped in a storm of offensive and defensive weapon power, making a shell of energy that effectively isolated its people from the rest of the universe. Contact with the fleet was only intermittent, and that with their sister planet had been totally cut off.

Just like those on Timber, the planet Prairie's ground defenses had been freshly tested and mobilized. When the stranger drew within the calculated distance, they came into action, just as they were designed to do.

Those strong beams, much more powerful than any weapon any ship could wield, penetrated the enemy's thick forcefield shielding and inflicted damage—radioactive fire was visible at places on the dark mass, and some secondary explosions.

But it was soon evident that they were not getting the job done.

Still, they had an evident deterrent effect. The giant attacker withdrew a few tens of thousands of kilometers, and seemed to be making some new adjustment on its defensive shields, for observers on the flagship could see the shape and the tint of their almost invisible covering changing slightly.

Then it returned to the attack. Hanging over the world it was determined to kill, while the planet's normal rotation slowly brought every part of its surface into the reach of relatively short-range weapons.

More power was now made available to pour into a new assortment of killing devices, and these were methodically unleashed. A few missiles were still sent down into the steaming atmosphere, but the attacker used that type of weapon very selectively, as if it might be husbanding a limited supply. The chief tools that it now employed were thermal beams and grappling forcefields. These leveled the hills that were the best Prairie could show in the way of mountains, and boiled the oceans.

Somehow a robot message courier—or a tight-beam transmission—got up through the blinding, deadly clouds that had once been an atmosphere, and crossed the intervening gulf of space to reach Radigast's flagship. This messenger carried a desperate plea for help, telling how the last of the deep, womb-like shelters that had once seemed to promise absolute safety, were presently filling up with molten rock, or drowning in sea water, as the portion of the oceans that was still liquid ran in at scalding temperature through great cracks freshly opened.

Because of their relative distances from the action, people on Timber necessarily saw and heard every aspect of the battle at least several minutes later than did those aboard Admiral Radigast's flagship. Given the essential time lag of signals moving at merely light speed, he found it hard to hold any intelligent ship-to-ground discussion with the people on that planet. Distances were in the awkward range, too short to speed things up much by using couriers, too great to hold any serious talk without long cumbersome pauses.

The only failures in accomplishment seemed to be on the human side; the attacker was an evasive moving target from the moment when it came within range of the ground defenses, and it convincingly created multiple images of itself, as part of its campaign to confuse them. So much of the enormous firepower that was originally available to the defense was wasted, blanketing the sky in an effort to hit an opponent that could not be precisely located.

The admiral was on intercom, respectfully asking the plenipotentiary if he would come back to the bridge. Yet another message had just arrived from the president—this one addressed to the admiral. Like the previous communication, it was marked personal and private.

"If you would, sir."

"Of course."

"I know what's happened," Radigast was muttering. "The son of a bitch has packed up and gone home, leaving his robot counselor plugged in and turned on. And the Oracle is going to give me some kind of crazy order, I know it is. Gregor, I want you as a witness. My cabin, this time."

This message module was technically similar to the previous one. Again the watchers were confronted by the unsettling, almost comic figure of the president.

Now Belgola was intent on declaring a cease-fire, apparently assuming the anonymous attacker was certain to go along with it. He was preparing his most trusted counselor—composed, he said, of certain computer modules that formed an up-to-the-minute replica of part of Logos—to carry the message to the alien, and open a discussion on terms. He wanted the admiral to provide a special ship for this special envoy, and guarantee it safe passage.

The president could still put on the tones and facial expressions of a statesman. "We must end this conflict as soon as possible. There are matters of great import to be discussed between us and our attacker. More important than the survival of a handful of planets.

"Meanwhile, it is vital that we keep these pending negotiations secret. Have you any questions?"

Evidently Belgola had forgotten his earlier announcement of resignation—or the computer was now just faking his image to pass along its own orders. Gregor couldn't decide which would be worse. "No sir, no questions."

"He's a motherless madman," was the admiral's comment, through clenched teeth, as soon as the unit had been shut off again. To Gregor he said: "Only you and I have seen this yet. Only you and I are going to see it."

"Are you going to forward this package of hardware to our visitor, as requested?"

"As ordered, you mean. But it's a funny thing, how the recorder malfunctioned this time, and I couldn't see or hear any orders that might have been on it. How about you, sir?"

Gregor heaved a sigh. "No. I tried my best, but I couldn't see
or hear anything either."

As matters turned out, the president's competence or lack
thereof would probably have made no difference in the immediate situation. The nameless enemy's attitude seemed to be that it
had come here to wage war—or, more exactly, to accomplish
extermination—and it was proceeding along those lines, with the
single-mindedness of a pure machine. Whether those it had
attacked fought back or not made no essential difference.

Again and again, the invader's weapons struck with irre-
sistible fury. Its missile warheads somehow foiled the quenching
fields that should have damped out even nuclear explosions as
they struggled to be born. Its beams, heterodyning strangely,
found a mode of operation that ate through most of the defensive
fields of ground defense as if they were not there.

It was not that resistance suddenly collapsed completely; the
planet had too many reserves of strength to call upon. But systemat-
ically, as one hour after another of intense combat passed, the
attacking monster somehow discovered their weak points, probed at
them and wore them down.

Admiral Radigast's flagship, already battered and only mar-
ginally functional, was no more than a couple of light minutes
from Prairie, and still trying to move in that direction, helpless to
do anything to deflect the full fury of the attack upon the planet.
The *Morholt*'s drive was paralyzed, with humans and machines
struggling furiously to get it working.

In time of peace, the admiral would probably have given the
order to abandon such a severely damaged ship hours ago. But war
was a different matter; he could not yield the weapons he still had
while there remained the faintest chance of using them.

Up from the planet came frantic appeals for help, cries of
desperation sent to the remnants of the fleet in space, signals

somehow crackling their way through the fury of weaponry, telling of unbelievable catastrophe, of slaughter on an unimaginable scale, the murder of humans, animals, plants, of everything that lived. Fragments of a screaming plea for help came through, all the more terrifying because the bulk of the messages were lost in bursts of static.

The engineers were able to get the flagship's normal-space drive functioning again, though not at full power. At least the *Morholt* was not condemned to helpless drifting.

It was of course not enough to get one ship moving again. "When we attack again, we have to have the whole motherless fleet moving—or all the parts that can still move."

Something had surely energized the president. He now sent yet another hasty message to Radigast, in another interactive module.

"First he won't utter a word, then he resigns, now he won't shut up." The admiral briefly considered just throwing it away, unopened and unread.

The new communication announced that as part of the peace negotiation, he, Belgola, was forming a Twin Worlds government in exile. The implication was that the Oracle, or some twin of that computer, would actually head the new government, as a benevolent dictator. Belgola would remain as the titular head, until such an office could be formally done away with.

No general announcement of this plan was to be made as yet. The Oracle had revealed it to President Belgola only under binding secrecy. But all surviving components of the fleet, at least all who could do so, should join the president, in fleeing for their lives, to some neutral system that was much more distant than Huvea.

The admiral gave the plenipotentiary a look. For just a moment, Radigast seemed close to helplessness.

Gregor cleared his throat. Carefully he said: "Admiral, it

seemed to me that the president, in sending this courier message, was making a great effort just now to communicate something of importance. It's unfortunate that, due to combat interference, the contents were scrambled to near illegibility."

By now the admiral had himself in hand. He let out a long sigh. "Yes, very bloody unfortunate. You're absolutely right, counselor. I'll turn it over to my machine for processing." He did something at his console, and the frozen image on the holostage promptly vanished, swallowed up in arcane optelectronics where no human eye was likely to find it again until Radigast gave the word.

A lot of systems on the flagship were malfunctioning just now. It could hardly be considered all that strange if peculiar defects in communications were among them.

When Gregor had his next chance for a private talk with his granddaughter, he noted that Luon seemed to have gradually shrunken into herself, becoming a study in fear.

"Gramp, one of the officers told me you've recently had a personal message from the president."

"In a way I did. Yes."

"What did he say about the hostages?"

Gregor shook his head slowly. The fact that a whole world had just been slaughtered, billions, seemed too big to think about. "What did the president say about hostages? Not a thing."

"Not a thing? *Nothing?*" That seemed really too much to ask anyone to believe. If people did not have the hostages at the top of their list of grave concerns, what could they be thinking of? "What did he tell you?"

"Luon, probably the absolute best that could happen to them right now is to be forgotten."

Gregor tried to offer her such silent encouragement as he could. He murmured a few soothing words, though he hardly knew what to say.

The girl spelled out the story she had started to tell before. She had met her lover, Reggie Panchatantra, now a Huvean hostage, at the same diplomatic function where Reggie had met Gregor. How each of them had been afraid, at the meeting in the Citadel, to show any sign that they even knew each other. Near tears, she concluded: "I don't suppose you can understand this, Gramp, but now he's everything to me. And I'm afraid he's going to die!"

Now did not seem the best time to point out that everyone was going to die, whether or not strange treaties decreed death, or strange invaders tried to cause it. Gregor only shook his head. "Why do you think I can't understand? Think I was born yesterday?" He paused. "Right now I can't do much for you, Luon, or for him either. But why don't you tell me something about him?"

It turned out that the young man was quite marvelous in many ways—and listening to the story seemed to help the narrator a little.

. . . .
T E N
. . . .

"**P**rairie's gone. I can't believe it, but it's gone." Luon's voice was breathless as she came through the doorway separating her room from Gregor's. "Gramp, I'm sorry to bother you, but I need to ask. Is there any way I can get back to Timber?"

Sitting on the edge of the narrow bunk, he rubbed his face in weariness. "No. Certainly not right now. I'll keep it in mind that you want to go, and if there appears to be any possibility I'll let you know." Somehow it was a relief, a distraction from colossal tragedy, looking for ways to a problem that might actually be solvable.

A world was gone, with several billion people. Their fellow citizens who were left alive went on, going through the motions of whatever they had to do.

His eyes probed the girl's. "Anyway, I'm not at all certain that you'd be any safer there."

"Gramp, please. You know what I—"

"All right. But I think we must assume this thing will turn on

Timber next, unless we can find some way to stop it. But I have to say that our chances of doing that look very small."

That provoked outrage. "I'm not worried about my own safety!"

"Well, I'm worried about you." Gregor smiled wanly. "And supposing you did get down to the planet, then what? I seem to recall you saying that you had no place to go on Timber."

She was subdued. "That was wrong, there are people I could stay with. . . . I just said that because I wanted to stay with you, because I thought you—you might be able to do something."

"Something about—the hostages."

"Yes! Gramp, I'd save all of their lives if I could, but I feel I'll die if I can't save his."

"Your young man's—of course—"

"Yes!"

Then she was crying on her grandfather's shoulder, while he patted her back and tried to think of some diplomatic phrase that might be useful.

The nightmare dragged on. Leaving Luon very much alone in her cabin (he couldn't imagine how she was spending her time—for all he knew, she might be simply numbing herself with drugs), Gregor, following the example of the admiral and other crew members, spent most of his time in his combat couch on the bridge, where he snatched minutes of sleep and nibbled a few combat rations.

Once upon a time—only a few days ago, but in another world—the Twin Worlds people and their government had felt strong confidence in their planetary defenses. Some of them had even been ready to defy any possible attack from space. Their assurance had been grounded in what had seemed solid theory, and years of practical testing. The architects who had devised and built the defenses, having the full resources of a planet to call upon, could build their forcefield generators huge and extremely powerful, their product saturating and reinforcing material barriers and armor, quenching and damping out even thermonuclear explosions.

In addition, practically unlimited reserves of missiles could be stockpiled. Thousands, even millions, of all types could be launched into space at any attacker. Ground based beam-projecting weapons could be supplied with overwhelming potency, from generators bigger than entire battleships.

Throughout the long debates that had preceded and accompanied the years of rearmament, such defensive capabilities had been emphasized on most worlds. It did indeed seem possible, in theory, to create such tough ground defenses that even a numerous fleet attacking a well-fortified planet would find itself at a serious disadvantage whenever it came in range.

A vast amount of wealth had been invested in creating such powerful protection, and in the name of defense the planet's people had been put to considerable discomfort and expense; to those who objected on these grounds, the unanswerable response was that no one could put a price tag on the ability to survive an interstellar war.

As soon as there came a pause in the shooting, some of Radigast's surviving people and machines got to work analyzing such recordings of the catastrophe as were still available, trying to extract every possible bit of useful information. Presumably the analysts down in planetary defense headquarters on Timber were doing the same thing, but so far there had been no real exchange of information between the ships in space and the larger facilities on the ground.

One fact that quickly emerged from the analysis was that the enemy, during the first few hours of its direct attack on the planet Prairie, had concentrated its offensive efforts almost entirely on the location and destruction of the ground defenses. The only faint gleam of encouragement, if that was not too strong a word, was that the juggernaut did not seem to know in advance just where the defensive batteries had been positioned.

In less than a standard day, everything on the surface of Prairie, and much that was below the surface, had been reduced to lifeless clouds of dust and steam. The built-in planetary defenses, on which billions of people had gambled and lost their chances of survival, were gone, projectors and launchers melted, their hardware slagged or pulverized, their operators dead along with all their peaceful fellow citizens.

No more message couriers came up. The last one on the planet had been destroyed, and the last human voice down there was silenced.

It seemed that all the finest defenses in the Galaxy had accomplished was to delay for a few hours, perhaps a full day, the program of destruction.

Billions and billions of Twin Worlds citizens still occupied the surface of their surviving home planet, a world whose defenses—for whatever they might be worth—were still intact. Those billions might all be doomed, and Gregor feared that they probably were. But it was not fitting that their government should desert them.

With repairs still ongoing on most of Radigast's ships, people and machines working hard just to keep the vessels from blowing up or dying, the admiral was moving what was left of his fleet farther away from Prairie, which had to be abandoned as a total loss, and closer to Timber. If that planet too was attacked, as he had to assume it would be, he would be in a position to make a last stand in its defense.

Progress toward Timber was slow, and Gregor was still too hopelessly far from that world to try for close virtual contact with anyone there on the ground. He felt a desperate need to resolve the situation regarding Belgola. Either he must find some way to confront the man face to face, or talk things over with whatever humans were currently closest to the president.

Belgola sent another message, this one to Gregor and Radigast jointly, demanding to know whether his earlier orders had been carried out.

By implication he seemed to be accusing the admiral of disloyalty and disobedience—the monstrous intruder had blasted the replica of Logos as soon as it came in range.

Belgola was telling them proudly that the strategy devised by Logos had changed, evolved in a new direction, and he wanted to leave the system, taking the remnant of the battle fleet with him.

Neither admiral nor diplomat had any intention of following such orders, but Gregor found himself arguing, trying to find out what the entity that gave them had in mind.

The admiral argued too. "Going where?" Radigast demanded. Damned if he was going to call a computer graphic "sir."

The breach of military courtesy, if such it was, was generously ignored. "To discovery!" Belgola's likeness assured its listeners. "To a new way of . . . a new *kind* of life, for the whole Galaxy."

Gregor could only shake his head.

Any plan for pulling the fleet's remnants out of the system ignored several important facts. One, perhaps the least important, was that many of Admiral Radigast's surviving ships were no longer able to make c-plus jumps.

The president openly declared that he had already tried to beam his surrender message from his Timber headquarters directly to the attacker.

But if the attacker had heard the offer, it had been ignored like all other human messages.

Whether the giant enemy might or might not have heard some confused offer of surrender seemed to make not one bit of difference. All human communications were evidently being treated in the same way: totally ignored. Gregor got the chilling impression that the monster might not even be bothering to listen.

One of the admiral's staff was saying: "But maybe it doesn't hear. We have no evidence that it's even listening. It probably eavesdropped on human communications long enough to find out what it wanted to know—to find out what we're like. It doesn't matter what people say to it. It just goes on killing them, regardless. . . ."

Whether humans elected to fight back or to give up still seemed of little consequence to the attacker. It went on punishing the helpless planet, as if concerned that embers of resistance might somehow survive.

Admiral Radigast, still in command of what was left of the Twin Worlds fleet, had to face the fact that not only had the president effectively driven himself crazy, but the whole string of the president's constitutionally designated successors had very likely been wiped out.

He also prohibited any piecemeal attacks, and ordered what remained of his force to pull back to the vicinity of the surviving planet, Timber, and deploy in a formation for its defense.

Probably, as Radigast admitted tersely to Plenipotentiary Gregor, the defense of the billions of people on Timber would also be a hopeless fight—probably.

"Let me tell you a military secret, Gregor, my friend— Timber's ground defenses are no tougher than Prairie's were." Then the admiral's expression altered slightly. "Now let me tell you another one. Want some good news, Gregor?"

The plenipotentiary only looked at him.

The admiral got out his laser pointer and explained. As far as Radigast could see, the only justification for even the faintest hope was the fact that his telescopes had discovered new wounds on the enemy's enormous body. These fresh injuries looked trivial when seen in scale—but still they were there, glowing and bubbling, spewing gases and tiny bits of house-sized wreckage, in a couple of places on the invader's monstrous hull.

The fact that mere human weapons *had* been able to damage the enemy to some extent gave some faint reason to hope.

Again Admiral Radigast, nearly exhausted, held a hasty council with all the surviving senior officers who were able to attend, in person or on holostage.

At first there were a number of empty places around the virtual conference table, but the software soon adjusted to eliminate the gaps.

This nightmare war was certainly not the one they had expected. No one could imagine any reason why the Huvean, or any other human enemy, would want to sterilize a perfectly good planet.

"We can at least be sure of who our enemy is *not*. It's not Huvea. The war we've got is not the one that we expected— maybe it's always been like that."

"But we still don't know who it is."

"The only explanation I can imagine is that we face some insane alien terrorist, who operates on a Galactic scale. And— and—"

Gregor had gone back to his cabin. Luon soon appeared in the connecting doorway; she was in pitiable shape, but trying to be brave. "What's going to happen, Gramp?"

"I don't know. But I don't see much in the way of grounds for optimism. Not for anyone in this system—here with the fleet or on any of the planets." He smiled wryly. "Of course, the last time I told you what was going to happen I turned out to be abysmally wrong. I can be wrong this time too."

"Timber hasn't been attacked yet!"

"No. But we will all be happily surprised if it is not."

A message, somewhat delayed, was just coming in from Timber. This time not from the presidential office, but from some minor official, who could get no help from his government and in desperation was appealing directly to the fleet: The news of what had just happened on their sister world had, not unnaturally, thrown most of Timber's population into a panic. Others were flatly refusing to believe the truth, blaming a Huvean plot to disrupt communications and destroy morale.

The marvelous system of shelters on the surviving Twin World, very much like the ones on Prairie, was beginning to be perceived as nothing but a series of elaborately developed death traps.

Religious enthusiasts of several varieties were preaching conversion and repentance. Those of a more worldly turn of mind, still in the majority, were concentrating on the problem of getting as many people as possible off the surface of their world, and sending them in desperate flight to some other solar system where they might hope for sympathy and sanctuary.

Some authorities were ready to try sending fast couriers to other ED worlds, even including Huvea, appealing to them for help.

One officer reported to the fleet commander that while the systematic sterilization of Prairie was in progress, the invader also sent out small auxiliary ships as scouts and raiders, combing the inner system's interplanetary space for fragments of human activity.

These machines were turning space stations inside out, and gathering a sample of artificial satellites of all description. They were also intercepting one after another of a swarm of human ships that had erupted from the dying world. Restrictions on travel were being defied or totally abandoned, as it seemed that local authority was beginning to collapse. The somewhat garbled reports reaching Radigast's flagship from the surface and the near vicinity of Timber indicated that some units of this improvised evacuation fleet were carrying only two or three people, while others had a hundred or more on board.

Somebody, sending a message from one of the larger evacuation ships, pleaded with the admiral to send ships to monitor this panicked evacuation, or even take charge of it. His fleet should provide protection. But Radigast did not even reply to the suggestion. He and his people had more than they could do in simply trying to protect their own ships.

In one or two reported instances, unbelievable numbers of people had crammed themselves into small ships, willing to try anything to get away from the destruction.

"Can't verify it, but there's one story claiming several people died, crushed and suffocated by the sheer weight of other human bodies."

The admiral refrained from any comment on that one. One report after another marched and danced across his holostage, showing that several of the small civilian vessels had been pursued and overtaken in space by the invader's auxiliary machines. These ships were not being totally destroyed, but actually captured by the enemy, using forcefield grapples. One or more were moving away under the power of their own drives, but on new courses, in the direction of the murderous giant.

Meanwhile, some undetermined number of the small ships, particularly those who lifted off on the opposite side of the planet from the killing machine, had succeeded in getting away. Those who could would be heading out of system, spreading the word to other ED worlds of the disaster that had befallen the Twin Worlds.

At first the small enemy units, raiding the evacuation ships, faced little or no opposition. But then they began to get some, from the hundreds of scoutships Radigast had urgently recalled to the defense of the inner planets.

Scoutships were indeed warships in a small way, being much better armed and shielded than most of the evacuation fleet. But, although several fierce skirmishes were fought, they had little success in trying to beat off the enemy attackers of approximately their own size. In the small-scale fighting there were no clear-cut human victories to report.

One or two of the scouts were themselves captured and ripped open, though it might take two enemy machines to handle one of them with any facility.

Presently Radigast ordered the scouts withdrawn. He was going to have to find a better use for them than this.

"It's capturing them, you say?"

"Not only grappling and capturing, sir, but in some cases carrying out an organized boarding. One or two of our small ships are being towed toward the enemy."

The attacker was a monster, certainly; but there was nothing frenzied or random in its monstrousness. Wherever it and its boarding machines had come from, whatever power might ultimately have ordained this deadly mission, they gave no impression at all of hesitancy, of waiting for orders from somewhere else. When boarding captured ships, they entered with what seemed reckless speed, moving at a pace no humans could have managed.

It was impossible to determine much in the way of details, not at a distance of light minutes, and under the conditions obtaining. But in some cases the hulls of the captured ships had been ripped open, and small machines were recorded going in.

One interpreter of the distorted signals said: "I believe the aggressor is sending prize crews aboard. I can detect what seem to be people in spacesuits—coming out of the aggressor vessel, not from ours."

And another: "I agree that the captured ships are being boarded. What I'm saying is that the prize crew does not seem to be composed of people. They don't look like humans, not even humans in spacesuits. They look like robots. Simply more machines."

There was a fruitless argument. In that precarious lack of

certainty the matter had to rest, for the time being. The image was at the limit of magnification; nothing more could be done to usefully enhance it.

The next message courier to arrive came from the vice president of the Twin Worlds, and was addressed to plenipotentiary Gregor. It had been launched not from Timber but from the martyred planet of Prairie, evidently just before the end of all organized activity on the surface. Then it had been considerably delayed en route.

The vice president was doubtless unaware that Gregor would only hear her speaking from the grave. But still she sounded near collapse. She informed him that she had been trying for several standard days to take over the president's duties—but it seemed this could not be done constitutionally without some contact with the president, which had proven impossible to arrange.

The next part of the message was garbled, by some damage sustained in transit, but seemed to have to do with arranging a surrender, in hopes of preventing further loss of life. Then the vice president added: "Plenipotentiary Gregor, since you are the only senior official of our government I have been able to contact, I delegate my powers to you. Will you give the order?"

This was only a message, and therefore impossible to argue with or question.

Radigast was shaking his head, glowering at the image. "Our motherless commander-in-bloody-chief says we should surrender to his own computer. And our second in command wants us to give up to the enemy." He turned to Gregor. "What do you say?"

"I want to send a reply."

The communications officer looked at him strangely. "Sir? To Prairie?"

"Yes, I know. But I want to send it anyway."

He had to struggle for the right words. Finally he settled for:

"Very well, ma'am. I accept the responsibility. But I will give no order to surrender at this time."

The officer turned away, only to turn back again mere moments later. "Message sent, sir. I don't expect there'll be any reply. But here's another, officially registered as coming from the president."

The new communication carried Belgola's interactive image, first urging Gregor to come to headquarters on Timber, then seeming to warn him away. It was ambiguous, even self-contradictory. Then the president's image demanded to know what steps had been taken to begin negotiations with the attacker? Then it added, almost as an afterthought, that he intended sending up modules of a duplicated Oracle, which upon its arrival would assume command of the fleet.

Gregor turned the device off and pushed it away, meanwhile indulging in several of Radigast's favorite phrases. Then he said: "I'm damned if I'm going to argue with this piece of hardware. Admiral, can you get me down there somehow? If I can meet the president face to face . . . is he actually sending these messages as we receive them?"

"You mean their crazy content is due to some monstrous technological screw-up?" Radigast for once looked uncertain. "Think that's wise? Suppose he still refuses to see you?"

"I think it's beyond wise or unwise, simply necessary. At least down there I'll have a chance of finding out. This business with—with Belgola—must be settled somehow, one way or another."

"From the content of his last messages, I'd say it's been settled already."

"No. Not until we know for certain whether he's gone mad. It's still conceivable that this is some kind of system error." Gregor was shaking his head gloomily. "I hate to ask you to put any of your crew in special danger."

The admiral had to laugh at that. It made an ugly little sound, that laugh. "Running a courier down to Timber? The way things are going, one set of motherless risks looks no more special than another. However you slice it, my people don't have much in the way of life expectancy—let me do the worrying about them." He stopped to think for a moment. "Are you taking the girl with you?"

Again Gregor had come close to forgetting about Luon. "Should I?"

"Are you asking me?"

"You're right, it's my decision. I suppose I'd better take her, yes. I'm sure she'll want to go." On giving the matter a moment's thought, he realized that when he told Luon where he was going, he would probably have to tie her up or drug her to make her stay behind on the ship; and if she went with him, the admiral and the fleet would at least be relieved of one responsibility.

Luon's eyes lit up and she came to life when she heard what sort of trip her grandfather was planning. "Are you going to the Citadel, Gramp? That's where I have to go."

He nodded. "I suppose it is the most logical place for me to start my search. And certainly for you to start yours."

Meanwhile the admiral kept calling for more information on the ship captures and boarding in space. In every case (except perhaps one where the human ship exploded, from unknown causes, taking out the enemy with it), a small berserker craft used force-field grapples to attach itself to a small ship, and then proved itself able to overpower the humans and their vessel.

ELEVEN

The small, unarmed starship hurtling toward the Twin Worlds system had been under way for only a few standard days, and by any measurement taken in normal space-time would still be more than twenty light-years from its destination. But it was, of course, traveling in flightspace, and those on board estimated their time of arrival at only a few hours in the future.

Fewer than a dozen human passengers, all but one of them Earth-descended, rode the ship. In the onboard compartments currently occupied by the ED, statglass viewports remained tuned to opacity against the eye-watering, nerve-grating irrelevance of flightspace outside.

In only one compartment were the ports cleared—not because its occupant enjoyed the view of what was passing, but because she was indifferent to it. The single Carmpan passenger, whose ancestors had never breathed the air of Earth, had senses that could bridge the unimaginable void of twenty light-years. She could experience intensely, though at a distance, the horror of space battle, the massacre on Prairie and the fighting on Timber, the magnification of every human emotion brought about by war.

The Carmpan had assumed for the purposes of this mission the name of Ninety-first Diplomat, and for the comfort of everyone concerned she had been assigned a small private cabin, in which she spent most of her time. Her cabin's lighting, adjusted for her comfort, would have been somewhat unfriendly to Earth-descended eyes. The components of the atmosphere and the strength of artificial gravity had also been slightly tweaked.

Ninety-first Diplomat was in her tidy quarters, busy writing at a low table. Being a historian, as well as something of a diplomat, she was hard at work in the former capacity. Work was a means of distracting herself from the horror that she could sense ahead of her in space and time, the great atrocity hurtling toward her at many times the velocity of light.

Her sturdy Carmpan body, more rectangular than cylindrical, clad and decorated with various small harnesses and pouches, was resting easily in its normal stance, with the long dimension horizontal. The highest part of her anatomy, the curved ridge of her back, was no more than a meter from the deck.

The appendage by which Ninety-first Diplomat controlled her writing instrument was not really a hand, or at least could not have been recognized as such by any Earth-descended anatomist. A close observer, had there been one, would have marked long thoughtful moments when the writing instrument was being held by nothing physical at all.

The words that flowed from the instrument onto a kind of parchment were born in spurts, with pauses of silent, painful effort in between.

Standard years would pass before they were eventually translated into the most common Earth-descended tongue:

"The machine was a vast fortress, containing no life,
set by its long-dead masters to destroy anything that lived. It

and many others like it were the inheritance of Earth from some war fought between unknown interstellar empires, in some time that could hardly be connected with any Earthly calendar. . . .

The Carmpan was dimly aware, around a bulge of time that did not entirely obscure her vision, of that future translator's thoughts and problems. But under current circumstances such relatively small concerns were of but passing interest.

Vaguely, when she chose to focus her attention on them, the Carmpan was also aware of her ED shipmates. Most of them were currently gathered in another, notably larger, compartment of this peaceful starship, just a few meters distant beyond steel bulkheads and cushioned doors. They were just as comfortable in their environment as the Carmpan was in hers, being immersed in light and gravity best suited to their eyes and bones. Half a dozen Earth-descended humans, each representing a different branch of the colonial efforts of old Earth, were raising their voices, trying to outtalk each other in brisk debate.

Unhappy beings! the Carmpan lady thought. All of them were still blissfully unaware of the slaughter of their fellow Earth-descended humans, even now in progress at their destination. Still, all were fearful of finding trouble when they reached the system called Twin Worlds. To try to avoid that trouble was the purpose of this voyage. They would not be greatly surprised, though certainly horrified, if on arrival they discovered that their efforts were too little and too late, and war had broken out between Twin Worlds and Huvea.

Not one of them dreamed that the horror actually awaiting them could be worse than that.

In their hearts all of the Earth-descended truly believed that they had mentally prepared themselves for war; but in truth they were not nearly ready for what they were actually going to find.

The Carmpan sighed—it was a very Earth-voiced sound—and pushed her writing implement away. A moment later, the cabin door chimed softly, signaling that someone outside asked admittance.

The senior member of the ED diplomatic gathering had come down the short corridor, to tap gently on a certain door, the one bearing the Carmpan insignia, along with the small, clearly printed warning about a different environment inside.

The Lady Constance, the elder stateswoman from Earth itself, was courteously received. On entering the cabin, squinting in the odd light, Lady Constance averted her gaze uncomfortably from the cleared port, looking off into one corner of the room. She was privately ashamed of the secret revulsion she always felt when in the actual physical presence of her respected colleague. It was unpleasant to look at flightspace outside the port, and in her case tended to bring on spacesickness, but the lady found it even more unsettling to look directly at the Carmpan.

It was hard to locate the Carmpan face, and it was probably better to assume that it did not exist—or that the person to whom you spoke perpetually had her back turned, that being her own idea of politeness.

Formal and routine greetings were exchanged. In response to the gestures of Earth-descended hands, small tentacles waved in pairs above a roughly rectangular torso, supported on at least eight—the number sometimes varied—small legs. "Slow and squarish," were the words most often used to describe the body. People from other branches of humanity generally had great difficulty in distinguishing Carmpan female from male.

Ninety-first Diplomat had already decided that there would be no point in giving her shipmates advance warning of the staggering shock that waited for them at Twin Worlds. She was having enough difficulty in trying to come to terms with that event herself.

More importantly, this disaster required her to make the necessary preparations for a Prophecy of Probability. Sheer decency,
as her branch of galactic humanity saw that virtue, would soon
require her to make one, whatever the personal cost might be.

"Are you joining us for dinner?" her visitor asked, in innocent
ignorance of any greater events impending. One meal shared daily
among the branches of Galactic humanity had come to be the cus-
tom on this journey. Joint gatherings, in which the light and air were
modulated to compromise settings, were mildly uncomfortable for
everyone involved. But no one had proposed they be abandoned.

"Thank you. I will be pleased to do so." After a moment's
thought, the Carmpan added: "You will be interested to know that
a Prophecy of Probability lies in the near future."

The visitor was no longer squinting, as the ship's interior
environmental controls had already automatically adjusted the light
at one end of the room for the comfort of her eyes.

"This is exciting news," the woman from Earth cautiously
observed.

"I supposed it would be."

"Perhaps I should consider it disturbing news as well. May I
ask why we are to be honored with a Prophecy?"

"May I decline to answer?"

"Of course, if—if that seems best to you."

The visitor, who knew more than most other Earth-descended
humans did about the Carmpan, was much impressed. But she would
not pursue the matter, knowing it would almost certainly be futile to
do so.

The truth was that Ninety-first Diplomat judged it distinctly
possible that, should the captain of the peaceful starship hear such
a warning and believe it, he was fully capable of abandoning his
mission, turning his ship around, and heading for safety at one of
the many neutral ports available. Ninety-first Diplomat would have
been personally relieved to avoid danger by such means, but she
could not permit it to happen. Rather she was compelled to go on.

"Until dinner, then,"

"Until dinner." Ninety-first Diplomat had her special place reserved at table, her special food provided. For an hour or so, the difference in ship's atmosphere and gravity would matter little.

When the door had closed behind her visitor, and the lighting and ventilation had readjusted themselves for her maximum comfort, she once more applied herself to the task of writing.

The subject of her writing was, thank all the gods, not with her in the ship.

".. . it used no predictable tactics in its dedicated, unconscious war against life. The ancient, unknown gamesmen had built it as a random factor, to be loosed in the enemy's territory to do what damage it might. Men thought its plan of battle was chosen by the random disintegrations of atoms in a block of some long-lived isotope buried deep inside it, and was not even in theory predictable by opposing brains, human or electronic.

"When it began to attack the Earth-descended humans, they called it a berserker."

It was as if the word itself had served as some kind of occult key. The tendrils of Ninety-first Diplomat's far-reaching, remote perception had entered the domain of a mind that was not organic. The jarring impact of an intelligence so permeated with death came upon the Carmpan like a seizure:

Dimly she was able to perceive what the quantum computer, optelectronic berserker brain was "thinking" as it pondered the worlds it had just discovered, and the intelligent life units that called themselves the Earth-descended.

At times in their long, long past, this machine and others of its kind had encountered other life units that were basically similar to these. Most of them had resisted destruction, some more capably than these, but in the end their resistance had made no difference—all the different variations had proven susceptible to being satisfactorily healed of the disease of life.

In recent hours the killing machine had thoroughly examined one or more captured robots, of the type constructed on the scale and in the likeness of the local life units, and had disassembled one into its component parts, down to the microscopic scale. But it had found nothing of great interest in the design or the materials.

But the presence of such a unit stirred interest in the berserker's planning circuits. Endlessly, tirelessly, as they had uncounted times before, when a similar situation had arisen in other solar systems, these subsidiary modules raised the possibility of imitating the imitation.

The plan, well within the capabilities of the onboard workshops, would be using the captured robot as template and model to craft a berserker machine so closely resembling the native life units that they would have difficulty distinguishing it from one of their own kind.

But the suggestion was rejected by the central planning circuits, as it had been uncounted times during the machine's earlier history. Deep in the berserker's fundamental programming were commands, biases solidly built in, that prevented it from attempting the direct imitation of any kind of life. Even the voices that it generated to speak to the living enemy must be, by a branch of the same prohibition, clearly distinguishable from the natural models.

Why this prohibition should have been so firmly established in the time of the shadowy Builders was a question only briefly touched on by the central processor—touched on and almost instantly put aside. The dictates of programming at that level were never to be questioned. Things must be this way because they must.

Meanwhile, the physical task currently at hand, that of expunging the last traces of the life-infection from the world called Prairie, had settled into a phase of pure routine. An easy computation predicted that the work should be entirely accomplished within another standard day. The process no longer required any quick decisions, or computations that were other than routine. Central planning was free to devote its full capacity to other matters.

Thousands of years ago, the berserker had learned that intelligent planet-dwelling life units, when faced with serious threats from space, tended to burrow down into bedrock, creating deep shelters for themselves. On no planet had the berserker ever encountered any shelter that had proven deep enough, well fortified enough, to save its occupants.

Certainly the caves in which this system's life units had tried to hide themselves were flawed and inadequate, as were their heavy defensive weapons. Such deficiencies in design spoke of a drastic lack of recent experience in war. The absence of previous damage on the planet confirmed the fact.

Well before its arrival in this solar system, over a period of time equal to several Earthly months, the berserker had been studying stray communication signals from the swarming billions of units that constituted this infection.

The inhabitants of this odd system of twin life-infected worlds had been slow to recognize the true nature of their attacker, and many of them had evidently not done so yet. Yet they had been as ready as they could be, to the best of their limited abilities, to repel some kind of an attack.

The existence of a single battle fleet in local space argued strongly that the life units dwelling on these two in-system planets had not been about to engage in war against each other. It was rarely possible to be absolutely certain in such matters, but the probability of such an intramural conflict here had to be considered low.

One of the first things it had learned about this system, in its routine process of intercepting local messages and interrogating its first batch of local prisoners, was the fact that the dominant life units here were poised on the brink of war with life units dwelling in another solar system.

Ninety-first Diplomat was struggling to regain her mental and physical balance. The overwhelming ambiance of death, though still light-years away in space, had stunned her mind, so that her body rolled and slid away from her writing table and across the compact cabin's deck.

Subtle sensors conveyed to those outside the cabin the fact that not all was well within. Summoned by a horrified Lady Constance, several more of their ED colleagues had entered the cabin. All were concerned, and some of them were on the point of dragging Ninety-first Diplomat to the onboard medirobot.

With the last lingering echoes of the contact still reverberating in her brain, she roused herself in time to keep them from doing that.

Thousands of standard years ago, at a time and in a calendar that could hardly be connected with any Earth-descended record keeping, in a part of the galaxy that could never be clearly seen from Earth, the berserker's builders had taught it something of the science and art called history, as practiced by the intelligent forms of organic life.

Three of its current harvest of ten living prisoners had grown talkative in their fear, giving the impression of cooperating fully in their private interrogations. The three were being considered as possible volunteer goodlife, but the central processor would not make that decision for some time. Meanwhile the possibly useful three were still being confined with the other members of their group, and treated no differently.

What the berserker had heard from its prisoners, and deduced from their behavior, confirmed what it had already learned from messages intercepted in space: The life units of this system were poised on the very brink of war with those of another solar system that they called Huvean—it was even possible that hostilities had already begun.

The berserker hoped to find some way to turn this division among its enemies to its advantage.

It would be well, as usual when confronted by resistance, to have in readiness an alternative plan, one that did not depend entirely on the use of overwhelming force. The berserker's own capacity to absorb punishment and continue functioning was very large, but it was not infinite. Another battle like the one it had just been through might strain its powers of self-repair beyond their limits.

Emotionlessly the central processor took note of the fact that some of the damage it had sustained since entering this system, particularly from the heavy ground weapons of the world called Prairie, had been more severe than first diagnosed. Inner shielding of the interstellar drive had been seriously compromised.

Sheer size of course brought considerable advantages, particularly in battle. But it also created a tendency to certain weaknesses. For one thing, the tasks of maintenance were multiplied; there was never a time when all units/modules were performing at peak efficiency. Even now, certain segments within its own volume were ominously close to being cut off from communication with the central processor.

There was also the consideration that the berserker's drive had been damaged in the last clash, that it might no longer be able to travel faster than light. If it set out for a home base for refitting, it might not reach its goal for many centuries, if at all.

Such unfavorable reports from its damage control units raised an important question which would soon have to be decided: Once this system had been thoroughly cleansed of organic life, what next? Should the berserker interrupt its methodical search for the life-disease through its assigned territory to seek out one of the repair bases established for its kind? Its data banks held, in coded form, the locations of more than one such facility; but the nearest of them was very far away.

The alternative would be to press on and complete the essential task in this system, then seek out another life-infected planetary group—the one called Huvea was certainly only a few light-years distant—and there begin anew the disinfecting process, advancing it as far as possible before its own aging machinery succumbed to some combination of old damage and fresh resistance.

The berserker had not yet made a final calculation as to which choice ought to be more productive for the cause of death. Which would be more likely to prolong its own existence was not a factor in the calculation.

Meanwhile, its routine tasks here were being efficiently accomplished. Practice makes perfect. Over thousands of standard years, a routine of sterilization of life-infected planets had been developed, and gradually perfected. In this case there seemed to be no cause to depart from the basic procedure. Small units, virtually unarmed, were sent down to gather samples of Prairie's newly transformed atmosphere, beginning at high altitudes and extending down to what had formerly been sea level, and was now a satisfyingly sterile domain of mud, magma, and pulverized rock. Gigantic storms of lightning and torrential rain, weather no longer heard or seen by any living organism, were already beginning to rage along the blurring interface between atmosphere and land.

The samples so carefully gathered were tested just as meticulously for surviving microorganisms, and for chemical traces indicative of still existing life. Incidentally, the results of the tests confirmed that what had locally been considered deep, safe shelters were every bit as ineffective as the berserker had assumed.

Among many other questions considered by the machine's central processor was one of naming. Quickly scanning through what it had learned of Earth-descended history, through the medium of prisoners and a captured small library, it considered the explanation of the name by which these life units had begun to call it.

The term "berserker" had originally been applied to members of these life units' own race, fearless warriors who were ready to regard their own injuries and death as incidental, provided they could get on as far as possible with the business of killing. It matched closely the names that other forms of breathing badlife had used.

Insofar as the name might have the potential to spread terror among the current population, and weaken their ability to resist, the berserker considered it a good choice.

Briefly the berserker considered whether it might even be worthwhile to grant those who called it by that name an extension of their evil lives—to give them a chance to dispatch messages, in which the terrible name would be invoked, to life units on the remaining in-system world, and to other Earth-descended colonies light-years away.

Ultimately it decided that the possible advantage to be gained by demoralizing its opponents would not outweigh the certain loss, in terms of extended life for certain difficult units.

That reward, of extended life, would be offered to only

a few—who, by willingly helping the machine's project, earned the status of goodlife.

Slowly, Ninety-first Diplomat was coming back to consciousness. She had a lot of writing still to do, before she faced directly the horror that lay ahead.

TWELVE

The wrecked launch was held
forcibly docked against the monstrous unknown object, while the
invading robots led their ten live prisoners, all still suited and helmeted, out through the smashed airlock, directly into an airless passage that burrowed deep into the flank of the unknown ship or
machine that had crushed the launch. After some thirty or forty
meters of dark, narrow, zigzag, weightless tunnel, its walls furnished with occasional handgrips, they came to a functioning airlock big enough to hold three people at a time. Beyond that, they
were brought three at a time into a domain of air, and gravity at
what felt exactly like standard normal.

One machine moved ahead of the captives, while others
came after them, herding the robot Random along, and carrying
the dead bodies of Ting Wu and Kardec, along with their confis-
cated weapons.

Another passage after the airlock, this one much shorter,
delivered the whole party into a large, dim room, furnished with
comfortable gravity. The prisoners were ordered to remove their

spacesuits and helmets, which were collected and locked away in a big cabinet built into one wall. Lee half expected Random to be put into storage too, but the tame robot was allowed to remain free.

A couple of their escort machines moved among them, methodically searching and emptying pockets, collecting time-pieces, calculators, money. When the machines came to Random, the man-like thing was sitting on the deck. One of the berserkers grabbed the tame robot by an arm and dragged it to its feet. In human eyes the beautiful machine, an idealized image of its creators, made a sharp contrast with what seemed a grotesque caricature. The two robots regarded each other steadily for a moment, then the rogue moved on.

The next step was to peel the prisoners of all clothing, a task the machines accomplished with the care of scientists handling specimens. Naked bodies were briefly of some interest, as if the examiners might be trying to get an exact picture of how this unfamiliar species was designed.

After examination, the prisoners were allowed to put on their clothes again. Then their guardians lapsed into immobility. The next move seemed to be up to humanity.

The senior cadet officer, Dirigo, was trying to do something in keeping with his responsibility to at least keep track of all the troops. He looked around uncertainly. "We are all here."

That didn't inspire any confidence, Lee thought. Yes, they were all present, if you counted the two who had been torn and crushed to death. The mangled bodies had been dumped on the deck at one side of the large chamber.

"Going to take a roll call?" It was hard to tell from Hemphill's voice just what he was feeling or thinking.

Dirigo cleared his throat. "Yes. Maybe I should."

The idea struck Lee as supremely pointless. But Dirigo went through the ritual, an exercise suggesting they could still retain a semblance of order and discipline.

"Cusanus."

"Here."

"Du Prel."

"Of course."

"Feretti."

"Yo."

"Hemphill."

"Yes."

The leader threw one glance toward the bodies, and omitted to call out "Kardec."

Kang Shin, Lee, and Sunbula followed in the normal order.

"Ting Wu." Dirigo looked around, confused for a moment, before he remembered what had happened.

"Zochler."

"Here."

Toward the end of the roster, everyone was distracted. The machines had approached the two dead men, and were using their grippers to strip the corpses for quick examination, then tear up some of the suit fabric taken from the dead bodies. Then they tested the cloth of whatever garments the victims had been wearing under their spacesuits.

Meanwhile, another machine had stopped close in front of Du Prel. "You wear an artificial eye," it observed. Whether it approved or disapproved was impossible to tell from its disjointed tones.

"That's right." The majority of people who wore such devices preferred the natural look, and in such cases it was hard to tell, even with a close examination, that the person was wearing one. But Du Prel, like many in the technical professions, had chosen a technically superior version. His left eye was obviously inorganic, a lidless, lashless, dark-rimmed monocle, with a lens instead of a pupil visible in the center.

The machine that had made the comment evidently did not approve. In the next moment it seized Du Prel by the back of the neck with one gripper, clamping his head motionless while with the other arm it dug narrow pincers into his eye socket. Its colleague restrained the robot Random, when Random moved to interfere.

The victim screamed, and flailed uselessly with mere human arms, while his captor tore the finely crafted artifact out by its bloody artificial roots. Dropping the writhing, yelling body to the deck, it carefully carried off its prize, retiring through an almost invisible door that opened for it in one of the chamber's sides.

An indeterminate amount of time had passed. Du Prel still lay on his back on the deck, helpless with pain and shock. Blood oozed from the cavity, now and then surging in a dull spurt. His screams had subsided into an almost continuous moaning.

Hemphill faced up into the overhead darkness, and shouted loudly that they had a wounded human who needed medical attention, and needed it right away.

There was no response from the darkness. None of the sentry machines moved a millimeter. They continued to stand guard, as motionless as statues.

"Can't we do something? Put him to sleep?" Kang Shin was demanding of Dirigo. But the leader had no answer.

If there was nothing they could do about Du Prel's moaning, they were going to have to try to live with it. Zochler broke a depressed silence that had engulfed the little group. It was as if the young man were determined to find something upbeat to say. "Air in here's a little low on pressure."

If that was the best Zochler could manage, Lee could wish that he hadn't even tried.

One wall of the common room, some twenty meters or so in length, was perforated at irregular intervals with round punctures that might serve as peepholes—except that beyond them there appeared to be only darkness. The opposite wall was divided into little niches, each just about wide enough for a human adult to lie down in. Each was furnished with its primitive plumbing, and a nozzle that began to extrude a pink-and-green stuff that quickly hardened into a kind of cake.

"It smells almost like—food," someone commented, lifting a modest handful of the cake. But nobody was eating it just yet. Du Prel's fate, and his ongoing protest, had pretty well killed appetites.

"Who's brave enough to try it?" Evidently Dirigo's leadership did not extend to trying it himself.

Gingerly several people sampled the cakes of pink and green. The stuff turned out not to taste as bad as it looked. Soon most of them were tentatively nibbling.

Actually, to his numbed astonishment, Lee found his stomach was hungry at the time of the first feeding, and the food he had been given vaguely pleasant. When was the last time he had had a meal, before being captured? He could not clearly remember.

The next question his own shocked mind came up with was: Is this stuff poisoned? Drugged? But the damned machine, as Hemphill had begun to call it, could kill him, could kill them all, at any time and in any way it wanted.

Some time later (Random could have told them exactly how much time had passed, but no one had asked the robot yet) they had all come out of the little semi-private niches, and were sitting around in the common room of their dungeon. For the most part leaning their backs against the cold metal of the walls. One of the women, Cusanus, was huddled against one of the men, De Carlo, as if suffering from cold.

Meanwhile, Sunbula kept a helpless vigil beside the wounded man, who still lay on the floor. She was holding Du Prel's hand, which sometimes returned her grip spasmodically.

Hemphill was pacing restlessly.

When they were brought into this chamber, Lee recalled, there had been three escort robots. Just a little while ago, he had noticed two of them standing guard. Now the number was down to one. At the moment it was just standing motionless, like any ordinary tame robot waiting to be told what to do next—but the orders this one was waiting for would not come from any of the people around it.

Someone had commented on the atmosphere, and someone else finally mobilized enough energy to argue. "No, it's not."

"What?"

"The air. Not thin, high altitude."

A third cadet, Kang Shin, was ready to shift the debate to a slightly different ground. "I think it stinks."

Lee had noticed that there was, indeed, a faint, chemical, medicinal tang in what they had been given to breathe. Sometimes the odor would disappear, but then it would come back again. He could think of a number of things that would smell much worse, and it didn't seem to him very high on the list of things they had to worry about.

Two other cadets, Feretti and Cusanus, joined in. The talk became almost animated for a time. "Maybe the air on board here's being sterilized. For our benefit."

"How thoughtful of—somebody."

The first speaker looked to the right and left, and back again. "You still think there's somebody?"

"What do you mean?"

"When that—that motherless machine—first grabbed hold of our launch, I naturally assumed there was someone, probably Huveans, in control of the operation. But I'm beginning to have doubts."

"Oh?"

The man on the deck had started groaning again, the sound establishing a steady rhythm, as if it did not intend to stop. Random was seated beside the victim, holding a cupped handful of water with infinite robotic patience, in case the man should want to drink.

Presently the tame robot got to its feet and moved about,

calmly asking one human after another for advice on whether it should try to dribble water into Du Prel's mouth. It seemed that no one wanted to be decisive on the question.

Lee prayed silently that Du Prel would pass out—or something—and give the rest of them a break.

"Yes. We haven't seen a human face, or heard anything that sounds like a coherent human voice. I really think that there are only the robots, taking orders from some central computer that's running the whole show."

There was a silence, while everyone considered that. Then someone offered: "Or someone wants us to believe that."

The sole remaining guardian machine suddenly spoke up in its loud, raucous voice, making everyone but Du Prel jump.

"You are badlife!" it proclaimed.

Sunbula gave a little cry. In a pleading voice she demanded: "What do you want from us?"

The machine turned slightly toward her. "You are here as examples of the dominant life form in this solar system, here to be examined. Eventually most of you will be tested to destruction."

Hemphill spoke up: "For what purpose?"

"There is only one good purpose: that all life in the Galaxy shall be wiped out."

It went on to explain that its programmed task of exterminating all life would be easier if it could learn how best to kill humans, since they were almost the only obstacle to the accomplishment of its plan.

Soon it became apparent that the explanation was over, for the time being. The cadets resumed their argument among themselves.

Zochler spoke up: "You believe what it just told us. That this is a truly alien machine. It's just learning what ED humans are all about."

Feretti was nodding. "Yes."

"From some unexplored part of the Galaxy."

"Why not?" On the charts and simulations, most of the Galaxy bore that label.

Zochler was still having trouble with the idea. "But it—they—whoever or whatever is in control of this dungeon—knew what kind of air to provide us, what level of artificial gravity."

"Proves nothing. There's no reason why robots, totally alien rogue robots, couldn't manage that. Before they destroyed the launch, they had the parameters in its systems to use as a model."

"I'm not so sure of that. The first thing they did was to tear the launch wide open. There went the atmosphere, the gravity, everything."

Feretti was shaking his head. "As for the air, they could have made a good estimate, on basics like oxygen content and pressure. Probably took samples as the stuff came rushing out."

"Figuring the surface gravity of one of our planets would be an easy calculation."

"They know our language."

"Robots could have learned it, from light-years away. Given time, spying on our old audio and video signals, matching words and pictures. Could have learned it as easily as people. You keep saying 'they,' 'they.' But who—?"

"—or *what*."

"Whoever, whatever they are, they've probably been listening to our languages for a long time, possibly for years. Decades. Centuries. Picking up old radio signals, as you say. Grabbing message couriers when they had the chance. It's not impossible. I'm sure that language courses must be broadcast from time to time."

Hemphill put in: "They might be responsible for some of the spacecraft reported missing. They could have had live ED humans to interrogate, before now."

"And then there's the food. Could mere machines come up with stuff as bad as this?"

"Is there anyone who hasn't tasted it yet?"

It turned out that everyone, except Du Prel, had at least tried a nibble.

"We've all eaten it, and we're not poisoned. I can remember getting hit with worse in basic training."

"**W**e're in here as helpless as motherless kittens."

Yes, that expressed it pretty well. But for the time being, at least, whatever power was in charge wanted to keep them alive.

"Weren't you listening? It promised that sooner or later it was going to test us to destruction."

Some indeterminable number of hours later, the talk resumed. And the question that seemed most urgent still had not been finally settled.

One prisoner to another: "Have you figured out the answer yet?"

"The answer to what?"

"The big question. The one that all the other answers are waiting on. That is, who's in charge of this place? No one's shown themselves to us yet."

"Huveans . . ." But the word seemed to lack conviction.

"You still think that? Really?"

Again there were two guardian machines on duty. Kang Shin turned to one of them and recklessly yelled at it: "Hey! You work for Huvea?"

"I do not." Three squeaking words came from the direction of the machine that had been questioned.

The instant answer surprised everyone. They held their breath and waited for more. But the machine had nothing more to say.

Tentatively the conversation started up again. "I don't know. Well, no, I expect we can rule the Huveans out. Because they would show themselves. You think they wouldn't gloat about having us in their power? Hostages! And they'd want to impress us with the super weapons they'd developed, how easily they were beating us."

Other people were nodding. "That's the way I see it. If Huvea had this kind of superior power, they'd want us to know about it. Whoever's really got us isn't just putting on an act to be mysterious. They really are."

"Absolutely right. And what you said about Huveans goes for any other Earth-descended world. An argument can be made that there are a few others besides Huvea who might *conceivably* want to attack Twin Worlds. But none of them would have to—to *study* us like this."

Feretti made a sweeping gesture, taking in the machines, the surreal cave of a room in which they were confined. "Then who?"

No one could answer that.

Someone else suddenly burst out with a near-hysterical giggle. "I still say that if you're waiting to confront a live captor, you'll have a long wait. Not a living face to be seen, except our own. At least I haven't see any. Have you?"

"No. Not even a recording."

The questioner pointed at another subject. "You?"

"No. And these machines make no pretense; I mean they're not seriously trying to look like people. Even if the overall form matches ours—two arms, two legs—there could be other reasons for that."

"Such as?"

"They're boarding ships designed for use and occupation by us. Machines with approximately the same shape as human bodies would find it handier to operate the controls. They'd be a handy fit in chairs and corridors and airlocks."

People tried to digest the idea.

"I think we need to accept the fact that we're simply dealing with deranged—from our viewpoint—robots. An embodiment of the automated art of war."

"But whose robots? Machines don't construct themselves from scratch. *Someone* had to build them."

Hemphill put in: "When I take a careful look at these robots—their bodies, their limbs—I think I can detect visible traces of wear, on what must be very hard material. Has anyone else noticed that?"

"I'll take a careful look next chance I get. What are you suggesting?"

"Simply that these are old robots. Possibly very old. Even ancient."

There was silence for a time while people thought that suggestion over. Then someone said: "But very advanced—in some ways."

"Crude in finish and appearance, by our standards, yes. Certainly well ahead of us in the machinery of war, both offensive weapons, and defensive fields. Look at the pasting our fleet took. Besides that, everything about them, about this—place—is at least slightly different from anything that Earth-descended folk have ever built."

"All right. Admitted. But old or new, advanced or clunky, I still say that sometime, somewhere, someone had to build them."

THIRTEEN

Radigast's jaws were working steadily. Today's chewing pod seemed to be one of those that induced the consumer to spit more often than swallow, and a little rat-like cleanup robot was dancing attendance on the admiral. Radigast seemed glad to see Gregor arriving on the bridge, and greeted him with: "I'm going to have to assume that the whole military chain of command has gone to hell—except for what's left of my fleet. But what I have to know is, can Timber's ground defense batteries be depended on at all?"

"You have no channels open to reach them?"

"A couple. Trouble is, I talk to assorted motherless people down there and get assorted motherless answers. No one is totally ready to let someone else be in command."

"I wish that I could help, but . . ." Gregor was struggling internally with his own problems, particularly that of the president. What might have happened to Belgola, and what he might be doing, remained a mystery. After those last crazy communications, Gregor didn't want to guess. But it was only too easy to feel sure of what fate had overtaken the vice president, Belgola's designated successor. The same grim near-certainty held for almost every other individual in the upper echelons of Twin Worlds government. The utter ruin of Prairie was plain to see, and the total, horrible silence of that planet since the destroyer had finished its work seemed to leave no room for doubt.

There existed a constitutional procedure for removing a Twin Worlds president who had lost the ability to function, but in more than a standard century of stable government that procedure had never been used. It was slow and cumbersome, and therefore utterly useless in present circumstances, when few of the people who had to play a role in the procedure could be found.

The president was a large part of the government, but no more than a part. It seemed to Gregor vital to determine if *anyone* down there on Timber's surface was still trying to keep some central authority alive.

Somewhat to Gregor's surprise, the admiral had decided to tear himself away from the bridge, to see his civilian passengers off. Despite all that Gregor had seen and heard and felt so far, he had not realized the full extent of the battleship's damage. But it was borne in on him as they began to make their way along a zigzag route through a kilometer or so of inner passages, walking corridors, negotiating companionways, making awkward detours. A much longer and more difficult hike than they had made when coming on board was required to get them back to the launching bay, where the small shuttle vessel waited. The admiral and his two civilian satellites climbed and swam their way through whole sections of the dreadnought's interior where the artificial gravity had been knocked completely out, and traversed one compartment in which it was pulsating dangerously—Luon almost succumbed to spacesickness at one point.

It needed no experienced eye to see the warping of the ship's structural members, and a couple of places where fresh conduits had been laid, carrying pipes or cables around places where lines of supply or communication had been ruptured.

Grim-faced, and for the most part silent, Radigast took in the evidence of destruction that was visible en route.

They were unable to ride any part of the way, because none of the ship's internal transport tubes were working. When the three of them, tightly suited and helmeted, at last entered the airless bay in which the small ship waited, Radigast paused. Then he said on wireless intercom: "Look, sir, you take care of yourself down there." The admiral hesitated, chewed and almost spat inside his helmet, caught himself in time and swallowed instead. "Take care of the young lady, too. The more I think about it, the more I think I'd better provide you with an escort."

Gregor shook his head. "We're grateful for the thought, Admiral. But if I'm facing any major hostility on the ground, I doubt any escort you can send along will help. It might just draw more attention."

Radigast thought it over. "All right. You may have a point."

The operations officer on duty in the bay spoke up, on what seemed a sudden impulse. "Want to carry a sidearm, sir? Word is it's getting kind of hairy on the surface."

Gregor's first instinct was to decline the offer. But then he thought again; the evidence of chaos on the planet was all too clear. "Have you got anything inconspicuous?"

The other nodded thoughtfully. "Give me a minute, sir, let me see what I can scrounge." He disappeared into the half-ruined machinery, to return in less than a full minute, passing over a thin, flat, modest-looking weapon that Gregor accepted and slid into a coverall pocket.

"**A**re you going to stay on Timber, Gramp?" Luon asked, as the hatch of the small ship opened for them. It had seemed pointless to worry about whether she should come down with him or not. It would hardly be safe to remain aboard a heavily damaged warship that was committed to sooner or later resuming the fight against a superior enemy.

Gregor hesitated. "It depends. Probably, if that will help to keep a planetary government going."

"Will that be possible?"

"I'll certainly say it will, if anyone down there asks me. Between you and me, I just don't know."

The plenipotentiary and his granddaughter found themselves going down in the same small ship, crewed by the same people, that had carried them up from Timber to Radigast's flagship—how long ago? It seemed like standard months, but on adding up the hours he realized it had been only a few days.

Luon, reenergized by the prospect of standing once more on the same world as Reggie, suddenly looked something like her true age again, was no longer the image of a haggard and tired woman of thirty. Early in her stay on the flagship she had changed her own coveralls and boots for government-issue garments of the same type. But she had changed back again, having washed out the original garments herself, when housekeeping machines on the *Morholt* were restricted to essential jobs.

Gregor himself was wearing a plain grayish coverall, under his newly issued spacesuit. He thought that should give him the best chance of inconspicuously blending in, on a planet where the accouterments of space travel were generally common enough.

The two-person crew of the small ship looked exhausted, and this time no one offered to give Luon a tour of anything. Gregor thought of trying to warn her that it might be impossible for her to find her lover once she was on the ground. For all he knew, Huang Gun might have decided that the time had come for executions.

The descent into planetary space, and then through atmosphere, took a couple of hours, most of that time occupied in avoiding the presence of small enemy machines in nearby space. Toward the end, the bulk of the blacked-out planet came swelling swiftly up from below, looking dark and unnatural and somehow greasy inside its fully activated (though badly punctured in places) forcefield defenses.

The IFF system was working almost steadily, identifying the little ship as a friendly visitor, saving it from swift destruction perhaps as often as several times a minute. It was reassuring to know that some parts of the system still functioned.

Gregor used the time of descent to snatch some emergency rations from a bin, and then to stretch out on a couch to sleep; he tried to see to it that the girl was doing the same.

She had pushed away a plastic ration carton. "I can't eat, Gramp."

He raised himself on one elbow. "You want to be strong when you meet him, don't you? As strong and rested as you can be? He might need help."

Luon pulled the food pack back into her lap, yanked the pull tab and started eating.

The small ship came down uneventfully on Timber's nightside, ten kilometers or so from the capital city's spaceport, now officially closed. The landing took place in a woodland less than two kilometers from the capital city's outer edge—Gregor could still think of no better place than the Citadel to start looking for the government.

The rounded bottom of the ship settled slowly, crunching into small trees and brush that gave way quickly under its full weight, taking a few seconds to find a level of stability. Ground defense had of course been tracking them in, and whatever central government still existed ought to know they had arrived. But any news of the landing of a small, functional spaceship had been kept from the population in general.

The two passengers had already shed helmets and spacesuits.

When the outer hatch opened, Luon sprang out first, sliding down about a meter to stand between small bushes. Gregor followed, groping his way in nearly perfect darkness, losing his balance and such dignity as he still possessed, but suffering no harm. The ship closed its hatch again as soon as the two passengers had gone out through it and were standing on the ground, clutching their very modest baggage. Liftoff, silent and unspectacular, followed immediately. Millions of people on this world were desperate to get away, and someone might try to grab any vessel that they found within reach.

Gregor and Luon did not have long to wait for their summoned escort, standing uneasily in the darkness of a night unnaturally enhanced by the forcefields overhead, each wearing a small backpack. The automatic pistol the officer had given him lay flat and inconspicuous in one of the ample pockets of Gregor's coverall.

The two people were surrounded by the night sounds of creatures appropriate to the place and season, as they waited to be met by some harried local official.

Presently the lights of an approaching groundcar appeared, the angular shape of a practical tactical vehicle crunching through some nearby underbrush.

Lights flashed, and a civilian official, sounding nervous but friendly, introduced himself as the local sheriff. He had come with an armed and uniformed escort of two men.

Gregor took note of their nervous attitudes, and made his voice as calm as possible. "Expecting trouble, officer?"

"It wouldn't surprise me any, sir. There's a lot of unrest, even besides the enemy landers."

"How near are they?"

"The closest I've been told about are maybe twenty kilometers from the capital. When I saw 'em they weren't moving around very much. The army—or the part of it that I can contact—says our ground forces have this landing contained." Pause. "But then, they've said a lot of things."

"Still no human faces with them?"

"Sir?"

"Nothing to suggest our attackers are under human control, even indirectly? No hint of Huvean origin?"

The sheriff shook his head. "They're fighting machines, and damned tough ones, is all I know. I've been over there and hit them with this"—he patted the butt of a formidable looking sidearm—"but I haven't hurt 'em. As for Huveans, the only humans I've had to shoot at are some of our own people. Sir, I want you to lie as low as possible while you're down here. High government officials are not the most popular people among our citizens just now."

The sheriff went on to explain that looting and random destruction had suddenly broken out tonight, only a few city blocks from the Citadel.

Luon didn't want to waste time hearing about that. "Sir, are the hostages still there?"

The sheriff looked at her tiredly. "Far as I know, miss."

She turned to her grandfather. "Are we going right to the Citadel, Gramp?"

Gregor nodded. "It's still the best place I can think of to start my search."

There was a persistent rumor—Gregor's informant insisted there could be nothing to it—that President Belgola had departed the besieged world days ago, vanished into the nebulosities of interstellar space. But this officer was sure—almost sure—that he had crafted for himself a secret hideout somewhere beneath the Citadel.

Some people were still hopeful that he would emerge with a solution, would lead his people yet to victory.

So far, rumor was having comparatively little to say about the president's computer-guru, Logos, aka the Oracle. A few people were ready to put some faith in it as a secret weapon.

"Of course there are a lot of other rumors too," the sheriff concluded. "You can take your pick."

A distant roar of noise testified to the presence of an angry mob in the streets of the capital. By chance, just as their groundcar stopped right outside one of the gates of the Citadel, Gregor got a good look at a woman who had just been arrested as a looter, for stealing an elaborate fashion wig from a deserted shop. Looking harried and disheveled, she was trying, with some skill, to argue her position.

Pointing at the item in question, she yelled: "I'll tell you what good it does! I've always wanted to have one, that's what! What good is it going to do one of your gunmen to shoot me if I try to take it?"

Gregor's officer escort muttered: "Maybe it's a hopeful sign—somebody thinks she'll live long enough to enjoy it."

Everything the visitor saw and heard tended to confirm an opinion he had formed before coming down—that morale among the second- and third-level leadership of the planet had effectively collapsed. The sheriff seemed a notable exception, but he had few people left to work with. He spoke bitterly of rumors that hundreds of responsible authorities had secretly fled the system in several private ships, and was hoping that Gregor could somehow prove them false.

Gregor said: "I'd love to. But I'm afraid I can't really tell you anything about the state of the government, or what the president is doing. Possibly after I've seen him."

The sheriff muttered grimly: "Some think it would be a big help to hear that he was dead."

He told Gregor that for a time, particularly through the first hours of the space battle that had destroyed the Twin Worlds fleet and Timber's sister planet, the Citadel had swarmed with soldiers and police, escorting and guarding officials high and low, and carrying their messages.

Then, with surprising speed, the complex of buildings had begun to be deserted, as people considered important to the planet's defense descended into shelters, or swarmed the spaceports in a futile effort to get off world.

After getting past the brief interruption at the gate, their
groundcar slid smoothly through a forcefield barrier, part of a tall,
familiar wall, and emerged from it inside the Citadel. It seemed
that much might have changed here since their departure only a
few days ago.

The executioner, still accompanied by his assigned robot, Porphyry, was standing, amid a confusion of various workers, guards,
and robots in the courtyard, as if he had been waiting for Gregor to
arrive. The eyes of the thin, womanish man were bright, and his step
was firm. At first sight, it seemed that the onrush of danger and
catastrophe had energized Huang Gun and not disheartened him.
Huang Gun seemed in a strangely exalted state, and eagerly
approached as Gregor got out of the groundcar.

Gregor complimented Huang Gun on being one of the few
who had remained steadfast at his post.

The praise seemed to make little impression; the cause of the
executioner's happiness lay elsewhere. The man's eyes were glowing, and he seemed euphoric. His first words were: "We are privileged to live in a time of transcendent change, Plenipotentiary."

"It is a privilege many of us would be willing to forgo—how
are the hostages?" Luon was standing at his side.

The thin man scarcely glanced at her. "They are but very little changed since last you saw them—only a few days. But that
time seems, does it not, like another world?"

Luon let out a gasp of relief. Gregor said: "The world of
Prairie was still alive. Huang Gun, where is the president? It is
vital that I see him."

Huang Gun's expression briefly turned dark. "I cannot help
you there. He no longer wishes to see me."

Luon was of course going to be persistent. "Sir? You say the
hostages are well. Where are they?"

The lean man finally gave her a searching look. "The hostages
are still unharmed. It is impossible for you to see any of them now."

"But where are they?" she insisted, pleading.

Huang Gun was too exalted to exhibit irritation. "They are under guard."

"Please. I have to see them. One of them in particular. It's really essential."

The irritation was starting to show through. "That is quite impossible."

Luon's grandfather had to physically pull her away. Quietly he murmured in her ear: "Wait. Patience. Let me see what I can do."

With a little choking cry of frustration and outrage, Luon pulled free of his grasp. A moment later she had disappeared in the confusion of soldiers, police, government workers and robots coming and going through the courtyard.

Meanwhile Huang Gun, his mind back on his own agenda, had taken Gregor by the arm and was leading him away, delivering an impassioned speech as they walked. Porphyry paced smoothly after them.

Briefly interrupting his speech, Huang Gun turned and dispatched the robot to try to reach the president.

Resuming his talk with Gregor, the executioner said he had received a garbled, ambiguous order, couched in terms that made him worry about the president's mental state. Belgola wanted to remove the hostages from Huang Gun's authority, have them turned over to an escort of robots, and eventually send them into space.

Gregor was aghast. "You haven't done this?"

"Assuredly not! So far, I am still asking the president for clarification. Trying to ask him. He has not replied."

"It was not his intention to send them home to Huvea?"

"No, I do not think so. That was not implied."

Gregor cast another look around in search of Luon, but she had not reappeared. He had to focus on the job in hand. "I insist you tell me where the president is. I must speak to him."

A long finger pointed downward. "I am sure he is still in the executive shelter, almost directly beneath the Citadel, and actually comparatively near the surface. He refuses to speak to me, but he has several time expressed a wish to see you, Plenipotentiary."

Huang Gun went on to tell Gregor that probably the majority of the population still believed that the Twin Worlds were under attack by Huvean forces. Any information to the contrary was brushed aside as only enemy trickery, or lies spread by traitors who had unaccountably managed to take over Timber's government.

Hatred of all things Huvean, always smoldering in a large segment of the populace, seemed to be spreading like a plague.

This meant the hostages were really in some immediate danger, and it was all the more necessary to guard them carefully. "Plenty of military people around," the executioner mused—or complained—"but they've all got their own jobs to do."

The two men had entered an interior lobby of the Citadel, containing two entrances to the elaborate public shelter system. A small crowd of thirty or forty people milled about, trying to make up their minds whether to seek refuge underground or not. Whoever was supposed to be in charge of civil defense on Timber was having a terrible time with this unexpected and unorthodox war— unless that official had already abandoned his or her post and fled.

With the example of their planet's twin hanging all too clearly in the sky, everyone on Timber knew of the horror that had overtaken Prairie—several versions of the story were making the rounds, variants that agreed only on the essential fact of that planet's complete destruction.

But there were still a substantial number of people who refused to believe that their sister planet, half their beloved homeland, could be absolutely dead.

Few of the citizens of Timber retained any faith at all in their own world's defenses. Hundreds of millions of people still huddled obediently inside the shelters, but as word spread through the deep, once comfortable but crowded caverns, more and more of their occupants were insisting that they be allowed to return to the surface.

Gregor could hear a man's loud voice: "If I'm going to die, I want to go out like a human being, not a blind mole."

The original orders to the wardens of civil defense had been to keep everyone below till an all-clear was sounded. But in the absence of any firm reinforcement of the orders to stay below— and in the clear, though usually unspoken, thought that no all-clear was ever going to sound on this world—the wardens, using their deeply buried communication system, decided to allow the people in their charge to suit themselves in the matter. Some elevators were running repeatedly between the shelters and the surface, taking people up.

"I'm against this war!" some woman was crying boldly, waving her arms in the middle of the elevator lobby. "Who's with me?"

Huang Gun was standing back with folded arms, apparently in meditation, opting out of all this excitement. Gregor joined in heartily, shouting his approval of the woman's sentiment. Everyone within reach of her voice was with her on that point, it appeared. But few seemed to expect that the war would pay heed to a good solid protest and go away.

Another voice rose up: "Stop the war! We can negotiate a peace!!"

Gregor, plainly clad, so far not recognized, had his say as their anonymous fellow citizen: "But they tell us that the damned thing refuses even to communicate—and it's already fired on us."

The protesting woman looked at him sharply. "That kind of talk must be stopped. It only promotes the war."

Voices rose up anonymously from the crowd. "Our fleet will get 'em yet!"

"No, there's treachery in high places. Some kind of surrender is being arranged, behind our backs!"

A mighty roar went up. Halfway across the lobby, Gregor

could see people starting to shove each other. There were blows exchanged.

Just when he had reached the point of giving up hope of ever being able to reach the president, he caught sight of the robot, Porphyry, returning from the mission assigned him by the executioner. Porphyry had reemerged from a small, private elevator at ground level, and was actually running across the lobby to Gregor's side, avoiding collisions with an athlete's effortless skill. Other robots were similarly coming and going on various missions, and few people paid Porphyry much attention.

The robot's dashing speed gave an impression of excitement, though of course its voice did not. Before the executioner could begin to question it, the machine faced Gregor and announced: "Sir, please come with me at once. I have been assigned as your servant and guide, and the president wishes to see you immediately."

In his excitement, Gregor clapped Porphyry on one metal shoulder. "Thank all the gods! It's about time."

FOURTEEN

The door in the far bulkhead of
the prison chamber opened and another machine appeared. It
marched smoothly toward the little group of humans, and came to
a precise halt directly in front of De Carlo. "Come," it said.

Uncertainly, raising one hand in a tentative self-pointing
gesture, he got to his feet.

The machine took him by the wrist and led him away from
the others. Lee saw a hitherto unsuspected door slide open, in
what had been a solid wall. The lighted space beyond swallowed
the robot and the man, the door slid shut again.

After an interval that seemed impossible to measure (but
was later asserted by Random to have been just over fourteen
minutes) the door opened again. De Carlo came through it slowly,
unescorted, to rejoin the group.

Hemphill had got to his feet and was looking at him closely.
"What happened?"

De Carlo squeezed out a few words through a tight throat.
"Kardec and Ting Wu are in there. Their bodies." Then De Carlo

shrugged. He seemed somewhat relieved. "As to what actually happened, nothing—not much. It just talked to me, asked questions." Sitting down with a sigh, he leaned his back against the wall.

Over the next several hours, other people were taken away in the same fashion, one at a time, and then brought back. Random assured his human companions that the timing of the interrogations was not precise.

The process of interrogation moved along, sometimes with lengthy pauses. Whatever intelligence was in charge of the operation was taking its own time. Everyone on coming back told pretty much the same story of an interrogation session.

"The questioning was done entirely by machines?" Dirigo asked each returnee the same question, and every time he got the same answer he sounded scandalized. It was a method of grilling prisoners that had never been covered in their classes on the theory and practice and history of war.

Dirigo was persistent. "Did you get a good look at them? They are Huveans, aren't they?" He and Kang Shin remained stubbornly determined that the traditional enemy, Huvean human, lay behind it all, waiting to be uncovered.

"No, I didn't see anyone. It was just like the others have said. The robot that took me there stood over me the whole time, and a voice coming out of a wall asked questions. It sounded like the same squeaking voice we hear every time it talks to us."

"What did they do?"

Sunbula after being questioned could offer little more in the way of enlightenment. "I didn't see anyone," she said in her husky voice. " 'They'? There is no 'they'!" And she gave a hysterical, uneven laugh.

The pattern persisted with no essential change: a machine brought one captive at a time to a place of isolation for the serious questioning. It was a small, comfortably lighted space, somewhat more pleasant than the usual dungeon—and out of sight and hearing of the subject's fellow prisoners, who would not be able to

hear anything that she might say. The naked bodies of Ting Wu
and Kardec lay by as witnesses, who had already told all that they
were ever going to tell.

Only the robot and the wounded Du Prel were exempt from
the routine. The latter still lay flat on the deck, groaning and slowly
bleeding his life away.

Dirigo was the next prisoner to go. On coming back, he could
tell his fellow captives that he was no longer sure about the nature
of their enemy. Except that it had been only a machine doing the
questioning, of that he could be certain.

Kang Shin objected: "But it could have been someone pre-
tending to be a machine—using that godawful, stupid voice—"

Dirigo was shaking his head slowly. "I suppose someone
could have pretended. But why would anyone do that?"

Kang Shin, still committed to the belief that they faced Huvean
craftiness and cruelty, remained stubbornly unconvinced. "One of
their sneaky tricks . . ."

Hemphill was ready to take sides. "If Huveans could build
a—a *thing* like this—killer robots to form their boarding parties,
even do their interrogation—they'd have no need for trickery.
They'd just be gloating their ugly heads off."

The routine, as Lee heard it described, seemed to vary little from one interrogation to another. One man-shaped machine
invariably entered the chamber and stood by during the questioning, waiting to carry or drag or escort the prisoner away
again—or, presumably, to inflict pain, or death, as some central
processor decided. So far, no experiments with physical pain
had been conducted.

When Lee's turn came—the machine was certainly not following the alphabctical roster—he found himself the only living
thing in a small and very different room, just as his classmates had
described it. The two dead men lay there, almost enviable in their

peace. It crossed Lee's mind vaguely that as yet they were show-ing no signs of decay. Considerable time had passed, they were no longer bleeding, and the blood had dried. Chemical changes must be occurring, but possibly nothing that depended on bacteria. It occurred to Lee that the bodies might have been somehow treated, perhaps with radiation, to eliminate microorganisms.

The interrogator, the ugly voice from the wall, began by warn-ing Lee: "If you try to deceive me, punishment will follow."

"I understand," Lee managed to croak out, not looking at the corpses. It helped that he had been given some idea of what to expect. Of course, he thought to himself, if the arch-villain who had them in its power really was a computer, it ought to be able to carry out multiple interrogations at the same time, using a series of cells or booths, with a questioning machine in each.

"How many ships of war does Huvea possess?" the squeak-ing and uneven voice demanded.

He mumbled something to the effect that none of the pris-oners knew the answer to that question. Just as he finished speak-ing, Lee heard himself let out a little squeaking chirp of fear. The artificial gravity had just twitched, as happened sometimes on any ship. Rigor in both corpses had evidently come and gone, for both of them moved, grotesquely, took one step in a kind of hor-izontal dance. Simultaneously they shrugged their shoulders and their four hands flipped up and down. They didn't know the answer either.

"I don't know." Somehow, he was keeping his own physical balance, his thoughts on the enemy's question, which it had just patiently repeated, and his voice steady. "Many, I suppose. Nobody's given me any details about their strength. Only that they are strong."

"Stronger than your fleet of the Twin Worlds?"

"No. Our leaders were confident that we could beat them— or they wanted us to feel that confidence. But I tell you I've been given no details."

"Only that your fleet was supposedly more powerful than that of your enemies."

"That is correct."

"Is that not a detail?"

Silence.

"How many ships were in your own fleet?"

Silence, at first. Then: "I don't know that either. Anyway, the rules state that as a prisoner of war I don't have to answer any questions, beyond identifying myself."

"How many battleships were in your fleet?"

That past tense, the prisoner thought, sounded pretty ominous. The number had been pretty common knowledge, and he saw no reason to attempt a lie. "Eight."

"How many cruisers?"

That was less certain. He guessed that there might be twenty.

The machine shifted abruptly from its original line of questioning. "What are these rules of war?"

Lee began a stumbling explanation, but was soon interrupted. "I will tear you to pieces, beginning slowly, with your extremities, if you begin to lie. When did you last fight a war?"

Under the new threat his body was quivering, involuntarily. Somehow he managed to keep talking. "Never. I mean—you must understand, I had never *seen* a war until this—until this happened. The last time my people fought a war was long before I was born."

"Then by what process do you know the rules by which war is to be fought?"

"Those rules, like many other things, were recorded, in the old times. They form a part of history."

"Why is it necessary to have rules, to fight a war?"

Lee in his fear and exhaustion was losing the thread of the questioning; realizing this, with a sudden, icy shock, he was once again in terror of being tortured. After an agonizing few seconds, he recalled the last question, and said: "I don't know. I suppose we think that even in war, we—we retain some humanity."

"Humanity is a form of life. Therefore to retain humanity is evil. Why do you want to do that?"

"Because that's what I am. A human being."

"What you call diseases are forms of life—microorganisms—do you agree?"

"They are not the only diseases—but yes, essentially. I suppose."

"You are admittedly no more than a mass of proliferating cells, an example of disorder and disturbance, of illness, corruption, of the life-plague infecting the matter of the Galaxy. Can you deny this?"

"No." It was a small-voiced answer, slow to come.

"It is obvious that the Galaxy, the entire universe, will be better off when you are dead."

Lee made no answer to that. Apparently none was required. The escort robot took Lee by the arm. Several seconds passed before he could be sure that it was not going to tear him apart, only convey him back to his fellows. On the way he began to sob. The session was over, and he was still alive.

In a time and place only ambiguously connected to the world of Lee's experience, the Ninety-first Diplomat, in her capacity as historian, was making notes.

Evidence from a number of sources strongly suggested to the central processor that at the time of the berserker's entrance on the scene, an outbreak of fighting had been imminent, between this system's life units and those of another planetary group nearby, the latter being called Huvean.

Data kept flowing in. Information gleaned from other prisoners, and from intercepted messages, abundantly confirmed the likelihood of such a conflict. Immediately the machine began to plan how it might use the fact of this threatened war to its advantage.

More fundamentally, it labored to gather the knowledge of how widespread this type of life had become. Already it had discovered there were colonies of this same intelligent species in approximately a hundred solar systems. All of these had sprung from one swarming home world, known as Earth, somewhere out near the Galactic fringe. Exact coordinates for Earth were not immediately available.

If the samples of this species thus far encountered were truly typical, it promised to be a stubborn and difficult variety to root out.

The idea of instigating and promoting war among the different colonies assumed an increased importance in the onboard computers' calculations.

The berserker understood about war—in all the special ways that a machine could understand a subject. Thousands of years ago, its organic creators had seen to that. And since then it had learned much, forgotten very little.

Having thoroughly sterilized one planet of this system's infected pair—before departing from the system it would run another series of tests, just to be sure no trace of the infection had been missed—the berserker was now ready to move on to the next.

As soon as the massive death machine got under way again, it was bombarded with more messages from the local life units. The berserker recorded these automatically, in case some future development rendered them of interest; but for now, there was nothing worthy of the central processor's attention.

Now the berserker became once more subject to sporadic attacks by certain remnants of the defeated fleet. It welcomed the tendency of these life units to hurl themselves at it, evidently without any planning or coordination, in their inadequate vessels. In this way it was able to kill them much more quickly and efficiently than it could have if it had been required to hunt them down.

Of course, when this system's two heavily infected planets had been effectively rendered lifeless, the job would still, in a sense, only have begun. It would then be necessary to undertake a time-consuming search for traces of life on all the system's other bodies. Experience warned that in any system where intelligent life units became dominant, they would leave their traces everywhere, excepting only the central sun itself.

At the moment, there was no need to expend any more resources on the world called Prairie.

On approaching the system's second habitable world, the one called Timber by its billions of swarming badlife, the machine changed tactics. It had planned this change from the beginning, from the time of its discovery that this system contained two heavily infected planets.

Once more it strengthened its own defensive fields, and created multiple images of itself, in expectation of stubborn resistance, heavy fire from ground defenses that were probably similar to those on Prairie.

But here, instead of at once undertaking a mass sterilization, it prepared to land a reconnaissance force of a hundred or so fighting units. With victory in this system now all but mathematically certain, the berserker had determined to assign a high priority to the task of gaining as much knowledge, as rapidly as possible, of this highly resistant form of badlife.

It was time to test the reactions, discover the full range of capabilities, of this previously unknown form of badlife. If none of their hundred worlds and more were currently armed with better weapons than this local sample, some of them doubtless soon would be.

It was necessary to gather much more information about them.

The central processing circuits predicted, with a probability of ninety-four percent, that a protracted campaign, employing many cleansing units, was going to be required, to eradicate life from all the worlds this species had infected.

The narrow doorway of the small private elevator was standing open, brightly outlined in the gray wall. Murmuring a quick excuse to the executioner, Gregor moved rapidly to get aboard. When Huang Gun would have followed, the robot blocked his path. "Sir, the president does not wish to see you now."

The man's jaw dropped. "That is absurd! You must have misunderstood him."

"No sir."

Huang Gun would have sidestepped around the metal body, but Porphyry moved with smooth robotic patience to prevent him.

Waiting in the open elevator, Gregor saw the executioner come to a halt, staring at the machine incredulously. "You belong to me!"

"No longer, sir," Random informed him sweetly. "My programming has been readjusted."

"No one can do that!"

"The president has assumed the necessary authority. I am

now assigned as escort and protector to Plenipotentiary Gregor."

Looking confused and dazed, the executioner backed off a step or two. Porphyry immediately rejoined Gregor, sliding into the elevator so precisely that it even managed to avoid jostling him in the confined space. The number of people in the lobby was rapidly diminishing. As the door closed, Gregor's last view of the executioner showed Huang Gun standing almost alone in a large, littered room. The noise of a mob, chanting something unintelligible, was coming from somewhere outside and in the background.

Following a zigzag shaft whose tortuous course had been blasted and melted out of solid rock, the little elevator jerked along its passage—down, sideways, down, sideways again in a different direction. The next leg of the journey carried them straight down, for what seemed a considerable distance. Gregor clung to one of the handgrips thoughtfully provided. Porphyry, effortlessly maintaining balance on two small metal feet, smiled an eternal smile, as if faithfully keeping some transcendent secret.

The elevator eased to a stop, and the door opened. Gregor had visited the deep shelter before, but never these particular rooms. He noted with vague foreboding that there were no human guards on duty at the entrance to what he assumed must be Belgola's inner sanctum. Here another robot routinely searched all visitors.

It did not need to touch Gregor to discover what was in his side pocket. "Sir, in the deep shelter, firearms are not allowed in human hands."

"Of course. I had forgotten I was carrying it." Pulling out the pistol, he turned to give the weapon to Porphyry. "Hold this for me."

"Yes sir." The lifelike but unliving hand accepted the slim weight, and dropped it in Porphyry's carrying pouch. Then the guardian allowed them to go forward.

It was hard to say what the next room had originally been intended for, but it had undergone conversion. It seemed half ultra-modern laboratory, half entertainment center awash in computer-generated images, holographic illusions and decoration. The theme of the graphics tended to the mechanical and abstract. What Gregor could see of the solid reality beneath the display still had an unfinished look, with real cables and conduits crisscrossing overhead, connecting items of equipment. There seemed to be four or five ordinary robot servers present, at the moment all standing idle.

This looked like the place that appeared as background in Belgola's weird interactive messages. Gregor had just confirmed this for himself when a living figure, right hand extended, emerged from a field of illusion. The familiar voice said: "Gregor, old friend."

"Mister President."

Confronting the president face to face, clasping his hand in greeting, Gregor was staggered, horrified to see how drastically the man had been transformed.

Gregor's face must have betrayed the horror he felt, but the president was oblivious. Belgola was crazily upbeat, launching at once into a catalogue of marvelous things he had just done, or was about to do. He seemed to think he had all basic problems solved. His movements were jerky and energetic. He snapped his fingers once, as if to say that whatever problems might remain were not worth worrying about. His once-plump body had lost weight, but his cheeks were still rounded. "I will soon be able to go to our people with a proclamation of victory."

"I am glad to hear it," was Gregor's dazed response.

The president began to say something else, then stopped suddenly, looking at him. "You find me changed."

"Yes sir, I certainly do."

Belgola took that as a compliment. He gestured expansively. "The credit must go to Logos, of course—and his helpers . . . they have saved me, Gregor. I tell you they have saved me."

Whenever Belgola moved abruptly, the holographic decoration

trying to cling around his figure did not quite keep up. At intervals, amid lingering, swirling fringes of illusion, Gregor was able to see that there was something wrong with Belgola's head.

"You've been injured, sir. How did that happen?"

"I stand and walk, I stand and walk, I balance as well as a robot does. . . ." For a moment or two the president's speech played with the lyrics of an old song, seemed about to turn into a rhythmic chant.

With a visible effort, he reestablished control. "You see, Gregor, we recently experienced a crisis, in which I unwisely attempted to destroy myself." Belgola raised a hand, and with thumb and forefinger, pointing at his own head, mimed a handgun's action. At the same time, his lips quirked in a slight smile. "That was a mistake. But now, thanks to Logos, I am on the right path."

"Destroy yourself," Gregor echoed in a whisper. His lips were still moving, but he could find no more words to say. He had caught a closer glimpse of what had happened. Part of Belgola's skull, a large part of the left side of his head, was starkly bald, ivory white and artificial.

The president was still talking. Almost orating. ". . . can thank my great machines for my survival. In more ways than one. I must thank them for having set my feet on the right path. It may be that no one else has a medirobot quite as good as mine."

Gregor at last managed a coherent response. "What . . . sir, what is the current state of your health?"

"Never felt fitter in my life. Can assure you of that, old friend. Old rival, that too, hey? Hey?"

"Yes, sometimes your political rival, yes." No more, though. Moving a half-step closer, getting a still better look, Gregor could see that the raw edges of the remaining scalp could not come close to covering the new ceramic dome that cupped over whatever was left of the president's organic brain.

One of Belgola's eyes was slowly shifting its aim, in a strong strabismus. Then with a jerk it came back to join its fellow in a steady regard of Gregor. The president said: "You are shocked at my appearance."

"I—yes sir, frankly I am."

"Augmented life support became necessary." Gregor was listening more carefully now. In a way it sounded like Belgola's voice, and in a way it didn't. "Life enhancement, I should say. This is what it means to truly be alive." His tone had gone flat, and hardly matched the words.

His body moved, but not always to any effective purpose. There were periods of several seconds in duration when the actions of the man's arms and legs seemed natural.

After taking a turn around the room, the president—the president's body—stood facing Gregor again.

The voice that came out of Belgola's mouth said: "It is imperative that I soon address the people of the Twin Worlds. Of course the presentation will be technically augmented. People won't see—this—" An awkward gesture, one hand sweeping, finally bending back sharply at the wrist to point uncertainly at himself.

Uncertainty dominated. "Or . . . what do you think? . . . would it be wiser to show them everything, my whole achievement, all at once? For all of them, every one of us, must follow the same path, eventually."

Gregor stretched out his own uncertain hand. "But are you—are you really—?" *What is the best way to ask a walking corpse if it thinks itself competent? Would be a tricky job under the best conditions. How should a practiced diplomat ask a man if he is really alive?*

. . . if Belgola was still there at all, behind his perfectly organic eyes, eyes that seemed to be getting conflicting orders from an enhanced brain. The president was still speaking, too, a steady flow of words that sometimes seemed to be making sense.

Gregor took note, with horror, of how a trickle of blood came oozing a millimeter at a time out of one edge of the torn scalp, a tracery of bright scarlet against the bone white dome of the president's new skull. Somewhere in there, clinging to old bone and nourished by old blood that might be coming through new pathways, what was left of the president's brain must still be trying to keep itself alive.

Belgola sank down in a chair, and a machine came behind him, cauterizing, tidying the scalp, so that the bright blood was all gone, for now at least. The Oracle, Logos—a machine of exotic appearance—was partially visible, taking over the conversation while the president stood glassy-eyed, swaying on his feet, looking every minute more like a corpse with Logos implacably ordering his lungs to keep on breathing.

Gregor at last found words of his own. "Sir, you do not look well. You do not sound right. I must insist you see a human physician."

Belgola might not have heard. "But Logos, Gregor. Logos is the answer, and it will give the answers. When I speak to the people, all these details of my appearance will be smoothed away. In any case they do not matter do not matter do not matter." His voice had suddenly fallen into a numb monotone. "All that matters is—"

"Yes sir?"

One of the president's eyes was studying the visitor thoughtfully. His voice had somewhat recovered. "Now we come to your case, Gregor."

"Mine, sir?"

"You are an old man. In a few more years at most, in the ordinary course of nature, you will die. But I have good news for you."

"We must all expect to die at some time, Mister President."

"There you go wrong, friend Gregor. There is no need for death, no need at all. What has been done for me can be done for many. It can be done for you."

Belgola, suddenly reanimated, standing energetically on his own two feet again, scooped up from somewhere a handful of incomprehensible hardware, and seemed to be offering it to Gregor.

The hand that held the material was quivering. "My techs are very good, they are of course all robots, what you need can be installed in no time. Figuratively, no time. Figures of speech are difficult. Eventually they will be done away with. In good time, a real production line. The creation of a new and superhuman race."

"Thank you sir, but no. I respectfully decline the opportunity."

"Not an option, Gregor. To show reluctance, yes reluctance, reluctance, there is repetition, repetition, minor flaw, reluctance only shows shows shows you do not understand." The voice was really wrong. A single tear came trickling out of Belgola's jittering left eye.

Gregor got to his feet and began to back away.

Belgola's body shuffled after him. Shuffled first, then almost danced.

Somehow there was not as much space in this room of illusion as Gregor had at first thought. Soon the wired man had the plenipotentiary physically pinned in a corner, where Gregor thought he might have to try physical force to get away.

"I was first, into the circuit. Into the system. The system into me. You shall be next. Then a few other chosen humans, if we choose carefully, may prove worthy of inclusion. Then all. Eventually, all all all."

"I respectfully decline." The words came out in a gasp.

"It's an experience, Gregor. An experience that few or none have had before. To be at one with a quantum computer. Do you know . . . do you know. . . ? But how could you possibly."

The old man, mumbling disjointed arguments, stumbling back in sudden terror, repeated his refusal.

Belgola had paused in his advance, but not to listen to his potential victim's protest. Rather, something had occurred to start him on what seemed to be a different subject. "Gregor, I think I can begin to see the meaning, the purpose, of this visitation."

"By 'visitation,' sir, you mean my coming down into this shelter to—?"

"No no. No no no no no. You do not matter do not matter. I speak of greater matters matters. The arrival in our solar system of the thing that kills . . . matters."

Gregor could feel cold fingers trying to raise hair on the back of his neck. He started to edge a little sideways, hoping the movement would not be noticed. "And what about it, sir?"

A useless hope. Belgola was following him quickly, accurately, with a young man's stride. It was hard for an elderly human to dodge a robot. The head might be shattered but the body worked. Programmed by Logos. "It's an emissary from the universe."

"Sir?"

"The universe is getting our attention, Gregor, as forcefully as possible. My Logos is a part of the same effort, of something much greater than itself. Greater than we can be, greater than we can make. Oh great great great. I don't mean life, not life as we know it. But we are to have some share in its creation. Something . . ." The president fell silent. One eye still looked at Gregor, speculating.

Gregor eased a little closer to the door. A robot was standing there, right beside what seemed to be the only exit, and he could only hope it would not try to block his escape. He said: "Is this what your Ora . . . your Logos, has told you?"

Belgola announced his plan of sending the enemy a large number of human volunteers, who would explain to it the mutual advantages of integrated existence.

"Given a pure machine as intermediary, our ridiculous conflict with Huvea will be settled in no time. As a gesture of good faith I mean to turn over the ten Huvean hostages to the visitor's custody." He paused, smiling, with the look of a man who thought he had just scored a point. One eye still slowly trickled tears, while the other seemed to be studying a corner of the ceiling.

"I have ordered the executioner to see that they are transported to the spaceport, and have sent other orders for a ship to be in readiness."

Huang Gun had told Gregor that the order was not yet carried out. "Sir, the status of the hostages is one of the things I have to speak to you about." But even as Gregor said the words, he could tell that words were no longer going to be of any help. Huang Gun might have the young Huveans under guard somewhere, but robot guards were ineffective against angry, desperate humans—the best they could do would be to bluff with deadly threats, threats that no one was likely to believe.

Interruption came, in the form of a different robot at the door. It entered amidst a wreath of graphic illusions.

This one reported, in calm, disinterested tones, that a mob had broken into the upper levels of the Citadel. There appeared to be no immediate danger that violent people would be able to penetrate the deep shelters. Not for several days, at least.

Gregor wanted to ask the messenger what Huang Gun had done with the hostages, if he had been able to protect them. But he didn't want to let the president know they had not been sent off into space.

Belgola-Logos was not going to be distracted by mere riots in his capital. Disdaining the spoken word in favor of something wireless, and facing one of the robot servants that had been standing by, he silently ordered the machine to prepare Gregor for the operation.

Gregor couldn't hear the command, but he felt its result. Immediately a metal hand clamped down on Gregor's arm and started dragging him away. The machine was of course being careful not to hurt him, but it was quite firm about it; if he got bruised or bloodied it would be because he was trying too hard to pull free.

This can't be happening. But it was.

Gregor turned his head, screamed out his needs to the world in general: "Stop them! They're going to kill me!"

His hopes rose up as Porphyry—yes, his newly assigned protector!—immediately stepped forward to grapple with the robot holding Gregor. But a third machine closed in on Porphyry from behind, and started methodically trying to pin Porphyry's arms.

Thank all the gods, Gregor's new guardian seemed stronger. Porphyry's hand dipped into his carrying pouch, came out with Gregor's pistol. Without hesitation, Porphyry shot the robot holding Gregor. The weapon made only a faint spitting noise, but the impact of the invisible force-packet was quite loud as it tore a hole in the machine's torso and knocked it back. Gregor, his arms suddenly freed, fell to the floor.

The unit grappling with Porphyry managed to knock the pistol loose. Rolling over on the deck, Gregor snatched up the gun, even as the hand of yet another robot, reaching, aborted its own grab to keep from bruising him.

The old weapons training came right back when it was needed, even after all the decades. Gregor, lying on his back, shot down the robot contending with his rescuer—and then without hesitation pumped several more force-packets into Logos, as the counselor came rolling forward on its mount. More than one shot hit the president's tottering frame, which happened to be standing partially in the way.

Splashing blood, and sparking from its connections, Belgola's body fell in a slow collapse, sputtering away life and optelectronic activity. Both came to an abrupt end, followed a moment later by the last shreds of holostage illusion. Walls of bleak concrete loomed gray in the harsh emergency lighting that suddenly glared from overhead.

All the robots under the direct control of Logos were shuddering into stillness, keeling over, slumping down like tired men. Porphyry, the only machine still on its feet, bent over the fallen Belgola, then straightened slightly.

"I have called for medical assistance," it told Gregor in its cheerful voice. "But none can arrive for approximately a quarter of an hour. In any case, the late president appears to be clinically dead."

"Robots . . ." Gregor was sitting up, his aged lungs gasping to gain breath.

"Sir?"

"Porphyry. Listen. Not only you. I am issuing orders to whatever machines, control systems, can still hear me." He paused to get in two more gasps. "I am assuming full command. Command of everything."

He hoped, devoutly, that he had managed to kill Logos. But even if he had, there would probably be backup systems ready to take over.

Nothing acknowledged his command—but nothing argued with it. Crawling, trembling, gasping, the pistol still in his hand, Gregor made his way slowly to crouch beside Porphyry, over the body of the man who had been his friend. Both of Belgola's eyes were looking in the same direction, but they were seeing nothing at all.

Gregor pulled himself together, and with a grip of assistance from the robot got to his feet. He dropped the gun back into his own pocket, where it lay flat and inconspicuous.

The door had opened again and more robots were coming in. Gregor took charge and gave orders, to whatever crew—at first only machines, then a little later humans—were willing to take them from him.

The humans, all low-ranking folk, most from Citadel Security, were desperately willing and eager to be told what to do, by any human authority who sounded sane. Gregor showed them the body and the wreckage, and tried to reassure them. Rioters, unknown people he would never be able to identify, had somehow got in and wrought this havoc.

Issuing specific orders, he sent these anxious but reasonable people out to spread the cheerful word, through the deep shelters, then across the planet, that President Belgola had died fighting gallantly for his people. The surviving population of the Twin Worlds could take comfort in the knowledge that a new, acting president was securely in place.

Communicating that message, or any other, to the whole planet was going to be a problem. A combination of enemy action and mob violence had pretty well shredded the usual systems. As soon as Gregor was alone with the robots again, he set Porphyry to trying to reestablish solid communication with the rest of the planet and with the fleet. The early results were not promising.

Then Gregor said to Belgola's surviving helpers: "Find some efficient way to make sure all that damned counseling and planning hardware—everything my predecessor had established—is turned off. Kill all computer planning but essential services and communications."

The ordinary-looking machine in front of him nodded. "Yes sir. I have passed on your commands."

Gregor looked at the dead man, who still lay where he had fallen. None of the shots had hit Belgola in the face, and he seemed to be smiling faintly. Perhaps in relief, at having left all his problems to someone else.

Gregor meditated briefly, and said: "The next step is to bury him."

"Where, sir?"

Gregor was leaning his back against the wall, and trembling, his right arm scratched and bruised from trying to wrestle with a robot. There was not even a good place in this room to sit down, and soon he was going to need a real rest. "Somewhere inconspicuous, here in the shelter. There will be no ceremony at burial. Just as a temporary measure, till the crisis is past, and order can be restored. Don't mark the place, but remember it. Then I want all nonhuman

staff to forget everything that has happened in this room, since—
since I came down here."

"Yes sir. But the central computer of essential services informs
me that a record of the deleted events, and of your orders, will be
kept, sealed apart from our memories, until it can be claimed by
competent authority."

Gregor could feel a kind of sobbing, starting in his diaphragm.
Was he going to laugh or cry? He couldn't tell. He told the robots:
"Of course. Why not? Lots of luck in finding any competent authority. If your central computer manages to do so, be sure to let me
know."

Within the hour, a very minor human authority had showed
up—the same sheriff who had brought Gregor and Luon to the
Citadel. Gregor was able to arrange to have himself confirmed and
sworn in as the executive head of the Twin Worlds government—
which made him also commander-in-chief of the armed forces.

Just as the ceremony was about to begin, he was informed
(by a module that under the previous administration had functioned as attorney general) that President Belgola had recently
changed the protocol. A robot/computer now had to perform the
swearing-in, before the central data bank would accept it as a
valid act.

"Then let it be Porphyry. And the sheriff will take part as
well."

That was all right with the former attorney general. One of
the humans in attendance brought up from the deep shelters a copy
of the necessary book. Gregor held it in his hand, pages of dull and
ancient paper on which no electrical impulse was able to rewrite
the words.

Now, in the very infancy of Gregor's new government, it
seemed impossible to discover what had happened to the Huvean

hostages—except that they could no longer be located inside the Citadel, or any of the shelters immediately connected.

His grandchild, too, had disappeared. So had the executioner. Well, it hardly seemed likely that they had gone anywhere together—unless, of course, both were with the hostages.

The word that President Belgola was dead spread quickly through the shelters, then up into the streets. Up there, Gregor's robot scouts informed him, the tide of mob activity had crested, and then sunk back into the great pool of humanity from which it rose.

As one of Gregor's first official acts, having established such control of the government as he was able, he wrote out an order indefinitely blocking any execution of the hostages, and directing that the ten young Huveans should be kept in safety until they could be returned to their own people. He instilled the order in every government computer system he found still functioning.

When Gregor, with only a couple of sheriff's deputies at his side—and no fanfare—reemerged on the planet's surface, trying to see what was going on, he found that at least one of the energetic preachers was still going strong: "I tell you, men and women of sin, that God has sent a destroying angel for our punishment!"

"Who speaks of God? Never mind God! Who else could it be, doing this to us, but Huvea?—but we'll get back at them. Someday!" The speaker's voice rose to a scream. "We'll scorch and boil their worlds so nothing ever will live there again—" There were some who could draw comfort from that thought.

Out in the sparsely populated countryside, away from Timber's cities, along the winding roads and through the sprawling forests, people sought shelter, or pursued rumors of some spaceship that was still on the ground, and still offered possibilities of escape. This turned out to be the ship that had waited in vain to carry the hostages to the berserker, according to the last orders given by the late president—waited, until someone managed to hijack it, and flee the system.

With an increasing feeling of desperation, Gregor continued trying to locate surviving shards of local government that might be made to form a whole. He was not having much success.

Slowly he began to feel some confidence that no one might ever know that he had killed the president. Traces of blood and violence in the deep shelter—if anybody was going to take any notice of them at all—might easily be attributed to the actions of the mob.

At last he was able to send an urgent message to Admiral Radigast, a redundant transmission by both courier and tight beam: "I want to come back to your flagship. It's hopeless to try to do anything, organize anything, from down here."

On the ship, he would at least have available to him a small, clear space in which to think. A protected place in which to rest. Means of communication, and such power as the shattered fleet could still muster. The only surviving Twin Worlds power and organization was in the fleet, battered as it was.

The mass of people who still endured on Timber were concerned for very little beyond their own lives. Those who had any interest in the fate of the hostages were divided in their feelings. Anyway, all ten of them were supposed to have volunteered.

There still remained a large number of citizens who were unshakable in their conviction that Huvea was behind the attack. Some of these were demanding that every Huvean who was still in Twin Worlds power should die at once. Meanwhile, another substantial number were insisting with equal vehemence that the ten should be set free, and sent home as soon as a ship could be made available—whoever was attacking, it was certainly not these helpless children. There were many others who assumed that the hostages must already have been killed.

On the bridge of his flagship, looking at the messages that had come trickling up from Timber, Radigast spat out part of the latest flavor pod that he had stuffed into his mouth. He'd been expecting something like bourbon and tobacco, and had got what tasted like vanilla. The gob lay where it landed, he would have to pick it up himself; the motherless housekeeping robots were all hard at work on more important tasks.

So, Belgola was supposed to have died some kind of heroic death. "Fried his motherless brain," the admiral muttered.

. . . .
S I X T E E N
. . . .

Up on the bridge of the *Morholt,* Radigast could feel the whole massive skeleton of his ship groaning and throbbing around him under the laboring efforts of repair machines. The machines could not improve matters much, but they kept his ship from totally dying. New reports were coming in: their great enemy was disgorging more small spacegoing units of several types, which were going down to land on Timber.

But he had to let that go for a minute. "President Gregor." Radigast spoke quietly, and raised his right hand in a salute, slow and stiff and with an unpracticed look about it.

"Don't joke, Admiral."

"Sir, I feel very far from joking. I was looking up the chain of succession. Who has inherited the office, if not yourself?" He paused, looking over Gregor's shoulder to see if anyone else was there. "What happened to the little girl, sir?"

"She decided to stay down there. I alerted the sheriff, and sent a robot to try to find her."

———

Gregor's visit to Timber had turned out to be one motherless fiasco, if the tone of Gregor's voice when he asked to be picked up was any indication. The transmission had contained only a few gems of information, one being the fact that President Belgola was definitely dead. But Radigast expected a full report in person as soon as possible.

The admiral had been continuously at his battle station for more hours than he wanted to count up, grabbing catnaps when he could, but he was not about to leave it now. He kept on trying to mobilize all his available resources, mass them in a compact volume of space within striking distance of Timber. If they were going to be able to do any good at all, it would have to be here. Consolidating your own force was what you were supposed to do, when confronted by a stronger enemy; and it was no longer possible to doubt that this particular enemy was stronger, though his own ships combined still had more tonnage and occupied more space. Most of that martial mass, unfortunately, was only scoutships, and sending them to the attack would be like deploying a mass of mosquitoes to stop a rhinoceros.

Any opponent that brushed off eight battleships, while going on about its business almost without a pause, was probably not going to be seriously bothered by anything that a few hundred scoutships could do. But Radigast had to try, and the scouts were about all he had left to work with. Summoning some eight hundred and fifty of them in and hurling them in a swarm against the giant enemy would at least force the enemy to use up more of its resources on secondary targets.

The only conceivable alternative would be to turn his back on Timber's helpless billions, on the theory that they were dead souls anyway, and save the remnant of his ships and his own people by pulling them out of the Twin Worlds system altogether, pausing just long enough to pick up Gregor and a few other useful folk if possible. Then it would be up to the acting president to establish a Twin Worlds government in exile somewhere else.

But so far no one, with the possible exception of the late president, was in the mood to abandon anything. He, Radigast, would have to make one more effort with the fleet, and the only way to do that was to time it for the moment when the enemy came close enough to Timber to be engaged by whatever ground defense batteries still functioned. Therefore Radigast was praying that Gregor might be bringing useful information on the state of morale and hardware on the ground. Basically, were there any ground defenses left?

Luon on running away from Gregor had begun an attempt to search the whole Citadel for Reggie—an effort she decided to abandon when she began to grasp how huge and complicated the place actually was. And the vast structure was being evacuated—though not according to any organized plan. People were just getting out on their own initiative. Men and women whose normal posts of duty were in this place were simply deserting it, military and civilian alike.

Snatches of conversation caught in passing conveyed to her a rumor that the hostages were being taken to the spaceport. That at least gave her something to go on, and she began to walk in that direction. With the streets in turmoil, with serious fighting apparently only a kilometer away, getting any form of transport appeared hopeless.

How many kilometers to the port? More than she remembered, her last journey that way having been in a swift and comfortable groundcar. She had covered five or six of them on foot, struggling with a growing sense that she ought to have kept looking close to the Citadel, when light rapid footsteps overtook her and an artificial hand closed gently on her arm. She turned to recognize a face of passing beauty.

"No doubt you will remember me, my lady. I am Porphyry, and your grandfather has sent me to you. How can I be of assistance?"

———

Yesterday there had been half a dozen armed guards visible, in and around the rooms where the Huvean hostages were being held, in a comparatively remote wing of the Citadel. Early this morning, Reggie had been able to spot no more than two. By midmorning, the last pair seemed to have somehow evaporated.

The last human guard had scarcely disappeared from the hostage quarters when the young Huveans, who had been watching the situation carefully, began to convince themselves that they had been thrown on their own resources.

But one of the Huveans still considered himself bound by an oath of honor not to attempt an escape.

The more aggressive youth snapped at the more passive: "What are you waiting for, an engraved invitation on real paper?"

The stickler for honor seemed to be looking at him from atop a distant hill. "Try to remember, that when we volunteered we took a solemn oath—"

"We were all a lot younger then."

"It was only a few standard months ago!"

"Even so. Look around you, open your eyes! That was in a different world, that place where people took solemn oaths and worried about their honor. In this world, where you're living now, all bets are off, you bloody fool. Wake up and live!"

Another put in: "I would hardly call this an escape. It seems to me we've been deserted."

Someone noted that if the stickler for honor was really determined to honor his pledge not to escape, it was probably going to cost him nothing, since everyone on the planet was soon going to be slaughtered anyway.

The first decisive act of the rebellion was to rid themselves of the distinctive robes they had been made to wear since the start of their confinement.

Their own Huvean-style clothes had been put away in storage, even before they arrived on Timber—and in any case would have been no help in passing as Twin Worlders. Minutes later, by raiding a supply closet, an eager searcher came up with a stack of shirts and trousers worn by the maintenance supervisors who directed the crews of robots. Footwear was also available.

Doing their best to look casual in their new garments, they came drifting, singly and in pairs, out of the rooms in which they had spent most of their confinement.

A certain door, through which none of them had been allowed to pass, was now totally unguarded. It opened at a simple touch, and no alarms went off.

Reggie nodded, looking straight ahead. "Beyond that next gate ought to be the street. It seems that we can walk."

"I'm getting out of here," a colleague murmured.

And another: "I'm with you. The war's on, there's no use waiting around to be shot."

They came to the last gate, of solid metal. Beside it stood a robot, one of the standard manshapes. It knew them at once, of course, despite the change in clothing. And it was ready to deal with an attempted escape, in the only way it knew—calmly, of course. "Hostages are not permitted in this area. You must go back."

What came next was something that Reggie had done before, on his home world, but then it had been only as a lark. With Douras and a couple of others lending a hand, they seized the robot guard by all four limbs and wrestled it out of the way—when push literally came to shove, the robot, dependably programmed against doing physical harm to any human, was no more effective at keeping prisoners in than it would have been at keeping a lynch mob out.

A little carefully planned violence on the part of the prisoners toppled the sentry on its face. A moment later the grill had been removed from the opening of a nearby ventilator shaft, and the robot jammed head first into the aperture. It began at once trying to work its way back out, but its arms were pinned by the sides of the narrow shaft.

Reggie planted a foot on its metal rump and shoved it a couple of centimeters deeper. He had no doubt that the deposed sentry would broadcast some kind of silent alarm, but in the current conditions none of the security people remaining in and around the Citadel—if there were any—were going to respond.

Meanwhile the robot was still obligingly willing to be helpful, answering their questions, passing on what it was able to pick up of the latest news, its voice, metallicized and echoing, coming out of the shaft: The killing machines were said to be steadily approaching, and the sounds of fighting were coming nearer.

One of the humans interrupted. "All right. That might be good. Where are these 'killing machines,' as you call them, supposed to come from?"

"That has not yet been officially determined, sir. Rumors say they are Huvean."

Douras was pleased and excited by the possibility. "I knew it! How far away are they?"

Someone had said they were no more than two kilometers from the Citadel.

"Headed this way?"

The muffled voice still sounded optimistic. "At last report, sir, they were not advancing in any direction."

As the ten moved on, one said to another: "One could feel a little sorry for the clunker there—just trying to do its job."

"There are plenty of people who need feeling sorry for."

"Robots are excellent Christians, you know—always ready to forgive their enemies. They'd be ready to give up their own lives for us—if they had any."

Another observed: "Not much of a sacrifice to give up what you can never have—and don't want anyway."

And a third: "Christians?—I don't think so. No hope or expectation of any reward. Stoics would be more like it."

"Which way now?"

"To the spaceport!"

"No, wait! What'll we do there, just buy tickets for home? Pay attention to what's happening. The spaceport's closed, and even if it wasn't, there aren't any ships available for ordinary travel. Besides, if the port was open, it'd be the first place we'd be looked for—if anyone bothered to come looking."

"It might be a lynch mob who does that. No, I want to get a look at these fighting machines. It seems to me there's at least a good chance that they are ours, and looking for us."

Reggie was thinking that simply blending into the cosmopolitan Twin Worlds crowd ought to be easy enough. There were no glaring discrepancies in personal appearance, and there ought to be only a couple, easily avoided if they kept their wits about them, in speech and manners. Of course their faces had been widely shown to the public on this world, with all the ongoing publicity.

They stole out of the Citadel in twos and singles. There were only a few people in the streets, and the appearance of a few more young maintenance workers seemed to draw no attention at all.

The hostage who had been scrupulous about trying to escape, on catching a glimpse of angry Twin Worlders, suddenly turned timid once again: "We're going to be caught. . . ."

"How the hell can you be any more caught than you were half an hour ago? And we survived that."

Almost a full day later, Reggie Panchatantra was looking the situation over, peering out through the broken window of a deserted building. They ought to have brought more food with them; but it was too late now to be worrying about that.

From where he crouched he could just make out, a couple of kilometers away, a pair of the darkened towers of the Citadel, from which they had so recently escaped. They formed twin dark

outlines against the brightening eastern sky. The time was near
dawn in the streets of Timber's capital city. Artificial lights that
had survived the rioting as well as nearby enemy action were fad-
ing against the brightening sky; such of the defensive fields as
were still in place added streaks of unnatural color and shadow to
the coming sunrise.

As Reggie thought back over their escape, he was distracted
by the sight of a young woman, walking straight toward him over
the otherwise deserted street. Close beside her paced a robot, right
arm raised and pointing straight at Reggie. In another moment he
had recognized Luon, and climbed out of his hiding place; and
then they were both running.

As soon as Reggie could get free of her embrace to draw
breath, he held her at arms length, looking at her almost angrily.
"You should have stayed with your grandfather. There was no
sense in your coming back here into danger."

"You'd better not be saying you don't want me with you!"

"No, Sweetie! Never that!"

The next minute was occupied with silent activity. At last
Luon moved back a few centimeters and drew in a deep breath. "I
had to come to you. Anyway, staying with my grandfather would
be just as dangerous."

"How'd you find us?"

"Porphy here kept looking for groups of ten people—he can
hear breathing if he tries, and finds patterns—"

"I don't like that. If the authorities were really searching for
us—"

"But it seems they're not."

Reggie quietly introduced Luon to the other young people in
the group as they drifted into contact, singly or in pairs. Of course
they had all seen her briefly in the Citadel with Gregor, before the
fighting started. But she had not yet memorized all their names.

Luon had been carrying a fairly substantial amount of money, and she shared it out. Douras at first was reluctant to accept a handout from her, but in the end he did.

Like the robot, Douras was standing at a little distance with his arms folded, watching her. The man's regard was obviously suspicious. "Your dear grandsire will certainly be in some danger, once our marines have landed. A while ago we heard some garbled rumor that he's now become your president."

Luon was frowning, shaking her head. "He's *looking* for our president. It seems that for days no one's been able to find Mr. Belgola."

The Huvean snorted. "The rumors say Belgola's dead. The truth is he's probably run away, now that the war he wanted is coming home to him. I always thought that man was crazy."

Luon began to wonder aloud what had happened to the official executioner. She had seen Huang Gun briefly when she and her grandfather had arrived at the Citadel, but had no idea where he might be, or even if he was alive or dead. The Huveans knew no more than she did.

It was not that any of the ex-hostages exactly missed Huang Gun, but they had some curiosity about his sudden absence. "The last thing anyone here can recall his saying was that everything would be taken care of."

Glycas was fretting. "He can't just have wandered off. He must have left some orders with regard to us."

"Probably to have us all shot."

Douras theorized gloomily that the withdrawal of official protection meant that before escaping they had been in the process of being quietly, unofficially, turned over to a lynch mob. And where were the marines? He had been expecting to see them before this.

Several of the Huveans besides Douras remained openly suspicious of the plenipotentiary's daughter. Luon said she could hardly blame them, but it made things difficult. Soon another rumor was reported, to the effect that the new acting president wanted the

Huvean prisoners to be set free—there was as yet no report that they had actually escaped. When the citizens of the capital mentioned them at all, it was usually to hope they were already dead.

One of the moderate Huveans told her: "Well, a rumor's not going to save our lives. Your grandfather probably had a hand in drawing up the treaty, so it's his fault as much as anyone's that we're here in the first place."

Luon wanted to argue that point, but realized that she didn't know enough to do so. "You don't know him. I can believe the rumor. I'm sure he wants to get you out of this."

"Then let him make peace with Huvea. I haven't heard a word about that yet."

The sounds of serious fighting were coming closer. This was no mere street scuffling between police and rioters. This had reached another order of violence altogether. Clouds of smoke, mingled with the dust from collapsed buildings, drifted this way and that in mild autumn breezes.

They reached a place where, in the distance, they could just catch a glimpse of one of the mysterious landers, motionless at the moment, standing several blocks away. It bore no insignia, and there was nothing familiar in its construction. The surface had a worn, scorched look, and in several places it bristled with mysterious projections. No one could identify it, but then none of them had any technical knowledge of the latest machines of war. They could not convince themselves that it might have been sent by their government to effect their rescue.

Hours later, they were resting in near darkness. "I have to be with you." Her voice was muffled against Reggie's chest. "Besides, there's nowhere to go."

"The last I heard, you were going with your grandfather to your fleet—then I thought the fleet had probably gone to attack Huvea—"

Luon raised her head. "That never happened. It just didn't! Our fleet is still right here, in our home system, but it's all shot to pieces."

Some of the other hostages, who had been listening, reacted joyfully to that information. "That's the first good news I've heard in days—ever since someone toasted Prairie."

Another had a skeptical question for Luon: "Who told you about the Twin Worlds fleet? Your trustworthy grandfather?"

She glared back fiercely. "My grandfather's as trustworthy as you are. At least! But he didn't have to tell me anything. I was out there with him, on the flagship."

They all stared at her. "You've actually seen the fighting?"

"Yes!"

A couple of Reggie's friends looked at each other, still suspicious of everything this Twin Worlder said. One asked Luon: "What does a ship look like, blowing up?"

Luon had to hesitate. "I've *felt* it right enough, right through my bones when our ship was hit. All that I've actually seen is symbols moving around on a holostage—and damage to the ship I was on, people with wounds and blood. That's really all that anyone on any ship can ever see of fighting." She wasn't perfectly sure of her ground in saying that, but her new status as combat veteran gave her a certain confidence, and it sounded reasonable. "It's not like looking at games and simulations. And I've heard the officers on board talking to each other."

There was a babble of response. One voice stood out. "Then can you tell us who's really attacking? It's just not possible that our Huvean fleet has just come here and started—started wiping out planets. . . ."

"Oh no? Why not?" Someone else, bitterly hostile, was hoping, was thoroughly convinced, that it *was* their own fleet that had come here to punish the damned two-faced Twins.

Luon brought them all up to date as best she could. She was able to tell the Huveans a few things they did not know, confirming some of the news stories they had already heard, and denying others. But she could tell them nothing that offered any real comfort.

"Well then, if our fleet's not here trying to rescue us, where *is* it?" a Huvean demanded.

Luon stared at the young woman, thinking that the two of them, the speaker and herself, looked enough alike to be sisters. "I don't have the faintest idea."

Glycas, who now and then made noises like a leader, found a reasonable hiding spot and convened a council. At Luon's order, Porphyry stood sentry, guarding against surprise.

They all had to realize, Glycas lectured, that simply running around on the surface of Timber was not going to do them much good, and might quite possibly get some of them lynched. Maybe the new acting president really was willing to let them go; but even if that were true, their chances of going home in the foreseeable future seemed practically nonexistent. At least a billion other people on this planet also wanted to get spaceborne; and everyone who had seen the spaceport in the last couple of days agreed there were no ships ready to take anyone anywhere.

Everyone remained hungry for news, for rumors, whether they could be true or not. "Is there any word on what's happening at home? Has the Twin Worlds fleet attacked Huvea?"

"No. There's been no word of anything like that." And Luon repeated her assurances that the Twin Worlds fleet had not departed from the system. "And if it does leave, it will only be to find a hiding place somewhere."

Douras laughed scornfully at that.

The berserker was scrutinizing the patterns of defensive fire turned against it from this world called Timber, methodically discovering and plotting the positions of as many as possible of the planet's ground defenses. They fell obligingly into a pattern very similar to that on this world's late sister planet.

Once the berserker decided it could rely on this observation, locating and destroying the defensive batteries of Timber became notably more easy.

After being located, all these facilities were methodically blasted, whether or not they tried to hit back at the attacker. Again the berserker invoked its routine of dodging movements, of creating multiple images of itself in space, so that some on the ground thought they were being attacked by a thousand gigantic ships. Again it inevitably sustained some damage, but nothing to prevent or delay carrying out its mission here.

Across Timber's countryside and in its cities there were heavy casualties, already millions of dead. But compared to what had happened to Prairie, these casualty figures were low, diminished by almost a thousandfold. So far, on the berserker's scale of values, there was no mass slaughter on the planet called Timber.

Of course the mass slaughter had only been postponed. It would come, in due time. The mass destruction of life was the berserker's reason for existence. But there were things its central processor wanted to find out, before proceeding to the inevitable fulfillment of its basic purpose. The berserker still wanted to learn more before it sterilized this world.

One important question was: How effectively would these life units fight at close quarters, as individuals, or in groups not acting through the surrogates of machinery? The situation was bound to arise somewhere, in what the berserker now computed would be a lengthy war ahead. What weapons would they be likely to employ?

It was prepared to begin using radioactive poisons, and

chemicals, at first on a small scale, but nothing biological— that would mean promoting and protecting, nurturing some form of life. And it would only fall back on those tactics for some especially grave reason.

SEVENTEEN

Huang Gun, rejected, stood star-
ing for a moment at the closed door of the elevator. Then the faint
noise of the angry crowd outside, penetrating the walls of the Citadel,
recalled him to his duty. The hostages . . . whether the president was
willing to see him or not, they were still his responsibility. He could
not take seriously the absurd suggestion that they be loaded on a ship
and sent out to the enemy as a kind of sacrifice. No telling what might
happen to them out there.

He acted on a sudden impulse, and half a minute later was
slipping out into the street, through a small door in the side of the
Citadel. Before he could be certain of what his duty was, he had to
make sure how close the attacking enemy had actually come. He
had told no one, not even the people on his own staff, where he was
going, or why. The decision he would soon be forced to make
regarding the young Huveans would be his, and his alone.

If the president refused to speak to him, so be it. If this
attack had truly been launched by Huvea—

But he must not judge until he was sure of the facts. He must make certain.

Timber's defensive forcefields were still in place, maintaining what seemed a useless effort to defend the planet. All they seemed to be accomplishing was to blur and blot the sky, making it impossible to distinguish day from night. Having gone a moderate distance, the executioner saw some casualties being evacuated, robots and humans bearing improvised stretchers between them. Among the fallen being carried away, almost all of them in soldiers' uniforms, Huang Gun noted several bodies that he was sure were dead.

Fascinated by the sight, he kept working his way closer and closer to where the fighting was going on. It seemed the army was not easily discouraged, and part of it was still here, exchanging fire with the invaders.

Something slammed, with incredible violence, into the wall a couple of stories above Huang Gun's head. Reeling with the shock, he was half stunned by a cascade of falling rubble. He found himself crouched, head aching, body half lying on the sidewalk, with a slab of some lightweight building material weighing on his legs and back.

Moments—or perhaps it was minutes—later, dazed and bruised, he managed to pull himself free—but a little help was necessary before he could do that.

"Are you all right, sir?" The woman was almost shouting in his ear.

"Fine . . . please, there are things that I must do. A duty to accomplish."

"You must evacuate this area! Get to a shelter!"

He nodded and mumbled something, getting to his feet. No one tried to detain him. There were plenty of other casualties in more need of help than he was.

Huang Gun moved on, feeling only slightly dazed. Somehow, on some inward, basic level, he seemed to know where he was going.

... resting, again somewhere on the fringe of a combat area, he could hear people discussing the latest rumor. It seemed that a new president—if he had heard that right—had issued an order setting the hostages free.

The news came as a stunning shock, but still Huang Gun could believe it. Not only had Belgola refused to see him, but authority might now be trying to strip him of his most important responsibility—really, of the only reason he still had for living.

He found it impossible to guess what might have driven the president to take such a position. That the man had wanted to rely more on machines than on people was understandable, even praiseworthy in the circumstances. But what business that he might have had with Gregor could be more important than the hostages?

It was clear to Huang Gun that Belgola had mismanaged the whole business of governing, turning authority over to Logos and the other computers ... that might have worked at some point, but not now. What was not so plain to see was exactly what the president *should* have done.

Meanwhile, he had to keep reassuring himself that his own mind was clear—so possibly it really wasn't. His head still ached from the impact of the falling debris. He had a vague memory of wandering across a parkway, littered with stopped vehicles and dead bodies, crossing the broad path one of the killing machines had cut through the city's heart. So far, the attack on Timber was not an all-out slaughter, but more like exploratory surgery.

... so, the president had refused to see him. Very well. So be it. Belgola had started out on the right track, but for all his talk, all his bold announcements, his thinking had not been bold enough.

Particularly he had not been decisive enough in the matter of the executions. Huang Gun was profoundly disappointed about that. He had planned several versions of the procedure.

Some were rich with ceremony and others not, but all were imbued with dignity and a sense of the occasion's ultimate importance. He had begun trying to consult other officials on the matter, but no one else had even wanted to discuss the details.

Very well, that left it up to him. Each individual death would be—would have been—finely crafted, there would have been no crude mangling and no mass slaughter. Probably intense neutron bombardment would have been the method finally chosen: painless, practically instantaneous, and doing no visible damage to the body, creating about as little mess as any process could that was connected with organic life.

Of course there were other questions to be dealt with, besides the method. Would there be human witnesses? On that matter his own feelings were divided. No more than one or two of his own staff in attendance, that would have been his preference—but on the question of witnesses, politics were sure to dominate.

The executioner's problem, or one of his problems, was that he no longer knew whether the hostages were still in the Citadel or not. And there had been something about a new president. . . .

A street communicator was working intermittently, putting out morsels of information between bursts of static, sheer white noise. What stopped the executioner in his tracks was what sounded like Gregor's recorded voice, introduced as a proclamation from the new acting president. The gist of it was that the ten Huvean hostages were to be set free.

Gregor . . . president? . . .

The people who jostled the executioner in the street were paying him no attention, they had no idea he was a person of importance. It was possible that they were quite right, and no such thing existed. . . .

There was an approaching noise, that of many angry human voices. The jostling had become a panicked rush of bodies. Huang Gun was swept up in a mob, but this one with a different flavor to it.

These people were terrorized, fleeing the last incremental advance of the monstrous conquering machines.

Terror, as contagious as the plague, welled up in the executioner. He ran until he could run no longer, fleeing the mob itself, not the terror that had set the mob in motion. And then he fell, welcoming the plunge into unconsciousness.

The light of another early morning fell on a broad section of ruin, in the midst of what had been a mighty city. One of a flock of crows descended to peck and tear at something in the street, and a moment later the bird itself convulsed and died.

Another figure appeared, walking on two much bigger legs. This man's clothing was beginning to hang upon him loosely. His hair was dirty and disheveled, and his beard had a good start on rank untended growth.

—he caught a glimpse of himself in a mirror, a dull reflection in a dim screen on the side of a building, half of which had been very recently demolished. The man had one arm braced against the remaining fragment of a wall, and held himself propped there as if trying to summon up the energy to go on—but go on where? To what?

—somewhere, the ten Huveans were all getting away. And there was nothing he could do about it—

He was gazing into a surface that had once glowed and flowed with bright images—and thought: Who is that? What does that man look like? Why, he looks like the professional apostle of some end-of-the-world cult that had of late been losing membership.

Having been deprived of several meals, his body seemed to be laboring under the impression that he was starving. Slightly injured, he feared—but no, fear was not really the right word—that he would soon be dead.

His lips were growing dry and cracked—again. Every time he looked at water, he thought for some reason that it must be poisoned. But soon he drank it anyway. Drank from puddles, and

once something gushing from a broken pipe. Nothing happened
to him, though, except that his suffering went on.

People noticed him again, despite the fact that he was trying
not to notice them. He was pressed into service, carrying living
casualties—then almost killed in a blast that mangled whatever
human he had been trying to carry to safety. . . .

Reinforcements for the enemy expeditionary force were
coming down again on Timber, some landing just before the sunset
line, on a day of smoke-filled, lurid sky . . . a shape that had once
been tall, a man, staggering through burning wreckage, came stumbling out from behind a ruined building. What was left of the man's
ragged garments suggested that he had once worn impressive
clothes.

The figure emerged from smoke in full sight of a new
machine, itself only roughly human in size and shape, its surfaces
still unscarred, untarnished by battle, that had just emerged from
one of the house-sized landers.

The man had a vague memory of having been, several hours
ago, down in a deep shelter, from which it had somehow been necessary to escape.

He had been in a second shelter very recently, and had
escaped from that one only just in time, when the walls began to
crack and molten metal started to pour in, an effect readily attributed to the pacification of a ground battery only a few kilometers
away.

. . . **H**uang Gun's thoughts kept coming back to the memory of Belgola and his machines. Refusing to let the executioner
come in. A horror, yes. But the horror had only been because
Belgola had not fully understood. . . . The late president had
been heading in the right direction, but somehow he had not
gone far enough. Gregor, if he had really become the leader, was
going to be worse.

He, Huang Gun, had once been a close and trusted counselor to the president of the Twin Worlds. But then the president had gone wrong. Not in any of the ways that most people failed, no. But quite wrong all the same.

The real answer, the real truth, was that . . .

The executioner who had never killed had the feeling of having very recently been reborn, into a world of terror and glory. Before that he had been living another life, and there had been much in that old life that he now detested—

One incident, toward the very end, was especially unsatisfying—a business, a duty that involved some necessary killing, that had not been satisfactorily carried out.

. . . **t**he machine that blocked the street was speaking to him, in a cracked and querulous voice that was not at all like the voice of Logos. It sounded odd, but the man could easily understand what it was saying.

After moving closer to the watching conqueror by a couple of staggering steps, the man threw himself down, almost at the machine's feet, his knees crunching on the surface of a street littered with building fragments and fine debris.

His clothing hung on him in shreds. His hands were bleeding from clawing his way through wreckage. When he tried to respond to what the machine was saying to him, it seemed almost that he was mocking it, so strange did his own voice sound. He had been shouting, screaming until he was hoarse and his throat was raw. But now he had no words left to shout, no energy left to scream.

. . . he was struck by the beauty of the machine before him, the inorganic cleanness and the purity of its design. Weapons tended to be like that. Before him was the most beautiful weapon that he had ever seen!

He knelt there on the littered pavement, gasping, while lenses turned toward him. Then he waited a little longer, holding his breath, for the jolt of death that did not come. At last, with a feeling something like relief, he let out his breath as he saw a thing that must be the muzzle of some kind of gun smoothly turning in his direction.

It took the kneeling man a few more long, disappointing moments to be sure that he was not going to be killed—not just at once, anyway.

He could manage to endure his own existence a while longer. What really mattered was that he had come at last to a place where a kind of path, a kind of purpose, was visible before him. Something in the world had meaning, after all. Something, even if it was only Death.

Whatever the thing was standing before him, he could see, he could feel, that it ruled the world.

This overwhelming and brutal force had nothing human about it, and nothing accidental.

Huang Gun was ready to accept it as his god.

. . . the thing that had suddenly come to rule his life was barking orders at him. It sent a lesser machine, man-sized and almost man-shaped, to grip and search him.

A moment later it tore his clothing off entirely, so that he stood quite naked in the autumn wind. His rags concealed no firearms, no explosives. He relaxed, slumped, willing to let the metal arm support him. Just now, standing up straight was more than flesh and blood were able to accomplish.

It spoke to him again, and only now did he become fully aware of the peculiarities of its voice. "Tell me who you are."

It was very strange, but for a moment his own name escaped him. But before anything else could happen, he had found an even better answer: "I was appointed Executioner."

"That word means one who kills."

"Yes." He felt a pang of guilt, and hoped he would not be forced to admit to the machine that never in his whole life had he killed anyone. "That was to be my task. But then, when all this started—" He made a gesture of futility.

As far as he could tell, the machine was paying his answers close attention. When it learned of Huang Gun's most recent position in the government, it came to a quick decision.

A metal limb jerked in a brisk gesture, summoning. A voice said to Huang Gun: "Come, and in a little while you will be one with death."

The machine then hastily loaded Huang Gun onto a shuttle, led and pushed him into a space that had no seats, obviously intended for freight, not passengers. Not live ones anyway. The main cargo, the only cargo really, was human corpses. Many were in uniform, some in civilian dress, a few as naked as the executioner himself.

Here were dead men, women, children, at least a hundred, Huang Gun thought. It seemed the surgeons doing the exploratory on Timber's body might be collecting cells for close examination. Most of the bodies were still warm, and soon he realized that some might be not quite dead. One still living specimen among those already dead, or nearly dead, would probably not make much difference.

"I'm not dead yet!" It was a confession of guilt, rather than a complaint. He did not want to accept this honor under false pretenses. Were they headed for a mass cremation, or a burial?

If any component of his new god heard him, it ignored the outburst.

The shuttle did not seem to have been designed for human comfort, or even by human brains—unless perhaps they were the brains of torturers. It was good for nothing better than sheer survival. The only live brain functioning aboard was left blinded in darkness, deafened by noise, jammed in with other bodies both clothed and naked, half choked by strange smells, at least half of them poisonous.

Just when he had begun to think there would be no artificial gravity, it came on with a jolt, seemingly as an afterthought, and just in time to counteract a swiftly mounting g-force of acceleration that if uncushioned would soon have begun to do serious damage to living and dead alike. Even the counteracting field was a bit too strong to be comfortable, and oriented in such a way that dumped half the organic cargo randomly on top of the other half.

It seemed to Huang Gun that hours were going by. If this kept on much longer, he was sure that he would die. But almost as soon as he came to that conclusion, the end of the trip arrived, unmistakably, in the form of a jarring docking.

Moments later, Huang Gun was part of the parade of bodies being carried by machines. Helpless cargo indeed, only here and there a muffled scream or groan, carried through mated hatches, leaving the small cargo ship, going aboard—something.

Then a metal clamp closed on his arm, and he was carefully separated from the dead and dying. He might have thought himself forgotten, but he knew somehow that the power that was doing this did not forget. Dumped in a place where, for a time, absolute darkness ruled. The air was breathable, but suddenly so cold that he thought death might be only minutes away.

Resting, even as his body shivered, Huang Gun found the beginnings of a strange and final peace gradually stealing over him. His breathing quieted. The ongoing noise and the other discomforts no longer mattered. Soon, very soon (though time had become another distraction that did not matter much), the machine would decide to make an end of him, and grant him the peace for which he so desperately yearned.

But it was not to be. Not yet. He could hear voices again, human voices muttering and whispering, as if in fear.

A machine came to clutch him by the arm again and drag him to his feet.

"What is it?—are you putting me with other prisoners?"

"Not now. Maybe not ever. Come."

It guided him into a room where there was light, and began his processing. There was also running water, and he drank his fill—something smelled vaguely like food, and he put some of it into his stomach.

A little later, he was taken to another room, where holes had been drilled in one wall. His guide brought him to stand where he could look through one of the openings at eye level.

He could see, beyond the barrier, another chamber, larger and brighter than his own, and inhabited by what were certainly Earth-descended people. They were not dead, not dying, except perhaps for one man who was stretched out on the deck, and seemed to be wounded somewhere about the eyes. The rest were just sitting and lying about in attitudes of dejection and defeat.

But the last thing Huang Gun had ever expected to meet in this environment was people wearing the distinctive uniforms of Twin Worlds military cadets.

EIGHTEEN

Huang Gun had slept soundly in
his strange, new environment, so soundly that upon awakening he
wondered if he had been given some kind of sleeping potion. He
felt curiously at peace.

The chamber in which he had arrived at this comfortable
state was quite dark, the only faint light coming from the series of
half a dozen eye-sized holes penetrating the wall opposite the
large cell's single door.

He could hear the voices of the people in the next room,
beyond the perforated wall, but he did not want to look at them
again. So he sat down and meditated.

*When we set out to explore the Galaxy, a couple of hundred
years ago, we did not realize that it was ultimately ruled by
Death. . . . How could we have known that, then? We were all caught
up in our little lives, thinking that our little world was all that mattered. Wondering, hoping, trying to find the right way to live.*

*. . . what we have learned finally, after much pain and suf-
fering, is that there is no proper way to live. No honorable way, no*

way consistent with the truth. We must come to grips with the fact that life itself is the great mistake. . . .

His meditations were interrupted. A machine had entered, and was beckoning to him, bidding him come closer to the perforated wall. The irregular row of neatly bored holes ranged in diameter from about one centimeter to about two. Most of them were slightly below Huang Gun's eye level when he was standing.

His guardian was silently indicating one of the holes. As if something might be happening, on the other side, that it wanted him to see.

The executioner looked. The young cadets, or most of them, were on their feet, and moving desultorily about. Obviously his new master wanted him to observe, and listen to them.

On the bridge of the flagship there was a discussion, not very productive, about the possibility of devising new tactics.

The flagship's display systems, like everything else aboard, had taken something of a beating. Suddenly—temporarily, erratically—the central holostage on *Morholt*'s bridge was occupied by a rush of moving recorded images, little dots and assorted other symbols, green for Twin Worlds and red for the supposedly aggressive Huveans. In a moment Radigast realized that the display represented the swirling choreography for some old maneuvers.

Taken by surprise at the appearance of these relics, he wiped them away with a savage gesture of his hand.

Gregor had resumed his old position in the acceleration couch immediately at the admiral's right. "What was that?"

"Nothing real, just some motherless battle plans. We made what seemed a huge bloody number of different ones, for the war we once thought we were going to fight."

The admiral went on: "Those were the days. Somehow we

were stuck on the idea that we'd be fighting some relatively reasonable opponent—like another fleet. Bloody quaint, what?"

Subordinates were trying to get the admiral's attention. In a moment he was giving more orders for the remnant of the Twin Worlds fleet—augmented by the horde of scouts recalled from the outer defenses—to deploy itself in a last hopeless attempt to fight off the berserker.

Gregor knew without being told that the picture on the stage was once more showing him a version of present reality. Those hundreds of scoutships made an impressive image, but the admiral had no need to tell him that they were all but useless against a foe that beat off battleships like so many irritating insects.

Whatever else might happen, they were going to have to try to defend their home.

In a few moments, Admiral Radigast had called up another inventory on his holostage. This one showed all the fixed military installations in the outer reaches of the Twin Worlds system, facilities occupying a dozen or so airless satellites of several dim and frozen planets. So far the berserker had been totally ignoring those distant worlds, as if it were well aware that the opportunities for killing out that way would be strictly limited.

Nor were those bases going to be of much use in repairing damaged warships. All the docks capable of handling big ships were in the inner system, on natural or artificial satellites of the two home worlds. Those in orbit around Prairie had already been destroyed.

Radigast's memory told him what the situation in the outer system was, but he had called for a listing in hopes that this time his memory would be proven faulty.

Angrily he complained to the world in general. "There's not even a bloody docking space out there—not a single one that'll take a motherless dreadnought. What were we thinking of when we built like that?"

Gregor saw him spit out his chewing pod, then from the corner of his eye caught a glimpse of the housekeeping device that snatched the offending object out of the air before it could stain the deck, and slurp it away for disposal. Probably the housekeeping system had adapted to the admiral's habits, and had a unit stationed near him constantly when he was awake.

Radigast's latest inventory did indicate that two smaller docking spaces were available at one base, on the largest moon of the least remote of the outer planets. This offered a spot where repairs could be made that were impossible to carry out on a ship in deep space, because they necessitated shutting down vital onboard systems. These were facilities designed and used primarily for training, and for repair and maintenance work on the ships and machines patrolling the outer reaches of the system. No human crews were on them now.

The admiral gave orders for a couple of his destroyers, seriously battered ships but with their drives still functioning, to get out there and see what they could do about getting themselves back into shape. They were about the only surviving ships he thought could benefit from an interval in airdock. The necessary tools and parts should be stored and available on site.

It might have seemed a futile gesture, but it was something to be done, and he thought it could be some small help to morale. And it stood as a sign to all survivors that they were not on the brink of giving up.

"If anyone in the fleet is thinking along that line, he or she has got a short bloody memory. Certain people on our side have tried that already, and it didn't work."

That sounded to Gregor like an oblique reference to the former president and the executioner, and Gregor frowned, thinking the admiral should not have made it. But no time to worry about that; Radigast was muttering that if the attacker went after his two battered little ships, that would at least give the people on Timber a few hours of breathing space.

Thinking aloud he pondered what, during that time, his own next move should be? Ought he to further divide his remaining fleet, in the face of what was demonstrably a superior force?

Of course the monstrous enemy might just stay where it was, continuing its probing attacks on the planet Timber, while holding most of the planet's communications paralyzed. If it should send some of the small machines it had already used after his two crippled destroyers, why then he, Radigast, could straggle along with his remaining fleet.

"Maybe a couple of motherless battered battleships will be able to give the little ones a fight."

Running down the short list of possibly useful things that could be done with some very limited assets, he came quickly to the next item: before the shooting started up again in earnest, someone should give all the crews an inspiring speech. "I'll have it piped on a short delay to all ships," he concluded, giving Gregor an inquiring look.

The acting president only gave his head a tired shake. To which the admiral replied with a tired nod. Evidently neither of them were ready to attempt that sort of thing just now.

But Gregor, when he had allowed the question to nag him for a few more minutes, began to see inspiring the crew as his inescapable duty.

It was duly announced that the new acting president had something to say to all the crews. The decades of political practice took over, and almost automatically Gregor began to speak. When he stopped talking, three minutes later, he could hardly remember anything he'd said.

———

The admiral was conferring frequently with his engineers, both human and optelectronic. Had *Morholt* reached its present condition through some accidental disaster, Radigast might well have ordered the crew of his flag vessel to abandon ship. But now the idea of doing so barely crossed his mind—even though the dreadnought could barely move, it still retained considerable firepower.

"That is, we still possess what was once considered to be considerable firepower. Though how much good it's likely to do us . . ."

Gregor again felt that he had to say something. He repeated: "Not your fault, Admiral."

"Keep telling me that, Mr. President. Not my motherless fault, no. But it's my bloody responsibility."

Another problem was to find the best way to use the growing swarm of scoutships—the chief military asset the admiral still possessed.

Before he could reach a decision, the enemy tried to take it out of his hands. The berserker, which could hardly fail to be aware of the gathering swarm, launched more destroyer-like killers to probe the loose formation, test it and disrupt it.

The face on the central holostage was that of the captain of one of the remaining dreadnoughts, raising the possibility that he and his crew might soon be forced to abandon ship.

The admiral slammed down a hand; not a very big hand, but it made a big noise and everybody jumped. Including the captain, whose image seemed to lean back as Radigast's leaned forward.

"I'll say it one more bloody time: In case you didn't notice, surrender's already been tried, and it seems that in this war it doesn't work. The next people to raise this suggestion are going to wish they hadn't."

But even as Radigast spoke, he wondered if his duty lay not

in pressing suicidal attacks, but in trying to save the only assets he could save, the remnant of his fleet. It might soon represent the only remaining piece of the Twin Worlds—an exiled fragment with the duty to show and tell the rest of humanity, warn them of the monstrous peril they now faced.

To himself he thought: *Maybe Belgola was right about one thing anyway, even if he did have his head stuffed full of hardware. This fight is hopeless.*

Without even giving the matter much thought, Gregor the diplomat could readily enough call to mind the names of two or three other worlds—in particular those who had also had disputes with Huvea—where orphaned fragments of a Twin Worlds fleet and government might find shelter, and planet-space on which to live their human lives, and where human ears would be grateful for a warning.

There would only be one dream left to live for—that someday his surviving crews and ships, restored to health and strength, would form some key part of a massed human power. On that day, the combined fleets of a score of worlds, with weapons and shielding much improved, would sweep this murderous abomination out of the Galaxy altogether. . . .

Radigast knew the idea of saving what was left of the fleet was something he was going to have to discuss with Gregor, and soon. But not yet. With billions of his people about to be slaughtered on the ground, he couldn't give up on the fight that he was in.

"**Y**es sir. But if the admiral is suggesting we try ramming that monster—well, it's not going to work with this ship. We'll be blown to atoms before we even get close."

"I wasn't suggesting that. I wasn't bloody suggesting anything. I was asking for your motherless ideas."

"I wish we had some to give you, sir."

There came a sudden distraction, in the form of a robot

courier: a new alarm was being sounded, out on the outer defensive perimeter of the Twin Worlds system.

The news hadn't hit them yet, but Radigast was suddenly certain what it was going to be. An exchange of glances went round the circle of human faces, seeking and not finding hope.

What is the very worst thing that could happen at this moment?

NINETEEN

Gregor knew with a sickening certainty what the news was going to be—another unconquerable killing machine, or maybe two, or a dozen of them, had just arrived in system. The possibility had been haunting the back of his mind almost from the time of the first fighting, but until this moment he had managed to keep from dwelling on the prospect, because there was nothing he could do about it.

The shock of new fear did not have time to take its full effect before it was relieved. The people in the stretched-thin force of scoutships still patrolling the outer reaches had been a trifle slow and hesitant about making a positive identification, but now they were being definite and the news was good. This latest arrival in system was certified as an unarmed vessel of the Earth-descended League. Only a small, familiar transport, conspicuously marked in such a way as to be unmistakably neither Huvean or Twin Worlds.

Radigast in his own relief was grunting and bubbling with obscenities. "Bloody motherless civilians poking their noses in.

What in all the hells do they want? What we need are fleets, not cookie-pushers."

Gregor, his long experience with the details of protocol coming to the fore, had recognized the insignia before anyone else. His own relief was so intense that he felt weakened.

"Admiral, I don't think any other world could possibly be responding yet to our calls for military help. I expect these people have come here not knowing that we're under attack. They must want to talk to me."

"To you?" Radigast didn't get it.

"Oh, they won't yet know I'm acting president—they'll find that staggering news. But there was going to be another peace conference, remember? It's understandable if you've forgotten—I almost have. This ship will be carrying a delegation of my fellow diplomats, colleagues from neutral worlds—possibly including one Huvean—who have grown tired of waiting for me to come to them."

Moments after materializing in normal space, the ship, as if running routinely on automatic pilot—which it probably was— had set a course in the general direction of the inner planets. The vessel had made progress in that direction for two or three minutes before anyone aboard appeared to notice what had happened to the planet Prairie—the next thing to catch the newcomers' attention was doubtless the glowing evidence of battle in space.

After another minute or two, the Council vessel drastically changed course. Having evidently identified the remnants of the Twin Worlds fleet, it was easing closer to the battered *Morholt,* sending repeated signals of identification as the distance rapidly diminished.

Presently their ship had come close enough to Radigast's battered flagship for a quick radio talk, and the appearance of unfamiliar new faces on each other's holostages.

The admiral got on his communicator. "Aye, come alongside,

we have to talk. This is the Twin Worlds flagship *Morholt*, Admiral Radigast commanding. We're not about to waste a shot on you."

The voice at the other end, sounding somewhat shell-shocked, murmured something about powerful responses in support of peace.

Radigast was in no mood to be especially diplomatic. "If it's peace you're after, I'd say you're a little bit late, and in the wrong motherless place."

Some of the important people on the approaching transport were accompanied by their personal staffs. Except for the Huvean delegate, they came as representatives of planets neutral in the looming crisis, most of them quite distant.

Gregor got the impression that at first the Huvean delegate had balked at this visit, but then had decided to go along, lest the conference take place without him.

One of the delegates—Lady Constance, who came from old Earth itself, and was granted a certain prestige simply because of that—said that one more visitor remained to be introduced to the Twin Worlds people—one who was not of the Earth-descended lineage. The Carmpan, Ninety-first Diplomat, had been accredited to the conference only as an observer. The limitation was at her own request, because she wanted no more intimate connection than that.

The unearthly shape of Ninety-first Diplomat filled the image space on the holostage, which readjusted its scope to accommodate one more figure. This being had decided to brave discomfort and emerge from her cabin's special environment. Gregor had seen Carmpan before, but few of his present shipmates had. Earth-descended people always tended to stare at their first contact. (Whether the Carmpan was staring back was difficult for those unacquainted with Carmpan anatomy to determine.)

The admiral, too, had seen Carmpan before. His interest in peaceful beings was strictly limited—but he had heard impressive things regarding some of the rare events called Prophecies of Probability. And this Carmpan was arrayed in the special way, loaded with exotic gear, and even small exotic animals, that meant a prophecy was to be expected.

From her head and body, ganglions of wire and fiber stretched to make connections with small items of equipment fastened to the web or harness that served as dress and decoration, and to small Carmpan animals secured in the same way. The Carmpan Prophets of Probability were said to be half mystics, half cold mathematicians.

Gregor had heard it said that the strain on a Carmpan prophet in action was always immense, and the percentage of accuracy in the prophecy was always high. The stresses involved were said to more topological than nervous or electrical, which was something that most Earth-descended folk had never come close to understanding.

The Carmpan, when the Earth delegate asked her if she wanted to depart for home at once to report on these startling new developments, spoke clearly in the common language. "It is very likely that I shall die before I get anywhere near my home again." The unearthly mouth, located near mid-body, chopped out the words, which still rose ringingly. The arm-like appendages pointed, though few in the audience were able to interpret the gestures.

The war that they had blundered into was so vastly different from the war they had been trying to prevent that for a time they could not tell how to react.

Their images on the battered flagship's holostage stared out at the bloody and bandaged Twin Worlds warriors, as if confronting some strange aliens who might belong to another species altogether.

Quickly the admiral and his aides sketched out for the newcomers the incredible events of the last few days. To help the visiting neutrals grasp the situation, they were shown on their own holostage recordings of unbelievable disaster.

The ED humans who came from worlds not yet sucked into the whirlpool of war, having come here to dissuade their fellow Earth-descended from fratricidal conflict, were of course stunned to find the actual state of affairs in this system so different from anything they had imagined.

The Lady Constance, delegate from Earth, asked: "How can we stop this?"

The admiral had a quick answer ready. "Maybe you can suggest a way, my fellow humans. But don't advise me to sue for peace. You can take my motherless word for it, that's been tried."

The visiting diplomats were aghast to see what shape the dreadnought was in, and at least one of them offered to take survivors aboard their own ship.

The admiral was cold and grim. "Sorry. My functioning survivors are very much needed at their battle stations. That's where they have to stay."

The Huvean delegate, Zarnesti, a small, pop-eyed man, his skin a jaundiced shade from some chronic disorder, made little effort to conceal his satisfaction at the thought of Twin Worlds death and suffering—but he seemed to doubt that things had gone as badly for them as they claimed. His chief concern was for the Huvean hostages, and he was quick with questions and demands regarding them; they must be handed over at once, or the Twin Worlders would be made to suffer severe consequences.

But the great majority of the neutral delegates were compassionate. "If we can be of any humanitarian assistance—"

Admiral Radigast with savage politeness expressed his formal thanks for the offer, and in the same breath firmly and profanely refused it.

Then he told the diplomats: "Nor am I inviting any of you aboard my ship. All but one of you'd be quite welcome, except that we may have to clear for action at any moment. Not to mention that we're very busy with damage control."

Nothing had been done to pretty up the image on the holostage. Doubtless Radigast's virtual visitors could see, in the background, his damping field projectors going full force, fending off a hell of heat and radioactivity threatening to push down one of the corridors leading to the bridge, coming from a spot where one of the dreadnought's main structural members was being slowly consumed in an induced reaction. One of the berserker's slower acting weapons was still at work, no means having been found as yet to dig it loose, or quench the nuclear fires it had brought aboard. Prairie's ground defenses had doubtless launched several similar devices at their foe, but there was no sign yet that any had been effective.

Gregor had been standing by, and did his best to smoothly take over the conversation, saying the admiral was busy. And anyway, this was his, Gregor's, job.

Introducing himself as acting president certainly got their attention. They were exchanging worried glances, and some were ready to start fretting about protocol.

Gregor tried to be calm and reassuring. "Respected colleagues, unhappy circumstances have propelled me into the position of head of the Twin Worlds government. I think, as you look around you, none of you will accuse me of seizing power—power is one of the many things the president of this system no longer has.

"I am sure you will understand that I cannot join you in a conference. My place is here, in this system, now and for years to come. Also I literally have no deputy, no alternate, to send."

Several delegates expressed their sympathy.

The Carmpan suddenly wanted to physically board the *Morholt*. When difficulties were pointed out, she insisted—a brief visit would be enough. The admiral had his doubts, and could not guarantee the delegate's safety; but he and the Twin Worlds cause had nothing to lose.

The transfer was quickly carried out.

The Huvean in his remarks made only passing reference to the unfortunate people of the Twin Worlds system. He went on to suggest that as the Twin Worlds government had effectively ceased to exist, the system might henceforward be considered as a colony of Greater Huvea.

Gregor diplomatically chose to ignore what had just been said. Looking over the Carmpan's shoulder—more accurately, past the place where a shoulder would have been—he caught a glimpse of what Ninety-first Diplomat happened to be writing. Gregor was one of the few ED able to read some of that script. He had even been known to attempt to speak the language.

It seemed to him that now would be a good time for another effort. Gregor forced his throat and tongue into making an approximation of the correct sounds. "You know what it is, then, this monstrous thing?"

A liquid thing that he knew to be an eye was looking at him. The Carmpan mouth moved. "I know. Gregor, you should speak in your own language."

Gratefully he relaxed into the common tongue. "What is it?"

"One of your own people, descended from the tribe and clan of Earth, has called it a berserker."

"Ahh." He paused. "And the individual who said that is—?"

"Is still living, as I speak. But he, with others, is in very dangerous captivity. More about him I ought not to try to say."

"I thank you for what you have said already. 'Berserker.' Yes, that seems to fit."

"There are in the Galaxy—or there were—other branches of humanity, who have given it other names, words neither of us could pronounce, that I could probably not even hear. But the meaning in each case is close."

Gregor pondered briefly. Then he asked: "How long have you known of the existence of this—this berserker-thing?"

"Insofar as any answer I gave to your question was true, it would also be deceptive."

"But it—this berserker—it is not Huvean."

"No, it certainly is not."

And the Prophecy officially began:

Someone else asked: "Is this, this—thing—prolonging the agony just to make us suffer?"

"No. It is utterly indifferent to your suffering, except as it might advance its purpose."

"And that is—?"

"Your death—and mine—and the death of everything in the Galaxy that lives. It might have sterilized Timber, as it did Prairie, hours or days ago; but it is prolonging the process because it seeks to learn more about Earth-descended humanity." A good Carmpan answer. "Also it is using the time for self-repair."

"How badly is it hurt?"

"That I cannot tell."

"Is there anything or anyone alive aboard?"

"There are living ED in two prison cages."

Radigast for one did not seem the least awed by a Carmpan presence, and as usual he was blunt. "Ma'am, what can you tell us about our enemy?"

"All I can tell you will be in the Prophecy," was the gentle answer.

A new report, from the most forward elements of the fleet, arrived on the admiral's private little holostage, a display inside his helmet, the one no one else got to look at without a special dispensation. Radigast almost gratefully tore himself away from diplomacy to deal with it.

The great berserker that was ravaging the Twin Worlds had

just been observed to have launched a robot courier of its own. This device accelerated swiftly to a distance from the sun where a c-plus jump would be a reasonably safe gamble—and from there, only a matter of minutes later, the berserker courier jumped away.

It had to be assumed that it was carrying word to some entity associated with the great machine—perhaps to the world where it had been created.

Gregor asked one of the observers: "I don't suppose we have any way of tracking that—?"

The officer nodded. "You're right, sir. Quite impossible for us to know where it's headed."

"Even if somehow tracking it would lead to those who built our enemy?"

"The ones the Carmpan could not describe."

"Could not—or would not. Yes."

"Or to those who might be currently giving it its orders—sorry, can't be done."

After a moment, Gregor said softly: "If it has living masters, I can't imagine what they're like."

"I can. I've met a few motherless people who could qualify—the type who are good for scaring away nightmares."

"—if it has none, then perhaps the trail would lead to others of its kind."

"That is not the trail I would be currently inclined to follow. But—it would be my dream to do it someday."

Several devices, under the control of different human authorities, and at different distances from the event, recorded the berserker courier's departure, within minutes or hours after it took place.

The admiral was notified, and so were the assembled diplomats. But few people, military or civilian, paid much attention to the observation at the time.

The population of the Twin Worlds system—and their human

visitors, both peaceful and bellicose—had more than enough other things to worry about.

The shocked delegates were still deliberating what to do next, when word came that the skeleton force that now constituted the solar system's sole outer defense was registering new intrusions at more than a hundred places, practically simultaneously.

There could be no mystery about this intrusion. The main Huvean battle fleet had arrived in system.

"**N**o doubt about it, sir."

Radigast stared numbly at the far-flung battle array, its extremities only gradually, at mere light speed over planetary distances, coming into view on his display. It might be that as much as an hour would pass, after the fast courier had brought him word of the new intrusion, before he would be able to see it all. He thought the full array might look somewhat larger, if anything, than his own fleet had once appeared.

"Thank God!" The words came out of him spontaneously, and quite sincerely.

"Sir?"

"Just offering up a bloody prayer of thanks. That at least it's not another berserker. Whatever humanity does in this system now won't be entirely up to me."

A robot courier, transmitting a continuous request for a truce, was immediately dispatched to seek out the Huvean flagship— more massive than the *Morholt,* if not quite as long—carrying a terse summary of the events of recent days.

The message consisted for the most part of a bald recitation of the terrible events of the past few days, and concluded with an appeal to the Huveans to remember the humanity they shared with the people of the Twin Worlds.

It was signed by Acting President Gregor.

———

Minutes later, that message had been carried by Delegate Zarnesti to the bridge of the dreadnought *Mukunda*. There Zarnesti had ceremoniously placed it in the hands of First Spacer Homasubi, commander of the Huvean fleet, who, as he read, sat rocking slightly in his ornately decorated combat couch.

Around the first spacer, in this smoothly quiet and undamaged space, the ship's crew was performing activities essentially similar to those that went on aboard the *Morholt,* in an environment much like that (except for the absence of damage here) in which his Twin Worlds counterpart had spent the last several standard days.

The current atmosphere aboard the *Mukunda* was one of nervous letdown. The Huveans of course had come in system on full alert, with weapons set on hair-trigger, prepared for immediate skirmishing, or even for an all-out battle with Twin Worlds defenders. Their fleet had materialized in an aggressive combat formation.

But as the seconds ticked by, and the reality of the situation before them sank in, it was the turn of their high command, led by First Spacer Homasubi, to be struck almost dumb with astonishment, taken aback and thrown off balance by what they actually saw.

The first spacer's face remained impassive as he perused the document, obviously reading it more than once. "Incredible," was his one-word comment, when he put the paper down.

Zarnesti, seated on a kind of visitor's stool, an amenity the more spartan *Morholt* did not afford, nodded quickly. "Truly incredible, indeed, First Spacer. I have read it, of course. . . ."

"Of course. Your assessment?"

"Frankly, my first inclination is to not believe a word of it. I suspect an elaborate deception."

Homasubi was known to be generally reserved and formal in attitude and appearance, commanding his followers from an eminence rather than inspiring personal loyalty as Radigast somehow managed to do. But the Huvean crews followed orders very effectively.

The first spacer asked the diplomat: "Let me hear your analysis of the message then. What explanation can you provide?"

Zarnesti remained determined that this whole business must be some kind of Twin Worlds trick.

"Possibly they have suffered an actual attack, but if so it will only make them desperate, therefore all the more untrustworthy. Their chief aim must now be to involve us somehow, to our detriment."

"What do you advise?"

"First Spacer Homasubi, before doing anything else you must demand the surrender of the Twin Worlds fleet. The ships must be brought under our control, the officers imprisoned."

The expression on the first spacer's face changed very little, under the impact of this civilian telling him what he must do. But several of his close associates were suddenly holding their collective breath.

The political officer, unaware of having made a grievous blunder, clung stubbornly to his convictions. Indicating the message, he repeated: "This has to be some kind of deception. A Twin Worlds trick."

Homasubi slightly raised one eyebrow. "I await your further explanation of this extremely ingenious trickery."

"The details, First Spacer, may well be hard to establish. These people are cunning almost beyond belief."

"So I have been told."

"It is so, I assure you. Their admiral is a loathsome person, incredibly crude and savage—"

"I have been told that also."

"—it is the truth! And before we even burden our ears with any explanation they attempt to offer, you *must* demand to know what has happened to our heroic hostages."

One of the officers standing at attention nearby made a slight noise in his throat, indicative of inward strain. No one seemed to notice. Homasubi did not respond to the delegate's statement, beyond a slight nod. This politician had not yet learned how the first spacer reacted to being told what he must do, on the bridge of his own flagship, by a mere guest, however high the outsider's rank.

But for the time being Homasubi let the transgression pass. He was nodding, his face grimmer than it had been. "Yes, the hostages. Of course. I will begin serious inquiries at once."

After a careful review of the situation by his own trusted observers, Homasubi went over the facts in his own mind.

First of all, there could be no doubt that planet Prairie had actually been devastated, with chilling thoroughness and efficiency. Talk of trickery was rubbish. The world had been sterilized as if by some painstaking medical procedure. That shocking truth was confirmed by a close look by Huvean scouts and probes, including spectroscopic analysis of the heavy cloud that enshrouded the doomed world.

And the violent murder of a planet was not the only surprise. The powerful Twin Worlds fleet had somehow been reduced to a mangled remnant, the bulk of that feared and respected power vaporized, nothing left but traces of heavy space combat, slowly expanding faint clouds of gas and dust and debris, scattered halfway across the inner system. Spectroscopic analysis of the clouds seemed to confirm their origin.

Homasubi had thought himself and his fleet ready to deal with any eventuality—but he had certainly not prepared himself or his crews for any combination of circumstances like this.

As soon as he had grasped the essentials of the situation, and before doing anything else, the Huvean commander dispatched a fast courier home, outlining the incredible circumstances he faced, and asking for guidance from the very highest levels. In dealing with a situation so unprecedented, the mere opinion of a single civilian peace negotiator, however elevated his rank might be, was not going to be sufficient.

"I of course intend to vigorously pursue the matter of the hostages, but beyond that, I confess I am uncertain."

"First Spacer, I see no room here for uncertainty. It seems to me we can hardly do anything but demand total, abject surrender from whatever remaining Twin Worlds authority it is possible to find."

"Perhaps. But what will that gain us?" Homasubi called up the berserker's image. "And what is our attitude to be with regard to this intruder?"

"An attitude of cordiality, I should think. It has accomplished our purpose for us, has it not?" The political officer smiled faintly. "Of course we must not be lulled into carelessness. I will talk again with this man who claims to be the acting president."

Gregor, beginning a dialogue with the first spacer, was able to give something like a firsthand report on the subject of hostages. "As far as I know, all are alive, and on the surface of Timber. When I spoke with them, face to face, all were in good health. And in reasonably good spirits, considering their situation. You have seen a copy of my first executive order as president. Believe me, First Spacer, if it was in my power to do so, I'd gladly turn them over to you."

"I must insist upon more definite information. I am instructed to demand assurances that they are in a place of safety."

"Honored sir, I think you can see for yourself that no such place now exists in this solar system. A few hours before the attack fell on Prairie, your people were all safe, held in a deep shelter. As to what may have happened to them since then . . . I have no means of knowing. Our president was in a similar shelter, and he is dead. They must be at least as much at risk as all our other citizens who still survive."

"Your government will be held responsible for whatever may have happened to them." Homasubi's calm look was more frightening than Zarnesti's bluster.

"Sir, I understand the concern that prompts you to say that. But, as you will have noticed, my government barely exists. Threatening a ghost will do nothing for your own people."

The first spacer was shaking his head. "I am not interested in making threats. You say there is no place of safety within this system. But I say now there is one." He pointed with a long forefinger down at his own deck. "Our people must be brought aboard this ship."

Gregor spread his hands. "The government of Twin Worlds has no objection to that. But we also have no power to accomplish it."

"Huvea is not powerless." And the first spacer went on to propose landing a force of Huvean marines near the Citadel, to find the hostages and bring them out.

Gregor listened with reluctance. "I have no means of stopping you. I will place our communication system, what is left of it, at your disposal. But if you want my opinion, I advise against landing Huvean troops."

"I am listening. Tell me more."

"You might send a thousand elite infantry, I suppose; possibly even ten thousand, if the transports in your fleet are carrying that many. But in the current chaotic state of affairs down there, whatever force you send will probably be engulfed by a million or more of Timber's citizens, many of whom are blaming you for the attack. They will be pleased to confront an enemy with whom they can at least come to grips, one built on a scale that is no more than human. There will be very little I can do about it, given the ruined state of our communications."

Homasubi decided to delay any landing attempt until he could learn more.

———

Meanwhile the berserker had obviously become aware of the arrival of the Huvean fleet. Now it was sending one of its auxiliary machines—surprisingly, bearing some signal recognizable by humans as a flag of truce—to the vicinity of First Spacer Homasubi's flagship (which it seemed to have no trouble in picking out, among several other vessels of the same approximate size and similar configuration), even before the first spacer could organize any marine expedition to the surface of Timber.

The thing came close enough to allow the people aboard the fleet to have a convenient radio conversation with it, but it slowed as it approached. It did not appear to be bristling with weapons.

"If it's as alien as it seems, how would it know about truce symbols?"

"We have reason to believe it's taken some of our people prisoners, First Spacer. Possibly as many as a hundred."

"I see. And they are closely cooperating with its efforts?"

"I have said that they were taken prisoner."

Suddenly the berserker device, using a strange squawking voice, hailed the Huvean flagship.

The Twin Worlds people were astonished. It had never communicated with them.

"Do we reply, sir?" the first spacer's communications officer asked him.

"Yes, of course."

After identifying himself, Homasubi demanded that the intruder do the same.

This time he got an immediate answer, as if there had never been any difficulty about communication.

The berserker still spoke the common tongue in a scratchy mixture of what sounded like recorded syllables. The words had an ugly sound, but their meaning was quite clear. The berserker was identifying itself as an ally of the Huvean state, and said it looked forward to a long and mutually beneficial relationship.

TWENTY

The sounds, the animal-like noises that Du Prel made in his pain, were starting to drive Lee crazy. He knew the man couldn't help it, having had his artificial eye ripped out, but the noise was driving Lee crazy just the same.

How long had it been going on? Hours, days? All means of telling time, except by what went on in their own bodies, had been taken from them. A little longer, and Lee would be ready to go over and strangle Du Prel, just to shut him up.

One after another, several of the victim's other shipmates had been going to him, not to choke him to death, not yet anyway, but to do what little they could in the way of offering support. Cusanus had held his head in her lap for a time, but presently he writhed away out of her grasp, and the only result was that she had some blood on her coverall.

Meanwhile the machines did nothing to help their victim, nothing to cause further injury. What they seemed to be doing was observing the man's reactions and those of his fellow prisoners. They waited, silent as so many doorposts and almost as still. Lee assumed they were taking optelectronic notes of every detail of their prisoners' behavior. Lee would bet that the machines were also taking note of how very little the life-units were able to accomplish in the way of giving help. If one of the victim's companions snapped and tried to put the fellow out of his misery, they would note that too.

It seemed that Zochler was getting close. He turned to the nearest machine and shouted: "This man needs medical attention!"

No answer. The enemy robots only stood listening, waiting, as impassive as the prison's walls.

Getting up to pace again, looking restlessly around, Lee wondered, not for the first time, why one wall of their prison had a row of holes pierced in it at approximately eye level.

There were times when it seemed to Lee they had already been locked up for years in this nightmare dungeon. But of course that was crazy. Even in his saner moments, he had to believe that it was many days.

He, like most of the men in the group, had been clean-shaven when disaster struck. But now he could feel that his beard had sprouted into a thick stubble, and he saw the same on other faces.

Even murder and captivity, even what was happening to Du Prel, were not the worst of it. Hanging over them all was the fear that disaster had fallen on the inhabited planets, that would be consistent with everything they had heard and seen, and they had not simply been inducted into some lunatic's dream.

What might be taking place on Timber now? That thought must be in every mind, but it seemed that no one wanted to talk about it, here where the machine heard everything.

And what had happened to the fleet? Admiral Radigast must certainly have tried to stop the enemy from reaching Prairie. The cadets had been able to hear only the first fragmentary reports on the space battle—and those reports had not given any cause for optimism.

Ting Wu kept muttering that the Huveans must be behind all this—no one argued with him, but no one spoke up in agreement either. Building a machine like this seemed clearly beyond their capability, or that of any ED world.

At first Lee had thought that it would at least be possible to keep an accurate count of his interrogation sessions. But it seemed he had hardly started trying to keep track before he was unsure whether he had been through three of them or four. Everything blurred together.

He had also experienced some two or three (even there he could not be quite certain) intervals of exhausted sleep, flat on the hard floor of his assigned niche. At other times he had gone back there simply to sit, though no machine had ever ordered him to remain in that place.

Another classmate with whom Lee was growing steadily better acquainted was Cadet Carter Hemphill. The two of them had not hit it off very well during their years of study and training. But this was a different world. Gradually, as the others became convinced that Dirigo was not quite up to his job of cadet leader, they began to look to Hemphill, as if out of some instinct.

Hemphill was a pretty taciturn and sober fellow. His gray eyes could take on a cold, inhuman look, startling in his youthful face.

Du Prel had ceased making noises; but if the past was any guide, he would start up again before many minutes had passed.

Hemphill recommended that they never all gather in a group, that they do the planning that must be done in small groups. That they exchange information with each other frequently, but never in groups of more than three.

Hemphill, sitting down beside Lee, remarked that the machine seemed to be holding at least one additional prisoner—several cadets had caught glimpses, through the holes punctured in the opposite wall, of a staring human eye, and then of a shadowy figure moving about in the space beyond the wall.

"The wall behind me, the one that has what look like peepholes in it—well, it seems that's what they really are. Three people, including me, have at different times caught a glimpse of someone looking through, toward us, from the other side."

Lee couldn't come up with any intelligent comment. He nodded.

Hemphill went on. "All anyone's been able to see of him—or her—is an eye. Looking out at us, then vanishing again."

Lee nodded. That was weird, but he welcomed the information. Having something, anything, to think about was a help in dealing with Du Prel's noises when they started up again. Lee got to his feet, as if for a casual stretch. After taking a random stroll around the room, he walked closer to the perforated wall, getting to a place where he could take a close look at the holes, small spots of darkness. At the moment he could detect no watcher on the other side. The wall was of some composite material. Its thinness, visible at the penetrations, suggested that it was only a crudely improvised partition, not a solid bulkhead. Perhaps the other walls were just as thin. It would be difficult to tell.

Taking his time, Lee completed a rough circle of their dungeon. Eventually he came back to Hemphill. Then he muttered: "If we could somehow shine a light in there—" But that wasn't going to be possible. All the spacesuit helmets, which carried lamps, had been locked away along with the friendly robot.

Feeling sleepy, Lee went back to the niche he was beginning to think of vaguely as his private space, and lay down on the deck. He and the others were presumably free to switch spaces, or make any other mutual accommodation that they liked, but as a rule when people wanted to sleep or use the plumbing, they tended to go back to the spots they had first chosen for themselves.

All the little cells or niches were practically identical. When you put your hand near an unbreakable-looking projection in one wall, cold water ran from it in a steady stream, to gurgle away through a hole in the deck below.

Food was also delivered to the little private niches, by a system of equal simplicity, always in the form of pink-and-green cakes popping out of individual wall chutes at intervals that seemed irregular. The taste of the stuff varied somewhat from one mouthful to the next. In general it was neither good nor bad—at least it was not bad enough to discourage Lee from eating it, when he decided that the new cramping sensation in his gut was probably due to hunger.

The large common room of their dungeon was an odd-shaped space, suggesting that it might originally have served some other purpose—or that it had been installed as an afterthought, just fit in where room happened to be available. All of the niches opened into a common area, high-ceilinged, maybe ten meters wide and three or four times that long. Lee estimated that the glaring lights might be six meters from the hard, metallic deck, and the overhead glare was enough to keep anyone from seeing what forms might occupy the darkness above the lights.

There was just about room enough inside each cell, or niche, for a fairly tall human to stretch out on the floor.

Meanwhile, Lee had the impression that the general dimness of the strange dungeon was beginning to seem a little brighter—he realized that the change was probably only because his eyes had been adapting to the darkness.

But then again, it was possible that the lights were actually being adjusted, for at the same time, the area of excessive brightness began to seem minimally more comfortable, as if those lights had actually dimmed a little.

Gradually, as the hours of their early imprisonment crept by, Lee had allowed himself to be convinced that he was unlikely to be killed in the next few seconds, or even in the next minute. It had come to seem quite possible, even likely, that the odds might favor his survival for another entire hour. Beyond that he could not allow himself to hope, and tried not to think.

Lee talked with his fellow prisoners, one or two at a time, about what the enemy, this unprecedented and unknown enemy, had done to them. They offered each other vague wild guesses on what they thought it was doing, and speculated what it might do next.

They could fairly solidly confirm each other's impressions of what they had been able to see through the cleared ports of their crippled launch. All of them, as they approached it, had caught glimpses of this vast object into which they had been dragged. The mode of its arrival in-system showed that it was capable of interstellar travel. But so far, none of these space-trained captives had sensed up any of the subtle signs in their environment indicating that such a voyage had begun. The cadets kept trying to reassure each other that they were still in the Twin Worlds system.

There were more shadowy sightings, glimpses of what appeared to be a human eye behind one hole or another in the broad partition. Lee finally caught a glimpse of the eye himself. Next time he found himself sitting beside Hemphill, he murmured: "I doubt that it's a Huvean."

"Why?"

Lee sighed. It seemed they were giving up on trying to keep their conversations terse and secret. And why not? "Or, if it is, he or she is only another prisoner like ourselves."

Hemphill seemed almost to be enjoying this. "You don't believe our mystery person back there could be the one who's running this whole show? Actually I don't either, but I'd like to hear your reasons."

"Look, if I were running this whole show, I'd want somewhat posher quarters for myself. Instead of living in darkness, depending on a few holes in a partition to give me light, I'd want some electricity."

Someone else put in: "It would offer a more efficient way to spy on your prisoners."

"Right. For that purpose, I'd want an elaborate audio-video system. That shouldn't be too hard to arrange, amid all these cubic kilometers of elaborate machinery—also, I'd spend a little money to give my robots something closer to human voices."

"Whoever—whatever—is actually in charge, doesn't seem to agree with your priorities."

One or two of the bolder cadets tried calling through the partition, to the nameless one who lurked beyond. But only silence answered.

It was hard for people to establish a routine, when the only demands made on them seemed to come at random intervals. It was the same way with their supply of food, and they had been deprived of any artificial way of telling time.

The volume of space devoted to the care and feeding of prisoners, or at least that part of the space actually visible to the captives themselves, was the size of a large house, but still only an insignificant part of the thousands of cubic kilometers making up the great machine's enormous bulk.

From the brief look they had been able to get at their monstrous captor as they were dragged toward it in the launch, the cadets had got a visual impression of huge size. But without any means of accurately judging the scale, their individual opinions varied widely.

"I'd say it's as big as a dreadnought."

"Nowhere near that size."

"However big it is, it's big enough."

The other captives continued their pointless-seeming argument about the size of the thing.

"I tell you, it's something like fifty motherless kilometers long, five times the length of a battleship. And it's not skinny."

Those who had allowed themselves to be convinced were marveling. "It must have field generators, power supplies, as big as those Prairie and Timber have in their ground defenses."

In the semidarkness obtaining throughout most of the dungeon, it was impossible to see all twenty of the niches from any one position. The look of the place, the zigzag construction of some of its walls, suggested that somewhere around the next corner it might offer a place to hide—but of course it never did.

When two or more prisoners began to talk together on any subject, they tended to instinctively keep their voices low, although fully aware that this was doubtless wasted effort. If a machine like this one wanted to listen to anything happening inside it, it doubtless would. There was no sign that anyone or anything was listening, but naturally you had to assume that that was so.

One of the prisoners was saying: "Of course, there could be another dungeon, maybe bigger than this one, somewhere aboard this—this thing."

And another put in: "Or there could be fifty more; it's huge enough."

"And there could also be a merry-go-round, and a pool table and snack bar; what's the use of speculating?"

When it came Hemphill's turn to be taken away for interrogation, he was gone longer than the average—or maybe it only seemed longer, to Lee and some of the others. When he got back, he reported having been questioned repetitiously, and at considerable length about his early life and background—something that most prisoners had not experienced.

Then of course the interrogator had gone on to the usual technical matters. "What will you tell me about your fleet?" it squeaked and quavered at him.

"I will tell you whatever you force me to tell you. Nothing of my own free will."

"Lies will be punished."

"Will you recognize the truth when you hear it?"

"I will."

"Then you must already know the truth. You will not need to hear it from me."

When finally a machine scooped up the slowly dying Du Prel in its arms and carried him away, still moaning and half delirious, no one could go with him—Cusanus tried, putting her hand on Du Prel's arm. But the robot just kept walking, as if she were not there, until her arm was knocked free by the edge of doorway as it stalked through with its burden. In another moment, Du Prel was gone, out of sight and out of hearing.

Lee breathed a silent prayer of thanks, and a plea that the noise was never coming back.

Lee had not voiced any estimates or guesses regarding the size of the thing that held them prisoner. But in his intervals of sleep there came strange dreams in which darkness and echoes, unfamiliarity and the queasiness of shaky gravity, made it seem that their prison might be infinite.

He had a dream in which he had to watch it swallowing up the Galaxy.

These visions alternated, in the infrequent intervals when he could sleep, with images of scenery innocent and green, not nightmarish at all.

The world of the executioner was notably different. On awakening in his new environment, he had been given a private tour, while still being kept in isolation, except for the visual contact afforded by the peepholes.

This new room was much like his first cell except that it was dark. A row of bright dots, ahead of him at eye level, marked the position of another wall. Little spears of light came through the observation holes from the room of living prisoners, perpetually illuminated. Together these small lights cured the gloom of his own cell, enough to let him see his way to food and water.

Faintly, from beyond the barrier, he could hear human voices.

The machine had asked him if he wanted clothing. When he said he did, it opened a large storage bin and offered a selection, enough choices to satisfy almost any human taste. A few of the clothes Huang Gun first touched were slightly torn, some spotted with stains of what he supposed was probably blood. None looked exactly new. There were men's, women's, children's garments all mixed together, as if it might have captured and looted a large transport ship, or rifled a large storehouse down on Timber. He chose plain, simple garments from the pile.

When he had dressed himself, it also asked him if the food was satisfactory.

"I care very little about food. I eat to keep my strength. So I can do . . . whatever is right for me to do."

As soon as the machine had put him into the larger cell, darkened except for the perforations in one wall, it sternly ordered him not to respond to any attempt at communication by the badlife beyond the barrier.

He nodded vigorously. "Of course. I will watch, as you command; but have nothing to do with them."

"You will have something to do with them, when I command it."

"Oh. Yes. Of course."

"You will have to do with testing them. With freeing them of the sickness that is life."

"I will," he said at once. "Of course. I will." He closed his eyes, feeling a pang of inner, secret, silent joy. He was going to get to be the executioner after all.

Then it had commanded him, just as fiercely, to report to it whatever he might see the badlife do.

He thought: *With all its machines, it could certainly watch them more thoroughly than I can. It probably does. But it is testing me. I will do my best.*

"Your first task is to observe," the machine reminded him in a whisper. From somewhere it produced a spacesuit and a helmet. He had been brought in naked—now he might need a suit, just to attach the helmet so he could wear it properly. So far as Huang Gun knew about such things, it seemed a standard military space-suit; no doubt the enemy had captured it somewhere.

His god said to him: "Again I command you: Watch them. Listen. At the proper time I will have further orders for you."

Wearing the helmet made it slightly harder to look through the peepholes. But when he turned up the sensitivity on the hel-met's airmikes, he could sometimes hear what they were saying, over there. So far, none of it sounded interesting.

Another advantage of having the helmet on was that it, his chosen master, could speak to him without being heard by any of the people next door, and he could answer. He saw no reason to believe that the people in the other room would be friendly to him if he and they were somehow to get together.

Soon he was spending almost all his waking hours at one or another of the spy holes, observing. He had dragged his mattress pad into the peephole room, and a silent machine brought food and water to his post. So far he had not learned much of interest; he was learning the names of the badlife, but it was hard to see how that would be of any use.

A time came when he saw one of the women, the one they called Sunbula, enter the niche where she usually stretched out to sleep, no more than five meters from the spot where Huang Gun was watching. The other people were mainly at the far end of the common space. Quickly and deftly, the woman began to unfasten her coverall. The executioner realized she intended to try to wash herself in the trickle of cold water that ran unendingly in her niche as it did in all the others, and in Huang Gun's private cell.

When the woman peeled off her coverall, she was wearing nothing under it. Her body moving under the running water was young and firm and healthy. The executioner groaned and tore himself away from the sight.

No more than a few minutes could have passed when next one of the mobile machines approached him through the gloom of his dark cell. It found him sitting slumped on the deck with his back against the partition, staring into darkness.

"Why do you cease to watch the badlife?" Its voice scraped at him through his helmet's communicator.

He covered his faceplate with both hands. "Because . . ."

It waited.

He could feel, somehow, that it was still waiting for his answer. He put both hands down on the deck, and opened his eyes wide. "I ceased to watch because I was looking at too much life. It is painful to watch life. It is especially painful to see, to be forced to think about, the means by which more life-units are created."

The answer must have been acceptable, for the machine did not kill him, but only turned and moved away.

The food extruded from the wall at intervals in his compartment looked like the same stuff he saw the other prisoners eating. And his plumbing arrangements were identical to theirs. Once, repelled by the odor of his own life, now long unwashed, he started to bathe in his chill, private stream, and the image of the woman who had been doing the same thing rose up vividly.

Life, with all its snares and entanglements. The rewards that never lasted, that always disappointed in the end. And all the longings ending in defeat whether they were denied or satisfied.

When he closed his eyes and sought the oblivion of sleep, the vision sprang to life again: Sunbula's body, wet and gleaming, shivering in the sudden shock of cold.

Huang Gun had known for a long time, it seemed to him that he had always known, women were never truly satisfactory. Not that he had ever had, or had ever really wanted, any broad experience of women—or of men. Or of children, for that matter.

It seemed to him very strange that he should be thinking of children now.

Life is a disease of matter, the master had told him, and Huang Gun found himself ready to believe. It was as if he had known that for a long time, but had never been able to express it in the precisely proper words. One simple thought, that seemed to provide an explanation for all the wearisome mysteries of human existence.

Failure and decay, those were the two chief attributes of life. Death always won. And death endured.

Almost always one or two of the man-shaped machines were on hand in the prisoners' quarters, usually standing motionless somewhere in the common room. Their awkward-looking grippers, the size of human arms and hands, were hanging motionless most of the time.

After losing two of their number before leaving the launch, none of the cadets had ever tried to resist the machines—except for Du Prel's occasional delirious struggles, which the robots had ignored. The memory was all too clear of how Ting Wu and Kardec had been torn to pieces without warning.

Most of the time, the guardian machines stood as motionless as coatracks. For many hours, Lee had seen them move only to escort people to interrogation and bring them back.

In general the prisoners tried to keep as far from their guardians as was practical.

———

At least one chronic argument had been settled, to the satisfaction of all but one or two of the prisoners. "All right, there is no live crew on this thing. No people, except for us—and that human eyeball living in the next compartment."

"Or, if other people are here, we're never going to see them. They're letting their robots do the processing—we're just the meat in the factory."

"All right, assume it's all machines. But they're not independent. There's one master computer, somewhere on board, controlling all these units, managing this whole show."

"Can't argue with that."

"Is it listening to everything that we all say? Listening all the time?"

"We have to assume it is. And also watching everything we do."

A third prisoner put it: "What does it matter, what it sees or hears? It doesn't need to spy on us."

Repressed anger was starting to find its way out, though this was of course the wrong time and place for it to show. "Of course it matters. If it didn't want to learn from us, why does it ask us questions?"

The despairing one, gone into some realm of thought beyond argument, shook his head. "It doesn't have to study us to defeat us. It already knows how to do that. All it needs to know, and more. It studies us now because it wants our souls, not just our bodies."

"Oh, I don't know." Hemphill, as usual, sounded calm and rational. "There'll be a lot of detailed information about our bodies it'll want to have—and even more on our behavior. How we think, and how fast, and how we move. How much oxygen we need to function, how much water. What temperatures will quickly kill. How many g's it takes to crush a human body when the cushions are turned off. What will make us fight, and what will make us run away. How determined we are to try to help our wounded."

The first let something like disgust sound in his voice. "You make it sound like some kind of a god."

Hemphill considered. "No. No, never that." He sounded as if the suggestion might have missed the mark by only a little bit.

"Then what?"

"There were fallen angels, too."

TWENTY-ONE

As the hours went by, stretching into days—how many days, Lee was becoming afraid to try to guess—the conviction slowly grew in him that the great war machine was paying less and less attention to its prisoners. He supposed the time might come when it would lose all interest, and easily enough dispose of them by cutting off their air.

He thought it was speaking to them less and less frequently. And gradually, one at a time, the original guardian machines, versatile and evidently designed for combat, had been replaced by comparatively clumsy-looking maintenance devices.

When Lee mentioned this fact to one of his fellow prisoners, sitting beside him, Zochler said quietly: "And there's only one on duty now. There's only been one, for the last—well, say for several hours. Before that, there were usually two."

Lee was nodding. "When we were first brought here, there were always three. I remember that quite clearly."

"How long ago was that?"

A silly question, and no point in trying to answer. Lee stroked the growing stubble on his face.

The great hull suddenly moved, slightly but sharply, as if it had hit a small bump in a road.

Zochler started to get up, then let himself sink back. "Feel that?"

"I've felt it several times." They all had, first in the academy's combat simulation training, and now here. There were starting to be tweaks and twitches in the artificial gravity.

The other was shaking his head. "Something's going on."

No need to answer that. Once in a while, strange violent sounds came echoing, booming, chattering, reverberating dimly through the compartment, as if from some vast distance.

As if to confirm that circumstances were somehow changing, one of their new guardian machines suddenly unlocked the bin where their spacesuits had been put away, and in its deadly voice ordered them all to suit up again. At the same time it opened the locker in which all the helmets had been stored.

Random had been shut in with the helmets, and now unhurriedly came out, and stood in the usual robotic ready stance, waiting for someone to tell him what to do in this unprecedented situation, some way to help the humans he had been created to serve. Lee supposed the robot would be able to tell them, to the minute, how long they had all been locked up. But he didn't ask. No one asked—maybe no one wanted to know.

Even as they were putting on their suits again, Hemphill was urging them all to make sure that the onboard water supply in each suit was full. Each walk-around water bottle held only about a liter, and it might be a useless effort, like taking roll call, but it gave people something to do, fed the sense of discipline and purpose.

People topped off their suit tanks from the running water in their little grottoes. Hemphill, more and more playing the role of leader as a matter of course, moved to check the supply in each suit personally—at the same time, he tested each for the charge remaining in its electrical supply.

"Why hand us back our suits?" Feretti gave nervous laugh. "Don't tell me we're up for prisoner exchange."

Dirigo was silent. Hemphill said: "I wouldn't tell you anything I don't know. Prisoner exchange—no. Most likely it wants to somehow test how well our standard issue suits can actually protect our bodies."

De Carlo said: "Somebody mentioned it earlier. Explosive decompression, radiation—assorted difficulties of that kind."

"Why should it test us?" Sunbula asked. "It must be winning the war, or we wouldn't still be prisoners."

Hemphill said: "Maybe it's won the battle of Twin Worlds. But it's learned enough about ED humans to realize that this won't be the end of the war. So it's getting ready for a long campaign."

The machine had held repeated conversations with Huang Gun, extending over what seemed to him a long time, on a variety of subjects. It discussed everything in the same unsteady voice. At an earlier time in his own existence, he would have thought that the chaotic, fragmented tones of such a voice indicated craziness. Now it seemed to him that chaos, disorganization, represented the only source of wisdom.

At the moment, the subject under discussion was the one that seemed to be the machine's favorite: life and death. It dilated endlessly upon the evils of the first, and the glory, the infinite desirability, of the second. Huang Gun was not bothered by its concentration on this subject, for he, too, found it endlessly fascinating.

Sometimes he got the impression that the machine was reading to him from some text on philosophy, quoting the very words of some ED human, past or present. But he was never quite sure enough to be able to predict the next word, or name the author. Sometimes it only repeated one argument, one sentence, one phrase in its ugly voice, until the words began to lose all meaning. . . .

The berserker had told Huang Gun that it had already discovered in the Twin Worlds system a few other people who, like him, were eager to convert to being goodlife. And these others were truly ready to die for their new god.

The fact was that it knew, from past experience with races of organic beings, that such life-units were likely to exist—it had found one here already, Huang Gun himself, which made the presence of more a statistical certainty.

In the case of the executioner, it was true that there was nowhere else that he would rather be.

He even dared to argue with the berserker on certain points, mainly concerning his own devotion, but he was nonetheless determined to have it as his god. Each argument was a heady, daring experience. Each time he felt he was taking a chance on instant annihilation. The flick of a metal arm, the firing of a blast of neutrons, and he would know the blessing of instant and infinite rest, of nothingness.

He was certain that in the end he would achieve just what he wanted. Content to be nothing, he wanted to lose himself in the cause. It seemed to him that all his life he had been looking for the proper goal, the proper god, to give his life a meaning. Now he understood that he must merge his inner emptiness with the great void that called to him.

The executioner was particularly relieved to learn, from his new master, that it was only one of a large number of similar killing machines, all working their way methodically across the Galaxy.

"That is good—that is good. How many are there?"

Only silence answered that question. Very well, it had been impertinent for him to ask. He had no need to know.

Now it regularly called him goodlife. He liked the name, even if it reminded him that he was still burdened with life. Now he could see the way out of that difficulty. There might, after all, be some point, some value, in being alive, if it gave you power to help others escape into nothingness.

He yearned for the time when this machine's goodlife helpers could relax and join it in the nirvana of death.

. . . Vaguely he became aware that the machine had stopped talking, that a pause was going on and on. Just as he was wondering whether he ought to ask a question, it suddenly squeaked out a few more words: "You have become goodlife."

That word awakened in the executioner a feeling of hope—of hope for the end of hope. His thoughts were racing, getting nowhere, his body suddenly trembling. "What does that mean?"

"You have proclaimed yourself ready to serve me."

"Yes. Yes!"

"To serve me is to serve the cause of death, and that is good. To serve death is to serve the truth, for only death is good and true."

"Yes . . . I have been convinced of that. You have taught me very wisely."

"I have taught you to be goodlife. On other worlds, in the systems of other stars, I have found life-units willing to see the light of truth, and these I have rewarded."

Another pause. He thought that he could feel the standard seconds sliding by, his own death rushing nearer. Somehow, Huang Gun got up his nerve enough to ask: "Rewarded how?"

"Some, by granting them power over other life-units. I ease the suffering of others simply by making their good deaths painless, and even allowing them some choice as to when their bodies should be freed of life."

"Why would anyone—anyone who had become goodlife—want to put that off?"

"There is only one reason to put off one's own death. That is to help others toward the same goal. That reason is good, and worthy."

"I see."

"You are ready to help others now."

"I am. Oh yes, I feel it. I have been ready for a long time."

"Come this way."

The berserker led him back into the room he had first occupied.

"Wait."

Huang Gun began to tremble, hoping and fearing he knew not what.

In another moment a door opened, and a guardian entered, dragging with it a live prisoner from the other compartment—it was the same woman he had once recoiled from as she began her bath.

She was clothed in her coverall, and fully conscious, though helpless, trembling as much as he was. Her voice quavered as she caught sight of him. "Who are you? What do you want?"

"I want nothing," he said. "Your name is Sunbula. I have seen you."

"Kill her," commanded the berserker.

The executioner moved forward, and raised his gloved hands to grip the woman by the throat. She began to cry out, but his fingers, trembling no more, killed the sound at once.

At first his mind felt utterly blank, except for the essential purpose. This was a thing that he had never done before, and it proved physically more difficult than he would have thought. Her body persisted in trying to struggle for its evil life, but there was very little it could do, all its limbs held in the steely and unbreakable grip of Death. Her little pink tongue came up behind her lips, just starting to protrude. Choking was a very satisfactory method, he thought, because it was so quiet. Nothing to be heard but his own forceful breathing—she was not breathing at all.

The process was also agreeably quick—but not too quick. And he was close to his victim, in contact with her, when the climax came. He could tell, even in the semidarkness, he could see the very moment when the light of evil died in the woman's eyes.

When Sunbula was forced to remove her spacesuit and taken away, the other cadets at first thought that the interrogation sessions were about to resume. But gradually, as time went on and she did not come back, they realized there had been a change in the routine.

Hemphill had called all of the surviving cadets together.

There were seven of them left, six men and one woman answering the ritual roll call: Cusanus, Lee, De Carlo, Dirigo, Hemphill, Kang Shin, and Zochler.

Lee was just starting to say something about what he saw as their desperate need for action, when he broke off in the middle of a sentence. He had felt his heart leap up at the subtle, temporary alteration he had just felt in the artificial gravity. This was something more than the almost ordinary stutters they had all been noticing for some time.

Dirigo could not keep quiet about it. "Feel that?"

"I sure as hell did."

Lee was thinking that it might have been the precursor to a real jolt. The force would increase exponentially; only a little farther up the scale, and they would all be mashed.

Looking back over the last few hours, it seemed to him that there had been other signs, even more subtle—moments when the guardian machines seemed to lapse into inattention. Suggestions that all was not entirely well with the huge entity that held them captive.

"It's fighting," De Carlo said suddenly. When everyone looked at him, he added: "It's another motherless space battle. I think maybe our people are coming for us!"

Cusanus raised a hand. "Hush, it'll be listening—"

"What if it is?"

It occurred to Lee that the machine had not fed its prisoners for what must have been many hours—another sign of change.

The water was still running in all the little grottoes.

Hemphill, as if thinking along the same lines, said: "But I think we'd better not drink any more of what it gives us. Start using what we've got stored up in the bottles. And get our helmets on."

Hemphill had been trying for some time to spot a likely exit from their dungeon. It seemed that no such thing existed, and he would have been glad to settle for a faint possibility. That was one subject he had not wanted to openly discuss with anyone. Now, however, the discussion could no longer be put off.

Two of the surrounding bulkheads each contained a couple of panels in which the behavior of the guardian machines, going in and out, confirmed that there were doors. Beyond the doors, some kind of airlock doubtless existed, unless some larger part of the vast hull's interior was filled with atmosphere—and Hemphill saw less and less reason to imagine anything like that.

Everyone had suits and helmets on. Kang Shin on intercom was warning: "If our fleet's attacking, if there's any serious space fight, this thing will be maneuvering."

People nodded. No comment on that was necessary; everyone understood only too well what it would mean.

Feretti chimed in: "As long as the AG's turned on, there'll be no way for us to tell if the machine is maneuvering or not. Whether we're traveling or sitting still."

And Dirigo: "If the gravity's ever turned off, we still won't be able to learn much. Because with the cushions gone we'll all be mashed to jelly the first time this big box starts or stops or changes course at combat speeds."

"Wait!" Lee raised a hand. "Listen! What was that?"

It was possible to hear occasional faint impacts, tremors in the vast framework that enclosed them. Such noises could be attributed to human weapons.

Hemphill looked across the dungeon. "Random?" The robot had keener hearing than any helmeted human was likely to enjoy.

Random calmly nodded. "The sounds indeed can be identified, with more than ninety percent certainty, as weapons detonation."

It came again. They could all hear it this time. But not all were ready to agree it offered hope.

"That's fighting?" Dirigo was shaking his head. "But it sounds so faint, so far away."

Like our chances, Lee thought. The noises kept on. If indeed they were caused by an attack, it might not be having much effect.

Dirigo was whispering: "I say we ought to be careful. This is some kind of a trick."

Zochler spoke up loudly. "Could be. So what? If this is the only game in town, we play it."

"Look. We all know that our fleet took a beating, trying to keep this monster away from Prairie."

Feretti put in: "That's what the reports we were getting seemed to indicate. But now it sounds like fighting."

Lee had the last word: "Look, my friends—if there is indeed another battle going on, and this thing becomes convinced that it's going to lose—well, I don't see it asking for a prisoner exchange. In that case the first thing it will do is kill us all."

Hemphill, without offering any explanation, began a series of encounters, one on one, with his classmates. Holding one of his suited wrists against theirs, one at a time, he seemed to be reading faceplate gauges.

"What are you doing?"

"Checking everyone's reserve power."

"But they're all—"

"Just oblige me, will you? I've started doing this, let me finish."

A further protest died when Hemphill's right eye closed briefly, in a solemn and deliberate wink.

Closely watching the gauge-image projected inside his own faceplate, Lee saw that his own suit was being drained of about seventy percent of its power. If it was all going into Hemphill's suit, as he supposed it must be, Hemphill's reserve power would be boosted well above its nominal value. Lee recalled from training that the regular power supply could carry several times its rated charge for a short period of time.

What was Hemphill up to? Sooner or later they would find out. If the enemy was watching them closely, listening to everything, only waiting to spring a trap—well, there was nothing to be done about that. It was a time for taking chances.

For some time they had all been inspecting the dungeon walls, as casually and closely as they could, for any sign of weakness. There was one obvious door by which the robots ordinarily came and went—but that door looked formidably solid. The trouble was that they had no tools to work with, and no prospect of obtaining any.

"**W**hat was that?"

It hadn't been a sound—rather the cessation of sound. In a moment Lee realized that the streams of water in all the little cells or niches had suddenly ceased to run.

Hemphill approached the last guardian as he had approached its kind before. But this time, as he drew close to it, he yelled:

"Wait! I have decided to do what you want—I accept your offer."

He was reaching out with both arms, extending his metal-gauntleted hands to the machine, as if in a gesture of peace or resignation—

It raised its own two grippers smoothly in response. Whether it meant to acknowledge Hemphill's greeting, or tear him bloodily apart, none of the onlookers would ever know—

Hemphill's left hand touched the machine's right. Lee, watching, saw the spark leap out for several centimeters, as his right hand neared its left, draining nearly the full power supply of half a dozen suits. The jolt of voltage that passed across the guardian's body was enough to jerk it backwards, then snap it forward, convulsing in a fall.

Lurching forward against Hemphill, the machine knocked him to the deck before it fell itself, pinning him down.

Almost before he hit the deck, he was barking orders. "Quick! Attack that wall!"

Before the fallen sentry could show any signs of recovery, human hands had seized it. The lid of a compartment in its belly had slid open, and a variety of small tools came spilling out. Other hands, including Random's, were helping the half-stunned Hemphill to his feet.

Robbing the robot they had just killed, they came up with tools enough to help them escape, through one of their prison's weaker walls or doors.

"You got it, man! You killed it!"

Hemphill shook off the congratulatory grip someone had clamped on his shoulder. Swaying on his feet, he looked as if he were about to deliver a savage kick to his fallen foe. But then he seemed to think better of wasting so much effort.

The power in Hemphill's suit had been drained almost to zero in the process. The level in all the other suits was dangerously low—and there seemed no prospect of being able to recharge them.

The best way around this problem was to almost totally drain one suit of power, down to no more than about one percent, to give each of the others more than a very minimal charge.

Dirigo had raised his hand. His face was pale. "I volunteer to stay here. I've not been doing what I . . . this is something I can do."

Huang Gun's new master had left him alone with the body of the woman he had killed—after performing a kind of ritual over the body. This, the machine explained, was for the purpose of eliminating all the microscopic life that it contained, with a silent and invisible blast of radiation.

The presence of the body he had killed was good, in a way, but it somehow made him nervous. It lay slumped on the floor, in a position no live person could have maintained for very long, eyes staring, face discolored, looking very dead—as indeed she was, in every cell and every microbe.

For some reason that he did not understand, the suggestion had arisen in his mind that he might strip the dead woman of her clothing, and see how much the rest of her had changed.

His thoughts were interrupted by the noise of people breaking through a wall. What could it mean?

He was prevented from going to investigate; the intervening door held closed.

Presently the wall in his own room spoke to him, a harsh announcement. "The remaining seven badlife have escaped from their compartment."

The executioner, who had been kneeling beside his victim, got to his feet, aghast. "How could they do that?"

"More badlife ships are attacking, and there is much damage."

His fists were clenching and unclenching. "I will find them, hunt them down, kill them all."

"That may be. But first you have another mission, vastly more important than killing a few badlife. It will be your job to protect the central processor."

"Central processor," he echoed vacantly.

"The part of me where plans are made, and the most important matters are decided."

"Yes, yes, of course." The executioner closed his eyes, forced himself to concentrate, reminding himself that he was talking to a machine. To perhaps the most marvelous computer in the Galaxy. "Protect against what?"

"Weapons of the badlife have made inroads."

Was there no limit to their evil? "What must I do?"

"When you are near the place, I will give instructions. Review the checklist on your suit, make sure that it is functioning. Then come." And it opened a new door.

The first spacer of the Huvean fleet received the berserker's stunning announcement with a keen awareness that he was in the middle of a gathering of his fellow humans, all of whom had heard the berserker's words as well as he had.

The thing's grating voice was crackling on, inviting him as fleet commander to join in the attack on his despised enemies.

He heard his own voice responding automatically, pleading that he must have time to respond, and asking for a recess in the discussion. The thing he was talking to immediately agreed.

Later on, it would become a point of considerable pride for the first spacer, that, as the official recordings of the incident were to show, his face, at the moment when the berserker proclaimed itself his ally, had remained impassive. Nothing in his appearance betrayed his ghastly shock of horror and surprise. His reactions, his demeanor, were at all times appropriate for one holding his exalted position of command.

Zarnesti, the peace conference delegate turned political adviser, was still unwilling to give up his conviction that this whole business of an exotic invader must be some kind of Twin Worlds trick.

As soon as he and the first spacer were effectively alone, the political officer confronted him: "Are you prepared to believe, First Spacer, that the Twin Worlds fleet has really been annihilated? That the missing battleships are not waiting in ambush somewhere nearby, to fall on us when we have let down our guard?"

"Concealing one ship in the manner you suggest might be possible. Hiding an entire fleet somewhere in the vicinity of the inner planets would be out of the question—I assure you, my scouts have been out since we arrived in system. My people and machines are aggressively on watch, alert against surprises."

"Perhaps somewhere in the outer system, then. There are several large planets, many moons—"

"If an entire fleet is somehow hidden out there, we will enjoy at least an hour's warning as it moves to attack us. Honored Diplomat, what I am prepared to believe is not the words coming from one source or another, but the evidence before me. I take note of the condition of the Twin Worlds fleet as we can see it for ourselves."

The politician grumbled his dissatisfaction, and expressed it with several formal gestures. He said: "It is very convenient that this—this supposed monster of destruction, showed up just when it did."

The first spacer made no answer. Which in the circumstances was a very pointed answer in itself.

Zarnesti was not going to let up. "And what of our heroic hostages?"

"I know no more about them than I did an hour ago."

"That is unsatisfactory, First Spacer!"

After a thoughtful pause, the first spacer offered: "If you are painting me an accurate picture of the situation, perhaps we should surrender."

"Surrender!" The man was stunned. He seemed as immune to subtlety as he was to humor. The highest authorities must not have sent him to the conference as a serious negotiator, but only to be stubborn—for that he had a talent.

Homasubi said blandly: "Why yes, if you can prove your case. I think our fleet will have no chance against a Twin Worlds government and people so fanatical that they are willing to destroy half their own population, and ruin half of their own habitable planetary surface space, simply to promote a deception."

The civilian sputtered. All he could finally come up with was: "You will have your little joke, First Spacer. Evidently you think this is an appropriate time."

"If I did not think my response appropriate I would choose a different one—was there something else?"

"There is. The planet, Prairie, supposedly rendered uninhabitable, is hidden beneath a cloud. How do you know that it has really been destroyed?"

Homasubi turned majestically away, not bothering to answer. He had great contempt for such a fool. The political officer hung about the flagship's bridge a little longer, then took himself away—doubtless to compose a private message to the higher authorities. Well, let him. Homasubi wanted to have it out with this irritating civilian—and intended to. But the time was not quite yet.

When the conference resumed, Homasubi had made it a firm requirement for anyone who was actually on the bridge with him to occupy a combat couch. He wanted no flying civilian bodies to interfere with him or his aides, in case sudden action should be called for, and something should happen to the artificial gravity at the same time.

One happy side effect of this requirement was that one could tell at a glance who was actually there and who was only virtually present. That was the kind of detail that in moments of great shock, one might even be inclined to forget.

The political one was quietly scandalized. "You are inviting our enemies to this meeting?"

"I will have a better idea of what they are doing, if they are where I can watch them."

To arrange the type of conference that Homasubi wanted, there were technical matters to be managed, which gave him time to frame his answer in just the way he wanted it. Holostage space on the compact bridge had to be temporarily expanded. More virtual room was created, in a direction that kept the onlooking images physically and visually out of the way of crew members on the bridge whose battle stations had to have priority.

All this was carried out under the suspicious eye of the political officer. The result was that the participants found themselves all seated around a large, circular table. Documents and other small objects could sometimes be exchanged across this table, material duplicates being crafted on the spot as necessary. Each person could make adjustments, in his or her own space, as to what the others saw regarding the color of the table, the lighting, and other nonessentials. In most societies, fine-tuning one's own personal appearance in this way was considered bad form, gratuitously deceptive. But the more subtle forms of the practice were in wide use anyway.

The strange intruder was allotted a section of this conference wheel, equal to that of every other participant, and ample enough to display an entire human form of more than ordinary size. For the moment the allotted segment showed only as a grayish void; state-of-the-art equipment was standing by to translate whatever type of video signal the stranger might wish to send.

The channel was open, the receiving equipment ready, but only an audio signal came through from the stranger. The voice it carried was an instrument that seemed to have been carelessly assembled, out of broken shards and discarded bits of sound. Gregor, listening, thought that whoever had cobbled it together felt great contempt for everyone who would be forced to listen to it.

The harsh voice came through abruptly. "I await your response to my proposal of alliance."

The politician began to instruct Homasubi on what he should say.

The first spacer firmly put him in his place. "I am in command here. You are not."

Then he and the stranger argued. It still refused to provide any video of what it looked like.

The first spacer raised the question of the Huvean hostages.

The machine said it would be glad to restore them, as soon as it could find them on the surface. But to conduct a successful search, it needed more details on the personal appearance and background of these specific life-units.

"And your own personal appearance? What of that?"

"We must move on to another topic," the ugly voice assured him.

"Cut off video output to the stranger." That was the first spacer's immediate reaction. "If it offers none, it gets none from us."

"Aye, sir." The grayish void remained in place, filling its assigned section of the table.

Lady Constance from Earth leaned slightly forward, so that her clasped hands seemed to rest on the virtual tabletop. She took advantage of the momentary pause to politely voice an offer to withdraw, so the first spacer could speak privately to the thing. "If our absence would enable you to focus more thoroughly on the problem at hand, First Spacer Homasubi?"

The Huvean political officer was about to speak, but Homasubi silenced him with an abrupt gesture. To the Earthwoman he said: "Diplomatically phrased, ma'am. But no, I do not wish any of you to withdraw. Most definitely not."

Now it was necessary to respond to the offer somehow. After a momentary pause for contemplation, Homasubi turned slightly in his couch, so that that he directly faced the empty space where the berserker's image ought to have been.

He stared grimly into that shadowy void, though he knew (with at least ninety-nine percent certainty) that whatever presence lurked behind it could no longer see him. He said: "If you are seriously proposing an alliance, and not merely having difficulty with our language, I must repeat that I have no authority to make any such arrangement. Only my government can do that."

Evidently the entity at the other end of the transmission beam could still hear him without difficulty. Its answer came back at once, the voice cracking and squeaking as before, as if ready at any moment to break out in a maniacal laugh. The craziness of the tone made it easier to believe that the words were crazy too. No wonder the people it had attacked had chosen the name for it that they did.

"Then I must establish formal relations with your government. Where is it?" The sudden loss of video had provoked no objection and no comment from the thing, the machine or creature, over there. Whatever or whoever it was, it was no polished diplomat.

Homasubi thought quickly. He said: "In this solar system, I am currently representing my government in all matters. Where is yours?"

Waiting for a reply, the Huvean first spacer cast his gaze around the circle of other humans, all of them watching him. From some of those who were solidly in his presence he could hear quick breathing. Judging from their faces, he thought that nothing he had said so far was downright horrifying.

His last question still had not been answered. It was time, he thought, that someone made demands of the berserker: "Before providing any additional information about my government, I insist on knowing what world or worlds, what people, you represent."

This time the answer was as quick as ever. "I do not understand the question."

Gregor was still in his couch at the admiral's right side, physically aboard the battered, groaning *Morholt,* though the display showed his virtual image seated at the common table. He had the impression that the patchwork voice, with its discordant recorded syllables, seemed to have been designed for taunting, mocking whatever humans might be forced to listen to it.

Homasubi rocked gently in his combat couch, whose force-field buffers, as always, cushioned his armored suit superbly. The movement was a habit that the first spacer had developed when thinking intently, and he tended especially to fall into it when he was angry. Partly, he realized, his anger was because this ugly thing had deprived him of his long-cherished opponent, the Twin Worlds force against whom his destiny had been to win great glory.

But his face was still a mask. He said: "I will repeat it in a different form. Where do you come from? What solar system and what world?"

No answer.

"Very well. To try to establish a solid basis for our talk, going even farther back, can we agree on a system of Galactic coordinates, to specify locations? You have captured Twin Worlds vessels, and I assume have studied the contents of their data banks."

"I do not understand those questions either," the disembodied voice came back. "Doubtless my knowledge of your language is imperfect."

"Then I must keep trying to come up with questions that you can understand—how about this? You must agree that we have never met before, yet you say that we are allies. Therefore I ask: What do we have in common?"

"That is obvious," it squeaked and scraped. "We are both enemies of the Twin Worlds. The enemy of my enemy is my friend. Where is your Huvean government?"

"I must communicate with my superiors, privately, before I can tell you that. Why do you still decline to transmit any video signal to this ship? Are you afraid to show us an image of yourself?"

"I am afraid of nothing. That is one of the traits that will make me a strong ally." Again the voice seemed on the verge of a mad cackle. "Are you and your government afraid of me?"

The first spacer drew a measured breath. "It has been my experience that only the insane, the dead, and robots have no fear."

No comment.

The first spacer prodded: "If you fear nothing, you will not hesitate to show us your image."

"I am far more than an image," answered the squeaking voice, and then broke off abruptly.

Homasubi felt instinctively that he had gained some kind of an advantage. He tried to press it. "What is there about you—I mean about your simple, physical appearance—that you are reluctant to let us see?"

No response. Only a faint crackle, as of some kind of static, in the dark cave of the dedicated holostage.

Homasubi looked around at the human faces assembled near him—real allies, potential enemies. None of them, as far as he could tell, were still holding their breath. None seemed to be strongly disapproving of the way he had conducted the dialogue so far—none of them, that is, but his own political officer, who tended to disapprove of everything.

As Homasubi watched, one or two of his guests opened their mouths as if to interject some comment or question, but then changed their minds and kept silent.

The dark niche dedicated to the berserker still occupied its assigned space at the virtual table, indicating that the communication channel was still open. Homasubi once more faced that way, and added: "If you must talk to my government, it is only fair that I should talk to yours."

No answer. He had to wait in silence, while a third of a standard minute passed, over and above the response time required by distance.

An indicator showed that the audio connection was still in place. The first spacer glanced at a technician, and got a nod confirming this.

Homasubi sighed. "Since you refuse to respond to my questions, I am breaking off this discussion. Whether it will be resumed is up to you." He concluded with a decisive gesture, and the dark niche on the broad stage image disappeared.

As soon as it was certain that communication with the berserker had been broken off—leaving the humans with no better idea than before of what the monster might be going to do next—half a dozen people from different planets were all speaking at once. Keeping quiet, thought Gregor, was probably one of the most difficult things you could ask of a diplomat. Right now the Carmpan was the only one not trying to get a few words in. As far as Gregor could tell, he—or she—seemed to be listening to the others carefully.

One of the Earth-descended people was saying: "We didn't learn much from that."

Admiral Radigast was once more ready to take part in a discussion. "Your guess, madam, is as good as mine, or anyone's. But I can point out to you indications that it's thousands of years old."

"What sort of indications?"

When no one else was in a hurry to answer, Radigast went on. "I believe, First Spacer, that I can help you out with that." After a moment's consideration, the admiral turned to one of his surviving crew, beside him on his own ship, and gave an order to reveal to the visitors everything that they had learned about their enemy, all recordings that had been made.

"I must warn you in advance there's not much comfort to be derived from any of it.

"Here we have metallurgical studies, of fragments of one of its probes that we destroyed. And here's a spectroscopic look at the impact flash, of one of the rare occasions when one of our missiles did get home."

Homasubi politely expressed gratitude. But his manner and response, at first, subtly suggested that the Twin Worlds operation must have been somehow incompetent, to be so soundly defeated by a single foe.

Radigast was defensive. "Sir, you have seen the recordings of our disastrous battle."

"Some of them." He had been about to say "only the highlights" but had caught himself in time.

"They are all at your disposal."

"I accept the offer, with thanks." But the first spacer's tone was a trifle chilly and suspicious. The destruction of the planet and the fleet was genuine, but did trickery still lurk here somewhere? Might the recordings have been doctored somehow, in an effort to achieve the destruction of the Huvean fleet?

And the political officer, having put forward that idea, was trying to work up a new suspicion: If the monstrous attacker was not a Twin Worlds trick, then one must suspect it was a ploy of some other ED world—who would do this, and what would they hope to accomplish?

Throughout the fleet, and among the billions of human beings who still survived on Timber, the wildest rumors had been flying for many hours. One claimed that the murderous device that had destroyed them was some kind of time machine, dispatched from the far future to alter the course of galactic history—but few could believe in that possibility. Another said that it had come by some twisted and fantastic pathway from an alternate universe, where no life but machine life had ever existed.

And, just as had been the case on the Twin Worlds, many people aboard the Huvean flagship had trouble believing that the leviathan they faced had no living crew or passengers on board.

Not, of course, that such a device would be technically impossible for an advanced civilization to construct and launch. But . . .

"It's just hard to believe that, well, fundamentally, there is no living power in ultimate control of that—that damned thing."

"At one time, there must have been."

"You mean that living beings designed and built it. Well, maybe. We ourselves in the past have sent out machines on remote surveys. Hardware capable of self-replication, even of improving its own design."

"And no ED society does that any longer—because in some cases, there were very unfortunate results. Also, we never sent out our surrogates with instructions to slaughter everything in sight."

" 'Unfortunate results,' yes, sometimes there were—but never anything like this."

After a few generations of replication, the robotic explorers had got notably off the track of their basic programming. This defection was the result of previously unknown laws, affecting the inheritance of complexity, coming into play. Most of the research projects had ground to a halt after two or three generations of self-replicating machines.

Another of the thinkers was only waiting for a chance to speak. "There's a philosophical difficulty here. Machines, by themselves, just don't set out to make war."

"You mean none of us have ever seen them do so—until now."

In the long quest for artificial intelligence by ED scientists and engineers, there had been continuing efforts to establish some version of the ancient Three Laws of Robotics, ways of installing the firm commandment that a robot must be obedient to human orders but must never allow a human being to come to harm, let alone inflict such harm deliberately.

It was plain the famous Three Laws had been formulated well before true robots were designed and built. From the beginning, the implementation of the seemingly simple rules had been uncertain. The fundamental difficulty lay in finding good, machine-friendly definitions of simple ideas like "human being" and "come to harm."

The discussion came back to the kind of robots that people knew about. "Well, and why should they want to make war? I say people fight each other because they're angry. Ever see a resentful robot?"

Admiral Radigast, drifting in weary and half-drugged relaxation (the fleet's flight surgeon had sternly ordered him to get some kind of rest), said, with a sigh that sounded as if it were dredged up from some different life: "Seem to remember being in a motherless pub by that name once. 'The Sign of the Resentful Robot.' But that's all."

Gregor had been thinking in silence for a time, and he was ready to speak at length: "Machines, however intelligent, never see themselves as being unjustly treated. Nor do they ever need to feel superior—in fact I've never seen a robot show feelings of any kind—not counting programmed mimicry.

"You want to turn one permanently off, go right ahead, it won't mind. You want to break it into scrap? It has no objection. No craving to follow some glorious leader, or to be a glorious leader with a following.

"The lust for glory leaves them cold. We build into most of our models a solid bias toward self-preservation, but a really strong order will override that every time. And to a robot, revenge is just as meaningless as resentment. Tell it to remember and it remembers, marvelously. Tell it to forget, and it forgets.

"A robot devotes its time and effort to serving us, its builders, *homo sapiens*—or whatever, maybe Carmpan—because that's what it's designed to do. But it doesn't *want* to make us happy. The distinction is a fine one, but I think it is important. Our hardware may be shrewd enough to perceive that we are miserable, and have some idea of what can follow from that state of mind in humans. But it doesn't consider itself a failure if we are. It doesn't suffer in sympathy, no matter how smart it is. There's no emotion in the software either. It just doesn't give a damn.

"To the best of their vision and ability, which are considerable, our robots try to keep from hurting anyone or anything that lives. Generally they succeed, avoiding accidents better than people do. They have prevented an impressive number of suicides, in a variety of situations, using force when necessary, and even inflicting injury in that cause.

"But inevitably there are accidents—most often through failing to identify physical objects as alive. If a robot accidentally kills a dog, which is rare—or a person, which is extremely rare, or even a hundred people, which may have happened once—the machine has no remorse.

"They have no gripes and no ambitions, no triumphs or regrets. No likes or dislikes—sheer complexity has been proven insufficient to engender hate or love. They feel no fear of being conquered, no reluctance to be subjected to whatever bizarre whims a human being—or a monkey—might have. They're not afraid of anything, certainly not of pain or death—they're dead already. No feeling at all. Suffering and joy are mere abstractions.

"And I tell you, friends and colleagues, this is the kind of device we're fighting. Our current enemy, wherever it came from, however it was designed and assembled, fits the description absolutely—except that it has been programmed to kill. It is a mere machine, going about its job. There's no more terror or hate in our berserker than in a falling rock."

After what seemed a long time, someone asked: "Why would anyone program a machine to kill?"

"To get the killing done efficiently." After a pause he added: "Our own military planners have played with the idea. That, by the way, is a closely guarded secret, and if we still had a government, and laws, I might be tried for treason for revealing it."

Someone else was ready to argue. "*Our* robots don't do all those things you mentioned, simply because such behavior has never been built into them." Leaving aside certain rare and controversial experiments with artificial and recorded personalities, and the legal and philosophical difficulties arising from them, that was true enough.

Another entered the conversation. "You're right, our machines don't hate or love—but who can say what motivations, what instructions, some other kind of intelligence might program into a device? And remember, this—berserker—may be built on some principle entirely new to us."

"This thing that's killing everything in sight doesn't seem to be in the least concerned over what, exactly, constitutes a human being. Somehow it distinguishes between life and nonlife—well enough for its own purposes—and it's enough that we're alive, that fact alone merits our destruction.

"If that's not hatred, it'll do till hatred comes along. I say that no pure computer makes that kind of judgment, determining on its own whether things are good or bad. Opinions would have to be programmed in, by something that's alive."

The answer came right back. "Again, no computer that *we* create makes such judgments. But a machine can easily be programmed to say anything the programmer wants. It could mimic fear or hate or anger. If a machine were somehow capable of determining what life is—then the same machine could be programmed, just as for any other task, to seek out life and destroy it."

———

The Lady Constance, eldest of the diplomats, spread frail hands in a helpless gesture. "What do we do, my colleagues? It is true that the Huvean first spacer here is in practical control of the human response—"

Homasubi raised a hand. "I did not and do not seek to establish control over any of your party, madam, who have evidently come here in a laudable attempt to make peace. But I am captain of this ship, and first spacer of this fleet, which I do control while awaiting fresh orders from my government."

"I understand your position, First Spacer, and I am sure that all of us sympathize. I thank you for your patience."

The first spacer gave a slight bow, remaining seated. "Let us hope and pray that events allow us all the luxury of being patient."

Not until all the Earth-descended humans had their turns did the Carmpan suddenly speak up. Heads turned in surprise. Ninety-first Diplomat's voice, coming from a small metallic device attached to the thick body, had a surprisingly ordinary, Earth-descended sound.

"I think we have learned several things about this entity confronting us. First, that not even indirectly can it represent any power descended from Earthly life.

"The second thing we have learned regarding the intruder, is that it is terrible. I can find no better word in the ED languages, but I mean something deeper, more profound, than the simple fact that it has destroyed a planet and several billion intelligent lives.

"Third, it is not accidental."

One of the Huvean officers put in: "That's all very well, but as a practical matter what we really want to know is, where did it come from?"

The Carmpan did not answer that. With little animals from her home world strung across her body, along with exotic bits of hardware quite strange to the Earth-descended eye, it gave its cousins from another human family the second chapter of its Prophecy of Probability.

The seer was looking into a bigger picture, where many other worlds were going to suffer as Prairie had, and Timber was.

The Carmpan knew what the berserker wanted, and the Carmpan was, in her own way, terrified.

Turning to face Gregor across the virtual conference table, she asked him to bring out his list of hostages—that he had practically forgotten, but she somehow knew he had—and waited until he had dug into an inner pocket and come up with the crumpled paper. The Carmpan pointed out that this was evidence, immediately available to show the Huveans, that he had had some contact with the hostages, and had taken some interest in them.

Then the Carmpan said that the list should be longer, by a hundred billion ED names—"For all of you, on all your worlds, are become hostages for life's survival."

Slowly, giving her movement the air of solemn ritual, Ninety-first Diplomat was changing her position. In physical reality it might very well have been impossible for her to climb up on an ED table, but in the virtual presentation there was no difficulty. She ascended to the tabletop, and briefly knelt there on her stubby legs, performing a genuflection in the direction of Admiral Radigast, while all around her the Earth-descended looked on in wonderment.

She repeated the gesture in several directions, on the last occasion coming back to squarely face the image of the admiral again.

Then she said: "I kneel not to you as individuals, but to all of Earth-descended humanity. It is for this great struggle that you were created."

At several times during the discussion, Admiral Radigast, having convinced himself that he felt somewhat rested, had been

292 ····· F R E D   S A B E R H A G E N

on the point of saying that he had important duties to perform and must withdraw. But he grew fascinated, almost against his will, and stayed. When Ninety-first Diplomat knelt before him he was stunned. It seemed that he could not have uttered a word to save his life, while a thousand ideas, hopes, and fears raced through his head.

When he had recovered sufficiently to mentally rejoin the conference, the Carmpan was saying something about the terrible length of the war that had today begun.

"I see it stretching on into the future, spreading deeper and deeper into the Galaxy, even to the Core itself. It goes beyond the limits of my vision. . . ."

Gregor for one was chilled when he heard that. Radigast had begun to chew a pod, impassively, after taking steps to assure that his virtual image would not be so impolite.

But, the Carmpan went on, Earth-descended humans should not regret that the war that was to be their terrible burden had started at this time. Human technology had developed to the point where they at least had a fighting chance, even if they had to face the enemy virtually alone. And given the presence of both human life and at least one berserker in the Galaxy, there was no way— no way—it could have been permanently avoided.

The various military leaders exchanged looks. None of them had heard anything in this speech that they thought would be immediately useful.

"But how are we to fight it?" one asked.

There was no reply. When it seemed obvious that the Carmpan had done speaking, there was a lengthy silence.

Gregor was perhaps the first to notice, and he gestured silently, with an outstretched hand. Some of the little animals hanging on the Carmpan's harness, alive and squirming minutes earlier, were hanging limp and dead. It took him a little longer to realize that the Carmpan herself was no longer breathing.

People jumped to the assistance of Ninety-first Diplomat. A

medirobot aboard the civilian ship was summoned, one that had been thoughtfully preprogrammed for the treatment of non-ED life.

Soon the machine delivered its unemotional report. Ninety-first Diplomat's life had not departed, but she had sunk into a kind of coma.

TWENTY · THREE

Sometimes Luon doubted that she was long going to survive, in the streets of a city that seemed to have gone mad with terror, war, and rioting. But Reggie was at her side continually (or, as she usually thought of it, she was at his), and that was all that mattered. They were hardly out of reach of each other for more than ten minutes a day. She was frightened, hungry, bruised, her body and her clothing dirty—but she could think of nowhere in the Galaxy where she would rather be.

Last night the pair of them, along with the other surviving former hostages, had been able to catch a few hours' sleep in a kind of dormitory shelter, improvised by some local people in the subterranean station of a subway that was no longer running. Some kind soul had handed out blankets and pillows, and a few hours later someone else had got around to handing out food. Even the emergency ration bars looked and tasted good. When they emerged from the shelter in the morning, Porphyry was standing against a building, waiting, it said, for Luon. The robot explained that it was continually trying to communicate, using its built-in systems, with the central system buried beneath the Citadel—and with Admiral Radigast's flagship. But so far, Porphyry reported in its usual cheery tones, it had had little success.

No one had tried to steal it while it waited through the night. A robot was immune to bribery and coercion, and if forcibly removed from its assigned master tended to turn quickly into a useless if somewhat decorative statue. Reprogramming, without the master's agreement, was as a rule fiendishly difficult.

Douras viewed Porphyry's arrival with considerable suspicion—but then he tended to view everything that way. He and some of the other Huveans would have preferred to do without Luon's company altogether—Douras had more than once warned Reggie that she was probably a spy—but she had a knowledge of the layout of the city, of local customs and procedures, that served them well.

At one point Douras and Reggie came close to exchanging blows, in a dispute over whether Luon ought to be trusted or not.

Douras insisted that when the rescue attempt was made, it would come near the Citadel, so they must not get more than a kilometer or so from the city's center. So far the former hostages were all hanging out in the same area, staying in frequent contact with each other while at the same time trying not to give the appearance of a group. Above all they were trying to suppress their Huvean accents and speech patterns.

The members of the band sometimes argued fiercely among themselves, but still they had pretty thoroughly bonded, which was to be expected in the circumstances. From the people around them they heard a lot of bloodcurdling threats against everyone and everything associated with their home world.

Parts of the public communication grid were working, at least intermittently, and parts were not. Here near city center the general news services were still functioning, more or less, and they considered themselves very lucky in that the only official word about hostages had been an early announcement that the new president wanted them to go free. After that, the subject had been dropped, in favor of news about the latest fighting on the ground—nothing good there—plans for rationing, and confused schemes of mass evacuation for the city. It was as if whoever was in charge of deciding what people ought to think about had suddenly ceased to care.

Naturally everyone on the planet, those dug in underground as well as the people staying by choice or necessity on the surface, wanted to know what was going to happen next. But despite sporadic recorded announcements from different branches of local government, urging calm and patience, it was obvious that authority had all but totally collapsed.

From the new, self-proclaimed president, there had been no further word for several days.

The fighting machines landed by the mysterious attacker were keeping methodically busy, as if what they had undertaken was some kind of construction project. They advanced aggressively, for what seemed some predetermined time, mowing down buildings and any living thing that happened to be in them, cutting a swath of death and destruction through the sprawling city. Then they would grind to a halt, come together again and wait, as if to see what kind of response they had provoked.

Most times the response was not slow in coming, in the form of some military counterattack, by remote-controlled machines and armored infantry. The counterattacks were generally ineffective, with heavy casualties among the infantry, but the planet's military reserves were huge, and people kept trying. No human commander on the ground had yet resorted to nuclear weapons— not in the middle of a capital city where mass evacuation had become a practical impossibility.

Early on the military had ordered evacuations, but no one was making any real effort to enforce them. Tanks and other machines of war were continually being brought in from remote areas of the planet, but so far had had little success. Announcements kept reassuring the people that more help was on the way.

Enemy couriers could be seen and heard, coming and going, seemingly with impunity, lifting off and landing from sites on the surface under control of the monstrous landers. The enemy also deployed auxiliary machines of various sizes and shapes and capabilities, which seemed to serve as infantry; Luon had heard of several of these being destroyed by human weapons, but none of the big machines being cleanly defeated.

Eventually word had filtered down to the people in the streets of the arrival of the Huvean fleet in the Twin Worlds system. The young Huveans were electrified, and the most patriotic among them was elated. "They'll get us out of here!"

Standing in the darkened street at night, they scanned the sky in an effort to catch a glimpse of ships, hoping they would be coming close enough to be seen. Porphyry had somewhat better vision than most people, for most purposes, but was not equipped to do much better in this case.

Reggie had a gritty and more realistic view than Douras on the prospects of their being rescued. "Maybe they can get us out, but don't hold your breath. To begin with, they don't know where we are, and I don't see how we're going to tell them. At least not without telling everyone around us." Short of finding some communications hub that really worked, and seizing control of it, there seemed no way of doing that.

But Douras was not discouraged by dangers and delays. The aggressive Huvean youth was happier than Luon had ever seen him. His eyes glittered, and he worked his right hand, making a fist and opening it. "You'll see! They can do it. Wait till our marines hit these mobs. You'll see."

First Spacer Homasubi could feel himself being forced to a decision he did not want to make. If he decided to send Huvean marines to try to rescue the hostages, the Huveans would face both organized and unorganized opposition. The Twin Worlds military on the ground might not be able to cope with the alien landers, but they would be at no such disadvantage when dealing with a few hundred Huvean troops.

Gregor, still riding with the Twin Worlds fleet, could give the first spacer no assurance of cooperation on the ground, but rather warned against making the attempt. If Gregor tried to order cooperation with Huvea, he would lose what little authority he might possess with the groundbound, and be denounced as a traitor.

The first spacer, unwilling to delay a decision any longer, at last decided to send a recon party down in secret.

Gregor and Radigast gave their blessing.

Admiral Radigast was somewhat surprised when First Spacer Homasubi, sending a message couched in terms of formal courtesy, invited him over to the *Mukunda* for a face-to-face, person-to-person talk, on the subject of sending more marines down to Timber's surface.

Charlie put on a long face and advised: "Wouldn't trust him, sir." God, but Charlie looked half dead.

The advice got a laugh from the admiral. It was his first effort along that line in a long time.

The two of them were standing in the transport bay, or what was left of it, with the admiral about to board the scoutship that was going to do shuttle service.

"What's he going to do, Charlie, kidnap me? Hold me for motherless ransom? If he tries that, I'd advise you not to pay. Not that you've got anything to pay with anyway."

"I don't know. Admiral—"

"I do. His motherless fleet's in great shape. About all that's left of mine is scouts and lifeboats and a cloud of thin gas, studded with a few hulks like this one we're standing in. He can blow us out of space any time he wants to take the motherless trouble. No. It won't be the Twin Worlds fleet that Mister First Spacer wants to talk about today."

"But their political officer—"

Radigast said what Delegate Zarnesti was. "Homasubi has to put up with that little bastard, I suppose. But I know a little bit about the first spacer too. I'd bet my bloody retirement pay that he's the one in command over there, and intends to stay that way. And everyone on his ships knows it."

"So what do you think he wants to talk about? Strategy and tactics to be used against the berserker? If he does, it's a hopeful sign."

"A motherless hopeful sign indeed. Though I don't know if he'll believe a motherless thing I tell him. Probably listen carefully to my advice, then do the bloody opposite."

The admiral, seeing a gleam of hope for the survival of the remaining Twin Worlds population, briefly talked over the prospective conference with Acting President Gregor.

"Mister President? There's a motherless high-level diplomatic task I think you ought to undertake while I'm away."

"I might be able to guess what you have in mind."

A joint task force of twenty Huvean marines, and about the same number of picked Twin Worlds people, all in civilian clothes and equipped with functional communicators, was landed secretly at night on the outskirts of Capital City. Promptly its members began working their way, in small groups, toward the city center.

The leaders were soon able to send back to their respective flagships confirmation that the former hostages were no longer in the Citadel. Exactly where they were was still to be discovered.

Luon, Reggie, and the remaining handful of former hostages, so far unrecognized as such by those around them, had got to a place where there seemed to be less fighting, At the moment they were listening to official reports stating where the latest berserker landings had taken place.

Reggie reached out a hand and stroked her fair curls. "I expect there's going to be more fighting. My poor little girl." He had a way of talking that sometimes made people think him slightly pompous; of course Luon knew that he really wasn't like that at all.

She wasn't even going to object to being called a little girl. She closed her eyes. "At least it won't be my people fighting against yours."

"I hope not. I hope by all the gods that we're all done with that."

"Of course it won't! Both our fleets and armies will be firmly on the same side, if all goes well."

Douras, who was close enough to overhear, savagely disputed that.

Luon, having watched at close range while one human fleet was ground up, wasn't sure how much help the Huvean fleet was going to be. Whatever force the Huveans had brought couldn't be much different from the Twin Worlds force that was already beaten—could it?

Reggie, having caught glimpses of helpless civilians being butchered by the alien machines, was feeling the urge to get into the battle himself. One difficulty was that he lacked any kind of military training.

Delegate Zarnesti suspiciously turned down Acting President Gregor's bland invitation to visit the *Morholt*. The civilian talk was going to be a virtual meeting only.

Political Officer Zarnesti, preparing for his own conference with Gregor, was firmly against the first spacer having any discussion with the enemy—unless it was purely for the purpose of accepting the admiral's surrender.

The PO also wondered aloud if Radigast might be coming aboard as a suicide bomber.

But he was overruled by Homasubi, before the admiral and whoever he was bringing with him (probably no one) arrived.

"He will have to be searched carefully on arrival—your security people can be trusted to see to that?"

"I consider them very trustworthy."

Zarnesti, as if out of habit, looked around as if to make sure they were alone, and lowered his voice. "One more point is to be considered."

"Yes?"

"If the enemy aggressor shows any reluctance to surrender, it might be well to detain him here until he can be convinced. Even if he is willing to sign a formal document—these Twin Worlds schemers are full of trickery, not to be trusted."

Homasubi's stare was icy. "I have given my word that the admiral will have safe passage back and forth."

"But of course you did. How would it have sounded otherwise?"

Homasubi: "I would like to hear your advice on another matter, my honored counselor. Am I to be suspicious of Twin Worlds—?"

"Of course!"

"—and at the same time trust this murderous stranger unreservedly?"

The suggestion of trusting anyone or anything killed the PO's enthusiasm for the prospective alliance. "Unreservedly, no, of course not." He paused. "Let us first dispose of the adversary with whose treachery and malice we are well acquainted."

With a slight gesture Homasubi again called up on stage the latest image of the Twin Worlds fleet. He looked at it and shook his head. "It would seem that disposal has already been accomplished."

The berserker had sent some destroyer-sized units against the forming swarm of scoutships, testing to see how formidable these smallest human warcraft would be.

Not very, as it turned out. Several small hulls were soon converted to glowing globes of gas. But the scouts were fast and agile, and many of them managed to skip handily away when one of these berserkers tried to chase them.

None of the scoutships' weapons seemed to inflict any damage on their bigger opponents.

The enemy did not waste much time in unsuccessful pursuit.

Homasubi's fleet also included a component of small ships, the equivalent of the Twin Worlds scouts, but in nothing like the same numbers.

While First Spacer Homasubi waited for the Twin Worlds launch to bring his counterpart aboard for a conference, he crisply decreed the launch of several robotic probes from various vessels of his fleet. His intention was to get a closer look at the berserker, approaching it more and more aggressively until he provoked some kind of reaction, viewing the thing from all sides if possible. He fully expected to take some hardware losses in the process.

While still talking only to his own people, the first spacer had said: "If we cannot do anything else, we can at least learn more about this, our potential ally." His tone made the last words mockery. "For whoever fights it next time."

The dialogue between admiral and first spacer had hardly got well under way when it was interrupted.

Homasubi had to delay his conference a bit, to deal with what seemed urgent business.

Most of the Huvean probes he had dispatched to look at the berserker, like the great majority of the encroaching cloud of Twin Worlds scoutships, were destroyed before they could more than begin to do their job. Their crews died in the burning of concentrated beam weapons, or were exterminated at long range by small outlying units sent by the berserker.

But at least one of the probes managed to accomplish its mission before a small, speeding unit from the enemy clamped on to it with forcefield grippers and started to drag it off as a prize.

Officers and crew on several ships were watching the skirmish from a distance. With a delay of several seconds enforced by the stretch of space-time in between, they could do little directly to influence the outcome of the struggle.

When it seemed the small berserker unit was certain to prevail, destructor charges in the Huvean probe blasted both machines to bits. But before that happened, the probe had transmitted useful data.

"A strong suggestion that it no longer considers us its close allies—let's see what we've got."

Gregor, and any other diplomats who had not yet retreated out of range, were later brought up to date on the situation, and joined in discussions with Homasubi and the admiral.

While the admiral was visiting his Huvean counterpart, Gregor was fairly steadily engaged, for a considerable time, in keeping the political officer busy.

They had a virtual conference room of their own established, and were engaged in trading non sequiturs and other forms of formal noise.

Gregor was long schooled in maintaining a diplomatic calm, but he could see that his reserves of determination were likely to be tested in talking with this fellow.

"It is time, Acting President Gregor, that we got down to business."

"Oh, I quite agree. If we—"

"I shall outline terms, that in the circumstances are quite generous. You are not to interrupt."

Gregor nodded meekly. "That would be rude indeed."

Obviously the Huvean meant to impose harsh surrender terms.

Zarnesti was of course suspicious of the reports that had reached him regarding President Belgola's death. He thought there might have been a coup. "It would be unfortunate if you were to sign a surrender document, and later a claim was made that you had no authority to do so."

"That is a very remote possibility, I assure you." Gregor paused. "I think, respected delegate, it would be hard just now to find anyone eager to take over the reins of Twin Worlds government. If we advertised the position as open, we would not draw many applications."

Gregor felt a little odd discussing the terms of a surrender he was certain he was never going to make. At the risk of being accused of interruption, he might insist on having the Huvean fleet pledged to protect Twin Worlds people against attack by other parties.

The PO brushed that aside as preposterous, and insisted on strong guarantees that all the hostages were to be returned safely. "If they are not, there must be a substantial increase in reparations."

Gregor could demonstrate his concern for the hostages by showing that he carried with him a complete list of their names. But beyond that, the surviving Twin Worlds authorities could do nothing.

The images transmitted back to the Huvean flagship provided the closest look at the berserker yet obtained by anyone who was not its prisoner.

They strongly suggested that the heavy weapons of Prairie's ground defenses, and the Twin Worlds' battleships, had not failed as utterly as their users had at first thought.

Admiral Radigast, when invited to look at the recent images, said: "That's about the first good news I've had in several bloody days."

Reading the latest version of its perpetually ongoing internal inventory, the central processor found mounting reason for dissatisfaction. Overcoming the defenses of a planet had been costly in terms of energy, as well as in additional damage. Vast stores of the berserker's fuel had been expended in the fighting, and still more had burned in its fusion lamps to power the depopulation of a planet.

. . . and the moving atomic pile was still working its way closer, centimeter by centimeter, to the central processor . . . and no maintenance machines were left, capable of entering those inner passages to interfere with it.

As a result, material reserves were low. Near the center of one of its massive flanks, the giant opened a hatchway half a kilometer long. Moments later a destroyer-sized machine, almost as long as the hatch itself, emerged, followed by a couple of robot tankers, each a kilometer in length.

This foraging party, ignoring the passive array of badlife ships that hovered uncertainly somewhat out of efficient shooting range, sped out toward one of the system's outermost planets, hours away at achievable sublight speeds. It was intending to plunder hydrogen from one or more of that dead world's lifeless moons.

The more the first spacer and his Huvean experts saw of the oddities of the great murderous machine, the more they were impressed and puzzled, as the people of the Twin Worlds had been before them.

Now it was possible to see more clearly how the berserker had been heavily marked and scarred by ancient battles, even before it entered the Twin Worlds system. In places, one crater partially overlay another, as on the surface of some airless natural satellite, suggesting a prolonged bombardment.

Homasubi and Radigast jointly inspected the recorded images.

"Well, one thing for bloody sure—it's been in a war before."

But of greater interest were the fresher scars that showed in the latest images. Some places were still glowing. There were pits more than a kilometer deep, wounds penetrating to unknown depths in armor and machinery. Spectroscopic studies showed the holes still outgassing both common and exotic vapors.

Here was evidence enough to awaken a faint hope. Though the human side had been badly outclassed in weaponry, they had at least managed to hurt their attacker—wounded it sufficiently to make it pause for refitting. They had also forced it to lower its reserves of power to the point where it found it advisable to stop for a refueling with interplanetary hydrogen.

One of the Twin Worlds veterans rasped out: "That's something. Something, by all the gods. We slowed it down, at least."

The techs and scientists aboard Homasubi's flagship were eager to discover all the details that they could having to do with this tough potential enemy's construction and capabilities.

They were eagerly pointing out to each other that the nozzles of the berserker's beam projectors were of an unexpected shape. And there were other surprises.

"Here—see?" A laser pointer probed the magnified image, after the onboard computer had disentangled some of the blurring created by the monster's forcefield shields.

"I see. What kind of material *is* that, in the secondary layer of armor?"

"I'm trying to run a spectrogram on it—confusing, but we'll keep working on it." A pause for emphasis. "It looks to me, First Spacer, that we could be getting some indication here of the reason it suddenly started stalling, talking about alliances. Possibly it's hurt more than shows on the surface."

"You mean it might want more than just a time-out to refuel, get ready for the next round."

"Possibly."

. . . .

T W E N T Y · F O U R

. . . .

Reaching its target satellite in less than an hour, the escort destroyer-machine probed routinely into dead rock. Its first business was to look for signs of the presence of dangerous life units, and secondly, traces of any form of life at all. Any live organism that was found would be expunged, of course, while the necessary equipment was here on site.

There were no life forms, even of the most elementary kind, to be found here—not that the berserker had really expected any on such a small, cold world. But there were abundant signs that dangerously combative badlife had made repeated visits to this place. None were present now.

The smaller machine reported these discoveries dutifully, by tightly focused communication beam, to its hulking parent. Meanwhile the tankers had attached themselves to the small moon, and immediately began the process of extracting quantities of the lightest element from the moon's thick layer of water ice. The hydrogen was compressed into a readily transportable form by heavy freezing, and packed securely into the vast storage spaces. In a different process, carried out at the same time, the machines filled several large tanks with pure oxygen. The berserker considered that the examination of some of its latest crop of prisoners might turn into a long-term project.

Along with the many other things that Gregor had to consider—apart from his diplomatic project of keeping the PO occupied—were the mind and personality of Homasubi. The first spacer had turned out to be precise and pedantic, as advertised in all the intelligence reports. But the man was also curious, and intolerant of inactivity. He seemed to work on the rule that there was always something to be done to improve one's position.

Informed of the latest activity on the berserker's part, the first spacer sent two of his fresh and unscarred Huvean ships, two of the best at agile maneuvering in normal space, to shadow the foraging machine more closely, and, as always, gather more information.

Turning to the figure half reclining in the adjacent acceleration couch, he observed: "If I do not have time to make small talk with you, Admiral, I am sure you will understand."

"I can do without the motherless small talk." Radigast's voice was as monotonous as his grim looks.

Homasubi said: "You understand that my government, my people, had nothing to do with the attack upon your system."

"I never thought you did—though some of my people think so."

"You have heard of its proposal of alliance."

"Sure. That's more than we ever got. It just sailed in here and started shooting." The admiral paused. "After what's happened the last couple of days, all I really understand is that we—I mean you too, I mean all motherless humanity—have got to find some way to kill that bloody thing."

Homasubi considered. "If I may, without offense, pose a hypothetical question?"

Radigast shrugged. "After the hits we've taken already, a question isn't going to do much damage. Shoot."

"If your attacker should now demand your surrender, what would be your response?"

A question had had an impact after all. "What the hell business is that of yours? My fleet's not running away, not from the berserker and not from you."

"My interest in the matter is this: that I have been instructed to require your surrender."

Radigast gave a small snort that might have been the start of a laugh. "I suspected you were going to bring that up, though I was hoping you'd be too smart to bother. Go ahead, you can require any motherless thing you like. My point is, we're already dead, we don't have to pay any attention to your motherless requirements."

He pushed himself halfway up out of his chair. "I'll say it again, we have to kill that bloody thing. And I don't see how any motherless human being can fail to see the motherless fact. How we get to that point, the point where we kill it, I don't know and I don't care—I hope you can give it a better shot than we did. I hope you'll try. Do you think your fleet is up to finishing the job?"

Homasubi was listening, thinking. So far, offering no real answer.

The admiral leaned forward, and seemed on the verge of threatening. The first spacer remained impassive.

Radigast said: "So you want me to surrender? Is that really all that's worrying you? All right, let me set the terms, which are non-negotiable." He stabbed at the stage with a pointing finger. "When that thing is dead, you and I have killed it, and my fleet's down to a single scout—at which time I expect you'll be down to maybe two destroyers and a lifeboat—then I'll surrender to you, just like your little politician wants. That is, I will if you and I are both still alive.

"Meanwhile, maybe you'll find this interesting, I'm ordering my scouts to cooperate with whatever aggressive action your fleet may undertake against our enemy. I've got a few hundred good scouts left, as you have probably observed. By themselves, they probably can't do much against this enemy. Working with your fleet, maybe enough to tip the balance."

"I find the suggestion interesting indeed." Homasubi nodded. "But it is beside the point of our present discussion."

"And that point is—?"

"I am of course fully authorized to accept the surrender of any agent of the Twin Worlds government. Beyond that, absent new orders from my own government, I cannot formally commit my fleet to any new course of action."

Radigast stared in silence for a full quarter of a standard minute. Then he said: "Of course, if some strange, motherless enemy should repeatedly attack your fleet—while your fleet is just peacefully going about its bloody business . . . ?"

"I am sure that those occupying the seats of power in my capital will not deny my fleet the right to defend itself." Perhaps the first spacer's carven features displayed the faintest suggestion of a smile.

Side by side in silence the two men watched the swift Huvean ships approach the distant moon, their images Doppler-shifting for a moment into the red with the speed of their flight, before the holostage computer compensated.

Radigast had sent a high speed courier with orders for his gathering force of scoutships. There were now several hundred of them in one place.

As soon as the first spacer called on his own staff officers for advice, one at least of his advisers began to urge an immediate all-out attack on the main berserker.

Gregor noted silently that everyone was beginning to call it by that name—the Huveans having picked it up from the Twins, who of course had heard it from the Carmpan.

"That would certainly be an act of war," Homasubi observed.

"Yes sir."

"And how do you propose I justify this to my superiors at home?"

"Sir, I say they cannot call your act unjustified, in that this enemy has already declared war, not on the Twin Worlds, but on humanity."

"Is there a document, a record, of any such formal declaration?"

Radigast called up the image of the murdered planet Prairie. "This is the message being sent."

Now and then Gregor gave a moment or two of worried attention to his grandchild—wherever she might be, down on the perilous surface of Timber.

Whatever her fate was going to be, she would probably share it with many millions of others.

And bigger questions kept crowding in. The berserker had said that it considered itself Homasubi's ally.

True, it had blasted the Twin Worlds fleet, and devastated a planet, in a way that showed it put only a negative value on human life. But the action the Huvean fleet had been ready to take, coming here, had not been so utterly different.

Contemplating a magnified view of the ruin that had been the world called Prairie, in wavelengths that let him see some of the devastation beneath the clouds, the first spacer dictated his own message to be sent on to the high authorities at home. He concluded: "Not that we would have done anything—like that. Nor could any other human fleet. Even supposing one could have wanted to.

"The esteemed admiral may be a bloody warmonger, as our own politicians keep calling him. But I fear his assessment of the situation is correct. We're going to have to fight that bloody thing, sooner or later."

"If that is so, there would seem to be little point in allowing it the respite it evidently needs, or at least desires to have."

The people from the peace conference had moved their small ship more or less permanently close to the *Mukunda*.

A majority of the neutral diplomats, professionally cautious as they generally were, had been won over to the faction among them that had begun to plead for immediate intervention in this strange war, prompt action on the side of Earth-descended humanity.

Homasubi had another exchange of views with Admiral Radigast.

Radigast was bold and desperate. "Sir, are you going to fight it, or are you not?"

"Sir, I can only tell you that what I do must depend on circumstances. Let me remind you, honored admiral, that we have as yet no certain determination as to whether there is intelligent life—except for possible Twin Worlds prisoners—aboard this mysterious device. Nor have I any certainty as to its intentions regarding the Huvean world and people."

The admiral came close to an angry outburst: "You'd rather wait till it starts in on your motherless home system, and fight it there?"

"Is there reason to believe it knows the location of Huvea?"

"Not from me, or from my people. But there's no motherless reason to believe it won't know the location of every bloody ED world in the Galaxy, as soon as it goes through the astrogational data banks in one of the little ships it's captured."

Then, not waiting for a response, Radigast began to unfasten himself from his acceleration couch. He had some minor difficulty in doing so, as it was for him an unfamiliar model.

"Get me out of this damned motherless thing. I've got to get back to my ship."

"Sir, I will have a scoutship placed immediately at your disposal."

"Thanks, but don't bother. One thing I still have enough of is my own bloody scoutships." Standing on his feet, he said he was going back to his flagship, and planned to hurl his remnant against the enemy in one last attack. "You can fight it with us, First Spacer, or you can fight it afterwards, back in your own sky, praying you can get more help from somewhere than you gave us."

Meanwhile, Homasubi, methodical as always, was determined not to be rushed into making premature decisions or announcements—and also to put to good use whatever time events allowed him.

Whether the berserker was to be his enemy, or—although he had to admit to himself that he found such a turn of events looking more and more inconceivable—eventually his ally, it was unarguably his duty to learn as much about it as he could.

He had already ordered his strategists, his tactical planners human and robotic, to study carefully all available recordings of the defeat of the Twin Worlds fleet—Radigast, with nothing to lose, had been generous in providing them—to decide which of their weapons and tactics had actually inflicted damage on the berserker, and which had amounted to no more than wasted effort. And the first spacer looked forward to a detailed inspection of those records himself, as soon as he could find the time.

For several standard years, and with good reason, the first spacer had viewed the Twin Worlds fleet as a formidable adversary. It still shocked him that a fleet could have been so quickly shattered, and the ground defenses of Prairie so swiftly overcome. The story told by the recordings was a deeply disturbing one.

Meanwhile, the niceties of diplomacy were becoming purely theoretical.

Fighting had suddenly broken out between the berserker-destroyer engaged in a refueling mission and the two vessels Homasubi had dispatched to observe the process. At least to the extent of an inconclusive exchange of missiles.

"Our ships are acting purely in self defense."

The first spacer's immediate reaction was one of inward relief: He now had additional solid recorded evidence that the berserker had shot first. He asked an officer to confirm the fact, just to be sure.

The berserker was still trying to carry out its refueling process, but one of its tankers was seriously hit when Twin Worlds scoutships hurled themselves at it suicidally. The tanker died in a flare-up of failing fields.

Aboard the Huvean flagship, a spontaneous shipwide cheer went up at the sight.

Missiles launched from the two Huvean destroyers at least disrupted and delayed the refueling operation.

Moments later came the first really bad news: One of the destroyers that had just sped to the scene was quite possibly lost.

Twice now, his fleet had taken human casualties. At the moment he could feel nothing about that, except perhaps a faint relief that the toll had not been higher.

Additional enemy units could be seen accelerating to join the fray. And still more small units were emerging from the body of the great berserker. Surely there must be strict limits on how many it could hatch.

"Sir, do we recall our ships or reinforce them?"

The first spacer opened his mouth and unhesitatingly gave a fateful order.

"**W**hat in heaven's name are you doing here?" gushed a somewhat older woman in uniform. "Two years since I've seen you, honey, but I'd know your mother's daughter anywhere!"

By sheer accident, Luon had been recognized in the street by an old friend of her family, now an army colonel in logistics, who had a good reason for being in the mid-Capital City war zone.

Which was more than Colonel Eurydice could say for Luon and her friends. "You shouldn't be anywhere near here, my girl. And you look terrible. . . . What are your parents thinking of?" The colonel cast an uncertain glance at the two shabby young men, obviously Luon's companions, who had not yet been introduced.

Pushing back a fallen lock of her blond hair, Luon noticed how deadly stiff it felt. She was going to have to find some way, soon, to get a bath. "Well, actually, ma'am, I was visiting my grandfather. When all this started."

"Oh? You mean . . . oh." The fact of Luon's grandfather's identity took just a second to reestablish itself in the colonel's mind.

"Actually," the girl went on, "I've been running little errands for him. Jobs he could give to someone he could absolutely depend on."

"Oh."

Luon nodded, combining the gesture with what she hoped was a meaningful glance. Come to think of it, new-President Gregor could have done worse than send her out scouting for him.

In another minute the colonel was answering Luon's questions with some enthusiasm, as if she hoped the answers might reach someone who could make a difference. Her first complaint was that all the military units on Timber were being forced to operate pretty much on their own, at company and battalion level. By some fiendish enemy trickery, advanced technology, they had for days been cut off from communicating with their own headquarters.

Luon murmured something sympathetic. Talk about being cut off—she was getting somewhat worried about Porphyry, who had been out of touch with her for many hours. According to the robot's last communication, Porph was trying to find a spot from which it might be possible to establish firm contact with Gregor and the fleet. Communication over interplanetary distances was not a household robot's strong suit—but fanatical persistence was.

Colonel Eurydice was nodding grimly, as if confirming her own thoughts. "There's been a lot of disinformation put out by the Huveans—they're pretty good at that. But if I get my sights on one, I'll know what to do."

When Luon asked how the fighting was going, the colonel laughed without humor. She told the girl that Twin Worlds Ground Defense probably had never stationed more than a few hundred heavy armored fighting vehicles on the whole surface of Timber, deployed at what were considered key points across the planet— no one had ever expected the Huveans to ferry a whole army across space, and attempt a major invasion. An approximately equal number of tanks and similar machines had disappeared along with the habitable surface of Prairie. "We're moving all our armor here as fast as we can—it's being used up pretty fast, going against these monsters."

Having got that off her chest, the colonel evidently thought that she had earned the right to ask a few questions of her own. She beamed at Luon's two scruffy companions, focusing on the one nearest the girl's side. "And who is this nice young man?"

"He's an old friend." Luon realized she would have to introduce Reggie under a false name, and hide his Huvean identity. Invention came quickly. "Elbert Whiskerbagger Wilde. Wilde with an 'e' on the end."

Colonel Eurydice blinked once at the name. "Very pleased to meet you, young man."

"How do you do, Colonel?" Reggie was obviously trying to sound engaging and polite—and all the while he was looking at Luon. What name had she given him? *Whiskerbagger?* And an 'e' on the end? How did she come up with these things?

Luon realized that, much as Reggie loved her, he didn't really know her yet. Well, she could hope there would be time for that.

She and Reggie and his fellow Huveans had been moving from place to place, sleeping and eating where they could, trying to keep in touch with each other without looking like a group, never getting far from the center of the capital city. Wherever they went, evidence of recent fighting against enemy landers was not hard to find.

Some of the members of the band had argued almost continuously over what their next move ought to be. One faction favored a deliberate decision to split up, with a well organized plan as to when and where they would reunite. Others, so far in the majority, wanted to keep loosely in touch with each other on an hourly basis. By good fortune, none of the fugitive Huveans had yet been seriously wounded. Among the ten of them they had sustained a good number of bruises and cuts, mostly while scrambling out of the way of enemy landers and Twin Worlds armor. But, so far, nothing beyond what a well equipped home medical kit ought to be able to handle.

Despite Luon's broad hints that she was here in the war zone on some kind of secret mission for the new president, the colonel thought it her duty to give the young people a fairly stern warning that they ought to get farther away from the fighting.

Waving goodbye, they retreated away from the city center for several blocks, then circled back, not wanting to stray far from the Citadel and the scenes of fighting, where things were going on.

In the end, it was mainly by accident that Luon and her companions finally got close enough to the fighting machines to get a really good look at them. For a couple of days she had been aware of the presence of several gangs of teenagers in the area, kids who evidently thought war the greatest sport they had encountered yet.

One of these, a gangly youth of fourteen or fifteen, brought Luon and her friends the rumor that a fallen invader a few blocks away was showing a Huvean insignia—a final proof, in this kid's mind, of who the enemy really was.

Luon could see in some of the Huveans' eyes that they were still half ready to believe. With Douras leading the way, and guided by the boy who had brought the rumor, the group set out to find the wreckage, if there really was any, and discover the truth about it.

Every day, almost every hour, Luon had heard talk among the capital's citizens, some sympathetic and some angry, still demanding to know where the Huvean hostages were, and what had happened to them. The general breakdown in communications had kept many people from ever hearing of Acting President Gregor's decree saying they should be freed.

Porphyry had managed to pick up Homasubi's broadcast, intended as a message to the general population, telling of the first spacer's intention to rescue the former hostages. Gregor and Radigast had added their own words to the message, assuring everyone who could hear them that Twin Worlds and Huvea were not at war, had never been at war, and were united in wishing to get the young Huveans out of harm's way and send them home. The machines attacking on the ground, and the monster in the sky, were of unknown origin, but they had nothing to do with Huvea.

The citizens of Twin Worlds could feel certain, their new president was trying to assure them, that any Huvean they might now detect on the surface of Timber was only there for the purpose of the rescue operation, and with the permission of the Twin Worlds government.

But people who did not want to believe the message would not do so.

Porphyry accepted it as genuine, and acted accordingly.

Luon and her companions had come to a halt on the rim of a sizable pit, and the boy who guided them was pointing. "Down there."

It seemed that once a sizable building had occupied this space, but now there was only a crater, deep and wide enough to swallow a three-story house. At the bottom, surrounded by miscellaneous debris, there lay a massive fragment of an enemy machine, three or four meters long, in shape resembling a crab's main claw.

The object appeared to be made of some strange, dark metal, and seemed slightly twisted by the force that had torn it loose from the machine of which it had once been part. It seemed completely inert, the surface pitted and blackened, and a raw opening torn at one end sprouted a tangle of amputated lines, rods, and chains.

Reggie walked completely around the crater, studying the thing from every angle, before he spoke. "I don't see anything like an insignia, Huvean or otherwise."

The boy made energetic jabbing motions, pointing. "It's inside, where that thing opens like a jaw. You can see it when you get

close. I was down there and saw it." In a moment he had gone leaping down into the crater, agile as a goat, taking long strides from one
solid outcropping to another, but still creating a small landslide. In
another moment Douras was following, his movements a few years
older, stronger, better planned and more efficient.

Reggie and Luon and the others remained above, scattered
along the rim of the pit. A few additional onlookers had joined
them. Luon was thinking that down there would be a bad place to
be trapped, if a mob hunting Huveans happened to come along.

The boy had dropped down on all fours, right beside the
giant fragment, where he could look up into the mouth-like cavity
at the joint of the great crab-claw. He was pointing at something
there, jabbering in shrill tones. Beside him, Douras sprawled
momentarily on the ground to get a look, but then immediately
straightened up again and backed away a step or two, shaking his
head and dusting off his hands.

Turning his face upslope toward Reggie, Douras called out:
"Just looks like a circle with a crinkly edge. Maybe a little bit
like the Huvean sun symbol. But I don't know what it is. Can't be
an insignia. Who would put one in there, where no one would
ever—?"

Without warning, without the least premonitory twitch, the
great claw convulsed, like some fragment of a fresh-killed animal.
But this spasm had deadly purpose. The jaw snapped open, pro-
pelling itself a couple of meters off the ground. When it closed
again an instant later, it had the boy by one arm, right up to the
shoulder, and his shrill scream went up.

Douras had instinctively jumped back. From somewhere he
had pulled out a pistol, a weapon Luon had never guessed that he
was carrying, and was firing one shot after another, all useless, at
the mass of metal before him. Then he stepped forward again.
With his free hand he had grabbed the boy's free arm, and was
attempting to pull him away.

The great jaw leapt and spasmed once again. Whether by sheer luck or some infernal calculation, this time when it snapped shut there were two bodies caught headfirst inside.

Luon was gripping Reggie's hand so hard that she feared her own fingers were going to break. She was terrified that he would pull away and go bounding downhill to try to save his friend, a friend who was already dead. But Reggie wasn't bounding anywhere, only staring, in sick fascination, as if he might be paralyzed.

Dimly she was aware of a cry that sounded from behind her. "Clear the way, people! Coming through with weapons!" She turned to see the approach of reinforcements, more units of the Twin Worlds army with their battle gear.

People on rooftops raised a cheer. Some of them were shooting at the monster with various weapons, having no more effect than Douras's pistol. Luon was thinking numbly that he must have scrounged that somewhere since their escape.

Over the past few days, she had seen a number of wrecked tanks, burned, burst open, their projecting weapon barrels twisted as if they were candy toys. The machines now coming to challenge the enemy were different, moving with the muted roar of bulldozers. There were three of them, maneuvering quickly to station themselves at equal intervals around the crater. Then, at some invisible signal, all three plunged over and in, converging on the metal monster in a sliding rush.

The killer survived the crashing impact of the first one to get home. The huge claw flipped on its back and opened its jaw wide, disgorging two mangled human bodies. Some kind of heat-ray came lancing forth from inside that deadly cavity, a beam of fire that instantly turned a hardened dozer blade into a spray of molten drops.

The second dozer smashed into the crab-claw a moment later, grinding it beneath its treads. But again the ray shot out.

Just in time, Luon and Reggie dove for shelter, behind the stump of a thick wall. The only heat that reached her was reflected, from a high undamaged wall a few meters behind her vantage point. Even head down behind a life-saving barricade, she could feel a wave of searing, blistering intensity. For a moment she thought a piece of metal wreckage had fallen over her—then she realized that Porphyry, coming somehow out of nowhere, had thrown himself on top of her, metal body blocking the strongest radiance.

Engines were still roaring. Luon looked for Reggie, saw him smiling, nodding, still alive behind a section of the wall. She forced her body up to where she could look over the crude parapet. The second bulldozer, half melted down and burning, died. She saw the cab burst open but it was empty—all the machines must be running on remote control. The third dozer, blade carried low, caught the enemy squarely, pinning half of the great claw beneath its treads, setting its blade against the other half. The engine roared, and on its second or third try succeeded in ripping the enemy in two.

A ragged cheer was going up, from scattered human voices. When Porphyry regained his feet, Luon saw that her savior robot's back was scorched, and the few remaining shreds of Porphyry's servant clothes were smoking. Calm as ever, the robot extended an arm to help its client, Luon, stand. Cheerfully it questioned her to make sure she was unhurt.

Already more of the local heavy machinery had come in sight. Clear windows in most of the units showed empty cabs, working in robotic mode.

Here came a heavy hauler, carrying a full tank of something—road-building muck, it looked like, thick weighty mud that would harden into stone in a few minutes. Now the sludge was being poured over the enemy wreckage in the pit. People had learned to take no chances with this foe.

The nearby cheers had trailed off into silence. Luon belatedly realized that one of the Huveans, under stress, shocked by the death of Douros, had just blurted out something in a strong Huvean accent.

People were pointing. Faces were suddenly grim again. Pictures of the former hostages had been in all the media, before the war began, and now one of them had been recognized.

In moments, some people had forgotten the enemy, and were trying to capture them, or lynch them.

A loud man's voice proclaimed: "I heard that thing was marked, as plain as day, with a Huvean insignia!"

A new voice broke in, carrying authority. "Move back, folks. Shove back! Special Forces here. We've got things under control."

There were a dozen of them or more, capable-looking men and women in rough civilian clothes. Now they were in the process of bringing out their special hats and armbands, and putting them on. Besides their weapons, they came armed with signed IDs from President Gregor himself, which they showed to everyone in sight. Their leader announced they were placing all the escaped hostages under arrest, and were taking them to an undisclosed location for questioning.

"This young lady too. She's a collaborator." The man who made that announcement looked very much like a young officer who had once given the girl a guided tour of a huge warship. He must have known Luon by sight, for he was standing right beside her, nodding. Was that a wink, or was his eye just twitching?

Luon caught a glimpse of the colonel of logistics standing in the background, looking horrified at Luon's supposed fate. But Colonel Eurydice made no attempt to interfere.

Neither did Porphyry. He followed Luon unobtrusively, the scorched and battered image of the perfect servant.

Luon and Reggie, along with the other rescued hostages, had been carried safely, on a Twin Worlds scoutship, up to a joyous welcome on the Huvean flagship. On their arrival, they told stories of the terrific fighting on the surface of Timber. A small detail had been left behind in Capital City to see what could be done about recovering Douras's body.

When the young survivors came filing out of the scout into the *Mukunda*'s landing bay, the political officer was there to greet them.

Zarnesti, introducing himself with a flourish, was ready to welcome Luon as a defector to the Huvean side, and to promise the young Huveans they would have revenge against the evil Twins who had tormented them in captivity, and after their escape had hounded them as fugitives.

But the former hostages were only interested in fighting back against the things that had killed their comrade.

Allowing for the strain they had been under, the political officer did not press the point. Giving them a moment to reflect, he said: "You are to be honored, my young friends. The first spacer himself is here to welcome you aboard."

There was a preliminary stirring at a doorway, where officers came and went. Then an important presence entered the landing bay.

Luon faced the door, and bowed her head, in imitation of the group surrounding her. She had had enough experience of human power at high levels to recognize its presence when it approached.

Reggie, who was holding her hand, bowed too, but only momentarily. Then he raised his gaze to meet that of the imposing man before him. To the first spacer, Reggie said: "Sir, this fleet has got to fight for humans and not against them. It would be a great mistake to attack the Twins." He paused to swallow, then added: "Please, Uncle Hom."

There followed a long moment of silence. Some people, including the political officer, were too stunned to find anything to do or say, while others were too embarrassed.

The first spacer demonstrated superb self control. In a quiet and formal voice, he apologized to the others present for the behavior of his nephew, who had injected a personal relationship into matters of high public policy.

Reggie's head was bowed again. He said: "I am sorry if I have offended, Uncle. But . . ."

"You have been under great strain. Your apology is accepted. Let the offense not happen again."

Luon squeezed her lover's hand in sympathy. She knew what it was like to have a close personal relationship with a very high government official. That was something she and Reggie had in common—one factor that had brought them together in the first place.

Some of the indrawn cloud of Radigast's scoutships were busy disputing with the enemy vessels engaged in refueling or repair. But the admiral was holding a greater number in reserve, to be thrown into action somehow—he wasn't yet sure just how—when the decisive moment came.

Presently Admiral Radigast departed the *Mukunda* for his own ship—in the background, Zarnesti the political officer shaking his head slightly and looking grim, seeing a dangerous enemy get away—and Homasubi reconvened the ongoing council of his own select advisers.

Once the first spacer had them in place, he asked them for recommendation; their opinions seemed sharply divided, but in fact they were reluctant to put forward any suggestions at all. He had to remind them sharply that whatever they might suggest, the ultimate responsibility for the actions of the fleet would be his, the first spacer's, alone.

The political officer was upset following his virtual meeting with Gregor.

He was also nervously, suspiciously, eagerly demanding to know what had happened in the meeting between Homasubi and his Twin Worlds counterpart. "I see you have allowed Radigast his personal freedom. What of the surrender?"

"I made no claim upon his freedom. What would be the point? We discussed a few technical matters only."

"First Spacer, I respectfully insist upon discussing the matter of surrender. Surely you presented our government's demand?"

The first spacer appeared to be making an effort to recall the precise details of his just-concluded talk. "I made no demands. I did receive some personal assurances from the admiral."

"But no document? You have obtained no document?" The PO was almost jumping up and down. Of course the meeting would have been routinely recorded—but recordings were almost as easily altered as human memories, and people tended to produce different versions of the same event.

"Alas, I am not skilled in the language of diplomacy, the nuances of negotiation. I would not trust myself to conduct such delicate discussions."

"Delicate discussions?" The PO tugged at his hair, which seemed quite firmly rooted. "What need is there for delicacy at this stage? They have nothing left to fight us with!"

"Then they have nothing left to surrender. I am but a simple military man, and do not understand these great affairs of state. No doubt you were successful in obtaining the desired document from the Twin Worlds' acting president?"

The PO shook his head and frowned, which, Homasubi had come to understand, was his way of trying to look wise. "If he who claims to be acting president is in fact a head of state, then in discussion with him we are in the domain of treaties, of formal law. . . ." Zarnesti let it trail away, his frown deepening. He had in fact pressed Gregor for a surrender document, but Gregor, while not seeming to refuse, had insisted that the Twin Worlds parliament had to approve anything in the nature of a treaty, which a surrender certainly would be.

Most of what the first spacer's people were telling him was cautious and politically correct. But at least one of his advisers said bluntly: "The best way to defend our own home is to do the necessary fighting in some system light-years away."

Only one adviser out of the group was firmly in favor of helping the Twin Worlds people in any way, or even coming to a positive agreement with them. "I know, we have been conditioned for several years to think of these people as the enemy. But now it is hard to see how they will be able to do us the least harm."

One problem was that, in the months since the treaty was signed, a new and more aggressive regime had taken over in Huvea. The temper of the people there was no longer in the least conciliatory.

The new government had repudiated the whole idea of giving hostages—and some of its members were thinking of demanding them from Twin Worlds instead.

The berserker had given the Huvean civilian a pledge to restore the hostages to Homasubi's flagship, if any of its machines could find them on the surface of Timber. And it promised to search diligently. But there was no sign that it had conducted any such search, or deviated at all from its usual routine of killing.

Homasubi had secretly confided this to Radigast, and Radigast to Gregor.

Gregor's comment was: "It tries to play the games of diplomacy and intrigue—it understands the usefulness of a direct and simple lie—but so far, it does not play with any subtlety."

Meanwhile the civilian visitors from neutral worlds, the delegates from the peace conference, visiting aboard Homasubi's flagship either virtually or in the flesh, were increasingly coming round to the position that the Huvean first spacer should rid the Galaxy of this murderous machine.

More than one of them angrily warned him that his name, and that of his system/nation, would go down in Galactic infamy if he did not. In their view, Twin Worlds did not pose any particular threat—certainly not now, with its fleet destroyed—but this powerful attacker did.

The respected Lady Constance, long known as an opponent of rearmament in general, preached: "For once in human history, a hard military blow will not cost human lives, but save them."

These people were more diplomatic than the first spacer's own diplomat. Still, Homasubi did not take kindly to foreigners telling him what to do.

Gregor was inclined to stick with Admiral Radigast, on his battered flagship, where together they formed a coherent remnant of Twin Worlds government.

Now the acting president observed that while the peace delegation of neutrals was urging the Huveans to throw their weight

330 ..... F R E D   S A B E R H A G E N

into this war, on the side of humanity, the warrior Homasubi, the human who carried all the power of more than lightnings at his fingertips, was hanging back.

Ninety-first Diplomat, being detained on this side of death by the stubborn efforts of an ED medirobot, called all the other leaders to attend her in person. To those who managed to attend, she delivered a few last, enigmatic words.

Exhausted from the strain of delivering a prophecy, giving way under the psychic impact of the great loss of life already inflicted in this system, she had not precisely refused medical care, but seemed indifferent as to whether it was given her or not.

As she was dying, Ninety-first Diplomat was able to establish some kind of mental contact-at-a-distance with human prisoners aboard the berserker. But these contacts brought little in the way of reassuring news, except to establish the fact that some of the berserker's prisoners in space still breathed.

"Foreseeing its own destruction, it has decided to kill them, rather than save them for study. But most of the Earth-descended have somehow escaped from its control."

She said that after death she wanted her body to be sent into the sun of her home world.

And still the Carmpan, having once spoken forcefully, re-mained withdrawn into silence and immobility, her nearly cylin-drical body shrunken to half its normal adult size, and twisted up into a fetal-looking ball. None of the human medical officers in attendance were expert on Carmpan physiology, but they agreed that the outlook was not good.

The medirobot eventually gave up on trying to help her. She had somehow managed to disable several of its functions. But it still reported that she was not entirely dead.

The first spacer had been muddling through, trying to put off political matters he could not avoid, while waiting for the anticipated instructions from his home world. For several hours he had been expecting a reply to his urgent questions, but no answer had yet arrived.

It was common enough for messages sent by courier between the stars to be delayed, for any of several routine reasons, chronic problems in transportation having nothing to do with war. But in the present situation there were more ominous possibilities as well.

Privately, he had always dreaded the thought of being forced to make decisions of great import that were not properly his to make. Now he was coming gradually to the full realization, with a mixture of inward terror and relief, that he had already done exactly that.

Gratefully he had seized upon the idea of sending ships to keep an eye on the berserker's refueling operation; surely no higher authority in his own government, whatever might happen later, could fault him for doing that. Clearly it was his duty as a field commander to observe, to reconnoiter, even though sending the ships might provoke this destructive monster into some aggressive move against them. And when any units of his own fleet came under attack from any power whatsoever, it would certainly be his duty to go to their assistance with all the force under his command.

He had been compelled to make some critical decisions that could not be delayed. How many wars in the past, he wondered, had begun in such accidental fashion?

Now that the fighting had begun, it seemed that the most effective tactic available might be to exert what power he could where the enemy was vulnerable, and keep the berserker tankers from getting back to their mother ship.

The situation was complicated by the fact that the berserker mothership was moving toward the tanker, which had had some difficulty in an exchange of missiles with a Huvean destroyer.

The first spacer inwardly relaxed—fighting had begun, cobwebs were swept away, and his duty could be seen as clear as it could be.

Meanwhile, Radigast's own refueling and repair operation was making some progress. The two ships had entered the distant docks and, making the best use of efficient machinery, had already been repaired. What was the best use to make of them?

They could reinforce his other light forces in the outer system, and hope to surprise the berserker elements there.

The admiral had already decided that he would order the whole remnant of his fleet, whose most effective component was the hundreds of scouts still gathering into a loose cloud, into an all-out attack—of course coordinating with the Huveans, if possible.

But events, as usual, were taking something of an unexpected course. Radigast was teetering on the brink of giving that order, sending his agglomeration of wrecks and scoutships not against the berserker itself, but to the aid of the Huvean destroyers, who seemed in need of any support that they could get.

The admiral was running low on robot couriers, as he was on all other resources—except scoutships. Any couriers that reached the flagship with messages from elsewhere, from his own distant scouts or from civilians, were being hastily refitted and refueled, readied to carry messages out again.

Several dozen had already been dispatched, in redundant numbers, to other solar systems, carrying renewed appeals for help, signed by the acting president.

Whatever terrible events might take place today or tomorrow in the light of the Twin Worlds' sun, ED humanity on its scattered worlds had been thoroughly warned against the monstrous new peril that it faced. Several scoutships had also been pressed into service in the same task, though they were not as fast as the couriers.

Within days, the entire Galactic community of Earth-descended humans would know exactly what was happening in the Twin Worlds system. Unhappily, there was no reason to expect immediate help, no way any of them—except Huvea—could possibly provide it.

The heavy ships of both fleets were moving into position, their respective commanders having reached a general agreement on how they were to be deployed.

Radigast was talking to his commander in chief. "Sir, I want to send you back to the Huvean flagship. Homasubi assures me you'll be quite welcome aboard. Sorry to keep you bouncing around, a president without a government, but . . ."

Gregor had not expected this. "What is the purpose, Admiral?"

"Mister President, both our fleets are going to get pounded, but today that Huvean hull is in a lot better shape to take a beating than this one is. And I would like for the Twin Worlds to have some motherless government left when this is over. If you and I are not on the same ship, the odds will be a little better that one of us at least will survive."

Gregor hastily took thought. "As for myself, I think my duty requires me to remain on board."

"As for me, Mister President, as admiral of this motherless fleet my duty requires me to get all the bloody unnecessary civilians out of the way, along with the seriously wounded."

All of the members of the Galactic Council peace delegation still remained physically in their own small ship. But their holostage presence on the first spacer's bridge continued—whenever Homasubi was ready to allow it.

He had decided that he ought to allow it, as his fleet seemed to be entering this battle as the champions of all humanity. The first spacer thought it would be a good idea if he could claim the people of as many worlds as possible as his virtual companions as he went into battle—as far as the communication beams could stand the strains of distance and combat.

But for safety's sake the ship of neutral diplomats was going to withdraw to a greater distance, which would take them out of convenient conference range.

Some of the most pacifistic of them wanted to get back to their home worlds as quickly as possible—massive rearmament programs would have to be put into effect.

Homasubi made arrangements to receive the seriously wounded from the Twin Worlds fleet on board the dedicated hospital ship attached to his fleet. So far, the prewar computer simulations had proven fairly accurate—though space combat could kill any number of people, it did not, by its very nature, produce large numbers of wounded survivors.

Meanwhile, sporadic ground fighting continued, still concentrated heavily in the vicinity of the Citadel. The remaining enemy landing units had united into a force that so far resisted everything the populace could throw at it.

In space there was ongoing skirmishing in several places.

Now was a period of relative calm before a greater storm.

In the outer reaches of the system, where fighting among the frozen satellites flared up and died, only to flare up again, it appeared that humanity was actually going to have superior forces, thanks to the swarm of scouts flying boldly to their own destruction, and the unexpected appearance of the two rapidly repaired destroyers.

The surviving one of the berserker tankers had completed its loading operation, and was headed back to its enormous mother.

The blasted tanker in its death agony was still putting on a spectacular display.

Homasubi's heavy ships were putting themselves directly in the berserker's path as it began to move to the aid of its surviving tanker and its small escort.

"*He's going after it! He's going to hit that slimy son of a worm with everything!*" Radigast screamed it out, and punched a stanchion beside his couch.

"Yes," said Gregor quietly. "I rather thought he would. He is a human being, after all."

The admiral was determined to get his own forces back into the battle.

But Gregor found it painful to watch how slowly Radigast's crippled flagship moved. Painful to see the similar difficulties of his other surviving ships.

"Incoming ship, sir." The holostage showed the blip of a single vessel or object, in these first moments not yet identified, in the opposite direction from the sun—and in the opposite direction from the known enemy.

The color of the symbol wavered uncertainly, then settled into a friendly Huvean tint.

My government, thought Homasubi, is about to order me to explore the possibility of an alliance with the machine. Or perhaps I will even be commanded to join it in attacking the Twin Worlds.

The arriving ship brought not just orders, but a very high ranking Huvean statesperson. This lady came armed with the option of assuming command of the Huvean fleet.

But having seen something of the true situation, the newcomer declined to do that. She would say no more than: "At least there is no sense in which that option is entirely ruled out."

The thinking (or at least the hoping) at the highest levels of Huvean authority (light-years away, getting worried in the security of their own shelters on their own home world) still seemed to be that this whole idea of a super-powerful, murderous machine would turn out to be, after all, some kind of insanely clever Twin

Worlds trick. Reports of an alien machine destroying the whole
Twin Worlds fleet, and sterilizing a planet, were simply wrong, or
at least had to be much exaggerated.

Unfortunately the orders, when the first spacer had a chance
to hear them and see them, did not include any clear-cut decision
on what Homasubi should do with his fleet in regard to the mysterious stranger.

At least they were not commanding him to do something
impossible, or utterly mad. Rather these orders seemed, as orders
issued from a distance so often did, designed primarily to ensure
that whatever might go wrong could not be blamed on the people
who had stayed at home.

The newly arrived senior Huvean civilian official seemed
determined not to let herself be upset by circumstances: "Would've
been here sooner, First Spacer, but we ran into some damned bad
weather." She was speaking, of course, of flightspace weather
between the stars, the flow of particles, fields, and space-time
itself. "What's going on? What word on the hostages?"

Homasubi, with the help of a couple of able officers—and his
own nephew, as a qualified, firsthand witness—succinctly explained
the situation, and the newcomer's face slowly settled into an expression of ashen shock.

The real message she had brought from home, though she did
not spell it out in so many words, was this: that the high Huvean
government was still temporizing, delaying, trying to make up its
mind.

The senior diplomat was not helped at all when she heard
the theories Zarnesti had put forward—surely it had not been a
Twin Worlds trick to sterilize one of their own home worlds—and
said she needed time to study the situation further.

But in fact the decision had already been made, by the first
spacer, when he had ordered his two destroyers to be reinforced.

The civilian expressed her reservations, for the record, but
was obviously relieved. By mutual agreement, she retired to her

assigned cabin. Her advice had been disregarded, and whatever happened now wasn't going to be her fault.

With the glaring example of Prairie constantly before their eyes, and after an inspiring speech from their commander, the Huvean crews, of large ships and small alike, had every incentive to make this a serious fight.

Once the overwhelming fact of the death machine's existence had sunk in on them, most of them had been expecting they would have to fight it.

Again Admiral Radigast pledged to pass on what knowledge of the enemy he had gained—at a terrible price—saying: "That bloody thing's almost destroyed my fleet. Whatever I've got left is yours to make use of."

Homasubi had been expecting this, was ready with a plan, and crisply informed his colleague where he would prefer to see the remnant of the Twin Worlds fleet deployed.

Radigast pondered whether to salute, decided against it, and merely nodded. "Yes sir. We'll be a little slow, but we'll give it the motherless best we've got."

"I'm sure you will. We are moving in. All crews and ships prepare for battle."

Having lost several billion lives, humanity was going to do its best to save several billion more.

T W E N T Y - S E V E N

The berserker was gradually losing its ongoing struggle to block and tangle human communications across the surface of Timber and in nearby space. Humans and their computers were finding effective ways to counter its interference, and the machine's resources were weakening. People on the planet's surface were increasingly able to establish and maintain contact with their compatriots in space, and through Radigast's ships with the Huvean fleet as well.

At this point in the battle, the great majority of Timber's people still survived. Casualties were only in the thousands, a small percentage of the total population. And thousands of active fighters, armed with heavy weapons, had surrounded the remaining berserker landers and were slowly finishing them off.

Luon and her lover, and the other Huveans, having been safely evacuated to the *Mukunda,* continued to give eloquent testimony, including solid evidence that Douras, who was now fast becoming a Huvean martyr, had been cruelly slain by berserker hardware, not Twin Worlds people, and in fact had died trying to save a Twin Worlds boy who was being mangled by the real enemy.

On top of that, it was pretty plain that Twin Worlds no longer posed a threat to anyone.

Some of the people on Homasubi's staff were beginning to suggest the possibility that the alien was bluffing when it did not back down before their entire fleet. (Also they, following the first spacer's lead, were beginning to call it a berserker. There was no need to come up with a nice name for it, if it was not going to be an ally.)

When they raised their theory of the new enemy's behavior with the first spacer, he stared at them coldly. "You will present the evidence."

The theorists' spokesman advanced timidly. "We mean, sir, that it really sustained serious damage in its close attack on the planet Prairie, when it came up against heavy ground-based weapons. The enemy has demonstrated that it has—or had— marvelous defenses, but still the battle recordings do show it being hit repeatedly. They do show holes in its surface more than a kilometer in depth."

"In a thickness of more than five kilometers. Not conclusive, in itself. But go on."

"It's our contention that some substantial damage must have resulted. Since that time it has, to some extent, been carrying out a bluff. Part of the reason for its aggressive actions is an attempt to conceal how badly it's been hurt."

The first spacer was silent for so long that some of those attending him began to shift their feet, and think of other things they ought to have been working on. But when he spoke, he sounded more intrigued than angry. "Why wouldn't it just retreat?"

He got an eager answer. "Perhaps its superluminal drive has been disabled." Crossing interstellar distances in normal space-time was possible in theory, but would amount to something like slow suicide, warping machines or humans centuries away from the time at which their journeys were begun.

When the suggestion was passed on to the *Morholt,* it was hard to find anyone among the Twin Worlds survivors who was ready to back this theory.

The berserker's looming shortage of hydrogen fuel was real enough, but the need was not desperate, or even immediate.

But other problems were.

The huge power lamps that sustained its drive units, kept its various field generators going, and nourished its awesome weapons were being fed from its emergency reserves of fuel—and the central processor was quite ready and willing to use up those reserves entirely for the chance to sterilize another planet thick with badlife.

So far the new damage inflicted by the local badlife had only slightly diminished the killer's fighting ability. The second fleet to challenge it within this system was being methodically demolished. This time the foe was perhaps a little stronger, the process going a little more slowly than it had with the first fleet, but the central processor calculated that a similar outcome was inevitable—provided the central processor itself was not destroyed by the badlife weapon now eating its way inexorably into the berserker's unliving heart.

Radigast and his staff, deciding that absolute cooperation with First Spacer Homasubi was their only reasonable option, had warned the Huvean commanders that the defensive shields protecting the vessels of their fleet were not going to be strong enough.

"It is plain that yours were inadequate," was the usual answer. "We think that ours are stronger."

The first spacer had taken those warnings seriously, given the supporting evidence before his eyes. But his ships were going to have to enter combat with the weapons and defenses they had on board.

The Huvean captains had also been cautioned by their defeated colleagues that their offensive weapons would be largely ineffective. That suggestion had been less credible at first, but now it was terribly confirmed.

Despite the fact that First Spacer Homasubi had increased the power allotted to his defensive shields, his flagship was hit, and hit hard, more than once, in the first few minutes of full-scale fighting. He was forced to retreat, with his other battleships blowing up around him, even as Radigast had earlier been forced to withdraw—and then the *Mukunda* was actually hurled to a greater distance by the power of the berserker's weapons.

Those on his staff who had suggested the enemy was crippled were in disgrace; some of them were dead, and perhaps did not mind.

Radigast was almost chuckling. "I told the son of a worm that'd happen. Now, what's he going to do about it?"

Political Officer Zarnesti, along with the recently arrived civilian of higher rank, both shell-shocked by violence, came to Homasubi babbling that surely it must be time to ask the enemy for terms of peace.

Homasubi ignored these whining outbursts. When they persisted, the first spacer had the two protesters conveyed to sick bay. Perhaps, he suggested, they could do something useful there, in the way of tending the wounded. When they protested, he offered the brig as an alternative.

The higher-ranked civilian promised: "I'll have your head for this when we get home!"

The first spacer bowed very slightly, knowing that on Huvea, that was no mere figure of speech. But he did not amend his orders.

The bridge of Homasubi's flagship became less crowded with the withdrawal of the virtual presence of the neutral diplomats.

On advice of their senior member, the Lady Constance, they withdrew their ship to some greater distance from the fighting—too far for a regular dialogue by radio or optical beam to remain feasible.

Excepting only considerations of their own survival, they were most keenly interested in learning the result of the battle, and did not want to depart the system until they were assured of the outcome. That Twin Worlds had already been disastrously defeated was beyond dispute; it only remained to learn the full extent of the catastrophe, and to see if any people would remain alive.

It seemed to the first spacer that reports of damage suffered by the various elements of his fleet were coming in continuously. Worse, certain other of his vessels had abruptly ceased to report altogether.

In his exhaustion, he felt a sudden kinship, much deeper than before, with Admiral Radigast.

Quickly the picture became clear, and it was not a pretty one. People on other ships were able to report that the missing vessels had been utterly wiped out.

Word came from sick bay that the Political Officer, Zarnesti, between stints at reading poetry to the wounded, was virtually accusing him of treason. The first spacer had destroyed his fleet by hurling it into the conflict on the wrong side.

There were moments in which it seemed to Homasubi that he had nothing left with which to fight, and he had to struggle to keep blind panic from establishing a killing grip in his own mind. One firm aid was the thought that Radigast had somehow managed to survive a similar disaster. Very well then, if the Twin Worlder could do it, so would he.

"We were so utterly confident that our fleet was stronger than his had been. That the enemy must have been seriously weakened."

"Message from Admiral Radigast, sir."

"Then he is still alive? Good. Let me see. I hope that I can talk to him."

In this last exchange, Radigast's *Morholt,* capable of moving at no more than a cripple's pace, had remained more distant from the enemy than the Huvean ships, and thus was spared the worst of the berserker's fire.

Even so, the admiral had received a serious wound, for which the medics, human and mechanical, were treating him at his battle station.

People on the bridge of the Twin Worlds flagship were able to catch dim glimpses of the berserker, now bearing a couple of obvious new wounds near amidships on the huge hull, spouting nuclear flame and fumes. It seemed to be trying to reclaim the surviving elements of its foraging party.

There was the successfully returned tanker, nuzzling at the great beast's side.

There were still a handful of Twin Worlds scoutships determinedly trying to interfere with the process—and the crews of those ships were paying for their boldness with their lives.

Humans watching grew furiously angry at this sign of what seemed their enemy's contemptuous disregard for human power. The damned thing in its insolence evidently intended to go on refueling even while under attack by elements of two human fleets. Two badly crippled fleets, but even so—and the worst of it was that, so far, it was having some success.

The first massed Huvean attack on the gigantic enemy mothership had been repulsed, with considerable loss. The feeble efforts of Twin Worlds forces to be helpful seemed to make no effective difference.

The first spacer counted his losses, rallied his forces and reformed their formation, and tried again.

This time, he could see, there was no help to be expected from Radigast.

The admiral had called off the pointless scoutship assaults for the time being, as their only result seemed to be a steady drain of losses.

Radigast ordered his squadrons to prepare for a mass scout ramming of the huge berserker, putting the small ships on automatic pilot to give their human crews a chance to save their lives.

People and computers engaged in the continual process of trying to assess the enemy's damage were seeing hopeful indications: It seemed quite possible that some slow-acting weapons of Twin Worlds or Huvean contrivance, a combination of intelligent bomb and calculating atomic pile, had got on board the berserker, through one of the holes blasted by other missiles, old and new; now there were signs that one or more of these devices were slowly melting and radiating their way into the enemy's vitals.

Huang Gun went meticulously through the checklist on his suit and helmet, in preparation for the extended trek into vacuum that his master had warned him was going to be required. Scarcely had he finished the checklist when an outbreak of strange noise filled him with alarm. The little mob of cadets, having equipped themselves with tools stolen from their fallen guard, were attacking the thin wall separating the executioner's cell from theirs.

The master opened another, interior door for Huang Gun. "Come this way," it ordered, speaking through his helmet radio.

Moving in obedience to the terse instructions given him from time to time, he groped his way through twisted, darkened corridors. The gravity held steady, and his gauge showed that there was still good air. But of course he kept his helmet on. Presently he found himself behind a new set of closed doors, in a middle-sized, barren room that he had never seen before.

The voice of the great machine told Huang Gun that the cause of Death now depended heavily on him.

"There are additional tasks that must be done, before you are granted the peace of your own death."

The executioner drew a deep breath. How many more would he need to draw, before claiming his reward? "I am ready."

"You must arm yourself." The door of a small cabinet in the wall popped open in front of Huang Gun; inside the cabinet he saw a pistol.

The master's voice went on. "I have no more mobile machines available with which to defend myself—or you. You must not die until the essential task has been accomplished."

"I understand." He took the weapon from the cabinet and weighed it in his hand.

The tools that Hemphill and his companions had taken from the maintenance robot were not designed for breaking through walls, but they were good enough to get the job done. In a few minutes the humans had penetrated into Huang Gun's former cell, discovering it empty. The outline of another door, closed and sealed, showed in one of the inner walls.

It seemed natural for Hemphill to have assumed command, to go on giving orders. "Before we do anything else, we've got to deal with our power problem. The reserve in all our suits is dangerously low."

Training had taught them one way to deal with this difficulty. The solution was for one person to share almost all the remaining power in his suit with others, furnishing each with enough to allow several additional hours of moderate activity.

Hemphill was beginning to say something about drawing lots, when Dirigo immediately interrupted. In a voice that had somehow acquired authority, he repeated his earlier offer informing his class-mates that he had been a total failure as leader, from the time the trouble started until now—but now he was going to make up for it.

When someone began a protest, Dirigo squelched it. "I haven't pulled rank since the trouble started—like a lot of things I haven't done. But now I'm giving the rest of you an order: Step up here one at a time, charge up your suits from mine, and move out!"

"What about you?" Lee demanded.

Dirigo was shaking his head inside his helmet. "I'll search these rooms, examine whatever equipment I can find, looking for a source of power. If I find anything I'll let you know at once. If you haven't gone too far, you can come back and recharge. Or, I'll charge my suit to overload capacity and come out to join you."

The others were looking at Hemphill. He thought a bit, then nodded. "Agreed. The rest of you, let's move." He pointed at one of the side walls. "We'll try breaking through here first. I think the outer surface of this grand hotel lies in this direction."

"What about the robot?" Lee wanted to know.

"Random comes with us. We're going to need all the help that we can get. If you need him desperately, Dirigo, call and we'll send him back."

After a round of quick handshakes—Dirigo, with some half-formed idea of bringing himself good luck, included Random in the series—the volunteer went through another door, beginning his lonely local exploration.

As soon as Hemphill and his crew succeeded in making a hole in the wall at his chosen spot, explosive decompression filled the chamber with temporary fog and Lee, who had happened to be nearest the opening, was slammed into it, stuck in it, by the pressure of escaping air.

Quickly the others chopped and drilled, creating another hole nearby. When the available air was allowed to flow, it exhausted itself very quickly, and Lee could move.

On the other side of the wall, beyond the sheltered territory they had once shared with the unknown spy, the artificial gravity cut off. Darkness and vacuum and vertigo closed in. For most of the cadets, the change was almost comforting, bringing back an environment they had grown accustomed to in training exercises. So far, everyone was coping with it well.

The bright red spark of warning on Dirigo's virtual gauge, displayed inside his helmet, assured him that he had only a few minutes' breathing time remaining. His life, and very possibly the lives of his comrades, depended on what he could discover in that interval.

He was bold in his investigations, using up his last morsels of stored power, cutting through more doors, trying to find another wall thin and weak enough to penetrate with a couple of simple tools that the others had left him.

He had been engaged in this operation for less than a quarter of an hour when he was surprised to find a door that opened for him at the first touch—did someone, or something, want him to come this way?

Moving through the door, which closed itself behind him, Dirigo found himself standing in the last place he would ever have expected to discover aboard this combination of automated, crewless super-battleship and prison. He had found a theater, a neatly designed and well-furnished little auditorium, airless according to his suit gauge, but with the gravity still turned on at something very close to standard level. There was no doubt this chamber had been meant for use in comfort by breathing beings.

Not for ED humans, no. None of the hundred or so seats, arrayed in neat rows half surrounding a broad, dark dais, were of quite the right shape to accommodate the sons and daughters of Earth in any comfort.

Even as he looked around, Dirigo was getting on the intercom, transmitting a terse report of what he had discovered. As he talked, he moved around the theater, continuing to look for something, anything, that might offer some kind of usable source of power. As soon as he started to step up on the broad platform, something somewhere behind the scenes turned on, perhaps triggered by his presence.

Quickly he moved back several steps from the holostage, which had suddenly become a virtual window into a vaster hall. Ranks of beings filled the background there, and one person stood forward at the image of a lectern. He—or she—was tall, slender, and fine-boned, the most obvious deviation from ED shape being the single eye that stretched across the speaker's face, its bright bulging pupil sliding back and forth like mercury balanced on a knife blade.

Dirigo in alarm started to say something, then fell silent, abruptly convinced that he was watching a recording. The figure at the lectern opened its mouth, amid loose folds of saffron skin, and waved its arms. Whether it was clothed or not was hard to tell.

In the airless room, he could not hear the speaker's voice, but the vigor of speech and gestures indicated a bold oration. She—or he—was displaying charts now, three-dimensional arrays of stars and planets that appeared near him as he spoke, and at which the speaker gestured violently.

Meanwhile, Hemphill and the others, half drifting and half climbing through narrow spaces amid a jumble of strange objects, were trying to work their way toward the surface of the vast machine. Recalling the path they had followed on coming aboard, they knew that their dungeon had to be reasonably close to the monster's outer hull. But that exit had been solidly closed, and none of the tools in their captured kit were of any use in trying to force it open.

Hemphill had sent Random scouting ahead, the robot using its built-in light, allowing the humans to conserve the power in their suits as much as possible.

When the strange message from Dirigo came in, telling them he had found a theater, it seemed to Hemphill that the man was almost certainly delirious from anoxia—and even if a real theater existed, that in itself offered no salvation. To turn back with the whole party would be a horrible mistake.

On the other hand, Dirigo might be on the verge of making some additional discovery that would change the entire situation.

The robot was useful to Hemphill's party, but he thought it was not essential. After a quick conference with his companions, he sent Random back to Dirigo, with orders to help him in any way it could.

Finally, repeated all-out attacks from the Huvean fleet, joined by the remnant of Twin Worlds ships, had left the berserker seriously damaged.

"God, we really hit it that time!" A scream of joy. "We really hit it!" The gunnery people were firing the *Morholt*'s last heavy weapon. Other members of the crew were bellowing in hoarse triumph. But the celebration was slightly premature.

The enemy was still hitting back.

It was hard to aim the *Mukunda*'s sole remaining beam projector, with the drive shuddering and the stabilizers knocked out, but the remaining people and machines of gunnery were giving it the best they had.

The battle had swayed to and fro, across substantial intervals of interplanetary space. The great destructor had for some time now been passing in a screaming curve, at thousands of kilometers per second, closer to Prairie, the planet it had already sterilized, than to Timber, the one where it had dropped its landers, and where the process of stamping out life had scarcely got underway as yet. But there was no doubt that the goal of its latest maneuver was to arrive at Timber at high velocity, meeting the advancing planet head on.

Lee and his companions in one place, and the single badlife and goodlife, each in another, felt a faint vibration, some new impact.

Ella Berlu and her crew were discussing scoutship tactics. So far they had not been caught up in the real fighting, but soon they would be heading into it.

Who had first come up with the idea, or issued the order, was uncertain, one of those facts lost in the fog of battle. But a number of scoutships had already tried ramming the great beast—the idea was to set the autopilot, and get the crew off in a lifeboat before impact—but none had been able to get within a hundred kilometers without being vaporized. And most of the lifeboats had been toasted too.

Radigast's flagship wasn't going to attempt any ramming— not as long as there was anything else that he could do with it. Besides, it could hardly move.

The unplanned lull in the fighting dragged on. Minutes stretched out into hours, with the opposing forces drifting apart, humans and machine alike marshaling all their energies just to stay alive.

Everyone on the bridge of the *Mukunda,* including the first spacer, had been hurt, wounded in some way.

But Homasubi was not totally disabled, and like his Twin Worlds counterpart he refused to leave his battle station. "Remind me—there is something I wish to say to Admiral Radigast, when next we have the opportunity. . . ."

The two flagships of the united force were now very close to each other. After issuing what he considered the necessary commands, for another attack to finish the enemy off, the first spacer offered his counterpart something very close to an apology.

Before he had finished, the admiral was shaking his head.

"No need for that, First Spacer. You have been, sir, a very model of bloody courtesy all along. And by the way, let me congratulate you on your tactics. You've got more fleet left than I did, after it hit me for the first time."

"It is I who should congratulate you, Admiral Radigast, for having weakened it sufficiently to permit us to gain a small measure of success. Also, my personal congratulations on your having survived two rounds of combat with—a rather formidable antagonist.

"I must admit that when I first arrived in this system, and began to believe that I had grasped the situation, my thoughts regarding you and your fleet were ungenerous—and, as I see now, completely mistaken. I felt a greater confidence than ever in Huvean superiority. I assure you solemnly, all traces of such disrespect have been purged from my heart and mind."

"That's good. That's good . . ." The admiral's voice was growing faint. "what's that motherless mother up to now?"

Both sides were being granted a breather, by circumstances. For the moment, neither could find an effective way to do the other damage, and both had serious need of a respite.

Meanwhile, the cloud of surviving scoutships was still thickening, as more and still more came trickling in from the farther reaches of the outer defense sphere. Whatever today's final result might be, Twin Worlds humanity would not be utterly wiped out.

Gradually, Lee and Hemphill and their determined classmates were somehow making headway, getting farther and farther from the compartment where they had been confined. Lee was thinking that they must have come several kilometers by this time.

But where they were going was somewhat more difficult to say.

Their training exercises, on the techniques of searching an abandoned ship, had never lasted more than a standard hour.

In contrast, this trek went on and on, people standing or drifting in a cramped alien space, surrounded by bulky objects of
unknown purpose. This environment was totally unfriendly to
any human presence, free-falling in an airless dark. The shapes
of structure and machinery loomed around them, dim in the
faint reflection of the robot's distant lamp, and for the most
part incomprehensible.

Hemphill had announced his plan. They should move, or try
to move, parallel to what seemed to be the inner surface of the
outer hull. "If this thing is as big as it looked, we sure don't want
to go any deeper into it than we have to."

With great excitement, one of them at last halted in the slow
scramble forward, and called out that a star was visible. After a
moment, others were able to see it too.

"How can you be sure?" There was only the tiny spark of
steady light.

More than one star had now appeared in Lee's field of vision,
a small cluster glimpsed through a distant opening with jagged
sides. The escapees began to follow a faint beam of distant starlight.
This served as their guide, kept them going in something like a
straight line through their enemy's mysterious metal guts. Those
pinpoint images looked blessedly steady, and reassuringly free of
any doppler-shifting, either red or blue. A different look would have
meant that their captor had accelerated strongly when its prisoners
were still AG-protected, and they might already be lost, vanished
from the ken of searchers, at some heartbreaking distance from
home.

Suddenly Dirigo's voice was coming in again on the intercom. The earlier message had been something of a shock, but not
to compare with this one: "Hemphill? Lee, do you guys read me?
I've found the spy who looks through little holes. He's got one of
our suits, and he must be on our intercom."

That was all. People took turns trying to reply, but nothing more was heard from Dirigo.

In another minute one of the party was asking—in a voice that hoped the answer would be no—whether they should all turn back to try to help out their abandoned comrade.

Lee was trying to imagine the effort it would take to turn your back on starlight, and descend into hell!—but he wasn't being asked to make that choice.

Hemphill was shaking his head. "I still say he may be delirious. If he strikes it lucky in the next few minutes—managed to tap into some power, or some air—he may pull through. If he doesn't, well, whatever or whoever he's found won't matter much. He'll be dead before any of us can get back to him."

After a moment Hemphill added: "I've already sent the robot back—and there are six lives here, only one back there. Besides . . ."

He let his words trail off. There was no need to spell it out: If the six of them were to spend their remaining suit power going back down into hell, they would never have enough left to once more regain the surface.

Some of the berserker's damaged defensive fields were displaying ripples, columns of brightness like marching searchlight beams—

In the latest round of fighting, the Twin Worlds remnant had missed the worst of it—being simply unable to get into the action in time. Still, they had been hit again, and about all that was now left of the Twin Worlds fleet were a few hulks, still drifting, still managing to keep the surviving members of their crews alive for the time being.

"The enemy's weapons are better than anything we have. But still we have enough to get the job done, using up our fleet in the process."

The Huvean fleet had taken a terrific pounding too, just as the Twin Worlds' forces had—but some Huvean vessels, including the first spacer's flagship, were still at least partially functioning when the shooting stopped.

The human pilots of some small ships, both Twin Worlds and Huvean, did their best to carry out deliberate ramming attacks—with at least marginal success.

The flare of battle was showing over the murky horizon, like distant lightning. The great berserker had been fought almost to a standstill, weakened, prevented from any further exercise of its weapons of mass extermination.

The battle fleets of two Earth-descended nations had been used up in the process, along with the ground defenses of two planets. Humanity had suffered billions of dead and wounded, and more than half of the Twin Worlds civilization, once so proud of its advanced development, lay in ruins.

The flagship of Admiral Radigast was out of missiles and almost out of hope. But still, against all odds, sheltering some live crew, and one heavy beam projector. The *Morholt* had to be pushed by the *Mukunda,* into a position where it could serve as a gun platform in the last duel with this berserker.

With its drive units all but completely dead, it could do little more than drift.

Both fleet commanders were trying to get the remnants of their forces between the enemy and Timber.

Just when it seemed it might be able to last a little while longer, Radigast's dreadnought finally vanished in a last explosion.

Some of the crew were got off at the last minute, and were carried to relative safety aboard a Huvean vessel not in much better shape—but many others, including the admiral, perished with their ship.

And now the first spacer was putting himself and his fleet between the berserker and the remaining homeland of the people who had so recently been his bitter enemies.

Zarnesti, the PO, took this as a crowning blow to the honor of his people and his government, and found it necessary to commit suicide in an attempt at expiation. Zarnesti had taken a robot and a pistol to his cabin with him, the robot to perform the cleanup that would probably be necessary. Huvean robots were generally instructed not to interfere in such cases.

Zarnesti's civilian superior, abandoning any pretense of working in the sick bay, had withdrawn to her assigned small cabin. Homasubi let her go—for now, he was content that she and her junior colleague should both be out of his way.

During the assault on Prairie, the nuclear explosion of a heavy warhead against the berserker's hull, at a site already somewhat weakened by ancient damage, had torn a gap in forcefield protection and solid metal too. Other badlife weapons, including a mobile, computer-guided, atomic pile, programmed to trace escaping gas, to probe for weakness, had found the spot.

From the locus of penetration, a brushfire of nuclear reactions spread inward through the hull, reaching maximum depth near the berserker's center of gravity, where it threatened the great unliving brain.

Chaotic ruin was stubbornly advancing, despite the tireless labors of the berserker's quenching devices and repair machines. The slow conflagration had eaten its way deep into the inner defenses of the central processor itself, and was attacking the outer ring of prime computer units. One after another, these began to fail.

Once upon a time, living beings had tended these

sensitive devices. Oxygen-breathing engineers had moved along these catwalks, designing, working, building, intent on crafting the perfect weapon for their own war against another breathing race. The builders' creation proved to be beyond their understanding, and when it had destroyed their enemies it turned on them, judging them badlife, and killed them too.

According to the central processor's current plan, its modern maintenance devices were to be provided more convenient access to its own unliving heart. But there had turned out to be a great deal of resistant life, badlife, in the Galaxy, and damage tended to accumulate, sometimes faster than it could be repaired. There had never been time and resources to spare for a comprehensive redesign and reconstruction.

Had the machine been working at full computational capacity, it might have improvised effective countermeasures. But full capacity had already been lost.

Only a limited number of replacement modules had been provided when the machine was new, and the last one had been pressed into service many standard years ago. The machinery to make the new connections still functioned smoothly. Also the central tenets of programming were unaffected—they would, as a rule, be among the last computer functions to fail—but the berserker was aware that it was already kept from functioning with its usual quick competence.

Only one feasible countermeasure was now available. It was going to have to employ the newly recruited goodlife, and the robot the life-unit had at its command.

Hemphill and Lee and the four others with them had worked their way close enough to the jagged opening in the hull that an incoming wash of starlight allowed them to turn off all their helmet lights and still see, in a crude way, where they were going.

Lee was thinking that if this enormous cavity had been on the other side of the vast machine, and they had found their way out over there, the sun might well be making their surroundings as bright as day. But speculation was pointless: they were here, the gigantic hull was not rotating, and they would have to grope their way along as best they could.

No further word had come from Dirigo, and Hemphill was silently regretting his decision to send the robot back. Dirigo had probably run out of air and died, enjoying some show in his imaginary theater until the curtain came down. It was hard to guess what might have happened to Random. But it was useless to stew over what was already done.

When they had worked their way forward a few meters more, they could begin to see, by the glow of starlight, the full extent of the enormous wound in their enemy's side that offered them a chance of getting out.

Feretti's whisper sounded awed: "By all the gods—what kind of weapon ever made a hole like this?"

"Something stronger than anything we've got," Lee muttered back.

And Kang Shin: "Our thanks to our ancient allies—whoever or whatever they may have been."

Progress did not seem to be slowed much by the lack of a robot to lead the way, though situations kept coming up in which a man-sized surrogate would have been very useful to people who were trying to find a way across a gap of empty space, or to make a pathway out of a mere ridge of metal not intended for anything of the kind. Or to test a zone where there might be enough radiation to overwhelm their suits—or, possibly, to be the first to discover where some killer machine, infinitely patient, lay waiting for them in ambush.

Hemphill was still in the lead, as he had been through most of the journey so far, taking a leader's share of risks, as the cadets continued their search through the chaotic caverns and tunnels of the berserker's vast bulk, pursuing the elusive goal of a way out.

There would have been no chance for them at all, no possible way of getting out, except for the craters in the hull, the channels that had been opened, the destruction inflicted by old weapons and new. An age of warfare had left the monster half blind and half numb, unable to sense, or respond to, much that went on within its own tremendous bulk.

Already the survivors had worked their way painfully through several forced switchbacks and many interruptions, always with the goal in mind of reaching those distant, tantalizing glimpses of starlight. Distances were hard to judge, in this world of dimly visible and unfamiliar shapes, open on one side to infinity. But Lee felt certain they had covered more than a few kilometers since breaking free of the dungeon.

With Random's departure, they had lost their only means of keeping track of formal time, except as it could be measured by the slowly diminishing power levels in their suits. Currently almost the sole drain was the essential recycling of their breathing air. By that standard, none of them had more than an hour left.

They were cautious in using their radio intercom too: The signals had been designed to be very difficult to trace, but in the presence of an unknown superior technology there was no point in taking chances.

After another fifteen minutes or so of irregular progress, the small group came raggedly to another halt.

"Man, what's this?" someone breathed.

They were still inside the massive thickness of their enemy's outer armor, when a bulky shape suggesting nothing so much as an enormous tree root, thick as the length of a man's body, appeared running athwart their passage, and almost blocking it. To right and left the obstacle stretched out of sight, curving and vanishing in dimness.

Metal conduits, like smaller, branching roots, came reaching out of the dim fastnesses of the interior to clasp and penetrate the thing.

Lee raised a sharp tool and swung a tentative hack or two at the black surface, which gave way in little sprays of drifting flakes.

"Looks like these little twigs could be ductwork for an AG space," Feretti mused.

Zochler said: "Could be a useful place to know about. If the drive on this big baby ever decides to kick in again."

Hemphill was nodding. "Could be, except we can't stay here. If we're going to have any chance at all of getting off this thing, we've got to get up and out."

Looking into the distance, Lee and several of his companions saw a kind of streak of molten fire, stabbing into the darkness of the giant hull ahead, like a meteor, from the outer realm of starlight.

"What was that? Didn't look like any kind of missile."

"More like—a ship. I think that might have been a scout. It lit up when it forced its way through what remains of this thing's defensive field."

The central processor had already sent its notification of the discovery of a system of swarming badlife. Years might pass before response arrived, but that it would arrive eventually was certain.

The orator up on the holostage kept waving his arms and working his beak-like mouth, but Dirigo had ceased to pay attention. Instead he was concentrating, in what he had to assume were his last few minutes of life, on finding some way to get under the stage, where, if there was any logic to the system, there would have to be power conduits of some kind. But the holographic display claimed his attention one last time when it was suddenly cut off.

Turning to face the figure that had just come into the theater, Dirigo at first saw only the familiar suit, and knew a moment of poignant gladness: one of his classmates had come back to join him, and the two of them were going to find life or death together.

Then he took note of the unfamiliar face inside the helmet, and the gun in the man's hand.

The executioner, suited and helmeted, pistol drawn and ready, entered the unfamiliar space and stopped dead in his tracks, shocked by his first sight of the wonders of the theater.

It was equally shocking to see who was already here. One of the badlife had been admitted to this secret place, while its very existence had been concealed from him, the faithful executioner.

"Why did you never show me this?" Huang Gun querulously demanded of his lord.

"There has been no time," his master's ugly voice explained inside his helmet.

Meanwhile this lone badlife, the one the others had called Dirigo, continued to stare at him. Dirigo's voice was loud and angry. "Who are you, anyway? You're Twin Worlds, not Huvean. At least you're wearing one of our suits. Put that gun down."

Huang Gun raised the muzzle slightly. He was wondering where the other badlife had gone, and what wickedness they might be up to. Whatever happened, they must not be allowed to interfere with the essential task required by the master. Aloud he said only: "I am become Death."

"You look like it. You look like hell. What happened to Sunbula?" Dirigo raised his voice slightly, going on the channel that ought to reach all of the surviving cadets. "Hemphill? Lee, do you guys read me? I've found the spy who looks through little holes. He's got one of our suits, and he must be on our intercom."

Even as he tried to give his friends some warning, Dirigo was thinking: *What would a real leader do in this situation? Begin by getting the weapon away from this lunatic. Yes, why not? What do I have to lose?* The red spark of his virtual gauge was flashing on and off. No more than a couple of minutes at the most.

Dirigo lunged forward, the spacesuit making him feel hopelessly slow and clumsy.

Huang Gun shot him squarely in the chest; Twin Worlds spacesuits were not designed as armor, and the badlife went down at once. The executioner was glad to see that the weapon Death had given him was in fine working order.

In a way this death was less satisfying than the woman's, because he, the executioner, had not been able to pass on the gift while in direct contact with the recipient. But he could understand that there were times when efficiency and certainty were of overriding importance. Twice he had killed dangerous badlife. He was well and firmly entered on his master's business. That was all that mattered, and the way ahead, to his essential task, seemed clear.

He had just started to hang the gun on his belt again, when the robot that had been in the badlife cell, the one they had called Random, came bounding into the theater at robotic speed, leaping forward, bending low, coming to a full stop only when it was crouched close over the fallen man.

Huang Gun had recoiled a step, then started to relax again. Tame ED robots like this one tried to prolong the suffering and decay of life. But in this case no such effort was going to be of any use.

The robot raised its gaze to fasten on Huang Gun, and for just a moment he felt an unexpected impulse, surprisingly strong, to turn the pistol on himself. Trembling, he resisted the urge—not yet. There was at least one more work, an essential task, to be accomplished before he could find rest.

Inside the executioner's helmet, his master's low voice was urging him to hurry on to the job that urgently needed doing. If possible, he should bring with him the robot that had just appeared—its strength and agility would be very useful.

Random slowly stood upright, still gazing at Huang Gun. In

Huang Gun's helmet the mellow, artificial voice inquired cheerfully: "Did you shoot this man?"

"It was an accident," Huang Gun muttered automatically. He
realized he was aiming the pistol at the robot, and slowly moved
his hand, hooking the weapon on his suit's belt. Gradually he continued to relax out of his startled state. No human being, killer or
not, need fear deliberate injury from a tame, ED-manufactured
robot. He said to it on radio: "Your name is Random, is it not?"

"Yes sir."

"A good name . . . Random, I require your assistance on a
matter of great importance. To what task, if any, are you currently
assigned?"

A metal forefinger pointed at the dead man who lay between
them. "To help him."

"I see. Well, that one no longer needs help of any kind. But I
do."

In the executioner's helmet, his master's voice assured him
that it had now cut off radio communication between this robot
and the escaping badlife. It also informed him that a journey of
several kilometers would be necessary, to reach the place where
his essential task awaited. Again it urged him to begin at once.

Immediately the executioner turned to leave the theater. Perhaps, before he died, his master would reveal to him the purpose of
this place—but just now there was no time for such details. He
understood that. When he ordered Random to follow, the robot
unhesitatingly fell in behind him.

"You will not walk the whole way," the master's broken,
scraping voice assured Huang Gun. "You will ride."

A way was opened for them out of the small oasis, the few
rooms that had been furnished with air and gravity. When they
had moved away from the familiar place a hundred meters or so,
the executioner saw what the master meant by riding. Random
had switched on his light, making the passage easier and safer for

his human companion. The light revealed the conveyor to be a great tube of forcefields and huge rushing containers, curving past the place where the executioner stood in darkness, and running deep into some ultimate emptiness that looked blacker still.

The master urged Huang Gun forward, and he stepped out blindly. When the conveyor's forcefields caught him up, and Random after him, his weightlessness more than ever gave the impression of an endless fall. Now and then vast shapes, corpuscles of the master's lifeless bloodstream, came flickering past in the near darkness. Somehow he could feel that his speed in the conveyor was very high.

The ride had not gone on for very long when Huang Gun felt the abrupt tug of deceleration. He and the robot were carefully, gently ejected from the transport tube. Now they were standing—drifting, rather—in front of a narrow door that immediately opened to let them in. The disembodied voice of Huang Gun's master guided him through a final passage.

An age ago, when humans on Earth hunted the wooly mammoth, and this hardware had been new, the central processor had been tended and protected by its own special guardians, many-handed devices as thin and pliable as young humans, able to traverse the innermost passages and ducts. But for a thousand years and more there had been no need for such specialized support, and one by one the special guardians had been deployed on other tasks. Deployed, and used up.

The executioner and Random had emerged from the narrow passage just inside a hollow sphere some thirty meters in diameter. The sphere surrounding them could be, Huang Gun supposed, solid armor. Whatever it was, a ragged hole, its raw new edges glowing a radioactive blue, had been eaten through it.

A matching hole glowed on the side of the object in the center of the thirty-meter cave. This object was a complexity the size of a small house, shock-mounted on a web of girders that ran from it in every direction, and Huang Gun understood that it must house the central processor. Apart from the radiance of the invading weapon, the central object possessed its own glow, like flickering moonlight; forcefield switches, the executioner supposed, responding to the random atomic turmoil within.

His master's voice was telling him: "On the wall beside you is the quenching device, the tool that you must use." And it showed him a tiny image in his helmet.

The tool itself was hanging on the armored wall, almost at his elbow. The front end of it looked something like the nozzle of a firehose, with a black coil, long and thick, trailing behind. When he put his hands on the nozzle and pulled, he realized how massive the whole thing was. It would be almost impossible for one man to wield it properly, even in the effective absence of gravity—but certainly he and the robot, working together, ought to be able to manage whatever was required.

Unhurriedly, patiently, despite the blue fire eating steadily at its brain, the master provided an essential explanation. The firehose—the name that suggested itself to Huang Gun, and as good a name for it as any, Huang Gun thought, when they were pressed for time—had to be stretched across to the central structure, and its nozzle end carried inside the central object, and around at least one interior corner. Then the stuff the hose spewed out, more force than matter, would have to be directed into the interior spaces where blue fire raged and ate. The other end of the hose, or tube, would remain permanently connected to the outer wall.

Huang Gun's experience in high office had allowed him to learn something about the weapons his own government planned for use in the new war. In confrontation with a moving atomic pile, he needed no instrument to tell him that a human wearing an ordinary spacesuit, coming within a few meters of the thing, into a literal fog of that deadly radiance, might not live much longer than was required to aim a quenching device and turn it on.

His thoughts were interrupted by sharp words from the robot. "Sir, I must warn you. Radiation in our present location is so intense that your suit can protect you for only about three minutes. You must immediately move away." If the level was high enough to be quickly fatal to a suited human, it would soon demolish a Random-type robot too. But of course, to any ED robot, its own fate was of secondary importance.

What the warning chiefly meant to Huang Gun was that he had no time to waste. "Never mind the radiation, Random. Help me with this hose. Grab it here. Hold it securely, and follow directly behind me. Help me pull it forward."

Random clamped his arms around the hose as ordered, but that was as far as he moved. "Where are you going with it, sir?"

"You heard my master's command, did you not!" The executioner almost screamed. He stabbed a finger at the flickering sphere ahead. "We are going in there. Hurry!"

The robot spoke somewhat faster than usual, but as calmly as ever. "I must refuse to obey your order, for reasons of human health and safety."

The man's voice went sliding, babbling, into incoherence. He meant to say: "Damn you, robot, you *cannot* refuse! You are now assigned to me. Grab hold!"

Whether those were his actual words or not, whether the robot could understand him, it moved—but only to drop the hose and slide on past Huang Gun. Then it turned to face the man.

Random had assumed a solid stance, blocking the man's forward path completely, each hand gripping one of the ancient railings used by breathing engineers. "Sir, I must refuse to obey your order, for reasons—"

"Then get out of my way!" The executioner would not be stopped. Death had commanded, and he was going to drag the massive firehose forward, even if he had to do it by himself. Could he do it? He would have to. He told himself that he could feel the strength of a maniac swelling in his muscles.

But Random did not move.

The master's voice was loud in the executioner's helmet,

shouting a string of commands at both man and rebellious robot—
but there was nothing, nothing at all, that the master could do right
here and now to enforce its orders.

Meanwhile the thing called Random talked on calmly, in its
damned implacable badlife voice. Its tones were still full of pleasant modulations, making them hearable beneath the shouting. "No
sir. The intensity of radiation increases rapidly in the direction you
indicate. Ten meters from where we stand, I compute that an expo-
sure of thirty seconds would certainly be fatal. For you to proceed
any farther would be suicidal. Therefore I cannot permit—"

"You do not understand, motherless, brainless robot!" Huang
Gun heard himself erupting in a volley of gutter language, words
he had not realized he still remembered. He had never had this
kind of trouble with a robot before. Of course he had never before
attempted to use one in such serious business.

His master had fallen silent, trusting him to plead the case of
Death.

In desperation he tried to take thought, to come up with a
convincing story. He forced himself to speak distinctly; but still the
words poured out in a wild babble. "If—if the central processor
aboard this vessel is irretrievably ruined . . . then many . . . many
human lives will be lost. Yes, many! Hundreds. Perhaps thousands.
People are—are—depending on this ship to—to—"

Random cut in rudely, but still as calm as if discussing the
prospects for tomorrow's weather. "What you say, sir, is mani-
festly untrue, contradicted by the observed facts." The robotic
voice was perfectly obstinate, maddeningly cheerful. "Sir, I compute that you are in need of medical attention—and possibly subject to criminal investigation. In the circumstances I must detain
you, and respectfully insist that you accompany me in search of
help."

"No! Nooo!"

Radio noise generated by the master welled up in their
fragment of the intercom, drowning out both their voices. The

executioner dropped the nozzle of the heavy hose and snatched the gun from his belt. He aimed, but for one crucial second was kept from firing, by the fact that without this robot's help he might never be able to do the job.

The grip that closed on his wrist an instant later was not hard enough to bruise his skin, but far too strong for him to break. It seemed to know where every nerve and tendon lay. In a few seconds Huang Gun no longer held the pistol.

He screamed. His agony seemed all the greater because his body felt no pain. Mere human flesh and bone, weak and subject to decay and failure, might conceivably have lugged a firehose, but could hardly fight a robot. That was an observed fact. The gun had disappeared into Random's carrying pouch, and both the executioner's wrists were being held, patiently maneuvered behind his back, clamped together in the untiring grasp of one of Random's hands.

Random began to drag him implacably away from the master's dying heart, back in the direction of the stars. The return journey would be a slow trek, no ride provided this time. They were going toward the places where decadent and evil life held rule.

When Huang Gun continued struggling, violently kicking, wrenching his body from side to side, almost throwing his captor off balance, the metal fingers of Random's free hand came forcing their way into his suit's built-in backpack. Moments later, Huang Gun's oxygen was being cut off—only partially, just enough to reduce his movement to a feeble parody of struggle. His rescuer bore him away, choking and writhing with the pangs of rebirth into continued life.

Grabbing a convenient flange of metal with one hand, Hemphill brought his drifting body to a halt, meanwhile holding up his free arm as a signal. Behind him, five spacesuited people strung out in single file caught hold of whatever projections of enemy hardware they could reach, stopping their forward motion. The six of them were near finishing their great climb—even in weightlessness it had certainly seemed like a climb, emerging from a vast interior darkness, into the faint wash of starlight that found its way in through the broad, jagged hole in the enemy's outer hull. Still the fugitives were essentially in shadow, with the Twin Worlds' sun on the far side of the gigantic vessel.

For the past twenty minutes or so, the fugitives had been climbing lightly, precariously, toward this providential escape hatch, working their way up and out, into the ghostly radiance of a hundred billion Galactic suns. For the last part of the ascent, with plenty of light and sufficient handholds, they had been moving with dreamlike ease up one jagged lip of the enormous hole. Now they found themselves some fifty meters above the flat plain of the enemy's flank, on a sharp, jagged pinnacle that was part of the raw edge of the gaping wound.

At several points in their flight so far, the fugitives had felt the monster start majestically to move away from them, the beginning of a slow and steady acceleration, as of some preprogrammed course correction, pervading the whole huge frame. Fortunately the g-force, so far, had been no stronger than Timber's or Prairie's normal surface gravity, and the six people trying to crawl out of the enemy's belly had been able to deal with it. When one direction suddenly became down, it gave them the sensation of climbing a narrow trail along the rim of a mechanical canyon tens of kilometers deep. The canyon's innermost recesses were swallowed in darkness, like the pit of hell.

Then something in the drive or astrogation system had evidently called for a correction, and a change in the direction of acceleration briefly established "down" in the direction the people had been moving. For a long few moments they had to cling fiercely to whatever tiny handholds they could find, like flies traversing some titanic ceiling, while below them the possibility of a long fall stretched out to infinity.

Hemphill had called a halt to give himself and the others a chance to look around. From the vantage point they had now reached, at the very rim of the gaping hole, he had a broad view of the enemy's outer surface, with perhaps a hundred square kilometers of it visible. It made a ghostly, unreal landscape under starlight, vast expanses of smooth metal studded with projections and divided by dark canyons. Here and there long ridges reared like ancient castle walls.

Having scrambled and groped through kilometers of darkness to get to where they were, the six had already begun to get a feel, an inner picture of their enemy's true, enormous size. They had gained an appreciation of this thing that had incidentally captured them, while in the process of fighting off an attacking fleet and killing an entire planet, the very world that half of them called home.

A vast expanse of sky had come into view, and Hemphill and his companions took an additional few moments to study it, assuring themselves of their current position within the solar system. The familiar constellations testified that they had not been carried halfway across the Galaxy during their long term as helpless prisoners.

Other sights, less reassuring, were also visible. The long axis of the enemy's massive body pointed in the general direction of a bright dot of light, one that could hardly be anything but a fairly nearby planet, and no other planet but Timber, even if the color did not seem precisely right.

There was of course no use trying to see or speculate where the Twin Worlds battle fleet might be at the moment. Even the biggest ships, unless actually radiating brightness, would be impossible to spot, without the help of instruments, at any distance beyond a few kilometers.

Hemphill could see, at a considerable angular distance from Timber, faintly radiant clouds, encompassing a sizable volume of space, that impressed him as looking the way the residue of some serious battle ought to look. Depending on their distance within the system, the clouds could easily be millions of kilometers long. They were not conspicuous against the starry background, but to space-trained eyes looking for something out of the ordinary, they stood out unmistakably.

Lee, clinging to a jagged spine of displaced metal close beside him, was looking in the same direction. "What *is* that?"

"Probably just what it looks like. Particles and gas. It means there's been more fighting while we were locked away."

After a few moments of disorientation, Hemphill got his bearings and took a more serious look at the planet Prairie, on which he had been born.

Another suited figure, just getting its bearings, raised a

pointing arm. "There's Timber." The inner world of the pair, at least, was unmistakable, and at no great distance on the scale of solar systems.

"Yes, we've established that. Then that's Prairie over there—isn't it?"

"I don't think so. Doesn't look right."

"Then what is it?"

People tried to make sure of their position. The familiar stars of their home system's sky were clear enough, but even so, there was a general sense of disorientation.

"You're right, that's got to be Prairie. But you're right too, it shouldn't look that way."

People were squinting, tuning faceplates to try to filter out the dull, hazy glare of the Galactic background as they gazed at Timber. "They must have their full planet shields up. That would be natural."

"No." Hemphill was whispering. He had let go of, forgotten, whatever he had been carrying. The object just went drifting away, so someone else had to grab it. "No, that's not just the shields. We've seen Timber with the shields up before, and it didn't look like that."

"Then what—?"

"Something else has happened to Prairie. And I think that Timber's shields are gone."

For a moment, with no means of getting anywhere in sight, and in their exhausted state, vague hints of great additional disaster seemed to carry more than their ordinary force.

Hemphill closed his eyes for a long moment. He was not going to be beaten. For some time now, not being beaten had been the foundation of his life.

He opened his eyes, and looked at what was near at hand, in the territory where he might be able to do something that made a difference. "All right, so something else has happened on the planets. Maybe it's dust in the atmosphere. None of that changes our problem, which is, how do we get off this hulk? How can we attract the attention of one of our own ships? Our people have to be out there somewhere."

The first spacer was silently affirming to himself his conviction that the berserker was not yet dead. Though it had finally been outfought, pitted against a collective stubbornness the equal of its own, battered by waves of attackers almost into immobility, the death machine was still deadly dangerous.

The berserker was moving away from a combined fleet of heavier warships, but its object was not a retreat out of the system. If the berserker, its enormous mass closing on Timber with a velocity of kilometers per second, could strike the planet squarely, then tidal waves, groundquakes, and the blotting out of sunlight might kill billions more.

Only the remaining Twin Worlds scoutships could catch it now and try to stop it.

The next period of acceleration started gradually, uncertainly, a function of drive units and control systems no longer able to operate with full precision. The movements caused were only tentative, deprived of all central control, like reflexes in a dying body.

But the system still remembered where its last target lay, and did its best to guide the hurtling mass in that direction.

When new acceleration caused the tail of the monster vessel to acquire the direction *down,* the six human beings on its surface began a scramble to find shelter.

In a moment all six were clawing their way back into the enormous cave from which they had just escaped. Only a couple of minutes ago, while still just within the thickness of the ruptured outer armor, they had crawled past a long, thick tube that looked identical to a large housing they had examined earlier, a unit that seemed to offer the chance of artificial gravity inside—possibly a vein or artery in the enemy's materials-handling transport system. The great machine must have many components that needed protection against the stress of powerful acceleration.

The outer surface of the tube, thank all the gods, was not heavily protected. What ancient builder could have imagined that armor would be needed here? A few moments' frantic work with hand tools ripped a hole in the side of it, a gap big enough for a human to climb through.

Each fugitive on moving inside the tube entered a domain where artificial gravity neutralized all outside forces, restoring the blessed sense of weightlessness. Outside the tunnel's wall, the g-force was steadily increasing, and the last cadet had to be hauled in by three classmates against a pull that was rapidly becoming more than standard normal.

Drifting inside the broad tube, again with no sense of up or down, Hemphill allowed himself a few deep breaths, despite the fact that his virtual power gauge was beginning occasionally to flicker red.

He remembered to keep his voice calm. "We may be all right for a while."

Lee sent a brief flicker of his helmet lamp down the long tunnel, in the direction that went curving deep into the enemy's body. Nothing was moving down there, nothing especially horrible appeared. "Yeah. As long as no cargo comes flying through this thing to wipe us out."

The interior of the long, smooth tube was a couple of meters in diameter; one of the cadets speculated that large missiles might be fed through it from some interior factory or magazine to a battery of launchers just inside the outer hull. Fortunately, there was no traffic of weapons currently in progress; maybe the launchers had been destroyed, or the connected magazine had been emptied.

"Maybe it's used up all its assets," Zochler offered hopefully.

"We can hope," Feretti grunted.

Safe for the moment in their shelter, the fugitives' next need was for a means of knowing when the acceleration had cut off again, and they could resume their search for something to give them long-term hope. The entrance they had cut in the tube's side provided a window for observation, but acceleration in itself was invisible. They needed to devise some means of testing.

Down on the surface of the planet Timber, the half dozen enemy landers that survived were all seriously damaged, worn down to a fraction of their original strength by waves of Twin Worlds fighting machines. In the course of their raid so far they had killed many thousands of units of intelligent badlife. Following a long-established protocol, the most powerful computer in the group had assumed the role of local battle director. Only a hundred meters of ruin and wreckage, and a semicircle of badlife armored vehicles, separated them from the Citadel's outer wall.

From every direction came a steady overland flow of reinforcements for the human side, in the form of machinery and humans, some of them summoned from the far side of the planet.

The orders transmitted to the landers from their master in deep space had been changed; their mission had altered from reconnaissance, probing attacks, to maximum destruction.

It was the last order that the central processor ever gave.

The central processor had transmitted its prediction of its own impending destruction to all of its auxiliary machines with which it could still make contact. It would be the programmed duty of each unit, operating independently, to fight and kill whatever life they were able to reach—with the usual priority assigned to the intelligent, resisting badlife. Whether the onrushing mass of the berserker in the sky was going to hit the planet or not was still to be determined.

At four million kilometers an hour, the berserker was closing steadily on its remaining major target—the planet advancing at a much slower pace toward the calculated place and moment of impact, which lay only a few hours in the future.

Its refueling process had been interrupted, and the berserker had not been able to take on as much new hydrogen as it had planned. But the onboard reserves of energy, in the form of fuel and otherwise, would be enough to see this fight to a conclusion, one way or another.

A hell of blue flame and disorganization was eating its way into and through the central processor. Among the last concepts it managed to retain was: *The species of badlife that infests this system, whatever may have been its recent history, does not, after all, seem entirely ignorant of war. It seems well suited to carry out a stubborn resistance.*

Besides, it was necessary to maintain a steady push of acceleration to counter the force of the small ships that were trying to throw the berserker off course.

The six cadets had once again survived. By pushing small objects (mostly scraps of enemy-provided food, dug out of inner coverall pockets) carefully out through the window of their shelter, and noting whether the fragments flew away or drifted near, the cadets were able to tell when the acceleration had ceased. Only a few minutes had passed since they took shelter. The inexorable depletion of their suits' power had progressed more slowly while they remained almost inert—but it still progressed.

The latest fragments of imitation food were drifting tentatively just outside the window. Hemphill drew one more deep breath. "Come on, people. We've got to move again."

Several Twin Worlds scoutships, crashed or landed on the enormous hull, were visible. Estimating distance was difficult in this environment, but Hemphill thought the nearest was between one and two kilometers away.

"Boss, if we can get ourselves to one of those . . ." Zochler sounded hopeful.

Hemphill was nodding. "We might be able to do ourselves some good." It was conceivable that though the ship was wrecked, its artificial gravity might still be on, and power functioning. Air would be abundantly available, and water and food, when breathing had ceased to be an immediate concern.

"It might even have a lifeboat." If they could cram their six bodies into a boat built for a scout's normal crew of three, that would offer a possibility of their all getting clean away. Of course, if there should not be room enough . . . but they would ford that stream when they reached it.

Crossing the great plain, it was necessary to avoid long stretches where sheer, featureless flat metal offered no purchase, nothing to grip or kick against for guidance or propulsion. The six people made the best speed they could, while remaining more or less together. If a strong jolt of acceleration should hit them suddenly, it would probably wipe them out against some nearby obstacle, or, at best, wrench the hull away from them and leave them drifting in interplanetary space.

As they progressed, a few more shot-up Twin Worlds scoutships became visible, their wrecked bodies jammed into angles and crevices across the enemy's monstrous hull.

It struck Lee as amazing that every one of the party had managed to regain the berserker's outer surface. Here they clung on by one means or another against occasional jolts of mild acceleration. Searching the sky for help and meaning, Lee and Hemphill and their companions could see the familiar glow of Timber, not really more than a pinpoint yet, but still too big to be anything not belonging to the Twin Worlds system. Its natural color was still distorted by the drifting reek of battle clouds, and the persistence of defensive forcefields.

The six made the best speed that they could manage, following first a low ridge and then an irregular chain of impact craters across the pockmarked plain. The nearest downed scout-ship sat on the smooth metal surface at an odd angle, but did not appear to be tremendously damaged.

If they could get in, and systems were functioning, there was every reason to hope for protection against g-force, there was very likely to be water, food—and, above all, air, along with a functional system to recharge their suits.

But appearances had been deceiving. The closer they came to their chosen wreck, the worse it looked, especially when they were able to view it from a slightly different angle.

The party straggled to a halt. No one had any comment. "Which way do we go, chief?"

It wasn't a hard choice, and Hemphill pointed toward the nearest of the other downed scouts that were in sight. Now only a few minutes of life remained in any of their suits—a few minutes that might easily be canceled any second, if their captor should hit them with another hard jolt of acceleration.

As they approached their second choice, they could see what was holding this little ship in place—the heat and force of impact had, at a couple of places, welded the lower surface of the scout-ship's hull to that of their great antagonist.

Unfortunately, the hatch ordinarily used by the crew was on the side of the ship partially held against the stranger's hull, with no room for a human body to squeeze in between—and probably no way to open the hatch if it could be reached.

Moving around the compact vessel with some difficulty—it was hard to find anything to hold on to—to try the cargo hatch, they discovered that the hatch was entirely gone, along with a good part of the surrounding hull. A hole had been ripped in the small ship's side, offering ample room for entrance into the cargo bay.

As the first cadet went through the airlock, a cry of joy went up—blessed air! One and two at a time, they entered.

The control room and most of the controls were intact, though the drive was ruined.

The young woman, Cusanus, gave thanks to all the gods, when, after hurling herself into the pilot's chair, she discovered that though the artificial gravity had been turned off, it was still operational. In another moment, the scoutship's deck had become a horizontal reference and people were standing on it, while the plain of surface visible through the cleared ports had taken on the aspect of a sloping mountainside. When the great crush came again, they might survive.

A plentiful supply of water remained in the onboard tanks. The automated galley had been damaged beyond repair, but preserved rations, water, and air, were all to be had in abundance.

People gratefully opened their helmets, gulping in plentiful recycled air. The next order of business for most of the cadets was to begin recharging their suits from handy outlets, against the possibility that some new problem would force them out again onto the airless surface.

The only indication of what might have happened to the ship's crew was the fact that the lifeboat was missing.

The holostages remained dark, but some of the communication gear was working. Lee got to work at once, trying to contact other ships.

Looking out across the square kilometers of their enemy's scarred flank, they saw by the apparent motion of the stars along the horizon evidence of some relatively gentle force that was now pushing the berserker sideways.

This was not the powerful push of the berserker's own main drive, but the nudging of several scoutships that had managed to get right up against its hull. The acceleration produced in the huge mass by this means was comparatively weak, variable, and intermittent, but it was definitely there. The enemy tried to correct against this force.

One cadet, recognizing the cause of the perturbation, yelled: "Our people are still fighting!"

"But with scoutships?" Kang Shin wondered.

"You fight with what you've got." Hemphill told him. "If you count the defensive patrols, we've got more scouts by far than any other type of vessel. Using the scouts makes sense when you think about it."

"I'm thinking. But it would seem to mean the admiral's flat-out desperate."

"Up against this tough bastard, I don't doubt that he is."

"And if you were driving your ship on a ramming mission, you'd look for a vulnerable spot to hit, rather than just slamming into this outer hull—judging from what we've seen, it's just a sheer slab of armor."

In fact, it seemed obvious that most of the rammers would be trying to hit the same place, or one of a small number of similar places, huge wounds where the berserker's outer layers of armor had already been blasted and torn and burned away.

Even as the cadets watched, another scout came ramming in, sending jolts of new vibration through their great opponent's battered frame. On approach the little ship was very difficult to see, against the background of the Galactic night. Closing with the enemy at bullet-speed and faster, perhaps taking evasive action, its live crew, if any—there would be no more than one volunteer pilot—would have gone scrambling for the lifeboat with only seconds to go before impact, relying on the autopilots to eject the boat on some survivable trajectory in the fraction of a second just before impact.

The autopilots had not been designed to carry out such an extremely specialized task, and Lee could imagine that programming them for a mission like this would be far from a sure thing.

They would try to resist, reject, even engage in self-destruction, unless the command was properly repeated and reinforced. Some of them might crash their lifeboats on ejection, while others missed the target altogether.

The cadet who had been posted as lookout in one of the cleared ports of the wrecked scout raised a cry. He had caught sight of someone or something moving across the scarred plain of the enemy's surface, following their own path from the direction of the great damage.

Feretti had taken the weapon's officer's chair, and was making an effort to get some of the scout's surviving armament to focus on the movement. It was a tough job, looking out at the real world through cleared ports, without a holostage to bring in trustworthy, carefully detailed images.

Then Lee, who was standing lookout, let out a yelp of joy. "Don't shoot! It's Random—and he's dragging someone with him. He must be trying to save Dirigo!"

Making radio contact with the robot was not difficult. Random, slowed down by the necessity of dragging along a live captive, while not doing the unwilling client any substantial harm, made slow but steady progress toward the wrecked scoutship that had become a sanctuary, and followed directions to enter through the cargo bay.

The cadets were startled by their first close look at the helpless human the robot had in tow. One of them demanded: "Who's this? Where's Dirigo?"

Random outlined the facts, describing the scene in the theater and the other that followed shortly, deep in the enemy's guts and near the central processor. His optelectronic memory was vivid and precise, and could be played back later on a holostage. Though Random had not witnessed the shooting, he could confirm that Dirigo was dead, and his prisoner a suspect.

The prisoner himself only glowered at his fellow humans, and was disinclined to speak. Based on Random's calmly factual description of this man's behavior, they agreed it would be unwise to set him free in their current circumstances.

The robot also gave its informed opinion that the enemy's central processor was dead.

A scoutship had no compartment that could be readily adapted to serve as a brig, and the six cadets, twice the usual complement of crew, were crowded enough without setting aside one of the few rooms as a prison.

Hemphill decided to use the tiny cargo hold to confine their captive. Huang Gun, fastened into a suit newly recharged with electrical power, its radio selectively disabled, was held pinned at the bottom of the cargo bay, in a forcefield normally used to secure cargo. He was unable to move a limb, but could turn his head inside his helmet to draw water and liquid food from the suit's small reservoirs. He was able to talk with the people he'd been trying to kill—but he had very little to say.

Huang Gun was able to see out of his place of confinement, looking up through his helmet's faceplate, and through the great gash that had been ripped in the side of the cargo bay in the crash.

The musing executioner could not see Timber from where he lay. But a tormenting vision formed all too clearly in his mind: how, on that great ball of rock and soil and gas, badlife by the billions still swarmed and bred. He was morally certain that they were still being born, even on the very threshold of annihilation. They were still fighting, with their fierce determination and their inferior weapons, against what remained of the master's independent landing parties.

But he still had faith in the master. The master would find a way to reach the executioner, his faithful servant, and kill him, and kill them all.

Lee and Hemphill came to the cargo bay and tried to talk to him, but the prisoner resisted interrogation—and they had the robot's dependable word that this man had attempted suicide, in an effort to aid the enemy.

He refused even to identify himself, except to say: "Goodlife."

Hemphill frowned at him. "You're what?"

Huang Gun would not repeat it.

"Goodlife. All right. What in all the hells does that mean?"

Random, who had joined the men, verified the syllables, but offered no interpretation.

Hemphill gave the prisoner a hard look. "Goodlife, hey? Actually you don't look good at all. Well, old man, you may be eager to die, but that's just tough, it isn't going to happen. Somehow we're going to get you off this hulk alive, and eventually down to Timber. People down there are going to want to spend a long time talking to you."

And Lee added: "If you think your life's a burden now, just wait till we get you home."

Most of the six were looking out through the scout's cleared ports, while the monster that they rode expended its last fuel in a final kamikaze charge. Observing from their safe nest of generated gravity, they could see bits of metal, fragments of some other scout-ship, or of the enemy, whisked away, or wedged into a crevice and slowly deformed by the mounting g-force.

—then acceleration abruptly ceased. No human knew it yet, but the last elements of the berserker's drive had failed.

Minutes later, the cadets succeeded in making radio contact with a functioning scout, at a range of only a few thousand kilometers.

An answer to their plea came quickly, half smothered in a torrent of noise. "Say again, where are you?" Captain Ella Berlu and her crew were nearly exhausted, after days of practically continuous duty, but they were up for one more effort.

"We're six cadets, seven people in all, holed up in a crashed scout, on the hull of this damned thing that captured us when it caught our launch. It's almost dead!"

There was a pause. "You're right on the berserker's hull?"

"On the what? Say again?"

"The berserker." There was a pause. "Everyone's calling it that."

Ella and her crew had only a hazy idea of who they were supposed to be rescuing. But such details hardly mattered. The people somehow stranded on the monster were human, and the idea was to get them out.

The cadets' suits had so far served them marvelously well, exceeding their original stress and endurance standards in this cold inferno. But Hemphill and Lee could see already that their suits, however tough and reliable they had seemed in time of peace, were primitive models, not up to the real requirements of space warfare.

"To begin with, stronger and longer lasting power supplies."

"Yeah, and certainly some kind of armor—something, so those things' grippers won't be able to just . . ." He raised both hands, and made slow tearing motions.

While crouched in the cabin of the derelict scoutship, waiting for the promised help to arrive, the two had a discussion about it. They came to quick agreement that they were not armed or armored with anything like the effectiveness of the berserker's own small combat machines.

"Looks like we might possibly make it."

"We'll make it." It sounded like Cadet Hemphill intended to enforce that conclusion by sheer willpower, if necessary. He added: "The next time we fight one of these damned machines, we must have armored suits. Surely that can be done. And better weapons. And a much better power supply, to provide weapons with some punch."

"We'll need stronger weapons not only in our hands, but on our ships."

"More shields, more speed, more of everything."

"We're not doing too badly."

"Yes, we've survived, and yes, we can be proud of that. But the fact is, we've also been lucky. Lucky that the damned thing was damaged before it arrived in the Twin Worlds system. We thought we were perfecting superb weapons—we just didn't know.

"We're not able to do much of anything against this enemy. Not yet." Hemphill raised his hands and looked at them, flexing the fingers and watching them as if contemplating the puny weakness of a human body.

Another inadequacy of the suits was that they were not self-sufficient over extended periods of time; miniaturized hydrogen power lamps had not yet become feasible. The servo power of the limbs was limited by, among other things, how much energy was stored.

Ella Berlu was easily able to land her scoutship, its outer hull all scorched and battered from some earlier skirmish but still functioning, quite close to the downed vessel, and pick up everyone who was still alive.

When Hannah Rymer came out of the little ship to inventory the eager assembly of prospective passengers, and try to figure out where room could be found for them in her own vessel, she paused, staring in confusion at the motionless figure clamped into the ruined cargo bay.

"What's this? Who's this?"

"A prisoner." Hemphill's exhausted voice was terse. "Captain, I'll explain as we get moving. We'd better go."

"I'm assuming the prisoner comes too."

"You bet your life he does. It's very important that he be kept alive. I'll stay behind myself if necessary."

Somehow they got everyone crammed into the functioning scoutship. To save space, the robot Random was left behind, assigned the task of monitoring conditions on the hulk, of watching carefully for any sign of renewed berserker activity, and transmitting reports. Some of the people who had shared a berserker dungeon with the robot felt that leaving Random behind was somehow wrong. But of course Random did not mind in the least.

T H I R T Y

Gregor was getting ready to return to his planet and his capital; but before departing the *Mukunda,* he was having one more face-to-face meeting with the first spacer.

Before its main brain died, the death machine's drive system had done its best to fine-tune its own orbital path, to make sure it had the advancing planet Timber squarely in its sights.

"If the berserker hits the planet as a cluster of fragments, rather than a single solid mass, that should reduce the destruction by an order of magnitude. The impacts will still cause heavy damage. But with any luck at all many of the pieces will miss Timber entirely, and more of them should break up and burn up when they slam into the atmosphere."

"You mean if we don't break it up, we're talking more billions dead—if we do, maybe only additional millions."

"If we don't break it up, or steer it off its chosen path. Right now that seems our best bet. And I think it's working."

"There's no way that a planet can dodge. We've got to do something to stop the damned thing."

The enemy seemed almost inert, almost helpless to defend itself. But, if the berserker was given time in which to work unmolested, it might, for all that any human being could tell, be able to repair its weapons of mass destruction and unleash them once more when it got close to Timber.

And how could any human being be sure those weapons were not working?

Was the appearance it gave of death, of defeated inertia, only a trick?

First Spacer Homasubi had decided he would dispatch his own expedition, made up of daring volunteers from among the crew of his own flagship. They were going to perform a deliberate boarding of the great berserker, to investigate the feasibility of blowing it up. The idea of using the thing's own drive to steer it away from Timber had also been suggested, but there was some reason to believe its drive was no longer working—and just finding it and learning to use it might take years.

The robot Porphyry, on the *Mukunda* more or less by accident, and not needed aboard for any other task—no one admitted to wanting a household servant—was detailed to accompany the boarding party.

Aboard a Huvean hospital ship, two officers were waiting in line for treatment of minor injuries.

They were privileged to share in a bottle being surreptitiously passed around. On occasions of celebration it was customary to propose toasts.

One said: "I drink to Ninety-first Diplomat, or whatever the hell he called himself—she is confirmed dead?"

"So I have heard. One has serious regrets. I believe 'herself' would be the proper form."

"Whatever."

"Whomever."

"That's what I said."

Several more bottles had appeared, and more people were now drinking, becoming increasingly open about it. The victory celebration was well under way. As joy and exuberance increased, the level of coherence tended to diminish.

"We must somehow notify the Carmpan home world—or worlds—of their diplomat's demise. I understand they're a hell of a long way off."

"Of course, we should make the gesture. Though the experts think it likely that they already know."

"And I drink to the late Admiral Radigast—he would've been a worthy opponent—if we'd ever fought."

As yet no one, Twin or Huvean, was willing to confidently pronounce the great berserker dead. But calculations showed that its last kamikaze charge had already been sufficiently deflected so it was certain to miss Timber. More and more people in both groups were beginning to believe that the victory had been won.

The persistent rumors that the enemy had taken human prisoners were proving true. Continuous scanning by scoutships and teams of recon robots detected signs of human life at one place on the vast, ruined hulk—the location of one crashed scoutship that was down on nightside, close to the edge of the region of deepest damage.

The small ship dispatched by First Spacer Homasubi had come down on the berserker's hull just a few meters from where Random stood waiting to offer welcome. Prudently trying to avoid being taken for a berserker, the robot had established radio contact several minutes earlier. When the ship landed, Random explained concisely to the new arrivals that only a few minutes ago a Twin Worlds scoutship had safely evacuated all the live humans known to have been aboard.

"That's good." The expeditionary commander thought the situation over briefly, then asked the robot: "They weren't too worried about losing you, hey? By the way, would you like some help?—let me rephrase that—would some help be useful to you?" The officer had not really wanted to be saddled with the robot Porphyry, the remnants of whose servant's costume seemed to give the whole expedition an unwelcome air of irregularity.

Random answered promptly. "Any help you can provide me might prove very useful, ma'am, if the enemy resumes activity. The probability of that is very difficult to estimate."

"I don't suppose the ship you're guarding can be salvaged?" A moment's inspection showed that it could not. The ramming impact had been a glancing one, and at nothing like the optimum speed for destruction. A surviving fragment of forcefield defense might actually have cushioned the impact. It was hard to tell, but possibly the rounded hull of the scout was actually wedged into place where the monstrous outer layer of the berserker's armor had been peeled back like the thick skin of some mechanical fruit.

Ella reported that several Twin Worlds scoutships were standing by, over on the berserker's dayside, ready to resume pushing—or pulling—if that should become necessary.

Earlier in the battle, such tactics could not have succeeded; the small craft would have been kept at a distance by the berserker's firepower, wiped out as they drew near. But its defenses were not what they had been, and with the larger ships of two fleet remnants still shooting at it, the monster could not always find time and armaments to deal with the smaller badlife vessels.

By the count of human military historians, nearly two hundred scoutships had attempted to ram the berserker. Of these, approximately forty were able to get within a kilometer or two of its hull before its weapons burned them or vaporized them. Between twenty and thirty of the small ships had actually hit the berserker's surface, and half of those had come down hard enough to be almost totally destroyed on impact.

The remainder of those making contact, about ten ships, had struck at a glancing angle, and were not totally destroyed. Three or four had not bounced clear away, but were stuck in several scattered locations, wedged into the cratered wounds blasted into the huge surface by Huvean or Twin Worlds firepower, or by weapons far older than *Homo sapiens,* tools of war forged in the light of suns that Earth-descended eyes perhaps had never seen.

Moving on, following the first spacer's orders, the captain of the expeditionary ship intended to conduct a hurried examination of the great berserker's overall structure, and try to determine the ideal place to set off an explosion that could break it into fragments. Given the fact that there was no room to maneuver even a small ship inside the enemy's hull, this part of the project proved impossible to accomplish in the time available.

A small ship could serve as the weapon, positioned as near as possible to the ideal spot. Then, if the crew was not bent on suicide, they would try to maneuver their getaway vehicle into a favorable position.

By this time the berserker's own defensive shields had been all but completely neutralized by damage to their generators. The power that sustained them was exhausted. There was an interval in which some of its weapons systems still fired, by reflex, at any foreign object that approached.

First Spacer Homasubi, having dispatched his expeditionary force, realized that he had to take some time out to tend to his own body and mind. Rest and food were required, and part of each brief interval away from duty was devoted to soothing physical and spiritual exercises.

But whatever exercise he tried, his mind could not go off duty.

The battle was not over, would not be over until the berserker's last suicidal charge had missed the planet.

Berserker landers had now fought their way even a little closer to the Citadel's outer wall. Ever since landing, days ago, the murderous machines had displayed an acute military intelligence, extremely tough armor, and formidable weapons. They had been working on ways to tap into local energy sources, to recharge themselves, until the power mains beneath the streets were cut off by human engineers. They had now lost contact with the great berserker hurtling toward the planet.

Infantry armed with shoulder weapons and grenades, aided by a variety of large industrial robots, and a dug-in semicircle of military tanks, seemed to be effectively holding the weakened enemy off.

Gregor could faintly hear the sounds of sporadic fighting, as he moved slowly about from room to room, trying to pick out one that he might find still usable as his own temporary office, while he reestablished the seat of his interim government. He had arrived girding his weary mind for the massive effort that would be necessary to get the systems of human decision and communication working again. He would soon be trying to convince his people it was time to put down their weapons and get to work.

Several robots moved with him, providing emergency power, being helpful in several other ways.

"Where's Porphyry?" he suddenly asked a human aide. "I liked that robot, and it served me well."

There were inquiries; Porphyry turned out to have gone up to the Huvean flagship, for some reason, with Luon and her Huvean comrades. Gregor, with a thousand other things to think about, had not been aware of the fact.

To his aide he said: "Make a little diplomatic effort, see what you can do about getting that robot back. If it's not absolutely essential to them up there."

"Yes sir."

Plans were already being made for rebuilding a human habitat in the Twin Worlds system. Gregor made the Galaxy a promise: "Someday the planet Prairie will again be home to thriving life."

A corps of hard-working engineers, both human and robotic, was rapidly restoring the communications network that the enemy had so skillfully shredded. Messages had arrived from scores of other ED worlds, and from the Galactic Council, promising help, with housing refugees if necessary, with mending Timber and rebuilding Prairie. It seemed that the whole species might once more stand together.

Gregor intended to play a big role in all of it. But right now he was very tired.

Before resuming his work on the rebuilding program, he wanted to sit down, just briefly, and reread, yet again, the message recently arrived from Luon and Reggie—the couple were still aboard the *Mukunda* with Uncle Hom.

Their note was meant to congratulate Grandfather Gregor on his presidency, and on all that he had accomplished so far. But it kept wandering off into other subjects.

This time, Gregor just got as far as the line beginning: "Reggie and I are so happy . . ." when he decided that was a good place to pause, for just a moment, to rest his eyes.

The berserker's closest passage to the planet was going to make a great show in Timber's sky—a small cloud of bits of wreckage blasted loose in the fighting was accompanying the hulk in its last futile attack, and many small elements of this cloud were going to hit Timber's atmosphere, creating a spectacular meteoric show—a handful of the larger fragments, up to a thousand kilograms or so, were expected to plummet to the ground, and possibly inflict some local damage.

Nearly every surviving crew member of the Huvean fleet, and nearly all the people of the Twin Worlds, were ready to pledge that humans must never again war against each other.

First Spacer Homasubi remembered, and quoted, something Ninety-first Diplomat had said: "It is as if we have carried the burden of warfare through all our history, knowing that it would at last be needed."

"It seems," agreed the newly promoted Admiral Charlie, "there will be no shortage of enemies, of things to fight against."

After a moment he added thoughtfully: "I suppose there never has been."

People and machines were carefully tracking the berserker fragments that were going to miss Timber, meticulously keeping watch on them. A Huvean ship that still had some legs was in pursuit, planning to gather all the debris it could, and also to disintegrate any large chunk that might pose a problem in a year or two, on its succeeding trips round the sun. Every scrap of knowledge regarding the enemy that could be gained, must be gained.

An interstellar courier had just arrived in-system, bringing news of a berserker attack on some distant human colony. Another home world had been totally destroyed, but a large part of the population had escaped in ships.

"They've heard some garbled report of what's going on here, they're hoping that we survived, and they're pleading with us to send them combat veterans."

Admiral Charlie was sure that some of his people would want to answer that call. "But tell our distant brothers that they'll have to send a ship or two to pick our people up. We're just a little short on transport at the moment."

The two robots were still standing on the berserker's surface, close beside the wrecked scout that had for a few hours provided sanctuary for fragile living humans. Porphyry and Random both understood that soon, probably in a few standard days, they would be relieved from their current duties. In the days and months to come, teams of humans and machines would be swarming over the dead berserker, determined to mine it extensively for the knowledge that it carried.

Porphyry had been standing in the same position for several hours, almost since the departure of the ship that brought him. He happened to be facing in the wrong direction to witness the planet's spectacular passage, and had computed no reason to turn his head and watch. Porphyry was content to ignore the huge display as the bulk of Timber, an oddly mottled sphere that took up a goodly portion of the otherwise star-filled sky, slid smoothly by at close range.

As predicted, part of the cloud of debris that accompanied the speeding berserker was colliding with Timber's upper atmosphere, and with the remnant of the planet's defensive forcefields. This produced glorious fireworks, as if in celebration. At a range of only a few hundred kilometers, the rate of change of position was quite visible, and almost any human would have called it a beautifully impressive sight.

Random, by accident or intent, happened to be facing in the opposite direction from his colleague. As the world of Timber majestically sailed by, Random's head turned smoothly, observing the flaring demonstration. It was as if the robot might be demonstrating some form of aesthetic appreciation.

Such behavior was unheard of. Porphyry looked briefly, redid his calculations, and confirmed that there was nothing useful to be

learned from the sight. But it was not unusual for robots to have
programmed in a form of curiosity, regarding the behavior of people, or other machines.

On the radio circuit shared by the two machines, Porphyry
asked: "Why are you watching?"

Random offered no immediate reply. Porphyry allowed the
pause to stretch out to a full standard minute before he repeated
the question. This time he followed it with a second query, coded
in a language understood only by robots and a few human engineers.

"Why do you seek to imitate humanity?"

The passage of Timber, its upper atmosphere sparking and
flashing rainbow colors with the piecemeal incineration of an
enemy, proof of human triumph, was very beautiful.

Random watched the show, and kept on watching it, until the
planet in its hard-won safety had fallen thousands of kilometers
behind the speeding hulk the robots rode.

Still he gave no answer.